The kiss deep⋯ ⋯⋯⋯ ⋯⋯⋯p on his part.

He wanted more. And he couldn't have stopped himself from taking it.

And then she was gone. Ripped away.

She bolted from the rocker, her chest rising and falling as she backed up against the split-pine railing surrounding the porch. "I'm sorry. I shouldn't have done that."

"But you did."

"I got caught up. That can't happen again."

Her expression glittered with undisguised longing. So why was she stopping?

"I heartily disagree. It's practically a requirement for it to happen again."

"Are you that clueless, Kyle? I'm your daughters' caseworker," she reminded him with raised eyebrows. "We can't get involved."

His body cooled faster than if she'd dumped a bucket of ice water on his head. "You're right."

Of course she was right. This wasn't about whether she was interested or not; it was about his daughters. What had started out as a half-formed plan to distract her from work had actually distracted *him* far more effectively.

And he wanted to do it again.

* * *

THE SEAL'S
SECRET HEIRS

BY
KAT CANTRELL

MILLS &
BOON

First Published in Great Britain 2016
By Mills & Boon, an imprint of HarperCollins*Publishers*
1 London Bridge Street, London, SE1 9GF

© 2016 Harlequin Books S.A.

ISBN: 978-0-263-91852-6

Special thanks and acknowledgement are given to Kat Cantrell for her contribution to the Texas Cattleman's Club: Lies and Lullabies series.

51-0316

Our policy is to use papers that are natural, renewable and recyclable products and made from wood grown in sustainable forests.The logging and manufacturing processes conform to the legal environmental regulations of the country of origin.

Printed and bound in Spain
by CPI, Barcelona

Kat Cantrell read her first Mills & Boon novel in third grade and has been scribbling in notebooks since she learned to spell. What else would she write but romance?

Kat, her husband and their two boys live in north Texas. When she's not writing about characters on the journey to happily-ever-after, she can be found at a football game, watching the TV show *Friends* or listening to '80s music.

Kat was the 2011 Mills & Boon So You Think You Can Write contest winner and a 2012 RWA Golden Heart® Award finalist for best unpublished series contemporary manuscript.

To Cat Schield. Thanks for all the collaboration
and for being my guide into the TCC world!

One

Royal, Texas was the perfect place to go to die.

Kyle Wade aimed to do exactly that. After an honorable discharge from the navy, what else lay ahead of him but a slow and painful death? Might as well do it in Royal, the town that had welcomed every Wade since the dawn of time—except him.

He nearly drove through the center of town without stopping. Because he hadn't realized he was *in* Royal until he was nearly *out* of Royal.

Yeah, it had been ten years, and when he'd stopped for gas in Odessa, he'd heard about the tornado that had ripped through the town. But still. Was nothing on the main strip still the same? These new buildings hadn't been there when he'd left. Of course, he'd hightailed it out of Royal for Coronado, California, in a hurry and hadn't looked back once in all his years as a Navy SEAL. Had he really expected Royal to be suspended in time, like a photograph?

He kind of had.

Kyle slowed as he passed the spot where he'd first kissed Grace Haines in the parking lot of the Dairy Queen. Or what used to be the spot where he'd taken his high school girlfriend on their first date. The Dairy Queen had moved down the road and in its place stood a little pink building housing something called Mimi's Nail Salon. Really?

Fitting that his relationship with Grace had nothing to mark it. Nothing in Royal proper anyway. The scars on his heart would always be there.

Shaking his head, Kyle punched the gas. He had plenty of time to gawk at the town later and no time to think about the woman who had driven him into the military. His shattered leg hurt something fierce and he'd been traveling for the better part of three days. It was time to go home.

And now he had a feeling things had probably changed at Wade Ranch—also known as home—more than he'd have anticipated. Never the optimist, he suspected that meant they'd gotten worse. Which was saying something, since he'd left in the first place because of the rift with his twin brother, Liam. No time like the present to get the cold welcome over with.

Wade Ranch's land unrolled at exactly the ten-mile marker from Royal. At least *that* was still the same. Acres and acres of rocky, hilly countryside spread as far as Kyle could see. Huh. Reminded him of Afghanistan. Wouldn't have thought there'd be any comparison, but there you go. A man could travel ten thousand miles and still wind up where he started. In more ways than one.

The gate wasn't barred. His brother, Liam, was running a loose ship apparently. Their grandfather had died a while back and left the ranch to both brothers, but Kyle had never intended to claim his share. Yeah, it was a significant inheritance. But he didn't want it. He wanted his team back and his life as a SEAL. An insurgent's spray of bullets had guaranteed that would never happen. Even if

Kyle hadn't gotten shot, Cortez was gone and no amount of wishing or screaming at God could bring his friend and comrade-in-arms back to life.

Hadn't stopped Kyle from trying.

Kyle drove up the winding lane to the main house, which had a new coat of paint. The white Victorian house had been lording over Wade land for a hundred years, but looked like Liam had done some renovation. The tire swing that had hung from the giant oak in the front yard was gone and a new porch rocker with room for two had been added.

Perfect. Kyle could sit there in that rocker and complain about how the coming rain was paining his joints. Maybe later he could get up a game of dominos at the VA with all of the other retired military men. *Retired*. They might as well call it dead.

When Kyle jumped from the cab of the truck he'd bought in California after the navy decided they were done with him, he hit the dusty ground at the wrong angle. Pain shot up his leg and it stole his breath for a moment. When a man couldn't even get out of his own truck without harm, it was not a good day.

Yeah, he should be more careful. But then he'd have to admit something was wrong with this leg.

He sucked it up. *The only easy day was yesterday.* That mantra had gotten him through four tours of duty in the Middle East. Surely it could get him to the door of Wade Ranch.

It did. Barely. He knocked, but someone was already answering before the sound faded.

The moment the door swung open, Kyle stepped over the threshold and did a double take. *Liam.* His brother stood in the middle of the renovated foyer, glowering. He'd grown up and out in ten years. Kyle had, too, of course, but it was still a shock to see that his brother had changed from the picture he'd carried in his mind's eye, even though their faces mostly matched.

Crack!

Agony exploded across Kyle's jaw as his head snapped backward.

What in the… Had Liam just *punched* him?

Every nerve in Kyle's body went on full alert, vibrating with tension as he reoriented and automatically began scanning both the threat of Liam and the perimeter simultaneously. The foyer was empty, save the two Wade brothers. And Liam wasn't getting the drop on him twice.

"That's for not calling," Liam said succinctly and balled his fists as if he planned to go back for seconds.

"Nice to see you, too."

Dang. Talking hurt. Kyle spit out a curse along with a trickle of blood that hit the hardwood floor an inch from Liam's broken-in boot.

"Deadbeat. You have a lot of nerve showing up now. Get gone or there's more where that came from."

Liam clearly had no idea who he was tangling with.

"I don't cater much to sucker punches," Kyle drawled, and touched his lower lip, right above where the throb in his jaw hurt the worst. Blood came away with his finger. "Why don't you try that again now that I'm paying attention?"

Liam shook his head wearily, his fists going slack. "Your face is as hard as your head. Why now? After all this time, why did you finally drag your sorry butt home?"

"Aww. Careful there, brother, or people might start thinking you missed me something fierce when you talk like that."

Liam had another thirty seconds to explain why Kyle's welcome home had included a fist. Liam had a crappy right hook, but it still hurt. If anything, Kyle was the one who should be throwing punches. After all, he was the one with the ax to grind. He was the one who had left Royal because of what Liam had done.

Or rather *whom* he'd done. Grace Haines. Liam had broken the most sacred of all brotherly bonds when he messed around with the woman Kyle loved. Afghanistan wasn't far enough away to forget, but it was the farthest a newly minted SEAL could go after being deployed.

So he hadn't forgotten. Or forgiven.

"I called your cell phone," Liam said. "I called every navy outpost I could for two months straight. I left messages. I called about the messages. Figured that silence was enough of an answer." Arms crossed, Liam looked down his nose at Kyle, which was a feat, given that they were the same height. "So I took steps to work through this mess you've left in my lap."

Wait, he'd gotten punched over leaving the ranch in his brother's capable hands? That was precious. Liam had loved Wade Ranch from the first, maybe even as early as the day their mother had dropped them off with Grandpa and never came back.

"You were always destined to run Wade Ranch," Kyle said, and almost didn't choke on it. "I didn't dump it on you."

Liam snorted. "Are you really that dense? I'm not talking about the ranch, moron. I'm talking about your kids."

Kyle flinched involuntarily. "My…what?"

Kids? As in children?

"Yes, kids," Liam enunciated, drawing out the *i* sound as if Kyle might catch his meaning better if the word had eighteen syllables. "Daughters. Twins. I don't get why you waited to come home. You should have been here the moment you found out."

"I'm finding out *this* moment," Kyle muttered as his pulse kicked up, beating in his throat like a May hailstorm on a tin roof. "How…wha…"

His throat closed.

Twin daughters. And Liam thought they were *his*? Someone had made a huge mistake. Kyle didn't have any children. Kyle didn't *want* any children.

Liam was staring at him strangely. "You didn't get my messages?"

"Geez, Liam. What was your first clue? I wasn't sitting at a desk dodging your calls. I spent six months in…a bad place and then ended up in a worse place."

From the city of Kunduz to Landstuhl Regional, the US-run military hospital in Germany. He didn't remember a lot of it, but the incredible pain as the doctors worked to restore the bone a bullet had shattered in his leg—that he would never forget.

But he was one of the lucky ones who'd survived his wounds. Cortez hadn't. Kyle still had nightmares about leaving his teammate behind in that foxhole where they'd been trapped by insurgents. Seemed wrong. Cortez should have had a proper send-off for his sacrifice.

"Still not a chatterbox, I see." Liam scrubbed at his face with one hand, and when he dropped it, weariness had replaced the glower. "Keep your secrets about your fabulous life overseas as a badass. I really don't care. I have more important things to get straight."

The weariness was new. Kyle remembered his brother as being a lot of things—a betrayer, first and foremost—but not tired. It looked wrong on his face. As wrong as the constant pain etched into Kyle's own face when he looked in the mirror. Which was why he'd quit looking in the mirror.

"Why don't you start at the beginning." Kyle jerked his head toward what he hoped was still the kitchen. "Maybe we can hash it out over tea?"

It was too early in the morning for Jack Daniel's, though he might make an exception, pending the outcome of the conversation.

Liam nodded and spun to stride off toward the back of the house. Following him, Kyle was immediately blinded by all the off-white cabinets in the kitchen. His brother hadn't left a stone unturned when he'd gotten busy redoing the house. Modern appliances in stainless steel had replaced the old harvest gold ones and new double islands dominated the center. A wall of glass overlooked the back acreage that stretched for miles until it hit Old Man Drucker's property. Or what had been Drucker's property ten years ago. Obviously Kyle wasn't up-to-date about what had been going on since he'd left.

Without ceremony, Liam splashed some tea into a cup from a pitcher on the counter and shoved the cup into his hand. "Tea. Now talk to me about Margaret Garner."

Hot. Blonde. Nice legs. Kyle visualized the woman instantly. But that was a name he hadn't thought about in— wow, like almost a year.

"Margaret Garner? What does she have to do with any—"

The question died in his throat. *Almost a year.* Like long enough to grow a baby or two? Didn't mean it was true. Didn't mean they were his babies.

It felt like a really good time to sit down, and he thought maybe he could do it without tipping off Liam how badly his leg ached 24-7.

He fell heavily onto a bar stool at the closest island, tea forgotten and shoulders ten pounds heavier. "San Antonio. She was with a group of friends at Cantina Juarez. A place where military groupies hang out."

"So you did sleep with her?"

"Not that it's any of your business," Kyle said noncommitally. They were long past the kiss-and-tell stage of their relationship, if they'd ever been that close. When Liam took up with Grace ten years ago, it had killed any fragment of warmth between them, warmth that was unlikely to return.

"You made it my business when you didn't come home to take care of your daughters," Liam countered, as his fists balled up again.

"Take another swing at me and you'll get real cozy with the floor in short order." Kyle contemplated his brother. Who was furious. "So Margaret came around with some babies looking for handouts? I hope you asked for a paternity test before you wrote a check."

This was bizarre. Of all the conversations he'd thought he'd be having with Liam, this was not it. *Babies. Margaret. Paternity test.* None of these things made sense, together or separately.

Why hadn't any of Liam's messages been relayed? Probably because he hadn't called the right office—by design. Kyle hadn't exactly made it clear how Liam could reach him. Maybe it was a blessing that Kyle hadn't known. He couldn't have hopped on a plane anyway.

Kyle couldn't be a father. He barely knew how to be a civilian and had worked long and hard at accepting that he wasn't part of a SEAL team any longer.

It was twice as hard to accept that after being discharged, he had nowhere to go but back to the ranch where he'd never fit in, never belonged. His injury wasn't supposed to be a factor as he figured out what to do with the rest of his life, since God hadn't seen fit to let him die alongside Cortez. But being a father—to twins, no less—meant he had to think about what a busted leg meant for a man's everyday life. And he did not like thinking about how difficult it was some days to simply stand.

Liam threw up a hand, a scowl crawling onto his expression. "Shut up a minute. No one wrote any checks. You're the father of the babies, no question."

Well, Kyle had a few questions. Like why Margaret hadn't contacted him when she found out she was pregnant. While Liam had little information on his whereabouts,

Margaret sure knew how to get in touch. Her girlfriend had been dating Cortez and called him all the time. She'd known exactly where he was stationed.

It was nothing short of unforgivable. "Where's Margaret?"

"She died," Liam bit out shortly. "While giving birth. It's a long story. Do I need to give you a minute?"

Kyle processed that much more slowly than he would have liked. Margaret was dead? It seemed like just yesterday that he'd spent a long weekend with her in a hotel room. She'd been a wildcat, determined to send him back to Afghanistan with enough memories to keep him warm at night, as she'd put it.

He was sad to learn Margaret had passed, sure. He'd liked thinking about her on the other side of the world, living a normal life that he was helping to secure by going after bad guys. But they'd spent less than forty-eight hours together and had barely known each other, by design. He wasn't devastated—it wasn't as if he'd lost the love of his life or anything. Not like when he'd lost Grace.

"We used protection," he muttered. As if that was the most important thing to get straight at this point. "I don't understand. How did she get pregnant?"

"The normal way, I imagine. Moron." Liam rolled his eyes the way he'd always done when they were younger. "Do you have any interest whatsoever in meeting your daughters?"

Kyle blinked. "Well…yeah. Of course. What happened to them after Margaret died? Who's taking care of them?"

"I am. Me and Hadley. Who's the most amazing woman. She's the nanny I hired when you didn't respond to any of my calls."

Reeling, Kyle tried to gather some of his wits, but they seemed as scattered and filmy as clouds on a mild spring day. "Thanks. That's… You didn't have to. That's above the call of duty."

Liam crossed his arms, biceps rippling under the sleeve of his T-shirt. "They're great babies. Beautiful. And I didn't do it for you. I did it because I love them. Hadley and I, we're planning to keep on taking care of them, too."

"That's not going to happen. You've spent the last ten minutes whaling on me about not coming home to take responsibility for this. I'm here. I'm man enough to step up." He set his jaw, which still throbbed. "I want to see them."

The atmosphere fairly vibrated with animosity as they stared each other down, neither blinking, neither backing down. Something flickered through Liam's gaze and he gave one curt nod.

"Fine." Liam called up the stairs off the kitchen that led to the upper stories.

After the longest three minutes of Kyle's life, he heard footsteps and a pretty, blonde woman who must be the nanny came down the stairs. But Kyle only had eyes for the pink bundles, one each in the crook of her arms.

Sucker punch number two.

Those were real, live, honest-to-God babies. What the hell was he thinking, saying that he wanted to see them? What was that supposed to prove? That he didn't know squat about babies?

They were so small. Nearly identical. Twins, like Kyle and Liam. He'd always heard that identical twins skipped generations, but apparently not.

"What are their names?" he whispered.

"Madeline and Margaret Wade," the woman responded, and the babies lifted their heads toward the sound of her voice. Clearly she'd spent a lot of time with them. "We call them Maddie and Maggie for short."

Somehow that seemed perfect for their little wrinkled faces. "Can I hold them?"

"Sure. This is Maggie." She handed over the first one and cheerfully helped Kyle get the baby situated without being asked, which he appreciated more than he could possibly say because his stupid hands suddenly seemed too clumsy to handle something so breakable.

Hey, little girl. He couldn't talk over the lump in his throat, and no one seemed inclined to make him, so he just looked at her. His heart thumped as it expanded, growing larger the longer he held his daughter. That was a kick in the pants. Who would have thought you could instantly love someone like that? It should have taken time. But there it was.

Now what? What if she cried? What if *he* cried?

He'd hoped a flood of knowledge would magically appear if he could just get his hands on the challenge. You didn't learn to hack through vegetation with a machete until you put it in your palm and started hacking.

"You can take her back," he said gruffly, overwhelmed with all the emotion he had no idea what to do with. But there was still another one. Another daughter. He found new appreciation for the term *double trouble.*

"This one is Maddie," the woman said.

Somehow, the other pink bundle ended up in his arms. Instantly, he could tell she was smaller, weighing less than her sister. Strange. She felt even more fragile than her sister, as if Kyle should be careful how heavily he breathed or he might blow her to the ground with an extra big huff.

Equal parts love and fierce devotion surged through the heart he'd already thought was full, splitting it open. She'd need someone to look out for her. To protect her.

That's on me. My job.

And then being a father made all the sense in the world. These were his girls. The reason he wasn't dead in a foxhole flopped out next to Cortez right now. The Almighty got it perfectly right some days.

"And this is Hadley Wade, my wife," Liam broke in with

the scowl that seemed to be a permanent part of his face nowadays. "We still introduce ourselves in these parts."

"It's okay," Hadley said with a hand on Liam's elbow. Her palm settled into the crook comfortably, as if they were intimate often. "Give him a break. It's a lot to take in."

"I'm done." Kyle rubbed his free hand across his military-issue buzz cut, but it didn't stimulate his brain much. He contemplated Hadley, the woman Liam had casually mentioned that he'd married, as if that was some small thing. "I don't think there's much more I can take in. I appreciate what you've done in my stead, but these are my girls. I want to be their father, in all the ways that count. I'm here and I'm sticking around Royal."

That hadn't been set in his mind until this moment. But it would take a bulldozer to shove him onto a different path now.

"Well, it's not as simple as all that," Liam corrected. "Their mama is gone and you weren't around. So even though I have temporary custody, these girls became wards of the state and had a social worker assigned. You're gonna have to deal with the red tape before you start joining the PTA and picking out matching Easter dresses."

Wearily, Kyle nodded. "I get that. What do I have to do?"

Hadley and Liam exchanged glances and a sense of foreboding rose up in Kyle's stomach.

With a sigh, Liam pulled out his cell phone. "I'll call their social worker. But before she gets here, you should know that it's Grace Haines."

Grace. The name hit him in the solar plexus and all the air rushed from his lungs.

Sucker punch number three.

Grace Haines had avoided looking at the date all day, but it sneaked up on her after lunch. She stared at the letters and numbers she'd just typed on a case file.

March 12. The third anniversary of the day she'd become a Professional Single Girl. She should get cake. Or a card. Something to mark the occasion of when she'd given up the ghost and decided to be happy with her career as a social worker. Instead of continually dating men who were nice enough, but could never live up to her standards, she'd learn to be by herself.

Was it so wrong to want a man who doted on her as her father did with her mother? She wasn't asking for much. Flowers occasionally. A text message here and there with a heart emoticon and a simple thinking of you. Something that showed Grace was a priority. That the guy noticed when she wasn't there.

Yeah, that was dang difficult, apparently. The decision to stop actively looking for Mr. Right and start going to museums and plays as a party of one hadn't been all that hard. As a bonus, she never had to compromise on date night by seeing a science fiction movie where special effects drowned out the dialogue. She could do whatever she wanted with her Saturday nights.

It was great. Or at least that was what she told herself. Loudly. It drowned out the voice in her heart that kept insisting she would never get the family she desperately wanted if she didn't date.

In lieu of a Happy Professional Single Girl cake, Grace settled for a Reese's Peanut Butter Cup from the vending machine and got back to work. The children's cases the county had entrusted to her were not going to handle themselves, and there were some heartbreakers in her caseload. She loved her job and thanked God every day she got to make a difference in the lives of the children she helped.

If she couldn't have children of her own, she'd make do with loving other people's.

Her desk phone rang and she picked up the receiver, accidentally knocking over the framed picture of her mom and dad celebrating their thirtieth wedding anniversary at a luau in Hawaii. One day she'd go there, she vowed as she righted the frame. Even if she had to travel to Hawaii solo, it was still Hawaii.

"Grace Haines. How can I help you today?"

"It's Liam," the voice on the other end announced, and the gravity in his tone tripped her radar.

"Are the girls all right?" Panicked, Grace threw a couple of manila folders into her tote in preparation to fly to her car. She could be at Wade Ranch in less than twenty minutes if she ignored the speed limit and prayed to Jesus that Sheriff Battle wasn't sitting in his squad car at the Royal city limits the way he usually did. "What's happened to the babies? It's Maddie, isn't it? I knew that she wasn't—"

"The girls are fine," he interrupted. "They're with Hadley. It's Kyle. He came home."

Grace froze, mid-file transfer. The manila folder fell to the floor in slow motion from her nerveless fingers, opened at the spine and spilled papers across the linoleum.

"What?" she whispered.

Kyle.

Her first kiss. Her first love. Her first taste of the agonizing pain a man could cause.

He wasn't supposed to be here. The twin daughters Kyle Wade had fathered were parentless, or so she'd convinced herself. That was the only reason she'd taken the case, once Liam assured her he'd called the USO, the California base Kyle had shipped out of and the President of the United States. No response, he'd said.

No response meant no conflict of interest.

If Kyle was back, her interest was so conflicted, she couldn't even see through it.

"He's here. At Wade Ranch," Liam confirmed. "You need to come by as soon as possible and help us sort this out."

Translation: Liam and Hadley wanted to adopt Maddie and Maggie and with Kyle in the picture, that wasn't as easy as they'd all assumed. Grace would have to convince him to waive his parental rights. If he didn't want to, then she'd have to assess Kyle's fitness as a parent and potentially even give him custody, despite knowing in her heart that he'd be a horrible father. It was a huge tangle.

The best scenario would be to transfer the case to someone else. But on short notice? Probably wasn't going to happen.

"I'll be there as soon as I can. Thanks, Liam. It'll work out."

Grace hung up and dropped her head down into the crook of her elbow.

Somehow, she was supposed to go to Wade Ranch and do her job, while ignoring the fact that Kyle Wade had broken her heart into tiny little pieces, and then promptly joined the military, as if she hadn't mattered at all. And somehow, she had to ignore the fact that she still wasn't over it. Or him.

Two

Grace knocked on the door of Wade House and steeled herself for whatever was about to happen. Which was what she'd been doing in the car on the way over. And at her desk before that.

No one else in the county office could take on another case, so Grace had agreed to keep Maddie and Maggie under the premise that she'd run all her recommendations through her supervisor before she told the parties involved about her decisions. Which meant she couldn't just decide ahead of time that Kyle wasn't fit. She had to prove it.

It would be a stringent process, with no room for error. She'd have to justify her report with far more data and impartial observations than she'd ever had to before. It meant twice as many visits and twice as much documentation. Of course. Because who didn't want to spend a bunch of time with a high-school boyfriend who'd ruined you for dating any other man?

Hopefully, he'd just give up his rights without a fight and they could all go on.

The door swung open and Grace forgot to breathe. Kyle Wade was indeed home.

Hungrily, her gaze skittered over his grown-up face. *Oh, my.* Still gorgeous, but sun worn, with new lines around his eyes that said he'd seen some things in the past ten years and they weren't all pleasant. His hair was shorn shorter than short, but it fit this new version of Kyle.

His green eyes were diamond hard. That was new, too. He'd never been open and friendly, but she'd burrowed under that reserve back in high school and when he really looked at her with his signature blend of love and devotion—it had been magic.

She instantly wanted to burrow under that hardness once again. Because she knew she was the only one who could, the only one he'd let in. The only one who could soothe his loneliness, the way she'd done back then.

Gah, what was she *thinking*?

She couldn't focus on that. Couldn't remember what it had been like when it was good, because when it was bad, it was really bad. This man had destroyed her, nearly derailing her entire first year at college as she picked up the broken pieces he'd left behind.

"Hey, Grace."

Kyle's voice washed over her and the steeling she'd done to prepare for this moment? Useless.

"Kyle," she returned a bit brusquely, but if she started blubbering, she'd never forgive herself. "I'm happy to see that you've finally decided to acknowledge your children."

Chances were good that wouldn't last. He'd ship out again at a moment's notice, running off to indulge his selfish thirst for adventure, leaving behind a mess. As he'd done the first time. But Grace was here to make sure he didn't hurt anyone in the process, least of all those precious babies.

"Yep," he agreed easily. "I took a slow boat from China all right. But I'm here now. Do whatever you have to do to make it okay with the county for me to be a father to my daughters."

Ha. Fathers were loving, caring, selfless. They didn't become distant and uncommunicative on a regular basis and then forget they had plans with you. And then forget to apologize for leaving you high and dry. Nor did they have the option to quit when the going got tough.

"Well, that's not going to happen today," she said firmly. "I'll do several site visits to make sure that you're providing the right environment for the girls. They need to feel safe and loved and it's my job to put them into the home that will give them that. You might not be the best answer."

The hardness in his expression intensified. "They're mine. I'll take care of them."

His quiet fierceness set her back. Guess that answered the question about whether he'd put up a token fight and then sign whatever she put in front of him that would terminate his parental rights. The fact that he wasn't—it was throwing her for a loop. "Actually, they're mine. They became wards of the state when you didn't respond to the attempts we all made to find you. That's what happens to abandoned babies."

That might have come out harshly. So what. It was the truth, even if the sentiment had some leftover emotion from when Kyle had done that to her. She had to protect the babies, no matter what.

"There were...circumstances. I didn't get any of Liam's messages or I would have come as soon as I could." His mouth firmed into an inflexible line. "That's not important now. Come in and visit. Tell me what I have to do."

"Fine."

She followed him into the formal parlor that had been restored to what she imagined was Wade House's former glory. The Victorian furniture was beautiful and luxurious, and a man like Kyle looked ridiculous sitting on the elegantly appointed chair. Good grief, the spindly legs didn't seem strong enough to support such a solid body. Kyle had gained weight, and the way he moved indicated it was 100 percent finely honed muscle under his clothes. He'd adopted a lazy, slow walk that seemed at odds with all that, but certainly fit a laid-back cowboy at home on his ranch.

Not that she'd noticed or anything.

She took her own seat and perched on the edge, too keyed up to relax. "We'll need to fill out some paperwork. What do you plan to do for employment now that you're home?"

Kyle quirked an eyebrow. "Being a Wade isn't enough?"

Frowning, she held her manila folder in front of her like a shield, though what she thought it was going to protect her from, she had no idea. Kyle's diamond-bit green eyes drilled through her very flesh and bone, deep into the soft places she'd thought were well protected against men. Especially this one.

"No, it's not enough. Inheriting money isn't an indicator of your worth as a parent. I need to see a demonstration of commitment. A permanency that will show you can provide a stable environment for Maddie and Maggie."

"So being able to buy them whatever they want and being able to put food on the table no matter what isn't good enough."

It was not a question but a challenge. She tried not to roll her eyes, she really did. But if you looked up "clueless" in the dictionary, you'd see a picture of Kyle Wade. "That's right. Liam and Hadley can do those things and have been for over two months. Are you prepared for all the special treatments and doctor's visits Maddie will require? I have to know."

Kyle went stiff all at once, freezing so quickly that she got a little concerned. She should really stop caring so much but it was impossible to shut off her desire to help people. This whole conversation was difficult. She and Kyle used to be comfortable with each other. She missed that easiness between them, but there was no room for anything other than a professional and necessary distance.

"Doctor's visits?" Kyle repeated softly. "Is there something wrong with Maddie?"

"Maddie suffers from twin-to-twin transfusion syndrome. She has some heart problems that are pretty serious."

"I…didn't know."

The bleakness in his expression reached out and twisted her heart. She wanted to lash out at him. Blame him. Those girls had been fighting for their lives after Margaret died, and where was Kyle? "Just out of curiosity, why did you come home now? Why not two months ago when Margaret first came looking for you? Or for that matter, why not when she first found out she was pregnant?"

She cut off the tirade there. Oh, there was plenty more she wanted to say, but it would veer into personal barbs that wouldn't help anything. She had a job to do and the information-gathering stage should—and would—stay on a professional level.

Besides, she knew he'd been stationed overseas. He probably hadn't had the luxury of jetting off whenever he felt like it. But he could have at least called.

Crossing his arms, he leaned back against the gold velvet cushions of the too-small chair, biceps bulging. He'd grown some interesting additions to what had already been a nicely built body. Automatically, her gaze wandered south, taking in all the parts that made up that great physique. Wow, had it gotten hot in here, or what? She fanned her face with the manila folder.

But then he eyed her, his face a careful mask that dared her to break through it. Which totally unnerved her. This darker, harder, fiercer Kyle Wade was dangerous. Because she wanted to understand why he was dark, hard and fierce. Why he'd broken her heart and then left.

"You got me all figured out, seems like," he drawled. "Why don't you tell me why I didn't hop on a plane and stick by Margaret's side during her pregnancy?"

Couldn't the man just answer a simple question? He'd always been like this—uncommunicative and prone to leaving instead of dealing with problems head-on. His attitude was so infuriating, she said the first thing that popped into her head.

"Guilt, probably. You didn't want to be involved and hoped the problem would go away on its own." And that was totally unfair. Wasn't it? She had no idea why he hadn't contacted anyone. This new version of Kyle was unsettling *because* she didn't know him that well anymore.

Really, she wasn't that good at reading people in the first place. It was a professional weakness that she hated, but couldn't seem to fix. Once upon a time, she'd thought this man was her forever after, her Prince Charming, Clark Gable and Dr. McDreamy all rolled into one. Which was totally false. She'd bought heavily into that lie, so how could she trust her own judgment? She couldn't. That's why she had to be so methodical in her approach to casework, because she couldn't afford to let emotion rule her decisions. Or afford to make a mistake, not when the future of a child was at stake.

And she wouldn't do either here. Maddie and Maggie deserved a loving home with a family who paid attention to their every need. Kyle Wade was not the right man for that, no matter what he said he wanted.

"Well, then," he said easily. "Guess that answers your question."

It so did not. She still didn't know why he'd come home now, why he'd suddenly shown an interest in his daughters. Whether he could possibly convince her he planned to stick around—if he was even serious about that. Kyle had a habit of running away from his problems, after all.

First and foremost, how could she assess whether the time-hardened man before her could ever provide the loving, nurturing environment two fragile little girls needed?

But she'd let it slide for now. There was plenty of time to work through all of that, since Maddie and Maggie were still legally in the care of Liam and Hadley.

"I think I have enough for now. I'll file my first report and send you a copy when it's approved." She had to get out of here. Before she broke down under the emotional onslaught of everything.

"That's it, huh? What's the report going to say?"

"It's going to say that you've expressed an interest in retaining your parental rights and that I've advised you that I can't approve that until I do several more site visits."

He cocked his head, evaluating her coolly. "How long is that going to take?"

"Until I'm satisfied with your fitness as a parent. Or until I decide you're unfit. At which point I'll make recommendations as to what I believe is the best home for those precious girls. I will likely recommend they stay with Liam and Hadley."

Without warning, Kyle was on his feet, an intense vibe rippling down his powerful body. She'd have sworn he hadn't moved, and then all of a sudden, there he was, staring down at her with a sharpness about him, as if he'd homed in on her and her alone. She couldn't move, couldn't breathe.

It was precisely the kind of focus she'd craved once. But not now. Not like this.

"Why would you give my kids to my brother?" he asked, his voice dangerously low.

"Well, the most obvious reason is because he and Hadley want them. They've already looked into adoption. But also because they know the babies' needs and have already been providing the best place for the girls."

"You are not taking away my daughters," he said succinctly. "Why does this feel personal?"

She blinked. "This is the opposite of personal, Kyle. My job is to be the picture of impartiality. Our history has nothing to do with this."

"I was starting to wonder if you recalled that we had a history," he drawled slowly, loading the words with meaning.

The intensity rolling from him heightened a notch, and she shivered as he perused her as if he'd found the last morsel of chocolate in the pantry—and he was starving. All at once, she had a feeling they were both remembering the sweet fire of first love. They might have been young, but what they'd lacked in experience, they made up for in enthusiasm. Their relationship had hit some high notes that she'd prefer not to be remembering right this minute. Not with the man who'd made her body sing a scant few feet away.

"I haven't forgotten one day of our relationship." Why did her voice sound so breathless?

"Even the last one?" he murmured, and his voice skittered down her spine with teeth she wasn't expecting.

"I'm not sure what you mean." Confused as to why warning sirens were going off in her head, she stared at the spot where the inverted tray ceiling seams came together. "We broke up. You didn't notice. Then you joined the military and eventually came home. Here we are."

"Oh, I noticed, Grace." The honeyed quality of his tone drew her gaze to his and the green fire there blazed with heat she didn't know what to do with. "I think we can both agree that what happened between us ten years ago was a mistake. Never to be repeated. We'll let bygones be bygones and you'll figure out a way to make this pesky custody issue go away. Deal?"

A mistake. Bygones. Her heart stung as it absorbed the words that confirmed she hadn't meant that much to him. Breaking up with him hadn't fazed him the way she'd hoped. The daring ploy she'd staged to get his attention—by letting him catch her with Liam, a notorious womanizer—hadn't worked, either, because he hadn't really cared whether she messed around with his brother. The whole ruse had been for naught.

Stricken, she stared at him, unable to look away, unable to quell the turmoil inside at Kyle being close enough to touch and yet so very far away. They'd broken up ten years ago because he'd never seemed all that into their relationship. Hadn't enough time passed for her to get over it already?

"Sure. Bygones," she repeated, because that was all she could get out.

She escaped with the hasty promise that she'd send him a set schedule of home visits and drove away from Wade Ranch as fast as she dared. But she feared it would never be fast enough to catch up with her impartiality—it had scampered down the road far too quickly and she had a feeling she wasn't going to recover it. Her emotions were fully engaged in this case and she'd have to work extra hard to shut them down. So she could do the best thing for everyone. Including herself.

Kyle watched Grace drive away through the window and uncurled his fists before he punched a wall. Maybe he'd punch Liam instead.

He owed his brother one, after all, and it sure looked as though Liam was determined to be yet another roadblock in a series of roadblocks standing between Kyle and fatherhood. Most of the problems couldn't be resolved easily. But Liam wanting Kyle's kids? That was one thing that Kyle could do something about.

So he went looking for him.

Wade land surrounded the main house to the tune of about ten thousand acres. There was a time when a scouting mission like this one would have been no sweat, but with a messed-up leg, the trek winded Kyle about fifteen minutes in. Which sucked. It was tough to be sidelined, tough to reconcile no longer being in top physical condition. Tough to keep it all inside.

Kyle found Liam in the horse barn, which was situated a good half mile away from the main house. *Barn* was too simplistic a term to describe the grandiose building with a flagstone pathway to the entrance, fussy landscaping and a show arena on the far end. The ranch offices and a fancy lounge were tucked inside, but he didn't bother to gawk. His leg hurt and the walk wasn't far enough to burn off the mad Kyle had generated while talking to Grace.

Who was somehow even more beautiful than he recalled. How was that possible when he'd already put her on a pedestal in his mind as the ideal? How would any other woman ever compare? None could. And the lady herself still got him way too hot and bothered with a coy glance. It was enough to drive a man insane. She'd screwed him up so bad, he couldn't do anything other than weekend flings, like the one he'd had with Margaret. Look where that had gotten him.

Grace was a great big problem in a whole heap of problems. But not one he could deal with this minute. Liam? That was something he could handle.

He watched Liam back out of a stall housing one of the

quarter horses Wade Ranch bred commercially, waiting until his brother was clear of the door to speak. He had enough respect for the damage a spooked eleven-hundred-pound animal could do to a man to stay clear.

"What's this crap about you wanting to adopt my kids?" he said when Liam noticed him.

Liam snorted. "Grace must have come by. She tell you to sign the papers?"

No one ordered Kyle around, least of all Grace.

"She told me you've got your sights set on my family." He crossed his arms before he made good on the impulse to smash his brother in the mouth for even uttering Grace's name. She'd meant everything to Kyle, but to Liam, she was yet another in a long line of his women. "Back off. I'm taking responsibility for them whether you like it or not."

Sticking a piece of clean straw between his back teeth, Liam cocked a hip and leaned against the closed stall door as if he hadn't a care in the world. Lazily, he rearranged his battered hat. "Tell me something. What's the annual revenue Wade Ranch brings in for stud fees?"

"How should I know?" Kyle ground out. "You run the ranch."

"Yeah." Liam raised his brows sardonically. "Half of which belongs to you. Grandpa died almost two years ago, yet you've never lifted a finger to even find out what I do here. Money pours into your bank account on a monthly basis. Know how that happens? Because I make sure of it. I made sure of a lot of things while you ran around the Middle East blowing stuff up and ignoring your responsibilities at home. One of those things I do is take care of Maddie and Maggie. Because you weren't here. Just like you weren't here to take on any responsibility for the ranch. I will not let you be an absentee father like you've been an absentee ranch owner."

"That's a low blow," Kyle said softly. Liam had always

viewed Kyle's stint as a SEAL with a bit of disdain, making it clear he saw it as a cop-out. "You wanted the ranch. I didn't. But I want my girls, and I'm going to be here for them."

Wade Ranch had never meant anything to him other than a place to live because it was the only one he had. Then and now. Mama had cut and run faster than you could spit, once she'd dumped him and Liam here with her father, then taken the Dallas real estate market by storm. Lillian Wade had quickly become the Barbara Corcoran of the South and forgot all about the two little boys she'd abandoned.

Funny how Liam had been so similarly affected by dear old Mama. Enough to want to guarantee his blood wouldn't ever have to know the sting of desertion. Kyle respected the thought if not the action. But Kyle was one up on Liam, because those girls were his daughters. He wasn't about to take lessons from Mama on how to be a runaway parent.

"Too little, too late," his brother mouthed around the straw. "Hadley and I want to adopt them. I hope you have a good lawyer in your back pocket because you're not getting those girls without a hell of a fight."

God Almighty. The hits kept coming. He'd barely had time to get his feet under him from being sucker punched a minute after crossing the threshold of his childhood home, only to have Liam drop twin daughters, Grace Haines and a custody battle in his lap.

They stared at each other, neither blinking. Neither backing down. They were both stubborn enough to stand there until the cows came home, and probably would, too.

Nothing was going to get fixed this way, and with Grace's admonition to prove he was serious about providing a stable environment for Maddie and Maggie ringing in his ears, he contemplated his mule-headed brother. He wanted help with the ranch? By God, he'd get it. And

Kyle would have employment to put on his Fatherhood Résumé, which would hopefully get Grace off his back at the same time.

"Give me a job if it means so much to you that I take ranch ownership seriously. I'll do something with the horses."

Liam nearly busted a gut laughing, which did not improve Kyle's grip on his temper. "You can feed them. But that's about it. You have no training."

And Kyle wasn't at 100 percent physically, but no one had to know about that. His injuries mostly didn't count anyway. It just meant he had to work that much harder, which he'd do. Those babies were worth a little agony.

"I can learn. You can't have it both ways. Either you give me a shot at being half owner of Wade Ranch or shut up about it."

"All right, smart-ass." Liam tipped back his hat and jerked his chin at Kyle. "We got a whole cattle division here at Wade Ranch that's ripe for improvement. I've been concentrating on the horses and letting Danny and Emma Jane handle that side. You take over."

"Done."

Kyle knew even less about cows than he did babies. But he hadn't known anything about guns or explosives before joining the navy, either. BUD/S training had nearly broken him, but he'd learned how to survive impossible physical conditions, learned how to stretch his body to the point of exhaustion and still come out swinging when the next challenge reared its ugly head.

You had to start out with the mind-set that quitting wasn't an option. Even the smallest mental slip would finish a man. So he wouldn't slip.

Liam eyed him and shook his head. "You're serious?"

"As a heart attack. I'll take my best shot at the cattle side of the ranch. Just one question. What am I aiming at?"

"We have a Black Angus breeding program. Emma Jane—she's the sales manager I hired last year—is great. She sold about two hundred head. If you want me to call you successful, double that in under six months."

That didn't sound too bad, especially if there was a sales manager already doing the heavy lifting. "No problem. Now drop the whole adoption idea and we'll call it even."

"Let me see you in action, and then we'll talk. I have yet to see anything that tells me you're planning to stick around. If you take off again, the babies will be mine anyway. Might as well make it legal sooner rather than later." Liam shrugged. "You made your bed by leaving. So lie in it for a while."

Yeah, except he'd left for very specific reasons. He and Liam had never been close, and Kyle hadn't felt as if he was part of anything until he'd found his brothers of the heart on a SEAL team. That's where he'd finally felt secure. He could actually care about someone again without fear of being either abandoned or betrayed.

He'd like to say he could find a way to stay at the ranch this time. But what had changed from the first time? Not much.

Just that he was a father now. And he owed his daughters a stable home life. They were amazing little creatures that he wanted to see grow up. With the additional complications of Maddie's health problems, he couldn't relocate them at the drop of a hat, either.

"I'm not going anywhere," Kyle repeated for what felt like the four hundredth time.

Maybe if he kept saying it, people would believe him. Maybe he'd believe it, too.

Three

Kyle drove into town later that night on an errand for Hadley, who had announced at dinner that the babies were almost out of both diapers and formula. She'd seemed surprised when he said he'd go instead.

Of course he'd volunteered for the job. They were his kids. But he'd made Hadley write down exactly what he needed to buy, because the only formula he'd had exposure to was the one for making homemade explosives. List in his pocket, he'd swung into his truck, intending to grab the baby items and be back in jiffy.

But as he pulled into the lot at Royal's one-and-only grocery store, Grace had just exited through the automatic sliding doors. Well, well, well. There was no way he was passing up this opportunity. He still had a boatload of questions for the girl he'd once given his heart to, only to have it handed back, shredded worse than Black Angus at a slaughterhouse.

Kyle waited until she was almost to her car, and then

gingerly climbed from his truck to corner her between her Toyota and the Dooley in the next spot.

"Lovely night, isn't it, Ms. Haines?"

She jumped and spun around, bobbling her plastic sack full of her grocery store purchases. "You scared me."

"Guilty conscience maybe," he offered silkily. No time like the present to give her a chance to own up to the crimes she'd committed so long ago. He might even forgive her if she just said she was sorry.

"No, more like I'm a woman in a dark parking lot and I hear a man speaking to me unexpectedly."

It was a perfectly legitimate thing to say except the streetlight spilled over her face, illuminating her scowl and negating her point about a dark parking lot. She was that bent up about him saying *hey* outside of a well-lit grocery store?

He raised a brow. "This is Royal. The most danger you'd find in the parking lot of the HEB is a runaway shopping cart."

"You've been gone a long time, Kyle. Things have changed."

Yeah, more than he'd have liked. Grace's voice had deepened. It was far sexier than he'd recalled, and he'd thought about her a lot. Her curves were lusher, as if she'd gained a few pounds in all the right places, and he had an unexpected urge to pull her against him so he could explore every last change, hands on.

Okay, the way he constantly wanted her? *That* was still the same. He'd always been crazy over her. She'd been an exercise in patience, making him wait until they'd been dating a year *and* she'd turned eighteen before she'd sleep with him the first time. And that had been so mind-blowing, he'd immediately started working on the second encounter, then the third. And so on.

The fact that he'd fallen in love with her along the way

was the craziest thing. He didn't make it a habit to let people in. She'd been an exception, one he hadn't been able to help.

"You haven't changed," he said without thinking. "You're still the prettiest girl in the whole town."

Now why had he gone and said something like that? Just because it was true didn't mean he should run off at the mouth. Last thing he needed was to give her the slightest opening. She'd slide right under his skin again, just as she'd done the first time, as if his barriers against people who might hurt him didn't exist.

"Flattery?" She rolled her eyes. "That was a lame line. Plus, I already told you I'd handle your case impartially. There's no point in trying to butter me up."

Oh, so she thought she was immune to his charm, did she? He grinned and shifted his weight off his bad leg, cocking his right hip out casually as if he'd meant to strike that stance all along. "I wouldn't dream of it. That was the God-honest truth. I've been around the world, and I know a thing or two about attractive women. No law against telling one so."

"Well, I don't like it. Are you really that clueless, Kyle?"

The scowl crawled back onto her face and it tripped his Spidey-sense. Or at least that's what he'd always called it. He'd discovered in SEAL training that he had no small amount of skill in reading a situation or a person. Before then, he'd spent a lot of time by himself—purposefully— and never paid much attention to people's tells. Honing that ability had served him well in hostile territory.

So he could easily see Grace was mad. At *him*.

What was that all about? She was the one who'd dumped him cold with no explanation other than she wanted to concentrate on school, which was bull. She'd been a straight-A student before they'd started dating and maintained her grade point average until the day she graduated a year after he had. Best he could figure, she'd wanted Liam instead and hadn't wasted any time getting with his brother once she was free and clear.

"You got something to say, Grace?" He crossed his arms and leaned against her four-door sedan. "Seems like you got a bee in your bonnet."

Maybe Liam had thrown her over too quickly and she'd lumped her hurt feelings into a big Wade bucket. And now he was giving her a second shot to spill it. He just wanted her to admit she'd hurt him and then say she was sorry. That she'd picked the wrong brother when she'd hooked up with Liam. Then maybe he could go on and meet someone new and exciting who didn't constantly remind him that Kyle, women and relationships didn't mix well. Maybe he'd even find a way to trust a woman again. He could finally move on from Grace Haines.

She licked her lips and stared at the sky over his shoulder. "I'm sorry. I'm not handling this well. The babies are important to me. All my cases are, but because we used to date, I want to ensure there's no hint of impropriety. All the decisions I make should be based on facts and your ability to provide a good home. So please don't say things like you think I'm pretty."

Something that felt a lot like disappointment whacked him between the eyes. She had yet to mention the episode with Liam. Maybe she didn't even know that Kyle had seen them together, or didn't care. No, he'd never said anything to her about it, either, because some things should be obvious. You didn't fool around with a guy's brother. It was a universal law and if he had to spell that out, Grace wasn't as great a girl as he'd always thought.

"Well, then," Kyle said easily. "Maybe you should transfer my case to someone else in the county, so you don't have to deal with my brand of truth."

She probably didn't even remember what she'd done

with Liam and most likely thought Kyle had moved on. He *should* have moved on. It was way past time.

She shook her head. "Can't. We're overloaded. So we're stuck with each other."

Which meant she'd checked into it. That was somehow more disappointing than her skipping over the apology he was owed.

No matter.

Grace was just a woman he used to date. That's all. There was nothing between them any longer. He'd spent years shutting down everything inside and he'd keep on doing it. Nothing new here.

And she had his babies and their future in the palm of her hand. This was the one person he needed on his side. They could both stand to act like adults about this situation and focus on what was good for the children. It would be a good idea to do exactly as he suggested to her and let bygones be bygones. Even though he hadn't meant a word of it at the time.

"You're right. I'm sorry, too. Let's start over, friendly-like." He held out his hand for her to shake.

She hesitated for an eternity and then reached out to take it.

The contact sang through his palm, setting off all kinds of fireworks in places that had been cold and dark for a really long time. Gripping his hand tight, she met his gaze and held it.

The depths of her brown eyes heated, melting a little of the ice in his heart.

Her mouth would be sweet under his, and her skin would be soft and fragrant. The moon had risen, spilling silver light over the parking lot, and the gentle breeze played with her hair. The atmosphere couldn't be more romantic if he'd ordered it up. He barely resisted yanking her into his arms.

Yeah, he was in a lot of trouble if he was supposed to keep this friendly and impartial. She was his babies' case-worker. But the fact of the matter was that he had never gotten over Grace Haines. He could no sooner shut down his feelings about her than he could pick up her Toyota with one hand. And being around her again was pure torture.

The next morning, Kyle woke at dawn the way he always did. He'd weaned himself off an alarm clock about two weeks into BUD/S training and hadn't ever gone back.

He lay there staring at the ceiling of his old room at Wade House. Reorientation time. *Not a SEAL. Not in Afghanistan. Not in the hospital*—which had been its own kind of nightmare. This was the hardest part of the day. Every morning, he took stock, so he'd know who and where he was. Then he thanked God for the opportunity to serve his country and cursed the evil that had required it.

This was also the time of day when he made the decision to leave the pain pills in the bottle, where they belonged.

Some days, that decision was tougher than others. There was a deep, dark place inside that craved the oblivion the drugs would surely bring. That's why he'd never cracked open the seal on the bottle. Too easy to have a mental slip and think *just this once*. That was cheating, and Kyle had never taken that route.

Today would not mark the start of it, either.

Today did mark the start of something, though. A new kind of taking stock about the things he was instead of the things he wasn't. *A father. A cattle rancher.* He liked the sound of that. It was nice to have some positives to call out. He needed positives after six months of hell.

Of course, Grace would be watching over his shoulder, and Liam was going to be smack in the middle of Kyle's steps toward fatherhood *and* ranching. The two people he distrusted the most and both held the keys to his future.

He rolled from bed and pulled on a new long-sleeved shirt, jeans and boots. Eventually, his wardrobe would be work-worn like Liam's, but for now, he'd have to settle for looking like a rhinestone cowboy instead of a real one. Coffee beckoned, so he took the back stairway from the third floor to the ground floor kitchen, albeit a bit more slowly than he'd have liked.

Hadley had beaten him to the coffeepot and turned with a smile when he entered. "Good morning. Sleep well?"

"Fine," he lied. He'd lain awake far too long thinking about how this woman and his brother wanted to take his kids away. "And you?"

"Great. The babies only woke up once and thankfully at the same time. It's not always like that. Sometimes they wake up all night long at intervals." She laughed good-naturedly and lowered her voice. "I think they plan it out ahead of time just to make me nuts."

Guilt crushed Kyle's lungs and he struggled to breathe. Some father he was. They'd agreed the night before that Hadley would continue in her role as Maddie and Maggie's caretaker until Kyle got his feet under him, but it didn't feel any more right this morning than it had then. His sister-in-law was getting up in the middle of the night with his kids, scant hours after he gave Liam and Grace a big speech about how he was all prepared to step up and provide a loving environment.

No more.

"I appreciate what you're doing for my daughters," he rasped, and cleared his throat. "But I want to take care of them from now on. I'll get up with them at night."

Hadley stared at him. "You have no idea what you're talking about, do you?"

"Uh, well…" Should he brazen it out or admit defeat?

God Almighty, he hated admitting any kind of weakness. But chances were good she'd already figured out he wasn't the brightest bulb on the board when it came to babies. "I'm going to learn. Trial by fire is how I operate best."

"They're not going to pull out AK-47s, Kyle." Hadley hid a smile but not very well and handed him a cup of steaming coffee. "Sugar and creamer are on the table."

"I like it black, thanks." He sipped and added *good coffee* to his list of things he was thankful for. "Tell me the things I need to know about my kids."

"Okay." She nodded and went over a list of basics, which Kyle committed to memory. Eating. Bathing. Sleeping. Check, check, check. Stuff all humans needed, but his little humans couldn't do these things for themselves. He just had to help them, the way he would a wounded teammate.

"Can I see them?" he asked. Felt weird to be asking permission, but he didn't want to mess up anything.

"You can. They're sleeping, but we can sneak in. You can be quiet, right?"

"Quiet enough to take out a barracks full of enemy soldiers without getting caught," he said without a trace of irony. Hadley just smiled as though he was kidding.

He followed Hadley to the nursery, a mysterious place full of pink and tiny beds with bars. The girls were asleep in their cribs, and he watched them for a moment, his throat tight. Their little faces—how could anything be that tiny and survive? A better question was, how did your heart stay stitched together when it felt as if it would burst from all the stuff swelling up inside it?

"I was their nanny first, you know," she whispered. "Before I married Liam."

What did a nanny even do? Was she like a babysitter and a substitute mom all rolled up into one? If so, that seemed like a bonus, and he'd be cutting off his nose to spite his face to relieve her of her duties. She could keep on being the nanny as far as he was concerned, as long as Grace was okay with it. She must be. Liam had hired Hadley, after all, and Grace seemed pretty impressed with them as a team.

"I'm not trying to take away your job," he mumbled.

Did she see it as a job? If she and Liam wanted to adopt the girls, she'd obviously grown very attached to them. Was it better to cut off their contact with the babies instead? Get them used to the idea?

If so, he couldn't do it. It seemed unnecessarily cruel and besides, he needed the help.

"I didn't think you were. It's admirable that you want to care for them, but there's a huge learning curve and they won't do well with a big disruption. Let's take it one step at a time."

He could do that. You didn't drop a green recruit into the middle of a Taliban hotbed and expect him to wipe out the insurgents as his first assignment. You started him out with something simple, like surveillance. "Can I watch you feed them?"

"Sure, when they wake up."

They tiptoed from the room and Kyle considered that a pretty successful start to Operation: Fatherhood.

Next up, Operation: Do Something About Grace. Because he'd lain awake last night thinking about her more than he'd wanted to, as well. Somehow, he had to shut down the spark between them. Or hose it off with a big, wet kiss.

Grace sat in her car outside of Wade House and pretended that she was going over some notes in her case file. In truth, her stomach was doing a cancan at the prospect of seeing Kyle again, and she couldn't get it to settle.

She'd gone a long time without seeing him. What was so different now?

Nothing. She was a professional and she would do her job. *Get out of the car*, she admonished herself. *Get in there and do your assessment.* The faster she gathered the facts needed to remove the babies from Kyle's presence and provide a recommendation for their permanent home, the better.

Hadley let her into the house and directed her to the second floor, where Kyle was hanging out with the babies. Perfect. She could watch him interact with them and record some impartial observations in her files.

But when Grace poked her head into the nursery with a bright smile, it died on her face. Kyle dozed in the rocking chair, Maddie against one shoulder, Maggie the other. Both babies were asleep, swaddled in soft pink blankets, an odd contrast to Kyle's masculine attire.

But that wasn't the arresting part. It was Kyle. Unguarded, vulnerable. Sweet even, with his large hands cradled protectively around each of his daughters. He should look ridiculous in the middle of a nursery decorated to the nth degree with girlie colors and baby items. But he looked anything but. His powerful body scarcely fit into the rocking chair, biceps and broad shoulders spilling past the edges of the back. He'd always been incredibly handsome, but on the wiry side.

No more. He was built like a tank, and she could easily imagine this man taking out any threat in a mile-wide radius.

It was a lot more affecting than she would ever admit.

And then his eyelids blinked open. He didn't move a muscle otherwise, but his keen gaze zeroed in on her. Fully alert. Those hard green eyes cut through her, leaving her feeling exposed and much more aware of Kyle than she'd been a minute ago. Which was saying something, given her thoughts had already been pretty graphic.

It was heady to be in his sights like that. He'd always

looked at her as if they shared something special that no one else could or would be involved in. But he'd honed his focus over the years into something new and razor sharp. Flustered, she wiggled her fingers in a half wave, and that's when he smiled.

It hit her in the soft part of her heart and spread a warmth she did not want to feel. But oh, my, it was delicious. Like when he'd taken her hand in the parking lot last night. That feeling—she'd missed it.

She'd lain awake last night imagining that he'd kissed her the way she'd have sworn he wanted to as they stood under that streetlight. It was all wrong between them. Kissing wasn't allowed, wasn't part of the agenda, wasn't what should happen. But it didn't stop her from thinking about it.

She was in a lot of trouble.

"Hi," she murmured, because she felt that she had to say something instead of standing there ogling a gorgeous man as he rocked his infant daughters against an explosion of pink.

"Hi," he mouthed back. "Is it time for our visit already?"

She nodded. "I can come back."

She didn't move as he gave a slight shake of his head. Carefully, he peeled his body from the chair, not jostling even one hair on the head of his precious bundles. As if he'd done it a million times, he laid first one, then the other in their cribs. Neither one woke.

It was a sight to see.

He turned and tiptoed toward the door, but she hadn't moved from her frozen stance in the doorway yet. She should move.

But he stopped right there in front of her, a half smile lingering on his lips as he laid a hand on her arm, presumably to usher her from the room ahead of him. His palm was warm and her skin tingled under it. The feeling threatened to engulf her whole body in a way that she hadn't been *engulfed* in a long time.

Not since Kyle.

Goodness, it seemed so ridiculous, but the real reason it hadn't been hard to stop dating was because no one compared. She was almost thirty and had only had one lover in her life—this man before her with the sparkling green eyes and beautiful face. And she'd take that secret to the grave.

Her cheeks heated as she imagined admitting such a thing to a guy who had likely cut a wide swath through the eligible women beating a path to his door. He hadn't let the grass grow under his feet, now, had he? Fathering twins with a woman he'd written off soon after spoke loudly enough to that question.

If she told him, he'd mistakenly assume she still had feelings for him, and that wasn't exactly true. She just couldn't find a man who fit her stringent criteria for intimacy. Call it old-fashioned, but she wanted to be in love before making love. And most men weren't willing to be that patient.

Except Kyle. He'd never uttered one single complaint when he found out she wasn't hopping into his bed after a few weeks of dating. And oh, my, had it been worth the wait.

The heat in her cheeks spread, and the tingles weren't just under his palm. No, they were a good bit more in a region where she shouldn't be getting so hot, especially not over Kyle and his brand-new warrior's body, laser-sharp focus and gentle hands.

Mercy, she should stop thinking about all that. Except he was looking at her the way he had last night, gaze on her lips, and she wondered if he'd actually do it this time— kiss her as he had so many times before.

One of the babies yowled and the moment broke into pieces.

Kyle's expression instantly morphed into one of concern as he spun toward the crib of the crying infant. Maddie. It was easy to tell them apart if you knew she was the smaller of the two girls. She'd worn a heart monitor for a long time but Grace didn't see the telltale wires poking out of the baby's tiny outfit. Hopefully that meant the multiple surgeries had been successful.

"Hey, now. What's all this fuss?" he murmured, and scooped up the bundle of pink, holding her to his shoulder with rocking motions.

The baby cried harder. Lines of frustration popped up around Kyle's mouth as he kept trying different positions against his shoulder, rocking harder, then slower.

"You liked this earlier," he said. "I'm following procedure here, little lady. Give me a break."

Grace hid a smile. "Maybe her diaper is wet."

Kyle nodded and strode to the changing table. "One diaper change, coming up."

He pulled a diaper from the drawer under the table, laid the baby on the foam pad, then tied the holding straps designed to keep Maddie from rolling to the ground with intricate knots. Next, he lined up the baby powder and diaper rash cream, determination rolling from him in thick waves. When the man put his mind to something, it was dizzying to watch.

With precision, he stripped the baby out of her onesie and took a swift kick to the wrist with good humor as he changed her diaper. It didn't help. The baby wailed a little louder.

"No problem," he said. "Babies usually cry for three reasons. They want to be held. Diaper. And…" A line appeared between Kyle's brows.

Then Maggie woke up and cried in harmony with her sister.

"Want me to pick her up?" Grace asked.

"No. I can handle this. Don't count me out yet." He nestled the other baby into his arms, rocking both with little murmurs. "Bottle. That was the other one Hadley said. We'll try eating."

Bless his heart. He'd gone to Hadley for baby lessons. He was trying so hard, much harder than she'd expected. It warmed her in a whole different way than the sizzle a moment ago. And the swell in her heart was much more dangerous.

The bottle did the trick. After Kyle got both girls fed, they quieted down and fell back asleep in their cribs. This time, he and Grace made it out of the room, but when they reached the living area off the kitchen, *flustered* was too kind a word for the state of her nerves.

Kyle collapsed on the couch with a groan.

"So," she croaked after taking a seat as far away from him as possible. "That was pretty stressful."

"Nah." He scrubbed his face with his hand and peeked out through his fingers. "Stressful is dismantling a home-made pipe bomb before it kills someone."

They'd never talked about his life in the military—largely because he was so closemouthed about it—and judging from the shadows she glimpsed in his expression sometimes, the experience hadn't softened him up any, that was for sure. "Is that what you did overseas? Handle explosives?"

Slowly, he nodded. "That was my specialty, yeah."

He could have died. Easily. A hundred times over, and she'd probably never have known until they paraded his flag-draped coffin through the streets of Royal. The thought was upsetting in a way she really didn't understand, which only served to heighten her already-precarious emotional state.

He'd been serving his country, not using the military as an excuse to stay away. The realization swept through her, blowing away some of her anger and leaving in its place a bit of guilt over never acknowledging his sacrifices in the name of liberty.

"And now you're ready to buckle down and be a father."

It seemed ludicrous. This powerful, strapping man wanted to trade bombs for babies. But when she recalled the finesse he used when handling the babies, she couldn't deny that he had a delicate touch.

"I do what needs to be done," he said quietly, and his green eyes radiated sincerity that she couldn't quite look away from.

When had Kyle become so responsible? Such an *adult*? He was different in such baffling, subtle ways that she kept stumbling in her quest to objectively assess his fitness as a parent.

"Did you give any thought to our discussion yesterday?" she asked.

"The job? I signed on to head up Wade Ranch's cattle division. How's that for serious?"

Kyle leaned back against the couch cushions, looking much more at home in this less formal area than he'd been in the Victorian parlor yesterday, and crossed one booted foot over his knee. Cowboy boots, not the military-issue black boots he'd been wearing yesterday. It was a small detail, but a telling one.

He'd quietly transitioned roles when she wasn't looking. Could it mean he'd been telling the truth when he'd said he planned to stay this time?

"It's a start," she said simply, but that didn't begin to describe what was actually starting.

She'd have to adjust every last thing she'd ever thought about Kyle Wade and his ability to be a father. And if she did, she might also have to think about him differently in a lot of other respects as well, such as whether or not he'd grown up enough to become her everything once again. But this time forever.

Four

Kyle reported to the Wade Ranch cattle barn for duty at zero dark thirty. At least he'd remembered to refer to the beasts as cattle instead of cows. Slowly but surely, snippets of his youth had started coming back to him as he'd driven to the barn. He'd watched his grandfather, Calvin Wade, manage the ranch for years. Kyle remembered perching on the top rail of the cattle pen while Calvin branded the calves or helped Doc Glade with injured cows.

Things had changed significantly since then. The cattle barn had been rebuilt and relocated a half mile from the main house. It was completely separate from the horse business, and Liam's lack of interest in the cattle side couldn't have been clearer. His brother had even hired a ranch manager.

Kyle could practically hear the rattle of Grandpa rolling over in his grave.

He'd always insisted that a man had to manage his own business and Calvin hadn't had much respect for "gentleman" ranchers who spent their money on women and whiskey and hired other men to do the work of running the ranch. Clearly Liam hadn't agreed.

The red barn dominated the clearing ahead. A long empty pen ran along the side of the building. The cattle must be roaming. Kyle parked his truck in a lot near a handful of other vehicles with the Wade Ranch logo on the doors. Easing from the cab, he hit the ground with bated breath. So far, so good. The cowboy boots were a little stiff and the heel put his leg at a weird angle, but he was going to ignore all that as long as possible.

He strolled to the barn, which had an office similar to the one in the horse barn. But that's where the similarities ended. This was a working barn, complete with the smell of manure and hay. Kyle had smelled a lot worse. It reminded him of Grandpa, and there was something nice about following in Calvin's footsteps. They'd never been close, but then Kyle had never been close with anyone. Except Grace.

The ranch manager, Danny Spencer, watched Kyle approach and spat on the ground as he contemplated his new boss.

"You pick out a horse yet, son?"

Kyle's hackles rose. He was no one's son, least of all this man who was maybe fifteen years his senior. It was a deliberate choice of phrasing designed to put Kyle in his place. Wasn't going to work. "First day on the job."

"We ride here. You skedaddle on over to the other barn and come back on a horse. Then we'll talk."

It felt like a test and Kyle intended to pass. So he climbed back into his truck and drove to the horse barn. He felt like a mama's boy driving. But he was in a hurry to get started and walking wasn't one of his skills right now.

Maybe one day.

Liam was already at the barn, favoring an early start

as well, apparently. He helped Kyle find a suitable mount without one smart-alecky comment, which did not go unnoticed. Kyle just chose not to say anything about it.

A few ranch hands gathered to watch, probably hoping Kyle would bust his ass a couple of times and they could video it with their cell phones. He wondered what they'd been told about Kyle's return. Did everyone know about the babies and Margaret's death?

Sucker's bet. Of course they did. Wade Ranch was its own kind of small town. Didn't matter. Kyle was the boss, whether they liked it or not. Whether he had the slightest clue what he was doing. Or not.

The horse didn't like him any better than Danny Spencer did. When he stuck a boot in the stirrup, the animal tried to dance sideways and would have bucked him off if Kyle hadn't kept a tight grip on the pommel. "Hey, now. Settle down."

Liam had called the horse Lightning Rod. Dumb name. But it was all Kyle had.

"That's a good boy, Lightning Rod." It seemed to calm the dark brown quarter horse somewhat, so Kyle tried to stick his boot in the stirrup again. This time, he ended up in the saddle, which felt just as foreign as everything else on the ranch did.

The ranch hands applauded sarcastically, mumbling to each other. He almost apologized for ruining their fun—also sarcastically—but he let it go.

Somehow, Kyle managed to get up to a trot as he rode out onto the trail back to the cattle barn. It had been a lifetime since he'd ridden a horse and longer than that since he'd wanted to.

God, everything hurt. The trot was more of a trounce, and he longed for the bite of rock under his belly as he dismantled a homemade cherry bomb placed carefully under a mosque where three hundred people worshipped. That he understood at least. How he'd landed in the middle of a job managing cattle, he didn't.

Oh, right. He was doing this to prove to everyone they were wrong about him. That he wasn't a slacker who'd ignored messages about his flesh and blood. That Liam and Grace and Danny Spencer and everyone else who had a bone to pick with him weren't going to make him quit.

When he got back to the cattle barn, Danny and the cattle hands were hanging around waiting. One of the disappointed guys from the horse barn had probably texted ahead, hoping someone else could get video of the boss falling off his mount. They could all keep being disappointed.

"One cattle rancher on a horse, as ordered," Kyle called mildly, keeping his ire under wraps. Someone wanted to know what he really thought about things? Too bad. No one was privy to what went on inside Kyle's head except Kyle. As always.

"That'll do," Danny said with a nod, but his scowl didn't loosen up any. "We got a few hundred head in the north pasture that need to be rounded up. You take Slim and Johnny and ya'll bring 'em back, hear?"

"Nothing wrong with my ears," Kyle drawled lazily. "What's wrong is that I'm the one calling the shots now. What do you say we chat about that for a bit?"

Danny spat on the ground near Lighting Rod's left front hoof and the horse flicked his head back in response. Kyle choked up on the reins before his mount got the brilliant idea to bolt.

"I'd say you started drinking early this a.m. if you think you're calling the shots, jarhead."

Kyle let loose a wry chuckle, friendly like, so no one got the wrong idea. "You might want to brush up on your insults. Jarheads are marines, not SEALs."

"Same thing."

Neither of them blinked as Kyle grinned. "Nah. The marines let anyone in, even old cowhands with bad attitudes. Want me to pass your number on to a recruiter? I'll let you go a couple of rounds with a drill sergeant, and when you come back, you can talk to me about the difference between marines and SEALs all you want. Until then, my last name is Wade and the only thing you're permitted to call me is 'boss.'"

Spencer didn't flinch but neither did he nod and play along. He spun on his heel and disappeared into the barn with a backhanded wave. Kyle considered it a win that the man hadn't flipped him a one-fingered salute as a bonus.

Now that the unpleasantness was out of the way, Kyle nodded at the two hands the ranch manager had singled out as his lieutenants, one of whom had fifty pounds on him. That one must be Slim. It was the kind of joke cowboys seemed to like. Kyle would probably be *jarhead* until the day he died after a recounting of his showdown with Danny Spencer made the gossip rounds.

"You boys have a problem working for me?" he asked them both.

Slim's expression was nothing short of hostile, but he and Johnny both shook their heads and swung up on their horses, trotting obediently after Kyle as he headed north toward the pasture where the cattle he was supposed to herd were grazing.

Then he just needed to figure out how to do it. Without alienating anyone else. Oh, and without falling off his horse. And without letting on to anyone that his leg was on fire already after less than thirty minutes in the saddle.

The north pasture came into view. Finally. It was still exactly where it had been ten years ago, but it felt as though it had taken a million years to get there, especially given the tense silence between Kyle and the two hands. Cattle dotted the wide swath of Wade land like black shadows against the green grass, spread as far as the eye could see, even wandering aimlessly into a copse of trees in the distance.

That was not good. He'd envisioned the cattle being easy to round up because they were all more or less in the same place. Instead, he and the hands had a very long task ahead of them to gather up the beasts, who may or may not have wanted to be gathered.

"How many?" he called over his shoulder to Johnny.

"A few hundred." Johnny repeated verbatim the vague number Danny Spencer had rattled off earlier.

He'd mellowed out some and had actually spoken to Kyle without growling. Slim, not so much. The man held a serious grudge that wouldn't be easily remedied. No big thing. They didn't have to like each other. Just work together.

"How many exactly?" Kyle asked again as patiently as possible. "We have to know if we have them all before we head back."

Johnny looked at him cockeyed as if Kyle had started speaking in tongues and thrown around a couple of snakes in the baptismal on a Sunday morning. "We just round 'em up and aim toward the barn. Nothing more to it than that."

"Maybe not before. But today, we're going to make sure we have full inventory before we make the trek." Kyle couldn't do it more than once. There was no way. "Liam didn't happen to invest in GPS, did he?"

Slim and Johnny exchanged glances. "Uh…what?"

"Satellite. RFID chips. You embed the chips in the cow's brand, for example, and use a GPS program to triangulate the chips. Technology to locate and count cattle." At the blank looks he received in response, Kyle gave up. "I'll take that as a no."

That would be Kyle's first investment as head of the cattle division at Wade Ranch. RFID chips would go a long way toward inventorying livestock that ran tame across hundreds of acres. That was how the military kept track of soldiers and supplies, after all. Seemed like a no-brainer to do the same with valuable livestock. He wondered why Liam hadn't done it already.

"All right, then." Kyle sighed. "Let's do this."

The three men rode hard for a couple of hours, driving the cattle toward the gate, eventually feeling confident that they had them all. Kyle had to accept the eyeball guesstimate from Slim and Johnny, who had "done this a couple of times." Both thought the number of bodies seemed about right. Since Kyle wasn't experienced enough to argue, he nodded and let the experts guide them home.

It was exhausting and invigorating at the same time. This was his land. His cattle. His men, despite the lack of welcome.

But when he got back to the cattle barn, Liam was waiting for him, arms crossed and a livid expression on his face.

"What now?" Kyle slid from his horse, keeping a tight grip on the pommel until he was sure his leg would support him.

"Danny Spencer quit." Liam fairly spat. "And walked out without even an hour's notice. Said he'd rather eat manure than work for you. Nice going."

"That's the best news I've heard all day." God's honest truth. The relief was huge. "He doesn't want to work for me? Fine. Better that he's gone."

Liam pulled Kyle away from the multitude of hands swarming the area by the barn, probably all with perked-up ears, hoping to catch more details about the unfolding drama.

"It's not better," Liam muttered darkly. "Are you out of your mind? You can't come in here and throw your weight around. Danny's been handling the cattle side. I told you that. This is his territory and you came in and upset the status quo in less than five minutes."

Kyle shook his head. "Not his territory anymore. It's mine."

"Seriously?" Liam's snort was half laugh and half frustration. "You don't get it. These men respect Danny. Follow him. They don't like you. What are you going to do if they all quit? You can't run a cattle division by yourself."

Yeah, but he'd rather try than put up with dissension in the ranks. Catering to the troops was the fastest way to give the enemy an advantage. There could only be one guy in charge, and it was Kyle. "They can all quit then. There are plenty of ranch hands in this area. I need men who will work, not drama queens all bent out of shape because a bigger fish swam into their pond."

"Fine." Liam threw up his hands. "You have at it. Don't say I didn't warn you. Just keep in mind that we have a deal."

His brother stomped to his truck and peeled out of the clearing with a spray of rock. Kyle resisted the urge to wave, mostly because Liam was probably too pissed to look in his rearview mirror and also because the hands were eyeing him with scowls. No point in being cocky on top of clueless.

His girls were worth whatever he had to do to figure this out.

Johnny approached him then. Kyle had just about had enough of cattle, his aching leg, difficult ranch managers and a hardheaded brother.

"What?" he snapped.

"Uh, I just wanted to tell you thanks." Johnny cleared his throat. "For your service to the country."

The genuine sentiment pierced Kyle through the stomach. And nearly put him on the ground where a day of hard riding hadn't. It was the first time anyone in Royal had positively acknowledged his time in the military. Not that he'd been expecting a three-piece band and a parade. He'd rather stay out of the spotlight—that kind of welcome was for true heroes, not a guy who'd gotten on the wrong end of a bullet.

Nonetheless, Kyle's bad day didn't seem so bad anymore.

"Yeah," he said gruffly. "You're welcome. You know someone who served?"

Usually, the only people who thought about thanking veterans were those with family or friends in the armed forces. It was just a fact. Regular people enjoyed their freedom well enough but rarely thought about the people behind the sacrifices required to secure it.

Johnny nodded, his eyes wide and full of grief. "My dad. He was killed in the first Gulf War. I was still a baby. I never got to know him."

Ouch. That was the kicker. No matter what else, Kyle and this kid had a bond that could never be broken.

Kyle simply held out his hand and waited until Johnny grasped it. "That's a shame. I'm sorry for your loss. I stood in for great fallen men like your dad and helped continue the job he started. I'm proud I got to follow in his footsteps."

The younger man shook his hand solemnly, and then there was nothing more to say. Some things didn't need words.

Kyle hit the shower when he got back to the house. When he emerged, Liam and Hadley asked if they could take the babies for a walk in their double stroller before dinner, and would he like to come?

A walk. They might as well have asked if he'd like to fly. He'd have a hard time with a crawl at this point. After the fishhooks Johnny had sunk into his heart, he'd rather be alone anyway, though it killed him to be unable to do something as simple as push his daughters in a stroller. He waved Liam and his new wife off with a smile, hoped it came across as sincere and limped into the family room to watch something inane on TV.

There was a halfway decent World War II documentary on the History Channel that caught his interest. He watched it for a few minutes until the doorbell rang.

"That was fast," he said as he yanked open the door with a grin he'd dare anyone to guess was fake, expecting to see Liam and Hadley with chagrined expressions because they'd forgotten their key.

But it was Grace. Beautiful, fresh-faced Grace, who stood on the porch with clasped hands, long brown hair down her back, wearing a long-sleeved sweater with form-fitting jeans. It was a hard to peel his eyes from her. But he did. Somehow.

"Hey, Kyle," she said simply.

His smile became real instantly. Why, he couldn't say. Grace was still a bundle of trouble tied up with a big old impossible knot. But where was the fun in leaving a tangle alone?

They'd agreed to forget about the past and start over. But they hadn't fully established what they were starting, at least not to his satisfaction. Maybe now would be a good time to get that straight.

"Hey, Grace." He crossed his arms and leaned on the door frame, cocking his busted leg to take the weight off. "What can I do for you?"

The sun shone behind her, close to setting for the day, spilling fiery reds and yellows into the deep crevices of the sky. As backdrops went, it wasn't half-bad. But it wasn't nearly as spectacular as the woman.

"We had an appointment. Earlier."

Kyle swore. He'd totally forgotten. Wasn't that just

dandy? Made him look like a stellar father to blow off his daughters' caseworker.

Fix it. He needed Grace's good favor.

"But you were off doing cowboy things," she continued. Her voice had grown a little breathy as if she'd run to the door from her car. But the scant distance between here and there sure didn't account for the pink spreading through her cheeks.

"Yep. Someone advised me I might want to find permanent employment if I hoped to be a daddy to my girls. Sorry I missed you." He raised a brow. "But it's mighty accommodating of you to reschedule, considering. 'Preciate it."

Good thing she hadn't wandered down to the barn so she could witness firsthand his impressive debut as the boss.

"No problem," she allowed. "I have to do the requisite number of site visits before I make my recommendations and I do want to be thorough."

Maybe there was room to get her mind off her recommendations and on to something a little more pleasant. *Before* she made any snap judgments about his ability to recall a small thing like an appointment with the person who had the most power to screw up his life. Well, actually, Grace was probably second, behind Kyle—if there was anyone who got the honor of being an A1 screwup thus far in this custody issue, it was him.

"Why don't we sit for a minute?" He gestured to the porch rocker to the left of the front door, which had a great view of the sunset. Might as well put Liam's revamp of the house to good use, and do some reconnaissance at the same time. Grace had to provide a report with her recommendations. He got that. But he wanted to know more about the woman providing the report than anything else at this moment.

"Oh." She glanced at the rocker and then over his shoulder into the interior of the house. "It would probably be best if I watched you interact with the girls again. Like yesterday. That's the quickest way for me to see what kind of environment you'll provide."

"That would be great. Except they aren't here. Liam and Hadley took them for a walk before dinner." Quickly, before she could ask why he hadn't joined them, he held up a finger as if a brilliant idea had just occurred to him. "Why don't you stay and eat with us? You can see how the Wade family handles meals. Meanwhile, we can hang out on the porch and wait for them to get back."

"Um…"

He closed the front door and hustled her over to the bench seat with a palm to the small of her back. To be fair, she didn't resist too much and willingly sank into the rocker, but as soon as he sat next to her, it became clear that *he* should have been the one resisting.

The essence of Grace spilled over him as they got cozy in the two-seater. It was too small for someone his size and their hips snugged up against each other. The contact burned through his jeans, sensitizing his skin, and as he tried to ease off a bit, his foot hit the porch board and set the rocker in motion. Which only knocked her against him more firmly so that her amazing breasts grazed his arm.

Actually, the rocker was exactly the right size for Kyle and Grace. Sitting in it with her might have been the best idea he'd ever had in his life.

Her fresh, spring-like scent wound through his head. They'd sat like this at her mama's house, but in the living room while pretending to watch TV on a Saturday night. It passed for a date in a place like Royal, where teenagers could either get in trouble sneaking around the football stadium with filched beer or hang out under the watchful eye of the folks. Usually Kyle and Grace had opted for the latter, at least until her parents went to bed. Then they got down to some serious making out.

He'd never been as affected by a woman as he'd been by this one. Even just a kiss could knock him for a loop. The memories of how good it had been washed through him, blasting away some of the darkness that had taken over inside. She'd always been so eager. So pliant under his mouth.

All at once, he wondered if she still tasted the same, like innocence laced with a warm breeze.

"Grace," he murmured. Somehow his arm had snaked across the back of the rocker, closing the small gap between them.

Grace's brown eyes peeked out underneath her lashes as she watched him for a moment. Maybe she was wondering the same. If that spark would still be there after all this time.

"How long will it be until Liam and Hadley are back with the girls?" she asked, her voice low.

"Later. Don't worry. We won't miss them."

"I, uh…wasn't worried."

She licked her lips, drawing his attention to her mouth, and suddenly that was all he could see. All he could think about. Her lips had filled out, along with the rest of her face. She'd grown into a woman while he'd been away, with some interesting new experiences shining in her eyes.

All at once, he wanted to know what they were.

"I've been wondering," he said. "Why did you become a social worker? I seem to recall you wanted to be a schoolteacher way back."

That was not what he'd meant to ask. But she lit up at the question. And the sunset? Not even a blip in his consciousness. Her face had all the warmth a man would ever need.

"I did. Want to," she clarified. "That's what I majored in. But I went to do my student teaching and something just didn't work right. The students weren't the problem. Oh, they were a bit unruly but they were fourth graders. You gotta expect some ants in the pants. It was me. There was no…click. You know what I mean?"

"Yeah." He nodded immediately. Like when he hit his stride in BUD/S training on the second day and knew he'd found his place in the world. "Then what happened?"

"I volunteered some places for a while. Tried to get my feet under me, looking for that click. Then my mom calls me and says a friend of hers needs a receptionist because the girl in the job is going out on maternity leave. Would I do her a huge favor for three months?"

As she talked, she waved her hands, dipping and shaping the air, and he found himself smiling along with her as she recounted the story. Smiling and calculating exactly what it would take to get one of those hands on his body somewhere. He wasn't picky—not yet.

"Turns out Sheila, my mom's friend, runs an adoption agency. She's been a huge mentor to me and really helped me figure out what I wanted to do with my life. See, I love children, but I don't like teaching them. I do like helping them, though. I ended up staying at the agency for four years in various roles while I got my master's degree at night."

"You have a master's degree?" That revelation managed to get his attention off her mouth for a brief second. Not that he was shocked—she'd always been a great student. It was just one more layer to this woman that he didn't know nearly well enough.

"Yep." She nodded slowly. "The county requires it."

"That's great."

"What about you? I know you went into the military but that's about it. You went into the navy, Liam said."

"I did." He shifted uncomfortably, as he did any time his years in Afghanistan came up among civilians. The top secret nature of virtually every blessed op he'd completed was so ingrained, it was hard to have a regular conversation with anyone outside of his team. "Special operations. It's not as glamorous as the media makes it out to be. I sweated a lot, got really dirty and learned how to survive in just about any conditions. Meanwhile, I followed orders and occasionally gave a few. And now I'm home."

Something flashed deep in her eyes and she reached out. Her palm landed on his bare forearm, just below the rolled-up sleeve of his work shirt. "It doesn't sound glamorous. It sounds lonely."

"It was," he mumbled before he'd realized it. Shouldn't have admitted that. It smacked of weakness.

"I'm sorry." Her sympathy swept along his nerve endings, burying itself under his skin. The place she'd always been.

The place he'd always let her be. Because she soothed him and eased his loneliness. Always had. Looked as if for all the things that had changed, that was one constant, and he latched on to it greedily.

"It's over now."

His arm still stretched across the back of the seat. The slightest shift nestled her deeper against him and a strand of her glossy hair fell against her cheek. He wasted no time capturing it between his fingers, brushing it aside, and then letting his fingers linger.

Their gazes met and held for an eternity. A wealth of emotions swirled in her eyes.

Her skin was smooth and warm under his touch. She tilted her face toward his fingers, just a fraction of a movement. Just enough to tell him she wasn't about to push him away.

He slid his fingers more firmly under her chin and lifted it. And then those amazing lips of hers were within claiming distance. So he claimed them.

Grace opened beneath his mouth with a gasp, sucking him under instantly. Their mouths aligned, fitting together so perfectly, as if she'd been fashioned by the Almighty specifically for Kyle Wade. He'd always thought that. How was that still true?

The kiss deepened without any help on his part. He couldn't have said his own name as something raw and elemental exploded in his chest. *Grace.* The feel of her—like home and everything that was good in the world, blended together and infused into the essence of this woman.

He wanted more. And he couldn't have stopped himself from taking it.

Threading both hands through her hair, he cupped her head and changed the angle, plunging into the sensation. Taking her along with him. She moaned in her chest, and answering vibrations rocked his.

She clung to him, her hands gripping his shoulders as if she never wanted to let go. Which was great, because he didn't want her to.

Her sweet taste flowed across his tongue as he twined it with hers, greedily soaking up everything she was offering. It had been so long since he'd *felt*. Since he'd allowed himself to be so open. Hell, he hadn't *allowed* anything. She'd burrowed into his very core with nothing more than a kiss, and he'd had little to say about it.

And then she was gone. Ripped away.

She bolted from the rocker, her chest rising and falling as she hugged the split-pine railing surrounding the porch with her back. "I'm sorry. I shouldn't have done that."

"But you did." Ruthlessly, he shut down all the things she'd stirred up inside, since it appeared as if she wasn't up for seconds.

"I got caught up. That can't happen again."

Her expression glittered with undisguised longing, and no, he hadn't imagined that she'd welcomed his kiss. That she'd leaned into his touch and begged for more. So why was she stopping?

"I heartily disagree." He smiled, but it almost hurt to paint it on when his entire body was on fire. And this woman was the only one who could quench the flames. "It's practically a requirement for it to happen again."

"Are you that clueless, Kyle?"

Clueless. Yeah, he needed to catch a couple of clues apparently, like the big screaming back-off vibes Grace was shooting in his direction.

"I'm your daughters' caseworker," she reminded him with raised eyebrows. "We can't get involved."

His body cooled faster than if she'd dumped a bucket of ice water on his head. "You're right."

Of course she was right. When had he lost sight of that? This wasn't about whether she was interested or not; it was about his daughters. What had started out as a half-formed plan to distract her from work had actually distracted *him* far more effectively.

And he wanted to do it again. That was dangerous. She could take his girls away at the drop of a hat, and he couldn't afford to antagonize her. Hell, she'd even told him she had to treat the case as objectively as possible, and here he was, ignoring all of that.

Because she'd gotten to him. She'd dug under his skin without saying a word. Talk about dangerous. He couldn't let her know she had that much power over him, or she might use it to her advantage. How could he have forgotten how much better it was to keep his heart—and his mouth—shut? That's why he stuck to weekend hookups, like the one he'd had with Margaret. No one expected him to spill his guts, and then he was free to leave before anyone got a different idea about how things were going to go.

That was the best he could do. The best he *wanted* to do. But he couldn't ditch Royal this time around when things got too heated. He'd have to figure out how to get past one more tangle in the big fat knot in his chest that had Grace's name all over it.

She thought he was clueless? Just a big dumb guy who couldn't find his way around a woman without a map? Fine. It served his purpose to let her keep on thinking that, while he flipped this problem on its head.

"Sorry about that, then." He held up his hands and let a slow grin spread across his face. "Hands off from now on."

Or at least until he figured out which way the wind blew in Grace's mind about the custody issue. He couldn't afford to antagonize her, but neither could he afford to let her out of his sight. Once he had curried her good favor and secured his claim on his children, all bets were off.

And when she mumbled an excuse about having other dinner plans, he let her leave, already contemplating what kind of excuse he could find to get her into his arms again, but this time, without any of the emotional tangle she seemed to effortlessly cause.

Five

The kiss had been a mistake.

Grace knew that. She'd known *while* she was kissing Kyle. The whole time. Why, for the love of God, couldn't she stop thinking about it?

She'd kissed Kyle lots of times. None of those kisses was seared into her brain, ready to pop up in her consciousness like a jack-in-the-box gone really wrong. Of course, all her previous Kyle kisses had happened with the boy.

He was all man now.

Darker, harder, fiercer. And oh, how he had driven that fact home with nothing more than his mouth on hers. The feel of his lips had winnowed through her, sliding through her blood, waking it deliciously. Reminding her that she was all woman.

Telling her that she'd yet to fully explore what that meant.

Oh, sure, she'd kissed a few of the men she'd dated before she'd become a Professional Single Girl. But those chaste, dry pecks hadn't compared with being kissed by someone like Kyle.

She couldn't do it again. No matter how much she wanted to. No matter how little sleep she got that night and how little work she got done the next day because she couldn't erase the goose bumps from her skin that had sprung up the instant Kyle had touched her.

When Clare Connelly called with a dinner invitation, Grace jumped on it, nearly crying with relief at the thought of a distraction. Clare was a pediatric nurse who'd cared for the twin babies in the harrowing days after their premature birth, and she and Grace had become good friends.

Grace arrived at the Waters Café just off Royal's main street before Clare, so she took a seat at a four top and ordered a glass of wine while she waited. The café had been rebuilt as part of the revitalization of the downtown strip after the tornado had tried to wipe Royal off the map. The owners, Jim and Pam Waters, had nearly lost everything, but thanks to a good insurance policy and some neighborly folks, the café was going strong. Grace made it a point to eat there as often as possible, just to give good people her business.

Clare bustled through the door, her long blond hair still twisted up in her characteristic bun, likely because she'd just come from work at Royal Memorial. Grace waved, and then realized she wasn't alone—Clare had her arm looped through another woman's. Violet McCallum, who co-owned the Double M Ranch with her brother, Mac.

Wow, Grace hardly recognized her. Violet looked beautiful and was even wearing a dress instead of her usual boots and jeans. It had been a while since they'd seen each other. Not since they'd all met at Priceless, the antiques and craft store owned by Raina Patterson, to indulge in a girls' night of stained glass making, which had been so much fun that Grace had picked it up as a new hobby.

"I had to drag her out of the house," Clare said by way of greeting, laughing and pointing at Violet. It was a bit of a joke among the three ladies as Violet and Grace had done something similar for Clare when she'd been going through man troubles. "I hope you don't mind."

"Of course I don't. Hi, Violet!" Grace jumped up and embraced the auburn-haired woman. Violet gave her a one-armed hug in return and scuttled to a seat.

Grace and Clare settled into their own seats. Grace signaled the waitress, then leaned forward on her forearms to speak to Violet across the table. "What are you using on your skin? Because I'm investing in a truckload. You look positively luminous!"

Violet flinched and gave Grace a pained smile, which highlighted dark shadows in her friend's eyes. "Thanks. It's, um…my new apricot scrub. I'll text you the name of it when I get home."

"Sure," Grace said enthusiastically, but it felt a little forced. Something was off with Violet but she didn't want to pry. They'd been friends a long time. If Violet wanted to share what was up, she would. "Give me your hand, Clare. Dinner can't officially start until we ooh and aah over your ring!"

A smile split Clare's face, and she stuck her hand out, fingers spread in the classic pose of an engaged woman. "Stand back, ladies. This baby will blind you if you don't give it the proper distance."

Clare had recently gotten engaged to Dr. Parker Reese, a brilliant neonatal specialist at Royal Memorial, where they both worked. Their romance had been touch and go, framed by the desperate search for Maddie's mother after the infant had been abandoned at a truck stop shortly after her birth. Margaret Garner had then gotten into her car and given birth to Maggie a little farther down the road, ultimately dying from the traumatic childbirth. So the twins had ended up separated. When Maggie ultimately went home with Liam and Hadley, they were unaware she had a sister. Thankfully, they'd eventually realized Maddie and Maggie were twins and thus both belonged with the Wades.

Of course, that had all been before Kyle had come home.

And that was a dumb thing to start thinking about. Grace pinched herself under the table, but it didn't do any good. The kiss popped right back into her mind, exactly the thing she was trying to avoid thinking about.

Kyle was a difficult man to forget. She should know. She'd spent ten years trying to forget him and had failed spectacularly.

"Tell us about the wedding," Grace insisted brightly. Anything to take her attention off Kyle.

Clare gushed for a minute or two until the harried waitress finally made her way over to the three ladies. The ponytailed woman in her early twenties pulled a pen from behind her ear and held it expectantly over her order pad.

"Sorry for the wait, ladies," she apologized. "We're short-staffed today."

"No problem," Grace tossed out with a smile. "This Chardonnay is fabulous. Can you bring two more glasses?"

"No!" Violet burst out, and then her eyes widened as all three of the other women stared at her. "I, uh, didn't bring my driver's license, and I know you have to see my identification, so no drinking for me. Water is fine anyway. Thanks."

"It's okay, Ms. McCallum," the waitress said cheerfully. "I know you're over twenty-one. You were two years ahead of my sister in high school and she's twenty-four. I'd be happy to make an exception."

Violet turned absolutely green. "That's kind of you. But water is fine. Excuse me."

All at once, Violet rushed from the table, snatching her

purse from the back of the chair as she ran for the rear of the restaurant toward the bathrooms. In her haste, she knocked the straight-backed chair to the floor with a crash that reverberated in the half-full café. Conversations broke off instantly as the other customers swiveled to seek out the source of the noise.

Violet didn't pause until she'd disappeared from the room. *What in the world?*

"I practically had to force her to come tonight," Clare confessed, her voice lowered as she leaned close to Grace and waved off the beleaguered waitress, who promised to come back later. "I guess I shouldn't have. But she's been holed up for a few weeks now, and Mac called me, worried. He mentioned that she'd been under the weather, but he thought she was feeling better."

That was just like Violet's brother, Mac McCallum. He was the kind of guy Grace had always wished she'd had for a big brother, one who looked out for his sister even into their adulthood. Back in high school, he'd busted Tommy Masterson in the mouth for saying something off-color about Violet, and the boys in Royal had learned fast that they didn't cross Mac when it came to Violet.

"We should go check on her," Grace said firmly. Poor thing. She probably had a stomach flu or something like that, and they'd let her run off to the bathroom. Alone. "Friends hold each other's hair."

When Grace and Clare got to the restroom, Violet was standing at the sink, both hands clamped on the porcelain as she stared in the mirror, hollow eyed, supporting her full weight on her palms as if she might collapse if the vanity wasn't there to hold her up.

"You didn't have to disrupt your dinner on my account." Violet didn't glance at the other two women as she spoke into the mirror.

"Of course we did." Grace put her arm around Violet

and held her tight as she stood by her friend's side, offering the only kind of support she knew to give: physical contact. "Whatever it is, I'm sure you'll feel better soon. Sometimes it takes a while for the virus to work through your system. Do you want some crackers? Cold medicine? I'll run to the pharmacy if need be."

A brief lift of Violet's lips passed as a smile. "You're so nice to offer, but I don't think what I've got can be fixed with cold medicine."

She trembled under Grace's arm. This was no garden-variety stomach bug or spring cold, and Grace was just about to demand that Violet go see a doctor in the morning, or she'd drag her there herself, when Clare met Violet's eyes in the mirror as she came up on the other side of their friend.

"You're pregnant," Clare said decisively with a knowing smile. "I knew it. That night at Priceless... I could see then that you had that glowy look about you."

Oh. Now Grace felt like a dummy. Of course that explained Violet's strange behavior and refusal to drink the wine.

Shock flashed through Violet's expression but she banked it and then hesitated for only a moment. "No. That's impossible."

"Impossible, like you're in denial? Or impossible, like you haven't slept with anyone who could have gotten you pregnant?"

"Like, impossible, period, end of story, and now you need to drop it." Violet scowled at Clare in the mirror, who just stuck her tongue out. "It's just an upset stomach. Let's go back to the table."

With a nod that said she was dropping it but didn't like it, Clare hustled Violet to the table and ordered her hot tea with lemon, then ensured that everyone selected something to eat in her best mother-hen style.

The atmosphere grew lighter and lighter until their food came. They were just three friends having dinner, as advertised. Until Clare zeroed in on Grace and asked point-blank, "What's going on with you and Kyle Wade?"

Grace nearly choked. "What? Nothing."

Heat swept across her cheeks as she recalled in living color exactly how big a lie that was.

"Funny," Clare remarked to Grace. "I'd swear I heard mention of a highly charged *encounter* with Kyle in the parking lot of the HEB the other night. Care to fill us in?"

Violet perked up. "What's this? You're picking up with Kyle again?"

"Over my dead body!" That might have come out a little more vehement than she'd intended. "I mean…"

"I haven't seen him yet," Violet said to Clare as if Grace hadn't spoken. "But when I went to the bank yesterday, Cindy May said he's filled out and pretty much the stuff of centerfold fantasies. 'Smoking hot' was the phrase she used. Liberally."

Clare waggled her brows at Grace. "Spill the beans, dear."

Heat climbed up her cheeks. "I don't have any beans to spill. His daughters are on my case docket, and we ran into each other at the grocery store. This is Royal. It would be weird if I *hadn't* run into him."

"I haven't run into him." Violet sipped her tea. "Clare?"

The traitor shook her head. "Nope."

"Well, the Kyle train has left the station and I was not on board. I don't plan to be on board." Grace drained her glass of wine and motioned for another one the moment the waitress glanced her way. Wow, was it hot in here, and she was so thirsty. "Kyle Wade is the strong, silent type, and I need a man who can open his mouth occasionally to tell me what I mean to him. If that's not happening, I'm not happening. But it doesn't matter because nothing is going on with us. He's trying to be a father and I'm working to figure out how to let him. That's it."

All at once, she realized she'd already made up her mind about his fitness as a parent. Kyle was trying. She'd seen it over and over. What could she possibly object to in his bid for custody? Nothing. Any objections would be strictly due to hurt feelings over something that happened a decade ago. It was time to embrace the concept of bygones and move on.

"Men are nothing but trouble," Violet muttered darkly.

"That's not true," Clare corrected. "The right man is priceless."

"Parker is one in a million and he's taken. Unless you're willing to share?" Grace teased, and tried really hard to shut down the uncomfortable squeeze of jealousy surrounding her heart.

Clare had met her Dr. McDreamy. Grace had nothing. A great big void where Kyle used to be, and nothing had come along in ten years that could fill it. Well, except for the one man whom she suspected would fill that hole perfectly. She just had no desire to let him try, no matter how much she wanted a husband and family of her own.

Eyebrows raised, Clare cocked her head at Grace. "So you're sticking by your single-girl status, huh?"

She didn't sound so convinced, as if maybe Grace had been kidding when she'd vowed to be a Professional Single Girl from now on.

"I've been telling you so for months," Grace insisted. "There's nothing wrong with high standards and until I find someone who can spell *standards*, it's better to be on my own."

Actually, her standards weren't all that high—a run-of-the-mill swept-off-her-feet romance would do just fine. If she was pregnant and in love with a man who desperately loved her in return, she'd consider her life complete.

"Hear, hear." Violet raised her mug of hot tea to click it against Grace's wineglass. "I'll join your single girl club."

"Everyone is welcome. Except Clare." Grace grinned to cover the heaviness that had settled over her heart all at once. There wasn't anything on her horizon that looked like a fairy-tale romance. Just another meeting with a man who was driving her crazy.

Grace drove to Wade Ranch the next day without calling and without an appointment.

She didn't want to give Kyle any sort of heads-up that she was coming or that she'd made a decision. Hopefully, that meant she could get and keep the upper hand.

No more sunset conversations that ended with her wrapped up in Kyle's very strong, very capable arms.

No matter what. No matter how much she'd been arguing with herself that maybe Kyle had changed. Maybe *she* had changed. Maybe another kiss, exactly like that first one, would be what the doctor ordered, and then she would find out he'd morphed into her Prince Charming.

Yeah, none of that mattered.

Kyle and his daughters—that was what mattered. That morning she'd spent two hours in a room with her supervisor, Megan, going over her recommendation that Kyle be awarded full and uncontested custody of his children. With Megan's stamp of approval on the report, Grace's role in this long, drawn-out issue had come to a close.

Hadley answered the door at Wade House and asked after Grace's parents, then let Grace hold the babies without Grace having to beg too much. She inhaled their fresh powder scent—it was the best smell in the world. Out of nowhere, the prick of tears at her eyes warned her that she hadn't fully shut down the emotions from her conversation with Clare and Violet last night.

If this meeting went as intended, this might be her last

interaction with Kyle. And the babies. They were so precious and the thought of only seeing them again in passing shot through her heart.

"I'm here to see Kyle," she told Hadley as she passed the babies back reluctantly. She had a job to do, and it wasn't anyone's fault except hers that she didn't have a baby of her own.

"He's at the barn. Expect that will be the case from now on." Hadley shook her head in wonder. "I have to say, Kyle is nothing like I remember. He had no interest in the ranch before. Right? You remember that, too, don't you?"

Greedily, Grace latched on to the subject change and told herself it was strictly because she wanted additional validation that she was doing the right thing in trusting Kyle with his daughters. "I do recall that. But he's taking over the cattle side, or so I understand."

"That's right. Liam's about to come out of his skin, he's so excited about the prospect of focusing solely on his quarter horses. He didn't think Kyle was going to step up. But Liam has admitted to me, privately of course, that he might have been wrong about his brother."

Liam saw it, too. Kyle had changed.

That was very interesting food for thought.

"Do you think Kyle would mind if I visited him down at the barn? I need to talk to him about the report I'm filing."

Grace was already on her feet before she'd finished speaking, but Hadley just nodded with a smile. "Sure. Bring Kyle back with you and stay for lunch."

"Oh. Um…" Grace stared at Hadley gently rocking both babies in her arms and realized that her recommendations were going to affect Hadley and Liam, too. And not in a good way. She hated the fact that she was going to upset them after they'd spent so much love and effort in caring for Kyle's babies in his stead. There was a long conversation full of disappointment in Liam and Hadley's future.

All at once, she didn't want this job any longer. She should have figured out a way to pass the case off the moment she'd heard Kyle's name over the phone when Liam called. But she hadn't been able to, and people's lives were at stake here. She'd have to figure out how to handle it.

"Thanks for the lunch invite, but I have to be getting back to the office. Maybe next time," she said brightly, and escaped before Hadley could insist.

The cattle barn was a half mile down a chipped rock path to the west of Wade House, and faster than she would have liked, Grace pulled into the small clearing where a couple of other big trucks sat parked. She wandered into the barn, hoping Kyle would be inside.

He was.

The full force of his masculine beauty swept through her as she caught sight of him through the glass wall that partitioned the cattle office from the rest of the large barn. He was leaning against the frame of an open door, presumably talking to someone inside, hip cocked out in a way that should seem arrogant, but was just a testament to his incredible confidence.

Working man's jeans hugged his lean hips and yeah, he still had a prime butt that she didn't mind checking out in the slightest. There might be drool in her future.

And then Kyle backed out of the doorway and turned, catching her in the act of checking out his butt. *Shoot.* Too late, she spun around but not before witnessing the slow smile spreading across his face. How in the world was she going to brazen this out? Heat swirled through her cheeks.

Kyle exited the office area with a clatter. His eyes burned into her back and she had the distinct impression his gaze had dipped below her belt in a turnabout-is-fair-play-kind of checkout.

"Hey, Grace," he said pleasantly.

She couldn't very well ignore his greeting, so she sighed and faced him, smug smile and all. "Hi."

"See anything you like?"

How was she supposed to answer that? *Men*. They all had egos the size of Texas and she certainly wasn't going to cater to inflating his further. He was lucky she didn't smack him in his cocky mouth. "Nothing I haven't seen before."

Except she really shouldn't have been all high-and-mighty, when she was the one who'd been ogling his butt. It was her own darn fault she'd gotten caught.

"Really?" His eyebrows shot up and amusement played at his mouth. Not that she was staring at it or anything, or remembering how dark, hard and fierce that kiss had been. "You've been shopping for cattle before?"

"Cattle?" She made the mistake of meeting his glittery green eyes, vibrant even in the low light of the barn, and he sucked her in, mesmerizing her for a moment. "I…don't think… I'm not here to buy cattle."

Her fingers tingled all at once as they flexed in memory of clutching his shoulders the other night during their kiss. And then the rest of her body got in on that action, putting her somewhere in the vicinity of hot and bothered. A long liquid pull at her core distracted her entirely from whatever it was they were talking about.

"Are you sure? That's what we do here at Wade Ranch. Sell cattle. Figured you were in the market since you came all this way."

"Oh. No. No cattle." Geez, was there something wrong with her brain? Simple concepts like English and speaking didn't seem to be happening.

Kittens. Daffodils. She had to get her mind off that kiss with something that wasn't the slightest bit manly. But then Kyle shifted closer and she caught a whiff of something so wholly masculine and earthy and the slightest bit piney, it nearly made her weep with want.

"Well, then," he murmured. "Why are you here if it's not to peruse the goods?"

Oh, she was *so* here to peruse the goods. Except she wasn't and she couldn't keep falling down on the job. "I wanted to talk to you."

"Amazing coincidence. I wanted to talk to you, too."

"So I'm not bothering you?"

"Oh, yeah. Make no mistake, Grace. You bother me." His low, sexy voice skittered across her nerves, standing them on end. "At night, when I'm thinking about kissing you again. In the shower, when I'm *really* thinking about kissing you again. In the saddle, when I think kissing you again is the only thing that's going to make that particular position bearable."

A stupid rush of heat sprang up in her face as she pictured him riding a horse and caught his meaning.

It was uncomfortable for Kyle to sit in a saddle. Because he was turned on. By her.

It was embarrassing. And somehow empowering. The thrill of it sang through her veins. Being in love with Kyle she remembered. Being a source of discomfort, she didn't. Sex had been so new, so huge and so special the first time around. They hadn't really explored their physical relationship very thoroughly before everything had fallen apart due to Kyle's strange moods and inability to express his feelings for her.

She suddenly wondered what physical parts they'd left unexplored. And whether the superhot kiss—which had been vastly more affecting than the ones ten years ago—meant that he'd learned a few new tricks over the years.

"You've been thinking about our kiss, too?" she asked before she thought better of it.

"Too?" He picked up on that slip way too fast, his expression turning molten instantly as he zeroed in on her. "As in *also*? You've been thinking about it?"

He was aiming so much heat in her direction she thought she might melt from it.

"Um..." Well, it was too late to back out now. "Maybe once or twice. It was a nice kiss."

His slow smile set off warning bells. "*Nice*. I must be rusty if that's the best word you can come up with to describe it. Let me try again and I can guarantee *nice* won't be anywhere in your vocabulary afterward."

Before he could get started on that promise, she slapped a hand on his chest, and Lord have mercy, it was like concrete under her fingers, begging to be explored just to see if all of him was that hard.

"Not so fast," she muttered before she lost her mind completely. "I'm here in an official capacity."

"Well, why didn't you say so?"

"You were too busy trying to sell me a side of beef, if I recall," she responded primly, and his rich laugh nearly finished the job of melting her into a big puddle. She shouldn't let him affect her like that. Quickly, she snatched her hand back.

"Touché, Ms. Haines." He crossed his arms over his powerful chest and contemplated her, sobering slightly. "Is this about my girls?"

She nodded. "I've provided my recommendations in a report to my supervisor. But essentially, I have no objections to you having sole custody of your daughters."

Kyle let out a whoop and swept her up in his arms, spinning her around effortlessly. Laughing at his enthusiasm, she whacked him on the arm with token protests sputtering from her lips. This was not the appropriate way to thank his caseworker.

And then he let her slide to the floor again, much more

slowly than he should have, especially when it became clear that there was very little of him that wasn't hard.

She cleared her throat and stepped away.

"Thanks, Grace. This means a lot to me." Sincerity shone in his gaze and she couldn't look away. "So it's over? No more site visits?"

"Well…" She couldn't say it all at once. Her excuse to continue seeing him would evaporate if she said yes. "Maybe a few more. I still plan to keep an eye on you."

The vibe between them heated up again in a hurry as he leaned into her space. "But if you're not my daughters' caseworker any longer, then there's no reason I can't kiss you again."

True. But she couldn't have it both ways. Either she needed an excuse to keep coming by, even though that excuse would prevent anything from happening between them, or she could flat out admit she was still enormously attracted to him and let the chips fall where they may.

One option put butterflies in her stomach. And the other put caterpillars in it. The only problem was she couldn't figure out which was which.

"I'm not closing the case yet," she heard herself say before she'd fully planned to say it. "So I'll come by a couple more times, just to file additional support for the recommendation. It could still go the other way if anything changes."

"All right." He cocked his head. "But if you've already filed the report, there's no issue with your objectivity. Right?"

And maybe she should just call a spade a spade and settle things once and for all.

"Right. But—" she threw up a hand as a smile split his face "—that's not the only thing going on here, Kyle, and you know it. We haven't been a couple for a long time, and

I'm not sure picking up where we left off is the best idea. Not saying never. Just give me space for now."

So she could think. So she could figure out if she was willing to trust him again. So she could understand why everything between them felt so different this time, so much more dangerous and thrilling.

He nodded once, but the smile still plastered across his face said he wasn't convinced by her speech. Maybe because she hadn't convinced herself of it, either.

"You know where to find me. If you'll excuse me, I have some cattle to tend to."

She watched him walk off because she couldn't help herself apparently. And she had a feeling that was going to become a theme very shortly when interacting with Kyle Wade.

Six

Kyle didn't see Grace for a full week, and by the seventh day, he was starting to go a little bonkers. He couldn't stop thinking about her, about picking up that kiss again. Especially now that the conflict of interest had vanished.

But then she'd thrown up another wall—the dreaded *give me space*. He hated space. Unless he was the one creating it.

So instead of calling up Grace and asking her on a date the way he wanted to, he filled his days with things such as learning how to worm cattle alongside Doc Glade and his nights learning which of his daughters liked to be held a certain way.

It was fulfilling in a way he'd have never guessed.

And exhausting. Far more than going for days at a stretch with no sleep as he and his boys cleared a bayside warehouse of nasty snipers so American supply ships could dock without fear of being shot at.

Kyle would have sworn up and down that being a SEAL

had prepared him for any challenge, but he'd been able to perform that job with a sense of detachment. Oh, he'd cared, or he would never have put himself in the line of fire. But you had to march into a war knowing you might not come out. Knowing that you might cause someone else to not come out. There was no room for emotion in the middle of that.

Being a father? It was 100 percent raw emotion, 24-7. Fear that he was doing it wrong. Joy in simply holding another human being that was a part of him, who shared his DNA. Worry that he'd screw up his kids as his parents had done to him. A slight tickle in the back of his throat that it could all change tomorrow if Grace suddenly decided that she'd made a mistake in awarding him custody.

But above all else was the sense that he shouldn't be doing it by himself. Kids needed a mother. Hadley was nurturing and clearly cared about the babies, but she was Liam's wife, not Kyle's. Now that the news had come out about Grace's recommendations, it didn't seem fair to keep asking Hadley to be the nanny, not when she'd hoped to adopt the babies herself.

It was another tangle he didn't know how to unsnarl, so he left it alone until he could figure it out. Besides, no one was chomping at the bit to change the current living situation and for now, Kyle, Liam and Hadley shared Wade House with Maggie and Maddie. Which meant that it would be ridiculous to tell Hadley not to pick up one of his daughters when she cried. So he didn't.

Plus, he was deep in the middle of growing the cattle business. Calving season was upon them, which meant days and days of backbreaking work to make sure the babies survived, or the ranch lost money instantly. He couldn't spend ten or twelve hours a day at the cattle barn *and* take care of babies. That was his rationale anyway, and he repeated it to himself often. Some days it rang more true than others.

A week after Grace had told him he'd earned custody of his daughters, Kyle spent thirty horrific minutes in his office going through email and other stuff Ivy, Wade Ranch's bookkeeper and office manager, had dumped on his desk with way too cheery a smile. The woman was sadistic. Death by paper cuts might as well be Ivy's mantra.

God, he hated paperwork. He'd rather be hip-deep in manure than scanning vet reports and sales figures and bills and who knew what all.

A knock at his door saved him. He glanced up to see a smiling Emma Jane and he nearly wept in relief. Emma Jane had the best title in the whole world—sales manager—which meant he didn't have to talk to people who wanted to buy Wade Angus. She handled everything and he blessed her for it daily.

"Hey, boss," she drawled. "Got a minute?"

She always called him "boss" with a throaty undertone that made him vaguely uncomfortable, as if any second now, she might declare a preference for being dominated and fall at his feet, prostrate.

"For you, always." He kicked back from the desk and crossed his arms as the sales manager came into his office. "What's up?"

With a toss of her long blond hair, Emma Jane sashayed over to his desk and perched one hip on the edge, careful to arrange her short skirt so it revealed plenty of leg. Kyle hid a grin, mostly because he didn't want to encourage her. God love her, but Emma Jane had the subtlety of a Black Hawk helicopter coming in for landing.

"I was thinking," she murmured with a coy smile. "We've mostly been selling cattle here locally, but we should look to expand. There's a big market in Fort Worth."

Obviously she was going somewhere with this, so Kyle

just nodded and made a noncommittal sound as he waited for the punch line.

"Wade Ranch needs to make some contacts there," she continued, and rearranged her hair with a practiced twirl. "We should go together. Like a business trip, but stay overnight and take in the sights. Maybe hit a bar in Sundance Square?"

First half of that? Great plan. Spot-on. Second half was so not a good idea, Kyle couldn't even begin to count the ways it wasn't a good idea. But he had to tread carefully. Wade Ranch couldn't afford for Kyle to antagonize another employee into quitting. Liam still hadn't replaced Danny Spencer, and Kyle was starting to worry his brother was going to announce that he'd decided *Kyle* should be the ranch manager.

"I like the way you think," he allowed. "You're clearly the brains of this operation."

She batted her lashes with a practiced laugh, leaning forward to increase the gap at her cleavage. "You're such a flatterer. Go on."

Since it didn't feel appropriate for the boss to be staring down the front of his employee's blouse, no matter how obvious she was making it that she expected him to, Kyle glanced over Emma Jane's shoulder to the window. And spied the exact person he'd been hoping to see. *Grace.* Finally.

He'd been starting to wonder if she was planning to avoid him for the next ten years. From the corner of his eye, he watched her park her green Toyota in the small clearing outside the barn and walk the short path to the door. His peripheral vision was sharp enough to see a sniper in a bell tower at the edge of a village—or one social worker with hair the color of summer wheat at sunset, who had recently asked Kyle to give her space.

"No, really," he insisted as he focused on Emma Jane

again. Grace had just entered the barn, judging by the sound of the footsteps coming toward his office, which he easily recognized as hers. "You've been handling cattle sales for what, almost a year now? Your numbers are impressive. Clearly you know your stuff."

Or she knew how to stick her breasts in a prospective buyer's face. Honestly, there was no law against it, and he didn't care how she sold cattle as long as she did her job. Just as there was no law against letting Grace think there was more going on here in his office than there actually was.

She wanted space, didn't she? Couldn't give a woman any more space than to pretend he'd moved on to another one. If he timed it right, Grace would get an eyeful of exactly how much *space* he was giving her. He treated Emma Jane to a wide smile and put an elbow on the desk, right by her knee.

Emma Jane lit up, just as Grace appeared in the open doorway of his office.

"Thanks, sweetie." Emma Jane smiled and ran one hand up his arm provocatively. He didn't remove it. "That's the nicest compliment anyone's ever given me."

Grace halted as if she'd been slapped. That's when he turned his head to meet her gaze, acknowledging her presence, just in case she'd gotten it into her head to flee. She was right where he wanted her.

"Am I interrupting?" Grace asked drily, and Emma Jane jerked back guiltily as she figured out they weren't alone anymore.

Yes, thank God. He'd have to deal with Emma Jane at some point, but he couldn't lie—he'd much rather have Grace sitting on his desk and leaning over strategically any day of the week and twice on Sunday.

"Not at all." Kyle stood with a dismissive nod at Emma Jane, whose usefulness had just come to an end. "We were just talking about how to increase our contact list in the Fort Worth area. We can pick it up later."

"We sure can," Emma Jane purred, and then shot Grace a dirty look as she flounced from the room.

"That was cozy," Grace commented once the sales manager was out of earshot. Her face was blank, but her tone had an undercurrent in it that he found very interesting.

"You think so?" Kyle crossed his arms and cocked a hip, pretending to contemplate. "We were just talking. I'm not sure what you mean."

Grace rolled her eyes. "Really, Kyle? She was practically draped over your desk like a bearskin throw rug, begging you to wrap her around you."

Yeah. She pretty much had been. He bit back a grin at Grace's colorful description. "I didn't notice."

"Of course you didn't." Her eyebrows snapped together over brown eyes that—dare he hope—had a hint of jealousy glittering in them. "You were too busy being blinded by her cleavage."

That got a laugh out of him, which didn't sit well with Grace, judging by the fierce scowl on her face. But he couldn't help it. This was too much fun. "She is a nice-looking woman, I do agree."

"I didn't say that. She's far too obvious to be considered 'nice-looking.'" Grace accompanied this with little squiggly motions of her forefingers. "She might as well write her phone number on her forehead with eyeliner. She clearly buys it in bulk and layers it on even at ten o'clock in the morning, so what's a little more?"

The more Grace talked, the more agitated she became, drawing in the air with her whole hand instead of just her fingers.

"So she's a little heavy-handed with her makeup." He waved it off. "She's a great girl who sells cattle for Wade Ranch. I have no complaints with her."

Grace made a little noise of disgust. "Except for the way she was shamelessly flirting with you, you mean? I can't believe you let her talk to you like that."

"Like what?" He shrugged, well aware he was pouring gasoline on Grace's fire, but so very curious what would happen when she exploded. "We were just talking."

"Yeah, you're still just as clueless as you always were."

There was that word again. *Clueless.* She'd thrown it at him one too many times to let it go. There was something more here to understand. He could sense it.

Before he could demand an explanation, Johnny blew into the office, his chest heaving and mud caked on his jeans and boots from the knee down. "Kyle. We got a problem. One of the pregnant cows is stuck in the ravine at the creek and she went into labor."

Instantly, Kyle shouldered past a wide-eyed Grace with an apologetic glance. He hated to leave her behind but this was his job.

"Take me there."

Liam had put Kyle in charge of the cattle side of Wade Ranch. This was his first real test and the gravity of it settled across his shoulders with weight he wasn't expecting.

He followed Johnny to the paddock where they kept their horses and mounted up, ignoring the twinge deep in his leg bone, or what was left of it. He could sit in his office like a wimp and complain about paperwork or ride. There was no room for a busted leg in ranching.

Kyle heeled Lightning Rod into a gallop and tore after Johnny as the ranch hand led him across the pasture where the pregnant herd had been quartered—to prevent the very problem Johnny had described. The expectant cows shouldn't have been anywhere near the creek that ran along the north side of Wade Ranch.

Kyle hadn't been there in years but he remembered it. He and Liam had played there as boys, splashing through the shallow water and gigging for frogs at dusk as the fat reptiles croaked out their location to the two bloodthirsty boys. Calvin had made them clean and dress the frogs when he found out, and they had frog legs for dinner that night. It was a lesson Kyle never forgot—eat what you kill.

They arrived at the edge of the pasture in a couple of minutes. A fence was down. That explained it.

"What happened?" Kyle asked as he swung out of the saddle to inspect the downed barbed wire and wooden stake.

"Not sure. Slim and I were running the fence and found this. Then he went to the creek to check it out. Sure 'nuff, one of the cows had wandered off. Still don't know how she got down there. Slim stayed with her while I came and got you."

"Good man. Hustle back to the barn and grab some of the guys to get this repaired," Kyle instructed, his mind already blurring with a plan. He just had to check out the situation to make sure the extraction process currently mapping itself out in his head was viable.

Johnny nodded and galloped off.

Kyle let Lightning Rod pick his way along the line of the creek until he saw Slim down in the ravine, hovering over the cow. She was still standing, which was good. As soon as a cow lay down, that meant they had less than an hour until she'd start delivering. They'd have to work fast or she'd be having her baby on that thin strip of ground between the steeply sloped walls and the creek. If the calf was in the wrong position, it would be too hard to assist with the birth, and besides, all the equipment was back at the barn.

Somehow, he had to figure out how to get her out. Immediately. Clearly, Slim had no idea how to do it or he wouldn't have sent Johnny after the boss. This was Kyle's battle to lose. So he wouldn't lose.

Kyle galloped another hundred feet to check out the slope of the creek bed walls, but they were just as steep all the way down the culvert as they were at the site where the cow had gone down. As steep as they'd been when he was a boy. He and Liam had slid down the slope on their butts, ruining more than one pair of pants in the process because it was too steep to walk down. But that had been in August when it was dry. In March, after a cold winter and wet spring, the slope was nothing but mud. Which probably explained how the cow had ended up at the bottom—she'd slipped.

Kyle planned to use that slick consistency to his advantage.

"Slim," he called down. "You okay for another few minutes? I have to run back to the barn to get a couple of things, and then we're gonna haul her out."

Slim eyed Kyle and then the cow. "*Haul* her out? That's a dumb idea. And not what Danny Spencer would have done."

Too bad. Wade Ranch was stuck with Kyle, not the former ranch manager. "Yep."

Not much else to say. It wasn't as if he planned to blubber all over Slim and ask for a chance to prove he could be as good as Spencer. He firmed his mouth and kept the rest inside. Like always.

The ranch hand nodded, but his expression had that I'll-believe-it-when-I-see-it vibe.

Kyle galloped back to the barn and found exactly what he was looking for—the pair of hundred-foot fire hoses Calvin had always kept on hand in case of emergency. They'd been retrofitted with a mechanism that screwed into the water reservoir standing next to the barn. The stock was too valuable to wait on the city fire brigade in the event of a barn fire, so a smart rancher developed his own firefighting strategy.

Today, the hoses were going to lift a cow out of a creek bed.

Kyle jumped into the Wade Ranch Chevy parked near the barn and drove across the pasture, dodging cows and the stretches of grass that served as their grazing ground as best he could. Fortunately, Johnny and the other hands hadn't fixed the fence yet, so Kyle drove right through the break to the edge of the creek.

By the time he skidded to a halt, the hands had gathered around to watch the show. There was no time to have a conversation about this idea, nor did Kyle need anyone else's approval, so if they didn't like it, they could keep it to themselves. Grimly, Kyle pulled the hoses from the truck bed and motioned to Johnny.

"I'm going to tie these to the trailer hitch and then throw them down to Slim. I'll rappel down and back up again once we have the hoses secured around the cow. You drive while I watch the operation. We'll haul her out with good old-fashioned brute strength."

Johnny and the other hands looked dubious but Kyle ignored them and got to work on tying the hoses, looping one end around the trailer hitch into a figure-eight follow-through knot. It was the best knot to avoid slipping and his go-to, but he'd never used it on a fire hose. Hopefully it would hold, especially given that he was the one who would be doing the rappelling without a safety harness.

When the hoses were as secure as a former SEAL could get them, Kyle tossed the ends down to Slim and repeated the plan. Slim, thankfully, just nodded and didn't bother to express his opinion about the chances of success, likely because he figured it was obvious.

Kyle waited for Slim to drop the hoses, and then grabbed on to one. His work gloves gripped better than he was expecting, a plus, given the width of the line. Definitely not the kind of rappelling he was used to, but he probably had more experience at this kind of rescue than anyone there.

He'd lost count of the number of times he'd led an extraction in hostile conditions with few materials at his disposal. And usually he was doing it with a loaded pack and weapons strapped to his back. Going down into a ravine after a cow was a piece of cake in comparison.

Until his boot slipped.

His bad leg slammed into the ground and he bit back a curse as a white-hot blade of pain arced through his leg. *Idiot*. He should have counterbalanced differently to compensate for his cowboy boots, which were great for riding, but not so much for slick mud.

Sweat streamed down his back and beaded up on his forehead, instantly draining down into his eyes, blinding him. Now his hell was complete. And he was only halfway down.

Muttering the lyrics to a Taylor Swift song that had always been his battle cry, he focused on the words instead of the pain. The happy tune reminded him there was still good in the world, reminded him of the innocent teenagers sitting at home in their bright, colorful rooms listening to the same song. They depended on men like Kyle to keep them safe. He'd vowed with his very life that he would. And he'd carried that promise into the darkest places on the planet while singing that song.

Finally, he reached the bottom and took a quarter of a second to catch his breath as he surveyed the area. Cow still standing. Hoses still holding. He nodded to Slim and they got to work leading the cow as close to the slope as possible, which wasn't easy, considering she was in labor, scared and had the brain of a—well, a cow.

The next few minutes blurred as Kyle worked alongside Slim, but eventually they got the makeshift harness in place. Kyle hefted the heavy hoses over his shoulder and climbed back up the way he'd come. The men had shuffled to the edge of the ravine to watch, backing up the closer Kyle got to the top. He hit the dirt at the edge and rolled onto the hoses to keep them from sliding back to the bottom.

He was not making that climb again.

Johnny grabbed hold of the hoses so Kyle could stand, and then made short work of tying them to the trailer hitch next to the other ends. He waved at Johnny to get in the truck. It was do-or-die time.

Johnny gunned the engine.

"Slow," Kyle barked.

The truck inched forward, pulling up all the slack in the hoses. And then the tires bit into the ground as the truck strained against the load. The cow balked but the hoses held her in place. So far so good.

The hoses gradually pulled the cow onto her side and inched her up the slope as the truck revved forward a bit more. It was working. The mud helped her slide, though she mooed something fierce the whole time.

Miraculously, after ten nail-biting minutes, the cow stood on solid ground at the top of the ravine. Kyle's arms ached and his gloves had rubbed raw places on his fingers, but it was done.

Johnny jumped from the truck and rushed over to clap him on the back, breaking the invisible barrier around Kyle. The other ranch hands swarmed around as well, smiling and giving their own version of a verbal high-five. Even Slim offered a somewhat solemn, "Good job."

Kyle took it all with good humor and few words because what was he supposed to say? *Told you so? That's okay, boys. I'm the boss for a reason?*

The ranch hands wandered off, presumably to finish the job of fixing the fence. Eventually, Kyle stood there, alone. Which was par for the course.

Was it so bad to have hoped this would become his new team?

No. The bad part was that if a successful bovine extraction couldn't solidify his place, he suspected nothing would. Because everyone was still waiting around for him to either fail or leave. Except Kyle.

Even Grace didn't fully believe in him yet, or she wouldn't have qualified her recommendations with a "We'll see," and the threat that she wasn't closing the case.

What more did he have to do to prove that honor, integrity and loyalty were in his very fiber?

Grace stood at the wide double door of the barn and watched horses spill into the yard as the hands returned from the cow emergency. They dismounted and loudly recounted the rescue with their own versions of the story. Seems as if Kyle had used fire hoses to drag the animal out of the ravine, which the hands alternately thought was ingenious or crazy depending on who was doing the talking.

Apparently it had worked, since one of the ranch hands had the cow in question on a short lead.

She should have left. She'd told Kyle what she'd come to say, witnessed an exchange between Kyle and another woman that she hadn't been meant to see, and now she was done. But you could have cut the tension in the barn with a chain saw, and she'd been a little bit worried about Kyle. Sure, he'd grown up on the ranch, but that didn't automatically make him accident-proof.

No one mentioned anything about Kyle, so he must be okay. But she wanted to see him for herself. Once she'd assured herself of it—strictly in her capacity as his daughters' caseworker, of course, no other reason—then she'd leave.

Finally, the truck he'd taken off in rolled into the yard and he swung out of the cab, muddy and looking so worn, she almost flew to his side. Except the little blonde bearskin rug beat her to it. Emma Jane. Or as Grace privately liked to call her—The Tart.

Like a hummingbird auditioning for the part of the town harlot, Emma Jane fluttered over to Kyle, expertly sashaying across the uneven ground in her high-heeled boots, which drew the attention of nearly every male still milling around the yard, except the one she was after.

Kyle pulled long lines of flat, muddy hoses out of the bed of the truck, dragged them to the spigot on the water tower beside the barn and attached one, using it to hose off the other.

Which was also pretty ingenious in her opinion.

Emma Jane crowded Kyle at the water tower, smiling and gesturing. Grace was too far away to hear what she was saying, but she probably didn't need to hear it to know it was along the lines of *Oh, Kyle, you're a hero* or the even more inane *Oh, Kyle, you're so strong and brave!*

Please. Well, yes, he was all of those things, no question, but Grace didn't see the point in shoving half-exposed breasts in a man's face when you said them.

The strong and brave hero in question glanced up at Emma Jane as he performed his task. And smiled. It was his slow, slightly naughty smile that he'd flashed Grace right after kissing her senseless, the one that had nearly enticed her back into his arms because it was so sexy.

It was a smile that told a woman he liked what he saw, that he had a few thoughts about what he planned to do with her. And there he was, aiming it at another woman!

That…*dog.*

Breathe, Grace. He was just smiling.

She crossed her arms, leaning forward involuntarily though there was no way she would be able to pick up the conversation from this distance, not with the clatter going on in the yard, all the hands still chattering and watering their horses at the trough running between the water tower and the barn.

Then Emma Jane placed her talons on Kyle's arm and he leaned into it. Something hot bloomed in Grace's chest as she imagined him kissing Emma Jane the way he'd kissed her. He said something to Emma Jane over his shoulder and she laughed. Grace didn't have to hear what was being said. He was enjoying Emma Jane's attention, obviously.

Or he was just washing a hose and having a conversation with his employee, which was none of her business, she reminded herself. She didn't own Kyle, and he'd certainly had female companions over the years who weren't Grace, or he wouldn't currently have two daughters.

She'd just never had that shoved in her face so blatantly before.

Now would be a great time to leave. Except as she started back to her car, Kyle stood and walked straight toward her, calling to one of the hands to lay the hoses out to dry before putting them away. Emma Jane trailed him, still chattering.

He was coming to talk to Grace. With Emma Jane in tow.

Or Kyle could be walking toward the barn. Grace *was* standing in the doorway.

But then his gaze met hers and the rest of the activity in the yard fell away as something wholly encompassing washed through her.

Seven

"Ms. Haines." Kyle nodded.

And then walked right past her!

Had she just been dismissed? Grace scowled and pivoted to view the interior of the barn. Kyle squeezed Emma Jane's shoulder at the door of the office and The Tart disappeared beyond the glass, presumably to go sharpen her claws.

Then he strolled across the wide center of the barn and disappeared around a corner.

Without a single ounce of forethought, Grace charged after him. She'd waited around, half-crazy with worry to assure herself he was okay, and he couldn't bother to stop and talk to her? How dare he? Emma Jane had certainly gotten more than a perfunctory nod and a platitude.

She skidded around the corner, an admonishment already forming in her mouth.

It vanished as she rounded the corner into a small, enclosed area. Kyle stood at a long washbasin. *Wet. Shirtless. Oh, my.*

Obviously she should have thought this through a little better.

Speechless, she stared unashamedly at his bare, rippling torso as he dumped another cupful of water down it. Water streamed along the cut muscles, running in rivulets through the channels to disappear into the fabric of his jeans.

Some of it splashed on her. She was too close. And way too far.

Every ounce of saliva fled from her mouth, and she couldn't have torn her gaze from his gorgeous body for a million dollars. She'd have *paid* a million dollars, if she'd had it, to stand in this spot for an eternity.

"Something else you wanted, Ms. Haines?"

She blinked and glanced up into his diamond-hard green eyes, which were currently fastened on her as he glanced over his shoulder. Busted. Again. There was no way to spin this into anything other than it was. "I didn't know you were washing up. Sorry."

Casually, he turned and leaned back against the long sink, arms at his side, which left that delicious panorama of naked chest right there on display. "That really didn't answer my question, now, did it?"

He was turning her brain mushy again, because she surely would have remembered if there had been talking. "Did you ask me a question?"

His soft laugh crawled under her skin. "Well, I'm trying to figure out what it is that you're after, Grace. Maybe I should ask a different way. Are you here to watch, or join in? Because either is fine with me."

Her ire rushed back all at once, melding uncomfortably with the heat curling through her midsection at the suggestion. "That's a fine way to talk after flirting with Ms. Cattle Queen."

Kyle just raised an eyebrow. "Careful, or a man might start to think you cared whether he flirted with another woman. That's not the case. Right?"

She crossed her arms, but those diamond-hard eyes drilled through her anyway. "Oh, you're right. I don't care." Loftily, she waved off his question. "It just seems disingenuous to make time with one woman mere minutes before inviting another one to *wash up*."

All at once, she had a very clear image of him dumping a cup of water over her chest and licking it off. The heat in her core snaked outward, engulfing her whole body. And that just made her even madder. Kyle was a big flirt who could get Grace hot with merely a glance. It wasn't fair.

She didn't remember him affecting her that way before. And she would have. This was all new and exciting and frustrating and scary.

"Maybe." That slow smile spilled onto his face. "But you're the one standing here. I'm not offering to *wash up* with Emma Jane."

"Yeah. Only because she didn't have the foresight to follow you."

"You did." He watched her without blinking and spread his arms. "Here I am. Whatever are you going to do with me?"

That tripped off a whole chain reaction inside as she thought long and hard about the answer to that question. But she hadn't followed him for *that*. Not that she knew for sure he even meant *that*. But regardless, he had a lot of nerve.

Hands firmly on her hips—just in case they developed a mind of their own and started wandering along the ridges and valleys of that twelve-pack of abs, which she was ashamed to admit she'd counted four times—she glared at him. "This is not you, Kyle. Liam? Yeah. He's a playboy and a half, but you've never been like that, just looking for the next notch in your bedpost."

There. That was the point she was trying to make.

He laughed with genuine mirth. "Is that what you think this is? Kyle Wade, playboy in training. It has a nice ring. But that ain't what's going on."

"Then by all means. Tell me what's going on," she allowed primly.

"Emma Jane is my employee. That's it." He sliced the air with his hand. "You, on the other hand, are something else."

"Oh, yeah? What?"

He swept her with a once-over that should not have been so affecting, but goodness, even the bottoms of her feet heated up. "A woman I'd like to kiss. A lot."

As in he wanted to kiss her several times or he just wanted to really badly?

She shook her head. Didn't matter.

"Well, be that as it may." She tossed her head, scrambling to come up with a response, and poked him in the chest for emphasis. He glanced down at her finger and back up at her, his eyelids shuttered slightly. "You wanted to kiss Emma Jane a minute ago. Pardon me for not getting in line."

"Grace." Her name came out so garbled, she hardly recognized it. "I do not want to kiss Emma Jane."

"Could have fooled me. And her. She definitely had the impression you were into her. Maybe because you were telling her jokes and letting her put her hands all over you."

"And maybe I let her because I knew you were watching."

"I— What?" All the air vanished from her lungs instantly. And then she found it again. "It was on purpose? Flirting with Emma Jane. You did that on *purpose*?" She was screeching. Dang near high enough to call dogs from another county. "Oh, that's…"

She couldn't think of a filthy enough word to describe it. *He'd been playing her.* Kyle Wade had picked her up and played her like a violin. Of course he had. She might as well have Bad Judge of Character tattooed on her forehead so people could get busy right away with pulling one over on her. And she'd waltzed to his tune with nary a peep.

And speaking of no peeps, Kyle was standing there watching her without saying a word, the big jerk.

"It was all a lie?" she asked rhetorically, because he'd just said it was, though why he'd done it, she couldn't fathom. "What were you trying to accomplish, anyway?"

His grin slipped as he pinned her in place with nothing more than his gaze. He swayed forward, just a bit, but his heat reached out and slid along her skin as if he'd actually brushed her torso with his.

She couldn't move. Didn't want to move. The play of expression across his face fascinated her. The heat called to her.

"No lies. See this," he murmured and wagged a finger between them, drawing her eye as he nearly touched her but didn't. "Just what you ordered. Space. Anytime you feel inclined to make it disappear, I'll be the one over here minding my own business."

Oh! Of all the sneaky, underhanded, completely accurate things to say.

Mute, she stared at him and he stared right back. He'd been giving her exactly what she asked for. Never mind that she'd rather drink paint thinner than admit he might have a point. And the solution was rather well spelled out, too.

She didn't want him to flirt with other women? Then close the gap.

There was no more running, no more hiding. This was it, right here. He wanted her. But he wasn't going to act on it.

They shared a fierce attraction and the past was in the past. She'd held him at bay in order to get her feet under her, to make sure he wasn't going to hurt her again. It was the same tactic she employed with her cases. If she wanted to be sure she wasn't letting her emotions get the best of her, wanted to be sure she was making an unbiased decision, she stepped back. Assessed from afar with impersonal attention.

This wasn't one of her cases. This was Kyle. As personal as it got. And the only way she could fully assess what they could have now was to dive into that pool. Wading in an inch at a time wasn't working.

Rock solid, not moving a muscle, he watched her. This was her show and he was subtly telling her he'd let her run it. Except he was also saying she couldn't keep talking out of both sides of her mouth.

Either she could act like a full-grown woman and do something about the man she wanted or keep letting their interaction devolve into an amateurish high school game.

She picked doing something.

Going on instinct alone, she reached out with both hands and pressed them to Kyle's bare chest, her gaze on his as she did it, gauging his reaction. His eyes darkened as her fingers spread and she flattened both palms across his pectoral muscles. Damp. Hot. Hard.

One muscle flexed under her touch and she almost yanked her hands back. But she didn't. He hadn't felt like this before. He was all man and it was a serious turn-on, especially because it was still Kyle underneath. When he was looking at her the way he was right then, as if the center of the universe had been deposited in his palm, it was easy to remember why she'd fallen for him. All the emotion of being in love with this man rushed back.

"There you go," she said breathlessly. "No more space."

"Grace," he growled, and she felt the vibrations under her fingers. "You better mean it. I'm only human."

Her touch was affecting him. *She* was affecting *him*. It was something she hadn't fully contemplated, but she did get that it wasn't fair to lead him on and keep dancing back and forth between yes and no.

"I mean it. If you want to kiss me, it's fine."

"*Fine*." There came that slow smile. "That's almost as bad a word as *nice*. I think it's time to fix your vocabulary."

All at once, Kyle's arms snaked around her, yanking her tight against his hard body. But before she could fully register the contact, his mouth claimed hers.

The crash of lips startled her. And then she couldn't think at all as his hands slid down her back, touching her, trailing heat along her spine, sliding oh, so slowly against her bottom to finally grip her hips and hold them firmly, pulling her taut against his body.

His very aroused body. The length of him pressed into her soft flesh as he kissed her. It was a whole-body experience, and nothing like the front porch kiss that she'd thought was so memorable that she couldn't shake it. That kiss had been wonderful, but tame.

This was a grown-up kiss.

The difference was unfathomable.

This kiss was hungry, questing, begging for more even as he took it.

Kyle changed the angle, diving deeper into her mouth, thrilling her with the intensity. His tongue swirled out, and instinctively, she met him with her own. He groaned and she felt it to her toes.

Kyle. She'd missed the feel of him in her arms. Missed the scent of him in her nose.

Except this Kyle wasn't like the warm coat she'd envisioned sliding into, wholly familiar and so comforting.

No, this Kyle was like opening a book expecting a nice story with an interesting plot and instead falling into an immersive world full of dark secrets and darker passions.

His hands were everywhere, along her sides, thumbs circling and sliding higher until he found her breasts beneath her clothes. The contact shot through her as he touched her, and then he shoved a leg between hers, tilting his hips to rub against her intimately.

This was not a kiss—it was a seduction.

And she had just enough functioning brain cells to be aware that they were not only in a barn, but she hadn't fully figured out what was supposed to come next. She didn't know what had changed that might mean things would work between them this time. She didn't fully trust that he was here for good, and even if he was, that he was going to meet her standards any better today than he had ten years ago.

Oh, he was certainly earning a ten in the Sweeping Her Off Her Feet category. But Happily Ever After carried just as much weight as Expressing His Feelings. And neither of those were on the board yet.

Breaking off the kiss—and nearly kicking herself at the same time—she pushed back and mumbled, "Wait."

His torso shuddered as he dragged in a ragged breath. "Because?"

"You know why." Her Professional Single Girl status was in jeopardy and she had to make sure he was worth the price of relinquishing it. Sure, he was hot and a really great kisser, but she didn't sleep around. An interlude in the barn didn't change that.

"I did not develop ESP at any point in the last ten years," he rasped, his expression going blank as he stared at her.

"Because of what happened before, Kyle." Exasperated, she stared at the wall over his head so his delicious chest wasn't right in her field of vision. "There's a lot of leftover emotion and scrambled-up stuff to sort out. I have to take it slow this time."

"Then you should leave," he said curtly. "Because I'm definitely not in the mood for slow right now."

She took his advice and fled. It wasn't until she'd reached her car and slid into the driver's seat that she realized leaving was the one surefire way to *never* figure out what they could have together.

Maybe slow wasn't any better an idea than space.

And at this moment, the only *s* word she seemed capable of thinking about ended in *ex*, which was the crux of the problem. She and Kyle had a former relationship and it muddied everything, especially her feelings.

Kyle stabbed his hands through his shirt, nearly ripping the sleeve off in the process.

Grace wanted to take it *slow* because of what had happened before.

Furiously, he fingered the buttons through the holes haphazardly, none too happy about having to spend the rest of the workday with a hard-on he couldn't get rid of, no matter what he thought of to kill his arousal—slugs, the Cowboys losing the Super Bowl, his mother. Nothing worked because the feel of Grace in his arms was way too fresh, and had been cut way too short.

Because of what had happened *before*. She meant when she'd fallen for Liam and he'd thrown her over. While Kyle appreciated that she wanted to figure out her own mind before taking things further with him, he wasn't about to stand by and let what happened in the past with his brother ruin the present.

Liam was married now and Grace should be completely over all of that. Bygones included forgetting about *everything* that happened in the past.

He didn't have any choice but to let it go for the time being. He had a job to do and men to manage.

By the time the sun set, the entire Wade Ranch staff was giving Kyle a wide berth. So the cow extraction hadn't earned him any points. Figured. His surly mood didn't help and he finally just called it a day.

When he got back to the main house, Liam met him in the mudroom off the back.

"Hey," Liam called as Kyle sat on the long bench seat to remove his boots, which were a far sight cleaner than they'd been earlier, but still weren't fit to walk the floors inside.

Kyle jerked his chin, not trusting himself to actually speak to anyone civilly. Though if anyone deserved the brunt of his temper, it was Liam.

"Hadley and I are flying to Vail this weekend. Just wanted to give you a heads-up." Liam's mouth tightened. "You'll be okay handling the babies for a couple of days by yourself, right?"

"Yep."

Liam hesitated, clearly expecting more of a conversation or maybe even an argument about it, but what else was there to say? Kyle couldn't force the couple to stay, and Maddie and Maggie were his kids. He'd figure it out. Somehow. The little pang in his stomach must be left over from Grace. Probably.

"Okay. We're leaving in an hour or so."

Kyle let the first boot hit the floor with a resounding *thunk* and nodded. Liam kept talking.

"I'm flying my Cessna, so it's no problem to delay for a bit if you need to talk to Hadley about anything."

The other boot hit the floor. Hadley had already imparted as much baby knowledge as she possibly could. Another hour of blathering wasn't going to make a difference. "Not necessary."

Liam still didn't leave. "You have my cell phone number. It's okay if you want to call and ask questions."

"Yep."

Geez. Was his brother really that much of an ass? Liam had taken care of the babies before Kyle had gotten there without anyone standing over him waiting for his first mistake. Did Liam really think babysitting was something only he could do and that Kyle was hopelessly inept? Seemed so. Which only set Kyle's resolve.

He wouldn't call. Obviously Liam and Hadley had plans that didn't include taking care of Kyle's children. Who was he to stand in the way of that? Never mind that Kyle had never even stayed alone in the house with the babies. Hadley had always just been there, ready to pick up the slack.

This was the part where Kyle wished he had someone like Hadley. His kids needed a mother. Problem was, he could only picture Grace's face when thinking of a likely candidate. And she was too skittish about *everything*. Mentioning motherhood would likely send her over the edge.

Finally, Liam shuffled off to finish packing or whatever, leaving Kyle to his morose thoughts. It was fine, really. So he'd envisioned asking Grace if she'd like to drive into Odessa for dinner and a movie. Get out of Royal, where there were no prying eyes. Maybe he would have even talked her into spending the night in a swanky motel. He had scads of money he never spent and he couldn't think of anyone he'd rather spend it on than Grace.

Guess that wasn't happening. A grown-up field trip didn't sound too much like Grace's definition of *slow* anyway, so it hardly mattered that his half-formed plan wasn't going to work out.

No matter. He'd spend the weekend with his daughters and it would be great. They'd bond and his love for them would grow. Maybe this was actually a good step toward relieving Hadley permanently of her baby duties. He could keep telling himself that she loved them and didn't mind taking care of his daughters all he wanted, but at the end of the day, it was just an excuse.

He'd decided to stay in Royal, taking a job managing the cattle side of Wade Ranch, and it was time for him to man up and start building the family life his daughters needed.

Liam and Hadley left in a flurry of instructions and worried backward glances until finally Kyle was alone with Maddie and Maggie. That little pang in his stomach was back and he pushed on it with his thumb. The feeling didn't go away and started resembling panic more than anything else.

God Almighty. Maddie and Maggie were babies, for crying out loud. Kyle had faced down a high-ranking, card-carrying member of the Taliban with less sweat.

He wandered into the nursery and thought about covering his eyes to shield them from all the pink. But there his girls were. Two of 'em. Staring up at him with the slightly unfocused, slightly bemused expression his daughters seemed to favor. The babies were kind of sweet when they weren't crying.

They couldn't lie around in their room all night.

"Let's hang out," he announced to his kids. It had a nice ring.

He gathered up Maggie from her crib and carried her downstairs to the family room, where a conglomeration of baby paraphernalia sat in the corner. He dragged one of the baby seats away from the wall with one bare foot and placed Maggie in it the way Hadley always did. There were some straps, similar to a parachute harness, and he grabbed one of Maggie's waving fists to thread it through the arm hole.

She promptly clocked him with the other one, which earned a laugh even as his cheek started smarting. "That's what I get for taking my eye off the ball, right?"

The noise she made didn't sound too much like agreement, but he nodded anyway, as if they were having a conversation. That was one of the things Hadley said all the time. The babies were people, not aliens. He could talk to them normally and it helped increase their vocabulary later on if everyone got out of the habit of using baby talk around them.

Which was fine by Kyle. Baby talk was dumb anyway.

Once Maggie was secured, he fetched Maddie and repeated the process. That was the thing about twins. You were never done. One of them always needed something, and then the other one needed the same thing or something different or both.

But here they were, having family time. In the family room. Couldn't get more domestic than that. He sat on the couch and looked at his daughters squirming in their bouncy seats. Now what?

"You ladies want to watch some TV?"

Since neither one of them started wailing at the suggestion, he took it as a yes.

The flat-screen television mounted to the wall blinked on with a flick of the remote. Kyle tuned to one of the kids' channels, where a group of grown men in bright colors were singing a song about a dog named Wags. The song was almost horrifying in its simplicity and in the dancing that would probably lace his nightmares later that night, assuming he actually slept while continually reliving that aborted kiss with Grace from earlier.

The babies both turned their little faces to the TV and for all intents and purposes looked as though they were watching it. Hadley had said they couldn't really make out stuff really well yet, because their eyes weren't developed enough to know what they were looking at, but they could still enjoy the colors and lights.

And that's when Maddie started fussing. Loudly.

Kyle pulled her out of her baby seat, cursing his burning hands, which were still raw from his climb out of the ravine. Liam's timing sucked. "Shh, little one. That's no way to talk to your daddy."

She cried harder. It was only a matter of time before Maggie got jealous of the attention and set about getting some of her own with a few well-placed sobs. Hadley could usually ignore it but Kyle didn't have her stamina.

Plan A wasn't working. Kyle rocked his daughter faster but she only cried harder. And there was no one to help analyze the symptoms in order to arrive at a potential solution. This was a solo operation. So he'd run it to completion.

Bottle. That was always Plan B, after rocking. It was close to dinnertime. Kyle secured Maddie in the chair again, forced to let her wail while he fixed her bottle. It seemed cruel, but he needed both hands.

He'd seen some guys wear a baby sling. But he couldn't quite bring himself to go that far, and he'd never seen Liam do it, either, so there was justification for holding on to his dude card, albeit slight.

Maddie sucked the bottle dry quicker than a baby calf who'd lost its mama. Kyle burped her and resettled her in her bouncy seat, intending to move on to Maggie, who was likely wondering where her bottle was.

Maddie was having none of that and let loose with another round of wails.

In desperation, he sang his go-to Taylor Swift song, which surprisingly worked well enough to ease his pounding headache. He sang the verse over again and slid into the chorus with gusto. The moment he stopped, she set off again, louder. He sang. She quieted. He stopped. She cried.

"Maddie," he groaned. "Tim McGraw should have been your daddy if this is how you're going to be. I can't sing 24-7."

More crying. With more mercy than he probably deserved, Maggie had been sitting quietly in her seat the whole time, but things surely wouldn't stay so peaceful on her end.

Feeling like the world's biggest idiot, he sneaked off to the kitchen to call Hadley. There was no way on God's green earth he'd call Liam, but Hadley was another story.

She answered on the first ring. "Is everything okay?"

"Fine, fine," he assured her, visualizing Liam throwing their overnight bags into the cockpit of the Cessna and flying off toward home without even pausing to shut the door. "Well, except Maddie won't stop crying. I've tried everything, bottle, rocking, and it's a bust. Any ideas?"

"Did you burp her?"

"Of course." He hadn't changed her diaper, but his sense of smell was pretty good and he didn't think that was the problem.

"Temperature?"

He dashed back into the family room, cringing at the decibel level of Maddie's cries, and put a hand on her forehead. Which was moronic when he'd been holding her for thirty minutes. "She doesn't feel hot."

"Is that Maddie crying like that?" Now Hadley sounded worried, which was not what Kyle had intended. "Take her temperature anyway, just to be sure. Then try the gas drops. Call me back in an hour and let me know how it's going."

"Won't I be interrupting?" He so did not want to know the answer to that, but it was pretty crappy of him to call once, let alone twice.

"Yes," Liam growled in the background. "Stop coddling him, Hadley."

Kyle muttered an expletive aimed at Liam, but his wife was the one who heard it. "Excuse my French, Hadley.

Never mind. I got this. You and Liam go back to whatever you were doing, which I do *not* need details about."

"We should come home," Hadley interjected. This was
accompanied by a very vehement "No!" from Liam, and
some muffled conversation. "Okay, we're not coming
home. You'll be fine," Hadley said into the phone in her
soothing voice that she normally reserved for the girls, but
whether it was directed at Liam or Kyle, he couldn't say.
"Call Clare if you need to. She won't mind."

"Clare?" Liam's incredulity came through loud and
clear despite his mouth being nowhere near the phone.
"She's already got plenty of babies that Royal Memorial
pays her to take care of. Call Grace if you're going to call
anyone."

Grace. He could get Grace over here under the guise
of helping with the twins and get to see her tonight after
all. Now that was a stellar idea if Kyle had ever heard one.
Not that he was about to let Liam get all cocky about it.
"Sorry I bothered you. Good night."

Kyle eyed the still-screaming baby. Fatherhood wasn't
a job for the fainthearted, that was for sure. Nor was it a
job for the clueless, and thankfully, Ms. Haines already
had him cast in her head as such. She thought he was clueless? Great.

Time to use that to his advantage.

Eight

When the phone rang, Grace almost didn't answer it.

The oven had freaked out. Worse than last time. It turned on and heated up fine, but halfway through the cooking cycle, the element shut off. Cold. Which described the state of her dinner, too. The roast was still raw inside and she could have used the potatoes to pound nails.

But there was no saving it now. The oven wouldn't start again no matter how much she cursed at it. She'd checked the power cord but it was plugged in with no visible frays or anything. Last time, she'd been able to turn it off and turn it back on, but that didn't work this time.

So why not answer the phone?

Except it was Kyle. His name flashed at her from the screen and she stared at it for a moment as the *wow* from earlier flooded all her full-grown woman parts. So this was taking it slow? Calling her mere hours after she'd broken off a kiss with more willpower than it should have taken—for the second time?

"This better be important," she said instead of hello, and then winced. Her mama had raised her better than that.

"It is." Something that sounded like a tornado siren wailed in the distance. "Something's wrong with Maddie."

That was *Maddie* doing the siren impression? *Relapse.* Her heart rate sped up. Those harrowing hours when they didn't know what was wrong with Maddie came back in a rush. Heart problems were no joke, and Maddie'd had several surgeries to correct the abnormalities.

"What's wrong? Where's Hadley?" She might be hyperventilating. Was that what it was called when you couldn't breathe?

"She and Liam went to Vail. I didn't want to bother them."

Vail? Suspicion ruffled the edges of Grace's consciousness. The couple had just gone to Vail a couple of months ago. Was this some kind of covert attempt to get Kyle to take his fatherhood responsibilities more seriously? Or an elaborate setup from the mind of Kyle Wade to get his way with Grace?

"Okay," she said slowly, feeling her way through the land mines. "Did you try—"

"Yep. I tried everything. She's been crying like this for an hour and it's upsetting Maggie. I wouldn't have called you otherwise." He was trying hard to keep the panic from his voice, but she could tell he was at the end of his rope. Her heart melted a little, sweeping aside all her suspicion.

It didn't matter why Liam and Hadley had gone to Vail. Maddie—and Kyle—needed help, and she couldn't ignore that for anything.

"Do you need me to come by?" She shouldn't, for all the reasons she hadn't stayed with him in the barn earlier that day.

Plus, and this was the kicker, he hadn't asked her to come over. Maybe it was supposed to be implied, but this was typical with Kyle. He had a huge problem just coming out and saying what he thought. That might be the number one reason she hadn't stayed in his arms, both back in high school and today.

Nothing had changed.

"That's a great idea," he said enthusiastically, and she didn't miss that he was acting as though it was all hers, and not what he'd been after the whole time. "I'll cook you dinner as a thank-you. Unless you've got other plans?"

Ha. If she couldn't hear Maddie's cries for herself, she'd think he'd set all this up. Grace glanced at her oven and half-cooked dinner, then at the lonely dining room table where she'd eaten a lot of meals by herself, especially in the past three years upon becoming a Professional Single Girl.

The timing was oh, so convenient. But even Kyle couldn't magically make her oven stop working at precisely the moment he'd asked her to come over for dinner. Thus far she'd avoided having any meals with him and his family because that would be too hard. Too much of a reminder that a husband and children was what she wanted more than anything—and that there was nothing on the horizon to indicate she'd ever get either one.

But this was an emergency. Or at least that was what she was going to keep telling herself.

"I'll be right there," she promised, and dumped the roast in the trash. If she freshened up her makeup and put on a different dress, no one had to know.

She drove to Wade Ranch at four miles per hour over the speed limit.

Kyle opened the door before she knocked. "Hey, Grace. Thanks."

His pure physical beauty swept out and slapped her. Mute, she stared at his face, memorizing it, which was silly when she already had a handy image of him, shirtless, emblazoned across her brain. She'd just seen him a few hours ago. Why did she have to have a reaction by simply standing near him?

"Where's Maddie?" she asked brusquely to cover the catch in her throat.

"Right this way, Ms. Haines."

Grace followed Kyle through the formal parlor and across the hardwood floor into the hall connecting to the back of the house. Why did it feel like the blind leading the blind? She didn't have any special baby knowledge. Most kids in the system were older by the time their cases landed on her desk, which brought back her earlier reservations about the real reason he'd called her. It wouldn't be the first time today that he'd manufactured a scenario to get a reaction from her.

In the family room, two babies sat in low seats, wide-eyed as they stared at the TV, both silent as the grave.

Grace pointed out the obvious. "Um. Maddie's not crying."

"I gave her Tylenol while you were on your way over here." He shrugged. "Must have worked."

"Why didn't you call me?"

"She didn't stop crying until a few minutes before you got here," he replied defensively, which was only fair. She'd heard Maddie crying over the phone. It wasn't as if he'd shoved Liam and Hadley out the door, and then faked an emergency to get her into his clutches.

She sighed. "I'm sorry. I'm being rude. It's just… I was convinced this was all just an elaborate plot to get me to have dinner with you."

Kyle blinked. "Why on earth would I do that?"

"Well, you know." Discomfort prickled the back of her neck as he stared at her in pure confusion. "Because you faked all that stuff with Emma Jane earlier today. Seemed like it might be a trend."

He cocked his head and gave her a small smile. "I called

you because it was the best of both worlds. I needed help with Maddie and I wanted to see you, too. Is that so terrible?"

Not when he put it that way. Chagrined, she shook her head. "No. But it just seems like I'm a little extraneous at this point. I should probably go. Maddie's fine."

"Don't be silly." His smile faltered just a touch. "She might go off again at any moment and Maggie could decide to join in. What will I do then? Please stay. Besides, I promised you dinner. Let me do something nice for you for coming all this way."

The panicky undercurrent had climbed back into his voice, bless his heart. She couldn't help but smile in hopes of bolstering his confidence. "It wasn't that far. But okay. I'll stay."

"Great. It's settled then." He held out his hand as if he wanted to shake on it but when she placed her hand in his, he yanked on it, pulling her toward the bouncy seats. "Come on, grab a baby and you can watch me cook."

Laughing, she did as commanded, though he insisted on taking Maddie himself. She gathered up Maggie, bouncy seat and all, and followed him to the kitchen, mirroring his moves as he situated the seat near one of the two islands in the center of the room, presumably so the girls didn't feel left out.

She kissed Maggie on the head, unable to resist her sweet face. This baby was special for lots of reasons, but mostly because of who her daddy was.

Wow. Where had that come from? She needed to reel it back, pronto.

"We'll let them hang out for a little while," Kyle said conversationally. "And then we'll put them to bed. Hadley has them on a strict schedule."

"Sure. I'd be glad to help."

It sounded great, actually. The children she helped always either had families already, or were waiting on her to find them the best one. Grace never got to keep any of the children on whose behalf she worked, which was a little heartbreaking in a way.

But here she was, right in the middle of Maddie and Maggie's permanent home, spending time with them and their father outside of work. The smell of baby powder clung to her hands where she'd picked up Maggie, and all at once, soft jazz music floated through the kitchen as Kyle clicked up an internet radio station at the kitchen's entertainment center. It was a bit magical and her throat tightened.

This was not her life. She didn't trust Kyle enough to consider where this could lead. But all at once, she couldn't remember why that was so important. All she had to do right this minute was enjoy this.

"Can I do something to help with dinner?" she asked, since the babies were occupied with staring at their fists.

Kyle grinned and pulled a stool from behind the island, pointing to it. "Sit. Your job is to keep me company."

Charmed, she watched as instructed. It wasn't a hardship. He moved fluidly, as comfortable sliding a bottle from the built-in wine refrigerator as he was handling the reins of his mount earlier that day.

The cork gave way with a *pop* and he poured her a glass of pale yellow wine, handing it to her with one finger in the universal "one minute" gesture. He grabbed his own glass and clinked it against hers. "To bygones."

She raised a brow. That was an interesting thing to toast to. But appropriate. She was determined not to let the past interfere with her family moment, and the future was too murky. "To bygones."

They both drank from their glasses, staring at each other over the rims, and she had the distinct impression he was evaluating her just as much as she was him.

The fruity tang of the wine raced across her tongue, cool and delicious. And unexpected. "I wouldn't have pegged you as a Chardonnay kind of guy," she commented.

"I'm full of surprises." With that cryptic comment, he set his wineglass on the counter and began pulling items from the double-doored stainless steel refrigerator. "I'm making something simple. Chicken salad. I hope that's okay. The ladies didn't give me a lot of time to prep."

She hid a smile at his description of the babies. "Sounds great."

Kyle bustled around the kitchen chopping lettuce and a cooked chicken breast, leaving her to alternate watching him and the twins. Though he drew her eye far more than she would have expected, given that she was here to help with the babies.

"I don't remember you being much of a connoisseur in the kitchen," she said as he began mixing the ingredients for homemade dressing.

They'd been so young the first time, though. Not even out of their teens, yet their twenties were practically in the rearview mirror now. Of course they'd grown and changed. It would be more shocking if they hadn't.

"In a place like Afghanistan, if you don't learn to cook, you starve," he returned.

It was rare for him to mention his military stint, and it occurred to her that she typically shied away from the subject because it held so many negative associations. For her, at least. He might feel differently about the thing that had taken him away from her, and she was suddenly curious about it.

"Did you enjoy being in the military?"

He glanced up, his expression shuttered all at once. "It was a part of me. And now it's not."

Okay, message received. He didn't want to talk about that. Which was fine. Neither did she.

"I'm at a stopping point," he said, his tone a little lighter. "Let's put the girls to bed."

Though she suspected it was merely a diversion, she nodded and followed him through the mysterious ritual of bedtime. It was over before she'd fully immersed herself in the moment. They changed the girls' diapers, changed their outfits, put them down on their backs and left the room.

"That was it?" she whispered as she and Kyle took the back stairs to the kitchen.

"Yep. Sometimes Hadley rocks them if they don't go to sleep right away, but she says not to do that too much, or they'll get used to it, and we'll be doing it until they go to college." He waved the mobile video monitor in his hand. "I watch and listen using this and if they fuss, I come running. Not much more to it."

They emerged into the kitchen, where the tangy scent of the salad dressing greeted them. Kyle set the monitor on the counter on his way to the area where he'd been preparing dinner.

He'd clearly been asking Hadley questions and soaking up her baby knowledge. Much more so than Grace would have given him credit for. "You're taking fatherhood very seriously."

He halted and whirled so fast that she smacked into his chest. But he didn't step back. "What's it going to take to convince you that I'm in this for the long haul?"

Blinking, she stared up into his green eyes as they cut through her. Condemning her. Uncertain all of a sudden, she tried to take a step back, but he didn't let her. His hands shot out to grip her elbows, hauling her back into place. Into his space. A hairbreadth from the cut torso she'd felt under her fingers earlier today.

"What will it take, Grace?" he murmured. "You say something like that and it makes me think you're surprised that I'm ready, willing and able to take care of my daughters. *Still* surprised, after all I've done and learned. After I've become gainfully employed. After I've shown you my commitment in site visits like you asked. This isn't about me anymore. It's about you. Why is this all so hard for you to believe?"

"Because, Kyle!" she burst out. "You've been gone. You didn't come home when Liam called you about the babies. Is it so difficult to fathom that I might have questions about your intentions? You just said the military was a part of you. What if you wake up one day and want to join up again? Those girls will suffer."

I'd suffer.

Where had that come from? She tried to shake it off, but as they stood there in the kitchen of Wade House with his masculinity pouring over her like a hot wind from the south, the emotions welled up again and she cursed herself. Cursed the truth.

Sometime between his coming home and now, she'd opened her heart again. Just a little. She'd tried to stop, tried asking for space, but the honest truth was that she'd never gotten over him because she still had feelings for him. And it had only taken one kiss to awaken them again, no matter how much she'd tried to lie to herself about it. Otherwise, that scene with Emma Jane would have rolled right off like water from a duck's back.

And she didn't trust him not to hurt her again. It was a terrible place to be stuck.

"Grace," he murmured. "I'm here. For good. I didn't get Liam's messages, or I would have been back earlier. You've got me cast in your head as someone with my sights set on the horizon, but that's not true. I want to live my life in Royal, at least until my daughters are grown."

He wasn't aiming to leave the moment he changed his mind. He was telling the truth; she could see it in his eyes.

Maybe she wasn't such a bad judge of character after all. Maybe she could let her guard down. Just a little.

The tightness in her throat relaxed and she took the first easy breath since smacking into him. "Okay. I'll shut up about it."

"Just to make sure, let me help you shut up."

He hauled her up and kissed her. His mouth took hers at a hard, desperate angle that she instantly responded to. Maybe she didn't have to resist if he wasn't going to leave again. Maybe she didn't have to pretend she didn't want more. Because he was right here, giving it to her. All she had to do was take it.

His hands were still on her elbows, raising her up on her tiptoes as he devoured her with his unique whole-body kiss. Need unfolded inside, seeking relief, seeking Kyle.

Yes. The darkness she sometimes sensed in him lifted as he dropped her elbows to encompass her in his arms, holding her tight. He backed her up against the counter to press his hard body to hers, thrusting his hips to increase the contact.

A moan bloomed in her chest, and her tongue vibrated against his as he took the kiss deeper, sliding a hand down her back, to her waist, to her bottom, molding it to fit in his palm. His touch thrilled her even as she pressed into it, willing him to spread the wealth. And then he did.

His hand went lower, gripping the back of her thigh, lifting it so that her knee came up flush with his thigh, which hiked her dress up, and *oh, my.* She was open to him under her skirt, flimsy panties the only barrier between her damp center and his very hard body.

He thrust his hips again, igniting her instantly as the rough fabric of his jeans pleasured her through the scrap of fabric at her core. Strung tight, she let the dense heat wash through her, mindless with it as she sought more. His mouth lifted from hers for a moment and she nearly wept, following him involuntarily with her lips in hopes of reclaiming the drugging kiss.

"Grace," he murmured, and dragged his lips across her throat to the hollow near her ear, which was so nice, she forgot about kissing and let her head tip back to give him better access.

He spent a long moment exploring the area, and finally nipped her ear lightly, whispering, "You know, when I said I wanted to live my life in Royal, I didn't picture myself alone."

"I hope not," she murmured. "You have two daughters."

He laughed softly, as she'd intended, and hefted her a little deeper into his arms as he lifted his head to meet her gaze. "You know that's not what I meant."

Of course she did. But was it so difficult to spell out what was going on his head? So difficult to say how he felt about her? She wanted to hear the words. This time, she wasn't settling for less than everything. "Tell me what you're picturing, Kyle."

"Me. You." He slid light fingertips down the sweetheart neckline of her dress until he reached the spot right between her breasts and hooked the fabric. "This dress on the floor."

Shuddering in spite of herself at the heated desire in his expression, she smiled. "Let's pretend for argument's sake I'm in favor of this dress on the floor. What would you say to me while you're peeling it off?"

The glint in his eye set off another shower of sparks in her midsection. "Well, my darling. Why don't we just find out?"

Slowly, he pulled down the shoulders of the dress, baring her bra straps, which he promptly gathered up, as well. She heartily blessed the impulse that had caused her to pick this semibackless dress that didn't require unzipping to get out of. Which might not have been an accident.

"Beautiful." He kissed a shoulder, suckling on it lightly, then following her neckline with the little nibbling kisses until she thought she'd come apart from the torture.

When she'd asked him to talk about what was on his mind, she'd been expecting a declaration of his feelings. This was so much better. For now.

All at once, the dress and bra popped down to her waist in a big bunch of fabric, baring her breasts to his hot-eyed viewing pleasure. And look he did, shamelessly, as if he'd uncovered a diamond he couldn't quite believe was real.

"Grace," he rasped. "Exactly like I remembered in my dreams. But so much more."

That pleased her enormously for some reason. It was much more romantic than what she recalled him saying when they were together ten years ago. He'd seen her naked before, but always in semidarkness, and usually in his truck. Bench seats were not the height of romance.

With a reverent curse, he brushed one nipple with his thumb, and her breath whooshed from her lungs as everything went tight inside. And outside.

"Kyle," she said, and nearly strangled on the word as he lifted her up onto the counter, spreading her legs and stepping between them. Then his mouth closed over a breast and she forgot how to speak as he sucked, flicking her nipple with his tongue simultaneously.

She forgot everything except the exquisite feel of this man's mouth on her body.

Her head fell back as he pushed a hand against the small of her back to arch her toward his mouth, drawing her breast deeper into it. She moaned, writhing with pleasure as the heat swept over her entire body, swirling at her core. Where she needed him most.

As if he'd read her mind, his other hand toyed with her panties until she felt his fingers touching her intimately. It was cataclysmic, perfect. Until he placed his thumb on her nub, expertly rubbing as he pleasured her, and that was even more perfect. Heat at her core, suction at her breast, and it all coalesced in one bright, hot pinnacle. With a cry, she crested in a long orgasm of epic proportions.

She'd just had an *orgasm* on the *kitchen counter*. She should probably be more embarrassed about that...

Before she'd fully recovered, Kyle picked her up from the counter and let her slide to the floor, then hustled her up the stairs to a bedroom. Heavy, masculine furnishings dominated the room, marking it as his, but a few leftover items from his youth still decorated the walls. He dimmed the light and advanced on her with his slow, lazy walk.

"Oh, there's more?" she teased.

"So much more," he growled. "It's been far too long since I've felt you under me. I want you naked. Now."

That sounded like a plan. The warm-up in the kitchen had only gotten her good and primed for what came next.

Breathless, she stood still as he peeled her dress the rest of the way from her body and let it fall to the carpet. She promptly forgot to worry about the extra pounds she'd gained in her hips and thighs since the last time he'd seen her.

He stripped off his shirt, exposing that beautiful torso she'd barely had time to explore earlier.

When his jeans hit the floor, she realized his chest was only part of the package, and the rest—*oh, my*. He turned slightly, holding one leg behind him at an odd angle, almost as if he was posing for her. Well, okay then. Greedily, she looked her fill, returning the favor from earlier when he'd gorged on the sight of her bare breasts.

In the low light, he was quite simply gorgeous, with muscles bulging in his thighs and a jutting erection that spoke of his passion more effectively than anything he could have said. The power of it coursed through her. She was a woman in the company of a finely built man who was here with the sole intent of pleasuring her with that cut, solid body. And she got to do the same to him.

Why had she waited so long for this?

"Grace."

She glanced up into his eyes, which were so hot, she felt the burn across her uncovered skin, heightening her desire to *get started* already. He was going to feel amazing.

"You have to stop looking at me like that," he rasped.

"Because why?"

He chuckled weakly. "Because this is going to be all over in about two seconds if you don't. I want to take my time with you. Savor you."

"Maybe you can do that the second time," she suggested, a little shocked at her boldness, but not sorry. "I'm okay with you going fast the first time if I get to look at you however much I want. Oh, and there's going to be touching, too."

To prove the point, she reached out to trace the line of his pectoral muscles, because how could she not? He groaned under her fingertips and that was so nice, she flattened her palms against his chest. "More," she commanded.

He raised his eyebrows. "When did you get so bossy?"

"Five minutes ago." When she'd realized she was a woman with desires. And she wanted this man. Why shouldn't she get to call a few shots?

With a small push at his torso, she shoved him toward the bed. And to his credit, he let her, because there was no way she'd have moved him otherwise. He fell backward onto the bed and she climbed on to kneel next to him, a little uncertain where to start. But determined to figure it out.

"Just be still," she told him as he stared up at her with question marks in his gaze. Then she got busy exploring.

What would he taste like? There was only one way to find out. She leaned down and ran her tongue across his nipple, and it was as delicious as she'd expected. He hissed as the underlying muscle jerked.

"Staying still is easier said than done when you're doing that," he muttered, his voice cracking as she ran her tongue lower, down his abs and to his thigh.

She eyed his erection and, curious, reached out to touch it. Hard and soft at the same time, it pulsed against her palm.

He cursed. "Playtime's over."

Instantly, he rolled her under him in one fierce move, taking her mouth in a searing kiss that rendered her boneless. She melted into the comforter as he shoved a leg between hers, rubbing at her core until she was in flames.

He paused only for a moment to sheathe himself with a condom, and then nudged her legs open to ease into her slowly.

Gasping as he filled her, she clung to his shoulders, reveling in the feel of him. This was so different than she remembered. The experience was so much stronger and bigger. The leftover emotion that she'd carried with her for the past ten years exploded into something she barely recognized. Before, Kyle had been in a compartment in her mind, in her heart. Something she could take out and remember, then put back when she got sad.

There was no putting this back in a box.

The essence of Kyle swept through her, filling every nook and cranny of her body and soul. No, he hadn't bubbled over with lots of pretty words about being in love with her. But that would come, in time. She had to believe that.

And then he buried himself completely with a groan. They were so intimately joined, Grace could feel his heartbeat throughout her whole body. They moved in tandem, mutually seeking to increase the pleasure, spiraling higher toward the heavens, and she lost all track of time and place as they lost themselves in each other.

The rhythms were familiar, like dancing to the same song so often you memorized the moves. But the familiarity only heightened the experience because she didn't have to wonder what would happen next.

Just as he'd done when they'd been together before, he stared into her eyes as he loved her, refusing to let her look away. Opening his soul to her as they joined again and again. The romance of it swept through her and she held him close.

This was why she'd fallen in love with him. Why she'd never had even the slightest desire to do this with any other man. He made her feel that she completed him without saying a word. Sure, she wanted the words. But times like this made them unnecessary.

Before she was fully ready for it to end, his urgency increased, sending her into an oblivion of sensation until she climaxed, and then he followed her into the light, holding her tight against him as they soared.

She lay there engulfed in his arms, wishing she never had to move from this spot.

Kyle must have been reading her mind, because he murmured in her ear, "Stay. All weekend."

"I don't have any of my stuff," she said lamely as reality nosed its way into the perfect moment.

"Go get a bag and come back."

It was a reasonable suggestion. But then what? Were they jumping back into their relationship as if nothing had happened and ten years hadn't passed? As if they'd dealt with the hurt and separation?

That was too much reality. She sat up and his arms fell away to rest on the comforter.

"I see the wheels turning," he commented mildly as he pulled a sheet over his lower half in a strange bout of modesty. "This is a beginning, Grace. Let's see where it takes us. Don't throw up any more walls."

She shut her eyes. Romance was great, but there was so much more that she wanted in a relationship. There'd been no declarations of undying love. No marriage proposal. Why did he get a pass that no other man got? She was caught between her inescapable feelings for Kyle and her standards.

And the intense hope that things might be different this time.

How would she ever find out if she left?

"Okay." She nodded and ignored the hammering of her pulse. "Let's see where it goes."

Nine

Kyle waited on Grace to come back by pretending to watch TV.

His body had cooled—on the outside—but the inside was still pretty keyed up. He wasn't really interested in much of anything other than getting Grace back in his bed, but this time for the whole night.

When the crunch of gravel sounded outside, breath he hadn't realized he'd been holding whooshed out. She'd come back.

He met Grace at the door, opening it wide as she climbed the front porch steps, her hair still mussed from their thorough lovemaking of less than an hour ago. Her face shone in the porch light, so beautiful and fresh, and his chest hitched as he soaked in the sight of her.

"Hey, Grace," he said, pretty dang happy his voice still worked.

He'd wondered if she might back out, call and say she'd changed her mind. She was still so skittish. She might have let him into her body but he didn't fool himself for a second that she'd let him into her head, or her heart. It wasn't the way it had been, when he'd been her hero, her everything. There was distance now that hadn't been there before and he didn't like it.

Of course, some of that was his fault. Not much. But a little. He didn't fully trust her, and while he'd sworn in theory to forget about the past, it was proving more difficult to do in practice than he'd thought it would be, so he didn't press the issue of the yawning chasm between them.

"Hey." She had a bag slung over her shoulder and a shy smile on her face.

Shy? After the temptress she'd been? It caught him up short. Maybe some of the distance was due to sheer unfamiliarity between them. As comfortable as *he* felt around Grace, that didn't mean she was totally in the groove yet. Plus, they didn't know each other as well as they used to. Ten years didn't vanish just because two people slept together.

"We never had dinner," he commented. "Come sit with me and we'll eat. For real this time."

She nodded and let him take her bag, following him to the table where he laid out silverware and refilled their wineglasses. They ate the chicken salad and polished off the bottle of wine, chatting long after clearing their plates. Grace told cute stories about the children on her case docket, and Kyle reciprocated with some carefully selected anecdotes about the guys he'd trained with in Coronado during BUD/S. Carefully selected because that period had been among the toughest of his life as his training honed him into an elite warrior—*while* he was fighting his own internal battle against the hurt this woman had caused. But he'd survived and wasn't dwelling on that.

Couldn't dwell on it. Liam wasn't a factor and he wanted

to do things with Grace differently this time. And by the time Kyle was done with her, she'd be asking, "Liam who?"

A wail over the monitor drew their attention away from their conversation and Grace gladly helped him get the girls settled again. It was nearing midnight; hopefully it would be the only time the babies woke up for the night.

Kyle didn't mind rolling out of bed at any hour to take care of his daughters, but he selfishly wanted to spend the rest of the night with Grace, and Grace alone. He got his wish. They fell asleep wrapped in each other's arms, and Kyle slept like the dead until dawn.

His eyes snapped open and he took a half second to orient. Not a SEAL. Not in Afghanistan. But with *Grace*. A blessing to count, among many.

Until he tried to snuggle her closer. White-hot pokers of pain shot through his busted leg as he rolled. He bit back the curse and breathed through it.

The pain hadn't been so bad last night, but of course, he'd been pretty distracted. Plus, he normally soaked his leg before going to bed but hadn't had a chance last night. Apparently, he was going to pay for it today.

All the commotion woke Grace.

"Good morning," she murmured sleepily, and slid a leg along his, which was simultaneously arousing and excruciating.

"Wait," he said hoarsely.

"Don't wanna." She stretched provocatively, rubbing her bare breasts against his chest, which distracted him enough that he didn't realize she'd hooked her knee around his leg. She fairly purred with sexy little sounds that meant she was turned on. And probably about to do something about it.

"Grace." He grabbed her shoulders and squared them so he could be sure he had her attention. "Stop."

Her expression went from hot and sleepy to confused

and guarded. Her whole body stiffened, pulling away from his. "Okay. Sorry."

"No, don't be sorry." Kyle swore. *Moron*. He was mucking this up and all he wanted to do was pull her back against him. Dive in, distract himself. But he couldn't. "Listen."

He took a deep breath, fighting the pain, fighting his instinct to clam up again.

He hadn't told anyone about what had happened to him in Afghanistan and didn't want to start with the woman who still had the power to declare him an unfit parent if he admitted to having a busted leg. But as he stared into her troubled brown eyes, his heart lurched and he had to come clean. This was part of closing that distance between them. Part of learning to trust her again.

She'd said she was going to let him keep his girls. He had to believe her. Believe *in* her, or this was never going to work, not now, not in a hundred years.

"I didn't tell you to stop because I wanted you to."

Her gaze softened along with her body. "Then what's going on, Kyle?"

"I got wounded," he muttered. Which made him sound as much like a wuss as he felt. "Overseas."

"Oh, I didn't know!" She gasped and drew back to glance down the length of his body, her expression darkening gorgeously as she took in his semiaroused state. "You don't *look* wounded. Everything I see is quite nice."

And now it was a fully aroused state. Fantastic. This was so not a conversation he wanted to have in the first place, let alone with a hard-on. "My leg. The bone was shattered. I had a lot of surgeries and they put most of it back together. But it still hurts, especially in the morning when I haven't stretched it."

Sympathy poured from her gaze as she sat up and pulled the sheet back, gathering it up in her hand as she sought the scar. When she found it along the far side of his calf, she touched the skin just above it lightly with her fingers. "You hid this last night. With the low light and striking that weird pose. Why didn't you tell me?"

"It's…"

How to explain the horror of being wounded in the line of duty? It wasn't just the pain and the fact that he wasn't ever going to be the same again, but he'd been unable to protect the rest of his team. He'd been unable to *do his job* because his leg didn't work all at once. A SEAL got back up when he was knocked down. *Every time*. Only Kyle hadn't.

Maybe he'd fail at being a parent, too, because of it. That was his worst fear.

"I don't like being weak," he finally said, which was true, if not the whole truth. "I don't like giving you ammunition to take away Maddie and Maggie. Like I might not be a good daddy because my leg doesn't work right."

"Oh, Kyle." She laid her lips on the scar for a moment, and the light touch seared his heart. "I would never take away your daughters because of an injury. That's ridiculous."

He shrugged, unable to meet her gaze. "You were going to take them away because I didn't come home for two months. But I was in the hospital."

"Well, you could have said that!" Exasperation spurted out with the phrase and she shook her head. "For crying out loud. Am I supposed to be a mind reader?"

Yes. Then he wouldn't have to figure out how to say things that were too hard.

"Now you know," he mumbled instead. "That's why I had to stop earlier. Not because I wasn't on board. I just needed a minute."

"Okay." But then she smiled and ran a hand up his thigh,

dangerously close to his erection. "It's been a minute. How about we try this instead, now that I know?"

The protest got caught in his throat as she rolled him onto his back and crawled over him, careful not to touch his leg, but deliberately letting her breasts and long curls brush his skin from thigh to chest. She captured his wrists and encircled them with her fingers, drawing his arms above his head, holding them in place as her hips undulated.

"What are you doing?" His voice scraped the lower register as she ignited his flesh with her sexy movements.

She arched a brow. "Really? I should hope it would be fairly obvious. Since it's not, shut up and I'll make it clearer for you."

He did as advised because his tongue was stuck to the roof of his mouth anyway. And then she leaned forward, still holding his wrists hostage, and kissed him. Hot. Open-mouthed. The kind of kiss laden with dark promise and he eagerly lapped it up. He could break free of her finger shackles easily, but why the hell would he do that?

She had him right where she wanted him, apparently, and since he could find no complaint with it, he let her have the floor. She experimented with different angles of her head as she kissed him, looking for something unknown and he went along for the ride, groaning with the effort it took to hold back.

Then she trailed her mouth down his throat, nipped at his earlobe and writhed against his erection all at once, slicing a long, hot knife of need through his groin. His hips strained toward hers, rocking involuntarily as he sought relief, and he started to pull his arms loose so he could roll her under him to get this show on the road. But she shook her head and tightened her grip on his wrists.

"No, sir," she admonished with a wicked smile. "You're not permitted to do anything but lie there."

This was going to kill him. Flat out stop his heart.

He got what she was doing. She wanted him to keep his leg still, while she did all the dirty work. Something tender hooked his heart as he stared up at her, poised over him with an all-business look on her face that was somehow endearing.

But he wasn't an invalid.

"I hate to break it to you, darling, but that's not happening." He flexed his hips again, sliding his erection against her bare, damp sex, watching as her eyes unfocused with pleasure. "I suggest you think about how you're going to get a condom on me with your hands occupied because I'm going to be inside you in about point two seconds."

"Don't ruin this for me." She mock-pouted and promptly crossed his wrists, one over the other, and held on with one hand as she wiggled the fingers of her free hand in a cheery wave. "I always dreamed of being a rodeo star. This is my chance."

He had to laugh, which downright ached. All over. "That's what's on your mind right now? Rodeo?"

"Oh, yeah." She leaned against his abs, holding on with her thighs as she fished around in the nightstand drawer and pulled out a condom, which she held up triumphantly. "I'm going for a ten in the bucking bronco event."

"I'll be the judge of that," he quipped, and then raised a brow at the condom. "Go ahead. I'm waiting."

In the end, she had to let go of his arms to rip open the foil package. But he obediently held his wrists above his head as she had so sweetly asked. Then there was no more talking as she eased over him, taking him gently in her hands to pleasure him as she rolled on the condom.

He groaned as need broke over him in a wave, and then she slowly guided him into her damp heat. He slid all the way in as she pushed downward and it was unbelievable. They joined and it was better than it had been last night.

Deeper. More amazing, because there were no more secrets between them.

She knew about his injury and hadn't run screaming for her report to revise it. She hadn't been repulsed by his weaknesses. Instead, she'd somehow twisted it around so they could make love without hurting his leg. It was sweet and wonderful.

And then she got busy on her promise to turn him into a bucking bronco, sliding up and down, rolling her hips and generally driving him mad with want. He obliged her by letting his body go with the sensation, meeting her thrusts and driving them both higher until she came with a little cry and he followed her.

Clutching her to his chest, he breathed in tandem with her, still joined and not anxious to change that. He held her hot body to his because he didn't think he could let go.

"You're amazing," he murmured into her hair, and she turned her head to lay her cheek on his shoulder, a pleased smile on her face.

"I wouldn't say no to thank-you flowers."

He made a mental note to send her a hundred roses the moment his bones returned and he could actually move. "Where'd you get that sexy little hip roll from?"

She shrugged. "I don't know. I've never done it before. It just felt right."

All at once, his good mood vanished as he wondered what moves she *had* done before with other men that she hadn't opted to try out on him. Like Liam. Was he better in bed than his brother? Worse? About the same? And yeah, he recognized that the burn in his gut was pure jealousy.

Totally unable to help himself, he smiled without humor and rolled her off him casually, as if it were no big deal, but he didn't really want her close to him right then. "It was great. Perfect. Like you'd practiced it a lot."

What an ass he was being. But the thought of Grace

with another man, some guy's mitts on her, touching her, put him over the edge. Especially since one of those Neanderthals had been his brother.

She quirked a brow. "Really? You're not just humoring me?"

The pleased note in her voice didn't improve his mood. What, it was a compliment to be well-practiced in bed?

"Oh, no," he said silkily. "You've got the moves, sweetheart. The men must line up into the next county to get in on that."

Not only was he jealous, he was acting as if he'd been a choirboy for the past ten years when there was nothing further from the truth. He'd been the king of one-night stands because that was all he could do. It wasn't what he'd wanted or what he'd envisioned for himself, but the reason he wasn't able to move on and find someone to settle down with was sitting in his bed smiling at him as if this was all a big joke.

But as always, he wasn't going to say what was really on his mind. That was how you got hurt, by exposing your unguarded soft places.

And then she laughed. "Oh, yeah. They line up, all right. As long as we're having confession time, I have one of my own."

He needed a drink first. A row of shots would be preferable. But it was—he scowled at the clock—barely 6:00 a.m., and the babies were going to wake up any second, demanding their breakfast. "We don't have to do this, Grace."

"No, I want to," she insisted. "You told me about your leg, which was clearly hard for you. I think this is just as important for you to know. I'm not practiced. At all. It's kind of funny you'd say that actually, since you're the last man I slept with."

Shyly, she peeked at him from under lowered lashes as she let that register.

He sat up so fast, his head cracked against the headboard. "You…what?"

She hadn't been with anyone since *him*? Since ten years ago? *At all?*

Grace nodded. "I guess you could say you ruined me for other men. But that's not the only reason. I just never found one I thought measured up."

To him. She'd never found another man she'd thought was good enough. Had he been working himself up for no reason?

Grace had never been with another man. She'd been a virgin when they met. Kyle Wade was Grace's only lover. The thought choked him up in a wholly unexpected way.

And then his brain latched on to the idea of Grace refusing suitors over the years and shoved it under the lens of what he knew to be the truth. His mood turned dangerously sharp and ugly again. "Well, now. That's a high compliment. If it's true."

Confusion crept across her expression. "Why would I lie?"

"Good question. One I'd like the answer to, as well." He crossed his arms over his thundering heart. "Maybe you could explain how it's possible that you've never been with another man, yet I practically caught you in the act with one. Liam."

Just spitting his name out cost Kyle. His throat tightened and threatened to close off entirely, which would be great because then he couldn't throw up.

"Oh, Kyle." She actually *smiled* as she tenderly cupped his face. "You've certainly taken your time circling around back to that. Nothing happened with Liam. I didn't think you'd even noticed."

"You didn't…" He couldn't even finish that sentence and jerked away from her touch. "His hands were all over you. Don't tell me nothing happened."

"First of all, we were broken up at the time," she reminded him. "Secondly, it was a setup, honey. I wanted to get your attention, and honestly, I was pretty devastated it didn't work. Liam was a good sport about it, though. I've always appreciated that he was willing to help."

Kyle's vision went black and then red, and he squeezed his eyes shut as he came perilously close to passing out for the first time in his life. *Breathe. And again.* Ruthlessly, he got himself back under control.

"A setup," he repeated softly.

She nodded. "We set it up for you to catch us. It was dumb, I realize. Blame it on the fact that I was young and naive. I was expecting you to confront me. For us to have it out so I could explain how much you meant to me. How upset I was that we weren't together anymore. It was supposed to end differently. But you left and I figured out that I wasn't all that important to you."

A setup. To force a confrontation. And instead, she'd decided his silence meant she wasn't important to him, when in fact, the opposite was true.

"Why?" He nearly choked on the question. "Why would you do something like that? With *Liam* of all people?"

His brother. There was a sacred line between brothers that you didn't cross, and she'd not only crossed it, she'd been the instigator. Liam had put his hands on the woman Kyle loved as a *favor*. Somehow, and he wouldn't have thought this possible, that was worse than when Kyle had thought his brother was just adding another name to his growing list of conquests. The betrayal was actually twice as deep because it had all been a *setup*.

The reckoning was going to be brutal.

"Because, Kyle." She caught his gaze and tears brimmed in her eyes. "I loved you. So much and so intensely. But you were so distant. Already seeking that horizon, even then. We'd stopped connecting. Breaking up with you didn't faze you. I figured it would take something bold to shake you up."

Yeah, it had shaken him up all right. "But *that*?"

He couldn't wrap his head around what she was telling him. He'd enlisted because of a lie. Because he'd felt as though he couldn't breathe in Royal ever again. Because he'd sought a place where people stood by their word and their honor, would take a bullet for you. Where he could be part of a team alongside people who valued him. And *found* that place.

Which wasn't here.

"Yeah. Like you used Emma Jane to make me jealous." She shrugged. "Same idea. Funny how similar our tactics are."

The roaring sound in his head drowned out her words. Similar. She thought the idea of Kyle flirting with a woman out in the open in broad daylight was the same as walking by Liam's bedroom and hearing Grace's laugh. The same as peeking through the crack at the door to see the woman he'd given his soul to entwined with his brother *on his brother's bed*.

"Go." He shoved out of the bed, ignored his aching leg and dressed as fast as he could. "I can't be around you right now."

"Are you upset, Kyle?" She still sounded confused, as though it wasn't abundantly clear that none of this was okay. And then her face crumpled as understanding slowly leached into her posture.

He couldn't respond. There was nothing to say anyway. *It wasn't the same.* He'd started to trust her again—no, he'd *forced* himself to forget the past despite the amount of pain he still carried around—only to find that her capacity for lies was far broader than he'd ever have imagined.

He slammed out of the room and went to make the babies' bottles because he couldn't leave as he wanted to. As he should. Grace would twist that around, too, and somehow find a way to rip his heart out again by taking his daughters away.

But he wouldn't give Grace Haines any more power in his life.

Since he couldn't leave, Kyle stewed. When Liam and Hadley returned from Vail the next afternoon, Kyle wasn't fit company.

Which made it the perfect time for a confrontation.

"Liam," Kyle fairly growled as he cornered his brother in the kitchen after Hadley went to the nursery to see the babies.

"What's up?" Liam chugged some water from the bottle in his hand.

"Grace fessed up." Crossing his arms so he wouldn't get started on the beating portion of the reckoning too soon, he shifted the weight off his bad leg and glared at the betrayer who dared stand there scowling as though he didn't know what Kyle was talking about. "Back before I went into the navy. You and Grace. It was a lie."

"Oh, that." Liam shook his head. "Yeah, you're a little slow on the uptake. That's ancient history."

"It's recent to me because I just found out about it."

With a smirk, Liam punched him on the arm. "Maybe if you'd stuck around instead of flying off to the navy, you'd have known then. That was the whole purpose of it, according to Grace, to get you to confront her. I was just window dressing."

"I went into the navy because of window dressing," Kyle said through clenched teeth, though how his brain was still functioning enough to spit out thoughts was beyond him. "Glad to know this is all a big game to everyone. I've been missing out. Where's Hadley? I'm looking forward to getting in on some of this fun. Would you like to watch while I feel up your wife or would you rather walk in on us?"

"Shut your filthy mouth."

Kyle was ready for his brother this time and blocked Liam's crappy right hook easily, pushing back on his twin's torso before the man charged him. "Not so fun when you're on the other side of it, huh?"

Chest heaving and eyes wild with fury, Liam strained against Kyle's immovable blockade. "What do you care? You ignored Grace to the point where she cried so much over your sorry hide, I thought she was going to dry up like an old withered flower."

"Aren't you the poet?" He sneered to cover the catch in his heart to hear that Grace had cried over him. And how did Liam know that anyway? It probably wasn't even true. This was all an elaborate bunch of hooey designed to throw Kyle off the scent of who was really to blame here. "I cared, you idiot. You're the one who didn't care about the big fat line you crossed when you put your hands on my woman."

"*Your* woman? I got a feeling Grace would disagree." Liam snorted and stepped back, mercifully, allowing Kyle to drop his hand from his brother's chest. Another few minutes of holding him back would have strained his leg something fierce. "What line did I cross? You broke up. You weren't even together when that happened, remember?"

"*She* broke up. I didn't," Kyle countered viciously. "I was trying to figure out how to get her back. Not so easy when a woman tells you she's through and then makes out with another guy. Who happens to be my brother. Which never would have happened if you'd told her no. *That's* the line, Liam. I would never have done that to you."

Something dawned in Liam's gaze. "Holy cow. You were in love with her."

"What the hell do you think I've been talking about?"

Disgusted with the circles and lies and betrayals, Kyle slumped against the counter, seriously thinking about starting on a bottle of Irish whiskey. It was five o'clock 24-7 when you found out your twin brother was a complete moron.

"You were in love with her," Liam repeated with surprise, as if saying it again was going to make it more real. "Still are."

Well, *duh*. Of course he was! Why did Liam think Kyle was so pissed?

Wait. No, that wasn't— Kyle shut his eyes for a beat, but the truth didn't magically become something else. Of course he was still in love with Grace. That's why her betrayal hurt so much.

"That's not the point." Nor was that up for discussion. It didn't matter anyway. He and Grace were through, for real this time.

"No, the point is that this is all news to me. Probably news to Grace as well, assuming you actually got around to telling her." More comprehension dawned in Liam's expression. "You haven't. You're still just as much of a jackass now as you were then."

Kyle was getting really tired of being so transparent. "Some things shouldn't have to be said."

Liam laughed so hard, Kyle thought he was going to bust something, and the longer it went on, the more Kyle wanted to be the one doing the busting. Like a couple of teeth in his brother's mouth.

Finally, Liam wiped his eyes. "Get your checkbook because you need to buy a clue, my brother. No woman is going to let you get away with being such a clam, so keep on being the strong, silent type and sleep alone. See if I care."

"Yeah, you're the fount of wisdom when it comes to women, Mr. Revolving Door. Do you even know how many women you've slept with over the years?" Cheap shot. And Kyle knew it the moment it left his mouth, but Liam had him good and riled. He started to apologize but Liam waved it off.

"That doesn't matter when you find the right one." Liam glanced up the back stairs fondly, his mind clearly on his wife, who was still upstairs with the babies. "But guess what? You don't get a woman like Hadley without knowing a few things about how to treat a woman. And keeping your thoughts to yourself ain't it. Look what it's cost you so far. You willing to spend the next ten years without the woman you love because of your man-of-few-words shtick?"

Yeah, he didn't blather on about the stuff that was inside. So what? It was personal and he didn't like to share it.

Keeping quiet was a defense mechanism he'd adopted when he was little to shelter him from constantly being in a place he didn't fit into, lest anyone figure out his real feelings. Some wounds weren't obvious but they went deep.

The old-fashioned clock on the wall ticked out the seconds as it had done since Kyle was old enough to know how to tell time. Back then, he'd marked each one on his heart, counting the ticks in hopes that when he reached a thousand, his mother would come back. When he reached ten thousand, she'd *surely* walk through the door. A hundred thousand. And then he'd lose count and start over.

She had never come back to rescue him from the ranch he didn't like, didn't comprehend. Nothing had ever fit right until Grace. She was still the only woman who ever had.

And maybe he'd messed up a little by not telling her what she meant to him. Okay, maybe he'd messed up a lot. If he'd told her, she probably wouldn't have cooked up that scheme with Liam. Too little, too late.

"We good?" Liam asked, his gaze a lot more understanding than it should have been.

"Yeah." Kyle sighed. "It was a long time ago."

"For what it's worth, I'm sorry."

Liam stuck his hand out and Kyle didn't hesitate. They shook on it and did an awkward one-armed brotherly hug that probably looked more like two squirrels fighting over a walnut than anything. But it was enough to bury the hatchet, and not in Liam's back, the way Kyle had planned when he'd stormed into the kitchen earlier.

"Listen." Liam cleared his throat. "If we're all done crying about your girlfriend, I've got something to tell you that's been rubbing me the wrong way."

"You need me to go underwear shopping with you so we can get you the right size?" When Liam elbowed him, Kyle knew they were on the way back to being brothers again instead of strangers. "Because you have a wife for that now."

"Shut up. This is for serious. There's an outfit called Samson Oil making noises around Royal and I don't like it. They're buying up properties. Even offered me a pretty penny for Wade Ranch. Wanted to make sure you're on the same—"

"You said no, right?" Kyle shot back instantly. This was his home now. The place he planned to raise his daughters. No amount of money could compensate for a stable home life for his family.

"Well, I wanted to talk to you first. But yeah. The right answer is no."

Relief squeezed his chest. And wasn't that something? Kyle had never thought he'd consider the ranch home. But there you go. The threat of losing it—well, he didn't have to worry about that, obviously.

"So it's a no. What's the big deal then?"

Liam shrugged. "I dunno. It just doesn't sit well. The

guy from Sampson, he didn't even look around. Just handed me some paperwork with an offer that was fifteen million above fair market value. How's that for a big deal?"

It ruffled the back of Kyle's neck, too. "There's no oil around here. What little there is has a pump on it already."

"Yeah, so now you're where I'm at. It's weird, right?"

Kyle nodded because his throat was tight again. It was nice to be consulted. As if he really was half owner of the ranch, and he and Liam were going to do this thing called family. He hadn't left this time and it might have made a huge difference.

It gave Kyle hope he might actually become the father his girls deserved. Grace, however, was a whole other story with an ending he couldn't quite figure out.

Ten

Grace kicked the oven. It didn't magically turn on. It hadn't the first time she'd hauled off and whacked it a minute ago, either.

But kicking something felt good. Her foot throbbed, which was better than the numbness she'd felt since climbing from Kyle's bed, well loved and then brokenhearted in the space of an hour. The physical pain was a far sight better than the mental pain.

Because she didn't understand what had happened. She'd opened her heart to Kyle again, only to be destroyed more thoroughly the second time than she had been the first time. This was a grown woman's pain. And the difference was breathtaking. Literally, as in she couldn't make her lungs expand enough to get a good, solid full breath.

Determined to fix something, Grace spent twenty minutes unscrewing every bolt she could budge on the oven, hoping something would jump out at her as the culprit. Which failed miserably because she didn't know what it was supposed to look like—how would she know if something was out of place? The oven was just broken. No matter. She wasn't hungry anyway.

She wandered around her small house two blocks off the main street of Royal. She'd bought the house three years ago when she'd claimed her Professional Single Girl status, and set about finding a way to be happy with the idea of building a life with herself and herself only in it. She had, to a degree. No one argued with her if she wanted to change the drapes four times a year, and she never had to share the bathroom.

The empty rooms hadn't seemed so empty until now. Spending the weekend with Kyle had stomped her fantasy of being single and happy to pieces. She wanted a husband to fill the space in her bed, in her heart. Children who laughed around the kitchen table. A dog the kids named something silly, like Princess Spaghetti.

A fierce knock sounded at the door, echoing through the whole house. She almost didn't answer it because who else would knock like that except a man who had a lot of built-up anger? At her, apparently. After ten years of turning over every aspect of her relationship with Kyle, analyzing it to death while looking for the slightest nuance of where it had all gone wrong, never once had she turned that inspection back on herself.

But she'd made mistakes, that much was apparent. Then and now. Somehow.

Only she didn't quite buy that what happened ten years ago was all her fault.

And all at once, she wanted that reckoning. Wanted to ask a few pointed questions of Kyle Wade that she hadn't gotten to ask before being thrown out of his bed two long and miserable days ago.

She yanked open the door and the mad she'd worked up faltered.

Kyle stood there on her doorstep in crisp jeans, boots and a work shirt, dressed like every other man in Royal and probably a hundred other towns dotting the Texas prairie. But he wasn't anything close to any other man the world over, because he was Kyle. Her stupid heart would probably never get the message that they were doomed as a couple.

He was holding a bouquet of beautiful flowers, so full it spilled over his hand in a riot of colors and shapes. Her vision blurred as she focused on the flowers and the solemn expression on Kyle's face.

"Hey, Grace."

No. He wasn't allowed to be here all apologetic and carrying conciliatory flowers. It wasn't fair. She couldn't let him into her head again, and she certainly wasn't offering up her heart again to be flattened. He didn't have to know she'd given up on getting over him.

"What do you want, Kyle?" She didn't even wince at her own rudeness. She got a pass after being shown the door while still undressed and warm from the man's arms.

"I brought you these," he said simply without blinking at her harsh tone. He held out the bouquet. "Thank-you flowers. Because I owed you."

Wasn't *that* romantic? She didn't take the bouquet. "You *owed* me? You definitely owe me, but not flowers. An explanation would be better."

Kyle dropped the bouquet, his expression hardening. "May I come in then? Your next-door neighbor is out on the porch with popcorn, watching the show."

"Mrs. Putter is seventy-two." Grace crossed her arms and propped a hip against the doorjamb. "This is all the fun she gets for the year."

"Fine." Kyle sighed. "I came to apologize. I shot first and asked questions later. It's the way I do things, mostly because people are usually shooting at me, too."

Not an auspicious start, other than the apology part. "And yet I still haven't heard any questions."

"Grace." Kyle caught her gaze, and something warm spilled from his green eyes that she couldn't look away from. "You meant something to me. Back then. You have to understand that I had a lot of stuff going on in my head that I didn't want to deal with, so I didn't. I shut down instead. That wasn't fair to you. But you were the best thing in my life, and then you were gone. I was a wreck. Seeing you with Liam was the last straw, so I left Royal because I couldn't stand it, assuming that you'd found the Wade brother you preferred. There was never a point when I would have confronted you about it."

Openmouthed, she stared at him. That was the longest speech she'd ever heard him give and it loosened her tongue in kind. "I get that I messed up with Liam. I was young and stupid. I should have been more up-front about my feelings, too."

Kyle nodded. "Goes for both of us. But I still owe you a thank-you. I joined the military because I wanted to be gone. I figured, what better way to forget Royal and the girl there than to go to the other side of the world in defense of my country? But instead of just a place to nurse my shattered ego, I found something I didn't expect. Something great. Being a SEAL changed me."

Yes, she'd seen that. He'd grown up, into a responsible, solid man who cared about his daughters. "You seem to have flourished."

"I did," he agreed enthusiastically. "It was the team I'd been looking for. I never fit in at the ranch. That's part of what was weighing me down back then. The stuff inside. I was contemplating my future and not seeing a clear picture of what I should do going forward. If you hadn't staged that ploy with Liam, I might never have found my unit. Those guys were my family."

The sheer emotion on his face as he talked about his fellow team members—it was overwhelming. He'd clearly loved being in the military. It had shaped him, and he'd soaked it up.

Her heart twisted anew. If he didn't fit in at the ranch, why had he taken over the cattle side? During one of her site visits, he'd told her that was his job now—he hoped to create a stable home for his daughters. He planned to stick around this time. Was that all a lie? Or was he just doing it because she'd forced him into it, despite hating that life?

"I don't understand," she whispered. "If you liked being in the military so much, why did you come home?"

"My leg." His expression caved in on itself, and it might have been the most vulnerable she'd ever seen him. She almost reached out to comfort him, was almost physically unable to prevent her heart from crying in sympathy at what he'd lost. He was hurting, and that was so hard for her to take.

But she didn't reach out. "You came home because you were injured," she recounted flatly.

That was the only reason. Not because he missed Grace and regretted splitting up. Not because he wanted his daughters, or the simple life on a ranch with his family. He'd been forced to.

And what would he do when he got tired of an ill-fitting career? What would happen when the allure of the great wide open called to him again?

He'd leave. Just as he'd done the first time, only he'd take his babies with him—there was no law that said he had to stay in Royal to retain custody. He'd go and crush her anew, once she'd fallen in love with three people instead of just one.

He hadn't confronted her about Liam ten years ago because he hadn't wanted to stay in the first place. Not for her, not for anything. If he had, he'd have fought for their love; she had no doubt.

Kyle could pretend all he wanted that he'd enlisted because he'd caught her with Liam, but that had been—by his own admission—the last straw. Not the first.

"Yeah." He jerked his head in acknowledgment. "I was honorably discharged due to my busted leg. I didn't have anyplace else to go. But when I saw Maddie and Maggie for the first time…and then you came back into my life… Well, things are different now. I want to do things different. Starting with you."

"No." Her heart nearly split in two as she shook her head. "We've already had one too many do-overs. You shot first and asked questions too late."

She'd begun to trust him again, only to have the carpet ripped out from under her feet. She couldn't do that again. She could be single and happy. It was a choice; she just had to make it.

"Don't say that, Grace." Kyle threw the bouquet on the wicker chair closest to the door and captured her hand, squeezing it tight so she couldn't pull away. His green eyes beseeched her to reconsider, hollowing her out inside. "I lie awake at night and think about how great it would be if you were there. I think about what it's going to be like for the girls growing up without a mom. It's not a picture I like. We need someone to keep us sane."

This was delivered with a lopsided smile that she ached to return. If only he'd mentioned the condition of his heart in that speech and how it was breaking to be away from her. How he couldn't consider his life complete without her. Anything other than a string of sentences which sounded suspiciously like an invitation to make sure Maddie and Maggie had a mother figure.

And she wanted a family so badly she could picture easily falling into the role of Mama to those precious babies. At what cost, though?

"You have Hadley for that," she said woodenly. "I'm unnecessary."

"You're not listening to what I'm saying." He held her hand against his chest, and she wanted to uncurl her palm so she could feel his heartbeat. "Hadley is Liam's wife. I want one of my own."

It was the closest thing to a proposal she'd ever gotten. She was certifiably insane for not saying yes. Except he hadn't actually asked her. As always, he couldn't just come right out and say what he meant. That's what had led to the Liam fiasco in the first place, and nothing had changed.

None of this was what she'd envisioned. Kyle was nothing like her father. What about her standards? Her grand romance and fairy-tale life? How in the world would their relationship ever stand the test of time with staged jealousy-inducing ploys and the inability to just talk to each other as their starting point?

"I can't do this, Kyle. I can't—" Her voice broke but she made herself finish. "I thought we were starting something and the moment things get a little rough, you bail. Just like before."

"That's an excuse, Grace." He firmed his mouth, and then pointed out, "I'm here now, aren't I?"

"It's too late," she retorted, desperate to get this horrific conversation over with. "We have too many trust issues. We don't even want the same things."

His green eyes sharpened as he absorbed her words. "How can you say that? I want to be together. That's the same."

"Except that's not what I want," she whispered, and forced herself to watch as his beautiful face blanked, becoming as desolate as a West Texas ravine in a drought. "Goodbye, Kyle."

And before she took it all back in a moment of weakness, she shut the door, dry-eyed. The tears would come later.

Now that Johnny and Slim had a grudging respect for Kyle as the boss, they got on okay.

Which was fortunate, because Kyle drove them all relentlessly. Himself included, and probably the hardest. Spring calving season was in full swing and eighteen-hour days fit with Kyle's determination to never think, never lie awake at night and never miss Grace.

At this point, he'd take two out of three, but the hole where Grace was supposed to be ached too badly to be ignored, which in turn guaranteed he wouldn't sleep. And as he lay there not sleeping, his brain did nothing but think, turning over her words again and again, forcing him to relive them because he deserved to be unhappy. He couldn't be with Grace because she didn't want to be with him. Because she didn't trust him.

All the work he'd done to get over his trust issues, and she'd blindsided him with her own. Because he'd left when life got too difficult. When all he'd wanted was to find his place in the world. And when that place spat him back out, he came back. To forge a new place, put down roots. It had been hard, one of the toughest challenges of his life, and yeah, when it got rough, he dreamed of leaving. But he hadn't. Only to have that thrown back in his face.

If it didn't hurt so bad he'd laugh at the irony.

A week after Operation: Grace had gone down in flames, Liam invited him to the Texas Cattlemen's Club for an afternoon of "getting away from it all" as Liam put it. Curious about the club his grandfather had belonged to, and now Liam, too, apparently, Kyle agreed, with the caveat that they'd only stay a couple of hours tops. The cattle weren't going to tend themselves, after all.

The moment Kyle walked into the formerly men-only club, the outside world ceased to exist. Dark hardwood floors stretched from wall to wall, reflecting the pale gold wallpaper that warmed the place. It was welcoming and hushed, as if the room was waiting for something important to happen. The sense of anticipation was compelling.

Kyle followed Liam to the bar, where some other men sat nursing beers. Kyle recognized Mac McCallum, who'd been Liam's buddy for a long time, and Case Baxter.

"Case is the president of the Texas Cattlemen's Club," Liam said as he introduced everyone around. "And this is Nolan Dane."

"Right." Kyle shook the man's hand. "Haven't seen you in ages."

"I'm back in town, practicing family law now," Nolan explained with a glance at Liam. "Your brother's a client."

Kyle nodded as his lungs hitched. Liam had a legal retainer who practiced family law? Didn't take a rocket scientist to do that math. When Liam had talked about papers and warned Kyle he'd need a lawyer, it hadn't been an idle threat. They hadn't talked about it again, and Kyle had hoped the idea of adoption had been dropped.

Obviously it hadn't.

But why stick it in Kyle's face like this? It was a crappy thing to do after all the hoops Kyle'd been forced to jump through to prove his worth as a father. *Especially* after they'd had their Come To Jesus discussion and Liam had apologized for the Grace thing.

Wasn't that indicative of Kyle's Royal welcome thus far? That's why he shot first. When he didn't, he invariably took a bullet straight into his gut.

Mouth firmly shut as he processed everything, Kyle took a seat as far away from Liam as he could. When the conversation turned to Samson Oil, it piqued his interest sufficiently to pull his head out of his rear long enough to participate. Especially when Nolan Dane excused himself with a pained look on his face.

"More offers for land coming in," Liam affirmed. "Wade Ranch included. I think we've got a problem on our hands."

The other men seemed to share his brother's concern. Kyle leaned in. "What does Samson Oil want? They have to know the oil prospects are slim to none around here. People been drilling for over a hundred years. There's no way Samson will find a new well."

Case Baxter shook his head. "No one knows for sure what they're up to. Fracking, maybe. But the Cline Shale property is mostly bought up already in this area."

"If you've got concerns, I've got concerns," Kyle said as his senses tingled again. "I know a guy in the CIA. Owes me a favor. I'll have him poke around, see what Samson Oil is up to."

The offer was out of his mouth before he'd thought better of it. He didn't owe these people anything. It wasn't as if they'd rolled out the red carpet for the returning war veteran. Or acknowledged that Kyle Wade owned half a *cattle ranch* and wasn't even a member of the Texas Cattleman's Club.

Royal clearly wasn't where Kyle fit, any more than he had ten years ago.

"I knew you'd come in handy." Liam fairly beamed.

"That would be great," Mac threw in. "The more information we have, the better. The last thing we need is to find out they're looking for a site to house a new strip mall after it's too late."

The expectant faces of the men surrounding him settled Kyle's resolve. He couldn't take it back now. And for better or worse, this was his home, and he had a responsibility to it. He shrugged.

"Consider it done." Kyle sat back and let the members

of the club do their thing, which didn't include him. If he kept his mouth shut, maybe everyone would forget about him. It wasn't as if he wanted to be a member of their exclusive club anyway.

But then Liam's phone beeped, and he glanced at it, frowning. When his grave and troubled gaze met Kyle's, every nerve in Kyle's body stood on end.

"We have to go," Liam announced. "Sorry."

Liam hustled Kyle out of the club and into his truck, ignoring Kyle's rapid-fire questions about the nature of the emergency. Because of course there was one. Liam's face only looked like that when something bad happened to one of his prized horses.

Liam started the truck and tore out of the lot before finally finding his voice. "It's Maddie."

All the blood drained from Kyle's head and his chest squeezed so tight, it was a wonder his heart didn't push through two ribs. "What? What do you mean, it's Maddie? What happened?"

Not a horse. His daughter. Maddie.

"Hadley's not sure," Liam hedged. Kyle gripped his forearm, growling. "Driving here. Causing me to have a wreck won't get you the information any faster. I'm taking you to Royal Memorial. Hadley said Maddie wouldn't wake up and had a really high fever. With Maddie's heart problems, that's a really bad sign because she might have an infection. Hadley called an ambulance and left Maggie in Candace's capable hands. We're meeting them there."

The drive couldn't have taken more than five minutes. But it took five years off Kyle's life to be trapped in the cab of Liam's truck when his poor defenseless Maddie was suffering. The baby was fragile, and while she'd been growing steadily, obviously her insides weren't as strong as they should be. His mind leaped ahead to all the ugly possibilities, and he wished his heart *had* fallen out ear-

lier, because the thought of losing one of his daughters—
it was far worse than losing Grace. Worse than losing his
place on his SEAL team.

Liam screeched into the lot, but Kyle had the door open
before he'd fully rolled to a stop, hitting the pavement at
a run. It was a much different technique from jumping
out of a plane, and his leg hadn't been busted on his last
HALO mission.

Pain knifed up his knee and clear into his chest cavity,
which didn't need any more stress. The leg nearly crumpled underneath him, but he ignored it and stormed into
the emergency room, looking for a doctor to unleash his
anxiety on.

The waiting room receptionist met him halfway across
the room. "Mr. Wade. Hadley requested that you be
brought to the pediatric ICU immediately. Follow me."

ICU? Shades of the tiny room in Germany where Kyle
had lain in a stupor for months filtered back through his
consciousness, and his stomach rolled involuntarily, threatening to expel the beer he'd been happily drinking while
his daughter was being subjected to any number of frightening people and procedures. The elevator dinged but he
barely registered it above the numbness. Liam and the receptionist flanked him, both poor wingmen in a dire situation. But all he had.

Finally, they emerged onto the second floor and set
off down the hall. Hadley rushed into Liam's arms, tears
streaming down her face. They murmured to each other,
but Kyle skirted them, seeking his little pink bundle, to
assure himself she was okay and Maggie wouldn't have
to grow up without her sister. The girls had already been
through so much, so many hits that Kyle had already
missed.

But he was here now. Ready to fight back against whatever was threatening his family. And that included his

brother. The adoption business needed to be put to rest. Immediately.

"Who's in charge around here?" Kyle growled at the receptionist, who must have been used to people in crisis because she just smiled.

"I'll find the nurse to speak to you. Dr. Reese is in with your daughter now."

The receptionist disappeared into the maze of hospital rooms and corridors.

Hadley and Liam came up on either side of Kyle, and Hadley placed a comforting hand on his arm. "Dr. Reese is the best. He's been caring for Maddie since she was born. He'll know what to do."

That was far from comforting. If only he could see her, he'd feel a lot better.

A woman in scrubs with balloon decals all over them emerged from a room and walked straight to Kyle. "Hi, Mr. Wade, I'm Clare Connolly, if you don't remember me. We've got Maddie on an IV and a ventilator. She's stable and that's the important thing."

"What happened? What's wrong with her?" Kyle demanded.

"Dr. Reese is concerned about the effects of her high fever on her heart," Clare said frankly, which Kyle appreciated. "He's trying to bring the fever down and running some tests to see what's happening. The last surgery should have fixed all the problems, but nothing is guaranteed. We knew that going in and, well, we're going to keep fighting. We all want to win this thing once and for all."

This woman genuinely cared about Maddie. He could see it in the worried set of her mouth. Nurses were never emotional about their patients, or at least the German ones weren't.

"Thanks. For everything you're doing. May I talk to the doctor?"

"Of course. He'll want to talk to you, too. We all want to see Maddie running alongside her sister and blowing out candles on her birthday cakes for a long time to come. When Dr. Reese is free, he'll be out," Clare promised, and extended her hand toward the waiting room outside the pediatric unit. "Why don't you have a seat until then."

Clare bustled back into the room she'd materialized from, and Kyle nearly followed her because the waiting room was for people who had the capacity to wait, and that did not describe Kyle.

But Hadley's hand on his arm stopped him. "Let the doctor do his thing, Kyle. You'll only be in the way."

Long minutes stretched as Kyle hovered outside his daughter's room. What was taking so long? Pacing didn't help. It hurt. Everything inside hurt. Finally, another nurse dared approach him, explaining that the hall needed to be clear in case of emergency. Wouldn't he please take a seat?

He did, for no other reason than it would be a relief to get off his leg. Now if only he could find something to do with his hands.

People began filtering into the waiting room. Mac Mc-Callum came to sit with Liam and Hadley, who promptly excused herself to fill out paperwork for Maddie, which she'd offered to do in Kyle's stead so he could be available the moment the doctor came out with news. Hadley's friend Kori came in and took a seat next to Liam.

They all had smiles and words of encouragement for Kyle. Some had stories of how Maddie was a fighter and how many people had sat with her through the night when she was known as Baby Janey. This community had embraced his daughter before they'd even known whom she belonged to. And now that they did, nothing had changed. They still cared. They were all here to provide support during a crisis, which is what the very best of neighbors did.

And then the air shifted, prickling Kyle's skin. He looked up.

Grace.

She rushed into the room, brown curls flying, and knelt by his chair, bringing the scent of spring and innocence and everything good in the world along with her. As he soaked up her presence, he took his first easy breath since Hadley's message to Liam had upended his insides.

"I came as soon as Hadley called me," she said, her brown eyes huge and distressed as her gaze flitted over him.

The muffled hospital noises and people and everything around them faded as they focused on each other. Greedily, he searched her beautiful face for some hint as to her thoughts. Was she getting any sleep? Did she miss him?

She slid her hand into his and held on. "I'm sorry about Maddie. How are you doing?"

"Okay," he said gruffly.

Better now. Much better. How was it possible that the woman who continually ripped his heart out could repair it instantly just by walking into a room?

It was a paradox he didn't understand.

She climbed into the next chair, her grip on his hand never lessening. Her skin warmed his, and it was only then that he realized how cold he'd been.

"What did Dr. Reese say?" she asked.

Did everyone in town know the name of his daughter's pediatrician? "He hasn't been out yet. The nurse, Ms. Connelly, said her fever might be causing problems with her heart, but we don't know anything for sure."

His voice broke then, as sheer overwhelming helplessness swamped him, weighing down his arms and legs when all he wanted to do was explode from this chair and go pound on someone until they fixed his precious little bundle of pink.

"Oh, no." Grace's free hand flew to her mouth in anguish. "That's the one thing we were hoping wouldn't happen."

He nodded, swallowing rapidly so he could speak.

"Thanks," he said. "For coming."

He wouldn't have called her. But now that she was here Grace was exactly what he'd needed, and he never would have taken steps to make it happen. What if she'd said no? But she hadn't, and he didn't care about anything other than sitting here waiting on news about his daughter with the woman he loved. Still. In spite of everything.

If only it made a difference.

Eleven

Grace normally loved being at Royal Memorial because 99 percent of the time, she was there because someone was giving birth. That was a joyous event worthy of celebration. Waiting on news about the health and well-being of Kyle's baby was hands down one of the most stressful things she'd ever done.

At the same time, it was turning into a community event, the kind that strengthened ties and bonded people together. And she hadn't let go of Kyle's hand once. People seemed unsurprised to see them together. Not that they were "together." But they were easy with each other in a way that probably looked natural to others.

Inside, she was a bit of a mess.

How many times had she replayed that last conversation with Kyle in her head, wondering if she'd been too harsh, too unforgiving? If her standards were too high? She'd finally had to shut it down, telling herself ten times a day that she'd stood up for what she wanted for a reason. Kyle wasn't a safe bet for her heart. He'd proven that over and over.

But being here with him in his time of need brought all the questions back in a rush. Because it didn't feel as if they were through. It felt as if they were exactly where they were supposed to be—together.

It was all very confusing. She just hoped that supporting him during this crisis didn't give him the wrong idea— that she might be willing to forget her standards. Forget that he'd stomped on her heart again the moment she'd let her guard down.

Grace had lost track of the hour and only glanced at the clock when Kyle's stomach grumbled. Just as she was about to offer to get him something to eat, Dr. Reese appeared at the entrance to the waiting room, looking worn but smiling.

The entire room ceased to talk. Move. Breathe.

She and Kyle both tightened their grip on each other's hands simultaneously. When he rose, she followed him to the edge of the waiting room, where Dr. Reese was waiting to talk to Kyle privately. She stepped closer to Kyle in silent support, just in case the news wasn't as good as the expression on Dr. Reese's face might indicate.

"I'm Dr. Reese." Parker held out his hand for Kyle to shake. "Your daughter is stable. I was able to bring the fever down, which is a good sign, but I don't know if it adversely affected her heart yet. I need to keep her overnight for observation and run some more tests in the morning after we've both had some sleep. She's a fighter, and I have high hopes that this is only a minor setback with no long-term effects. But I'll know more in the morning."

"Call me Kyle. Formality is for strangers," Kyle said, and his relieved exhale mirrored Grace's. "And any man who saved Maddie's life is a friend of mine. Can I see her?"

Parker nodded instantly. "Sure, of course. She's asleep

right now, but there's no reason you can't stay with her, if you want—"

"Yes," Kyle broke in fiercely. "I'll be there until you kick me out."

That meant Grace wasn't going anywhere, either. If there were rules about that sort of thing, someone could complain to the hospital board, the mayor and Sheriff Battle. Tomorrow. No one was going to stand between her and the man who needed her.

Unless Kyle didn't want her there.

Would be weird to spend the night in the hospital with a man she'd told to get lost?

But then he turned to her, his expression flickering between cautious optimism and fatigue. "I'm glad you're here."

And that decided it. It still might be weird for her to stay, but he needed her, and she could no sooner ignore that than she could magically fix Maddie's frightening health problems.

They gave the others a rundown of the situation and implored them to spend the night in comfort at their homes with a promise to call or text everyone with more news in the morning. With hugs and more murmured encouragement, one by one, the full waiting room emptied out. Kyle smiled, shaking hands and accepting hugs from the women, while Grace watched him out of the corner of her eye to ensure he was doing okay.

What she saw surprised her. His small smile for each person was genuine and he returned hugs easily. For someone who hadn't wanted to come home, he'd meshed into the community well enough. Did he realize it?

Hadley stayed where she was.

"Liam and I will wait with you," she insisted, stubbornly crossing her arms.

Liam quickly hustled Hadley to her feet with a hushed

word in her ear. Whatever he said made her uncross her arms but didn't get her moving out of the waiting room any faster.

"I appreciate that," Kyle said. "But it's not necessary. You've done enough. Besides, I need someone I trust at home with Maggie, so Candace can get back to her house-keeping. That's the most important thing you can do for me."

Grace's heart twisted as she got more confirmation that she'd made the right decision in leaving Maddie and Maggie with Kyle—he clearly had both his daughters' interests in the forefront of his mind.

"Candace is trustworthy," Hadley countered. "She's watched Maggie plenty of times."

Liam captured his wife's hand and pulled on it, his exaggerated expression almost comical. "Sweetie, *Grace* is staying with Kyle."

Comprehension slowly leached into her gaze as Hadley finally caught her husband's drift. She started shuffling toward the exit. "Well, if you're sure. We'll be a phone call away."

And then they were gone, leaving Grace alone with Kyle. There was still tension between them but for now, the focus was on Maddie. This was the part where they'd be adults about their issues, just as they should have been all along, and get through the night.

"Guess they thought they'd leave us to our romantic evening," Kyle commented wryly as he nodded after Hadley and Liam. "I'm pretty sure that's why they went to Vail. To give me the house to myself for the weekend in hopes that I'd call you."

Not to get him to step up for his girls. That wasn't even necessary, probably hadn't been from the beginning. Liam and Hadley had gone to Vail for *her* benefit. Hers and Kyle's. And it would have been perfect if she and Kyle had only hashed out their issues before getting involved again, instead of hiding behind their defense mechanisms.

That's why she couldn't give him the slightest false hope that she was here because she wanted to try again. The problem was that she might have given *herself* that false hope.

For all her conviction that she'd made the right decision to walk away from him, something inside kept whispering that maybe it wasn't too late to take a step toward talking about their issues.

"Will you go with me to see Maddie?" Kyle's eyes blinked closed for a moment. "I'm not sure I can go in there by myself."

He'd been stalling. How had she missed that? Because she was busy worrying about what was going on with the state of their relationship instead of worrying about the reason they were here: Maddie. Some support system she was.

Grace smiled as she took his hand again, holding tight. "I'm here. For as long as you need me."

When his eyes opened, he caught her up in that diamond-hard green gaze of his. "Grace," he murmured, "come sit with me."

Meekly, she complied, following him into the hospital room where Maddie lay asleep in a bed with a railing. It looked so much like her crib at home, but so vastly wrong. Machines surrounded her, hooked to wires and tubes that were attached to her tender skin. Grace almost couldn't stand to internalize it.

Clare was checking something on one of the machines and smiled as they came in. "She's doing okay. Worn out from the tests. That couch against the window lies flat, like a futon, if you plan to stay. I have to check on some other patients but we've got Maddie on top-notch monitors, and I'll be back in a couple of hours. Press this button if you notice any change or need anything."

She held up a plastic wand with a red button at the end. Kyle nodded. "Thanks. We'll be fine."

Then Clare bustled out of the room, leaving them alone with Maddie.

"I would trade places with her in a New York minute," Kyle said softly, his gaze on his daughter. "I would *pay* if someone would let me trade places. She's so fragile and tiny. How is her body holding up under all of those things poked into her? It's not right."

Grace nodded, her throat so raw from holding back tears, she wasn't sure she could speak.

All at once, he spun toward her, catching her up in his desperate embrace, burying his head in her hair. She clung to him as his chest shuddered against hers while they both struggled to get their anguish under control.

"I'm sorry," she whispered, forcing the words out.

"Thank you for staying with me. My life was so empty, Grace," he murmured. "For so long, I was a part of something, and then I wasn't."

"I know." She nodded. "You told me how much the military meant to you."

"*No*. Not that. *You*." Fiercely, he clasped her face in both palms and lifted her head and spoke directly to her soul. "Grace. Please. We have to find a way to make it work this time because I can't do this without you. I need you. I love you. I always have."

And then he was kissing her, pouring a hundred different meanings into it. Longing. Distress. Passion. Fear.

She kissed him back, because *yes*, she felt those things, too. He was telling her what she meant to him, first verbally and then through their kiss, and she was finally listening. But this was how it was with them. She got her hopes up and he dashed them.

What could possibly be different this time? She took

the kiss down a notch, and then pulled back. "Sit down with me and let's talk. For once."

That was *not* what she'd meant to say. She should have said no. Told him flat out that they were not happening again. But the eagerness on his face at her suggestion— maybe talking was that start toward something different than what she'd been looking for.

"We're not so good at the talking, are we?" he asked rhetorically, and let her lead him to the couch. They settled in together and held hands as they watched the monitors beep and shush for a moment. "I'm sorry about Emma Jane."

That was so out of the blue, she glanced at him sideways. "I've already forgotten that."

"I haven't. It was low. And totally unfair to both of you. I apologized to her, too." He stared at Maddie, his gaze uneasy. "I wish I had a better excuse for why I did it. I have a hard time just coming out and saying what's going on with me."

She bit her tongue—hard—to keep from blurting out, *Hallelujah and amen.* She didn't say a word. Barely.

"It doesn't come naturally," he continued, his voice strained, and her heart ached a little as he struggled to form his thoughts. "I'm used to being stomped on by people I trust, and I guess I have a tendency to keep my mouth shut. My rationale is that if I don't tell people what I'm feeling, I don't get hurt."

The tears that had been threatening spilled over then, sliding down her face as she heard the agony in his words. He fell silent for a moment, and she started to give him a pass on whatever else he was about to say, but he glanced at her and used his thumb to wipe the trail of tears from her cheek.

His lips lifted in a wry smile. "Guess what? It doesn't work."

Vehemently, she shook her head, more tears flying. "No,

it doesn't. If I'd just told you how I was feeling ten years ago instead of breaking up with you and then pulling that ridiculous stunt with Liam, we'd be at a different place. Instead, I hurt both of us for no reason."

All of that had been born out of her own inability to tell him what was going on with *her*. They were so alike, it was frightening. How had she never realized that?

"I've already forgotten that," he said, and this time, his smile was genuine and full.

"I haven't," she shot back sarcastically in a parody of their earlier conversation. "I spent ten years trying to forget you, and guess what? It doesn't work."

"For the record, I forgave you way before I ever showed up at your door with those poor flowers."

Chagrin heated her cheeks. That was mercy she didn't deserve. Actually, none of this was what she deserved—which would be for Kyle to walk out of this room with his daughter and never speak to her again.

Instead, it looked as though they were on the verge of a real second chance. *Please, God. Let that be true.*

"I'm sorry about the flowers. I was just so hurt and mad. It never even occurred to me that part of the problem was that I wasn't opening my mouth any more than you were. I don't even have a good excuse. So I'm trying to do things differently this time. Starting now." She covered their joined hands with her other one, aching to touch him, to increase the contact just a bit. "I have a hard time with separating what I think something should look like from reality. I wanted you to be dashing and romantic. Sweep me off my feet with over-the-top gestures and babble on with pretty poetry about how I was your sun and moon. Silly stuff."

Saying it out loud solidified that fact as she took in Kyle's still closely shorn hair that the military had shaped. He'd traveled to the other side of the world in defense of his country, seeing and doing things she could only imagine. What could be more dashing and romantic than *that*?

"I'm sorry I don't do more of that," he said gruffly. "You deserve a guy who can tell you those things. I can try to be better, but I'm—"

"No," she broke in, even as her voice shattered. She wasn't trying to make him into someone different. He was perfect the way he was, and she'd finally opened her eyes to it. "You do something wonderful like bring me flowers, and I don't even take them. I'm just as much to blame for our problems as you are. Probably more. You'd never have left if I had just told you every day what you meant to me."

Kyle was never going to be like her dad, who left notes all over the house for her mother to find and surprised her with diamond earrings to mark the anniversary of their first date. She doubted Kyle even *knew* the anniversary of their first date.

The way Grace felt right now, none of that stuff mattered. She had a man who demonstrated his love for her in a hundred subtle ways if she'd just pay attention.

He tipped her chin up with a gentle forefinger and lightly laid his lips on hers. When he finally pulled back, he said, "But I'm not sorry I left. I gained so much from that. Foremost, the ability to come back to Royal and be a father. I was lost and being a SEAL is how I found myself. I might never have had the courage to enlist if things hadn't shaken out like they did. I'd never have had Maggie and Maddie. There was a higher power at work, and I, for one, am very grateful."

She nodded because her heart was spilling over into her throat, and she wasn't sure her voice would actually work.

Her "standards" had been a shield she'd thrown up to keep other men away, when all along her heart had belonged to this man. And then she'd kept right on using her standards as an excuse to avoid facing her own failures.

There was so much more to say, so she forced herself to open her mouth and spill all her angst about the possibility of Kyle leaving again, which had also been an excuse. It was clear he was here for good—what more proof did she need? But that didn't magically make her fears go away, much as being in love didn't magically make everything work out okay.

He let her talk, holding her hand the whole time, and then he talked. They both talked until Clare came back into the room to check on Maddie, then they talked until Maddie woke up howling for a bottle. When she fell back into an exhausted sleep, they talked some more.

When dawn peeked through the window, they hadn't slept and hadn't stopped talking. Grace had learned more about the man she loved in those few hours than in the entire span of their relationship. Even though Kyle hadn't said *I love you* again—which honestly, she could never hear often enough—and in spite of the fact that he would never be a chatterbox about his feelings, it was hands down the most romantic night of Grace's life.

If only Maddie had miraculously gotten better, it would have been a perfect start to their second chance.

When Clare Connelly came into Maddie's room shortly after dawn, Kyle had to stand up and stretch his leg. With an apologetic glance at Grace, he stood and paced around the hospital crib where his daughter lay.

He didn't want to lose that precious contact with Grace, but she didn't seem to be in a hurry to go anywhere. That could change at a moment's notice. He wished he could express how much it meant to him that she'd stayed last night. His inability to share such feelings was one of the many things that had kept them apart.

"Dr. Reese will be in shortly," Clare told them. "Why

don't you go get some breakfast while I change Maddie. You need to get some air."

Kyle nodded and grabbed Grace's hand to drag her with him, because he wasn't letting her out of his sight. Last night had been a turning point. They were in a good place. Almost. Grace deserved a guy who could spout poetry and be all the things she wanted. But she was stuck with him. If she wanted him. Nothing had been decided, and along with the concern about Maddie, everything weighed on him. He was exhausted and emotional and needed *something* in his life to be settled.

They grabbed a bite to eat and about a gallon of coffee. When they returned to Maddie's hospital room, Liam and Hadley were waiting for them. Perfect.

"Any news?" Hadley asked anxiously. "I hardly slept. I was sure we'd get a text at any moment and have to rush back to the hospital."

"Nothing yet. The doctor will be here soon. I guess we'll know more then," Kyle said.

As if Kyle had summoned him, Dr. Reese strode down the hall and nodded briefly. "I'm going to start some more tests. I'll be out to give you the results in a bit."

The four of them watched him disappear into Maddie's room. What was Kyle supposed to do now? Wait some more to find out what was happening with his daughter?

Liam cleared his throat. "Hadley and I talked, by the way. We ripped up all the adoption paperwork. We're formally withdrawing our bid for custody of your daughters. It's pretty obvious you're the best father they could hope for, and we want you to know we're here for you."

Somehow he managed to blurt out, "That's great."

Grace nodded, slipping her hand into his. "He's an amazing man and an amazing father. I wouldn't have recommended that he retain custody otherwise."

Their overwhelming support nearly did him in. He'd

left Royal to find a new team, a place where he could fit in and finally feel like a part of something, only to learn that there really was no place like home.

"Just like that?" he finally asked Liam and Hadley. "You were going to adopt Maddie and Maggie. It can't be easy to live in the same house and realize what you've missed out on."

He wouldn't take to that arrangement too well, that was for sure. If they'd somehow gotten custody, there was no way he'd have stayed. And he'd have ruined his second chance with Grace in the process. Leaving was still his go-to method for coping. But if things went the way he hoped, he had a reason to stay. Forever.

Hadley shook her head. "It's not easy. It was one of the hardest conversations we've had as a couple, but it was the easiest decision. We both love them, so much, and want the absolute best for them. Which means *you*. They're your daughters. We're incredibly fortunate for the time we've had together, and besides, you're not going anywhere, right?"

"No." Kyle tightened his grip on Grace's hand. "I'm not. Royal is where I belong."

The words spilled from his heart easily, despite never dreaming such a thing would be true.

"Then it will be fine," Liam said. "We're still their aunt and uncle, and we expect to babysit a lot in the future."

"That's a deal." Kyle shook his brother's hand and held it for a beat longer, just to solidify the brotherly bond that they were forging.

Hadley and Liam waited with Kyle and Grace, chatting about the ranch and telling stories about Hadley's cat, Waldo. Finally, the doctor emerged, and Kyle tried to read the man's face, but it was impossible to tell his daughter's prognosis from that alone.

Quickly, he stood.

"She's going to make a full recovery," Dr. Reese proclaimed. "The tests were all negative. The fever didn't cause any more damage to her heart."

Everyone started talking at once, expressing relief and giving the doctor their thanks. Numbly, Kyle shook the doctor's hand and stumbled toward Maddie's room, determined to see her for himself to confirm that she was indeed fine.

After a few minutes, Grace forced him to go home with her so he could get some sleep, but he couldn't sleep. Now that he could stop worrying about Maddie so much, he couldn't get Grace's comments about being swept off her feet out of his mind.

They'd talked, and things were looking up, but no one had made any promises. Of course, it hadn't been the time or place. They'd been in a hospital room while his daughter fought for her life.

But he owed Grace so much. And now he had to step up. This was his opportunity to give her everything her heart desired.

When Hadley called Grace to invite her to a horse show Friday night, Grace actually pulled the phone away from her ear to check and make sure it was really Hadley's name on the screen.

"I'm sorry. Did you say a horse show?" Grace repeated. "There's no horse show scheduled this time of year. Everyone is busy with calving season."

In a town like Royal, everyone lived and died by the ranch schedule whether they worked on one or not. And Kyle had been conspicuously absent for the better part of a week as he pulled calves, worked with the vet and fell into bed exhausted each night.

He always texted her a good-night message, though, no matter how late it was. She might have saved them all, even though not one had mentioned talking about the future. It had been almost a week since the hospital, and she and Kyle had had precious few moments alone together since then.

That's what happened when you fell in love with a rancher.

She'd hoped he might be the one calling her for a last-minute Friday night date so they could talk. It wasn't looking too promising since it was already six o'clock.

"Don't be difficult," Hadley scolded. "Liam is busy helping Kyle and I need some me time. Girls' night out. Come on."

Laughing, Grace said yes. Only Hadley would consider a horse show a girls' night out activity. "Your middle name should be Horse Crazy."

"It is," Hadley insisted pertly. "Says so on my birth certificate. I already asked Candace to watch the girls, so I'll pick you up in thirty minutes. Wear something nice."

Hadley was still acting in her capacity as the nanny, though often, Grace dropped by to spend time with the babies. She and Hadley had grown close as a result. Close enough that Grace felt totally comfortable calling Hadley out when she said something ridiculous.

"To a horse show?"

"Yes, ma'am. I will be dragging you out for a drink afterward, if you must know. Be there soon."

Grace chuckled as she hung up. As instructed, she donned a pink knee-length dress that hugged her curves and made her look like a knockout, if she did say so herself. Of course, she wasn't in the market to pick up an admirer, but it didn't hurt to let the male population of Royal eat their hearts out, did it?

The only arena in Royal large enough for a horse show was on the west end of downtown, and Grace was a bit surprised to see a full parking lot, given the timing.

"How come I haven't heard anything about this horse show before now?" Grace asked, her suspicions rising a notch as even more trucks poured into the lot behind them. This arena was normally the venue of choice for the county rodeo that took place during late May, and it held a good number of people.

"Because it was last-minute," Hadley said vaguely with an airy wave. "Liam has some horses in the show, and that's how I found out about it."

"Oh." There wasn't much else to do at that point but follow Hadley into the arena to a seat near the front row. "These are great seats."

"Helps to have a husband on the inside," Hadley acknowledged with a wink.

The grandstand was already half-full. Grace waved at the continual stream of people she knew, and hugged a few, like Violet McCallum, who was looking a lot better since the last time they'd seen each other. Raina Patterson and Nolan Dane strolled by, Raina's little boy in tow, as always, followed by Cade Baxter and his wife, Mellie. The foursome stopped to chat for a minute, then found seats not far away.

The lights dimmed and the show started. Sheriff Battle played the part of announcer, hamming it up with a deep voice that was so far removed from his normal tenor that Grace had to laugh. And then with a drumroll, horses galloped into the arena, crisscrossing past each other in a dizzying weave. It was a wonder they didn't hit each other, which was a testament to the stellar handling skills of the riders.

Spotlights danced over the horses as they began to fall into a formation. One by one, the horses galloped to a spot in line, nose to tail, displaying signs affixed to their sides with three-foot high letters painted on them. *G-R-A-C—*

Grace blinked. The horses were spelling her name. They

couldn't be. And then the *E* skidded into place. The line kept going. *W-I-L-L.*

Something fluttered in her heart as she started to get an inkling of what the rest of the message might possibly spell out. No. It couldn't be. "Hadley, what is all of this?"

"A surprise," Hadley announced unnecessarily, glee coating her voice. "Good thing you took my advice and wore a pretty dress."

Y-O-U. The last horse snorted as he pranced into place. And then came the next one. *M—*

Holy cow. That definitely was the right letter to start the word she fervently hoped the horses were about to spell. All at once, a commotion to her right distracted her from the horses. The spotlight slid into the stands and high-lighted a lone man making his way toward her. A man who was supposed to be in a barn at Wade Ranch. But wasn't, because he was here.

The last horse hit his mark and the sign was complete. *Grace, will you marry me?* It was the most beautiful thing in the whole world, except for the man she loved.

Her breath caught as Kyle arrived at her seat, wearing a devastating dark suit that he looked almost as delicious in as when he was wearing nothing.

She didn't dare look away as he knelt beside her and took her hand. "Hey, Grace."

Tears spilled from her suddenly full eyes, though why Kyle's standard greeting did it when nothing else thus far had was a mystery to her. "Hey, Kyle. Fancy meeting you here."

"Heard there was a horse show. It so happens I own a couple of horses. So here I am." He held up a small square box with a hinged lid. "Okay, I admit I set all this up be-cause I wanted to do this right. I love you, Grace. So much. I want nothing more than to put this ring on your finger right now, in front of all these good people."

Yes, yes, yes. A thousand times yes. There was never a possibility of anything other than becoming Mrs. Kyle Wade. She'd never expected a romantic proposal. She'd have been happy with a quiet evening at home, but this… this took the cake. It was a story for the ages, one she'd recount to Maddie and Maggie until they were sick of hearing it. Because she was going to get to be their mother.

"I'd be okay with that," she said through the lump in her throat.

"Not yet." To her grave disappointment, he snapped the box closed and pocketed it. "You asked to be swept off your feet."

And then he did exactly that. As he stood, he gathered her up in his arms and lifted her from her seat, holding her against his chest as if he meant to never let go.

She'd be okay with that, too.

The crowd cheered. She noted Hadley clapping out of the corner of her eye as Kyle began climbing the stairs toward the exit, carrying Grace in his strong arms.

Kyle spoke into her ear. "I hope you won't be disappointed, but you're missing the rest of the show."

She shook her head, clinging to Kyle's amazingly solid shoulders. "I'm not missing anything. This is the best show in town, right here."

Looked as if she was an excellent judge of character after all.

Once he had her outside, he set her down and pulled her into his embrace for a kiss that was both tender and fierce all at the same time.

When he let go, she saw that a long black stretch limousine had rolled to a stop near them. "What is this?"

"Part of sweeping you off your feet," Kyle acknowledged. "Now that Maddie has fully recovered, I'm whisking you away on a romantic weekend, just you and me, to celebrate our engagement. But I want to make it official."

Then he pulled the box from his pocket and slid the huge emerald-cut diamond ring onto her finger. It winked in the moonlight and was the most beautiful thing she'd ever seen. Except for the man she loved. "Tell me this is forever, Kyle."

He nodded. "Forever. I'm not going anywhere. I'm a part of something valuable. I'm a cattle rancher now with orders pouring in for the calves I've helped deliver. The Texas Cattlemen's Club voted me in as a member earlier today. My daughters are thriving, and I'm going to get the best woman in the world as a wife. Why would I want to leave?"

"Good answer," she said as the tears flowed again. "But if you did decide you wanted to leave for whatever reason, I'd follow you."

"You would?" This seemed like news to him for some odd reason.

"Of course. I love you. I know now I could never be happy without you, so…" She shrugged. "Where you go, I go. We're a team now. Team Wade, four strong. And maybe more after we get the first round out of diapers."

He laughed softly. "I like the sound of that. Keep talking."

* * * * *

"I am not an actress.

"I can't make this engagement believable. I won't be the only one who finds our decision to marry a total farce."

She reached for the door as if to end the conversation on that note.

He reached for her, bracketing her with his arms. Stopping her from exiting the vehicle.

"No one is going to doubt that you have my attention." The space around them seemed to shrink. He noticed she remained very, very still. "That much is going to be highly believable."

She swallowed hard.

"Do you believe me, Adelaide?" He wanted to hear her say it. Maybe because it had been a long time since someone questioned his word. "Or shall I prove it?"

Her eyes searched his. Her lips parted. In disbelief? Or was she already thinking about the kiss that would put an end to all doubts?

"I believe you," she said softly, her lashes lowering as her gaze slid away from his.

* * *

His Secretary's Surprise Fiancé
is part of the Bayou Billionaires series—
Secrets and scandal are a Cajun
family legacy for the Reynaud brothers!

HIS SECRETARY'S SURPISE FIANCÉ

BY
JOANNE ROCK

First Published in Great Britain 2016
By Mills & Boon, an imprint of HarperCollins*Publishers*
1 London Bridge Street, London, SE1 9GF

© 2016 Joanne Rock

ISBN: 978-0-263-91852-6

51-0316

Our policy is to use papers that are natural, renewable and recyclable products and made from wood grown in sustainable forests.The logging and manufacturing processes conform to the legal environmental regulations of the country of origin.

Printed and bound in Spain
by CPI, Barcelona

While working on her master's degree in English literature, **Joanne Rock** took a break to write a romance novel and quickly realized a good book requires as much time as a master's program itself. Today, Joanne is a frequent workshop speaker and writing instructor at regional and national writer conferences. She credits much of her success to the generosity of her fellow writers, who are always willing to share insights on the process. More important, she credits her readers with their kind notes and warm encouragement over the years for her joy in the writing journey.

To Catherine Mann, my longtime critique partner, for inviting me to dream up a Mills & Boon Desire series with her. We've brainstormed many books together over the years, but this was a special treat since we both got to write them! Thank you, Cathy, for being a creative inspiration and a wonderful friend.

One

Dempsey Reynaud would have his revenge.

Leaving the football team's locker room behind after losing the final preseason game, the New Orleans Hurricanes' head coach charged toward the media reception room to give the mandatory press conference. Today's score sheet was immaterial since he'd rested his most valuable players. Not that he'd say as much in his remarks to the media. But he would make damn sure the Hurricanes took their vengeance for today's loss.

They would win the conference title at worst. A Super Bowl championship at best.

As a second-year head coach on a team owned by his half brother, Dempsey had a lot to prove. Being a Reynaud in this town came with a weight all its own. Being an illegitimate Reynaud meant he'd been on a mission to deserve the name long before he became obsessed with bringing home a Super Bowl title to the Big Easy. A championship season would effectively answer his detractors, especially the sports journalists who'd declared that hiring him was an obvious case of favoritism. The press didn't understand his relatives at all if they didn't know that his older brother, Gervais, would be the first one calling for his head if he didn't deliver results. The Reynauds hadn't gotten where they were by being soft on each other.

More important, his hometown deserved a championship. Not for the billionaire family who'd claimed him as their own when he was thirteen. He wanted it for people who hungered for any kind of victory in life. For people who struggled every day in places like the Eighth Ward, where he'd been born.

Just like his assistant, Adelaide Thibodeaux.

She stood outside the media room about five yards ahead of him, smiling politely at a local sportswriter. When she spotted Dempsey, she excused herself and walked toward him, heels clicking on the tile floor like a time clock on overdrive. She wore a black pencil skirt with gold pinstripes and a sleeveless gold blouse that echoed the Hurricanes' colors and showed off the tawny skin of her Creole heritage. Poised and efficient, she didn't look like the half-starved ragamuffin who'd been raised in one of the city's toughest neighborhoods. The one who used to stuff half her lunch in her book bag to share with him on the bus home since he wouldn't eat again until the free breakfast at school the next morning. A lot had changed for both of them since those days.

From her waist-length dark hair that she wore in a smooth ponytail to her wide hazel eyes, framed by dark brows and lashes, she was a pretty and incredibly competent woman. The only woman he considered a friend. She'd been his assistant through his rise in the coaching ranks, her salary paid by him personally. As a Reynaud, he wrote his own rules and brought all his resources to the table to make a success of coaching. He'd been only too glad to create the position for her as he'd moved from Atlanta to Tampa Bay and then—two years ago—back to their hometown after his older brother, Gervais, had purchased the New Orleans Hurricanes.

There was a long, proud tradition of nepotism in football from the Harbaughs to the Grudens, and the Reynaud family was no different. They'd made billions in the global shipping industry, but their real passion was football. An obsession with the game ran in the blood, no matter how much some local pundits liked to say they were dilettantes.

"Coach Reynaud?" Adelaide called to him down the narrow hallway draped in team banners. Her use of his title alerted him that she was annoyed, making him wonder if that sportswriter had been hassling her. "Do you have a moment to meet privately before you take the podium?"

She handed him note cards, an old-fashioned preference at media events so he could leave his phone free for updates. He planned to brief the journalists on his regular-season roster, one of the few topics that would distract sports hounds from grilling him about today's loss in a preseason contest that didn't reflect his full team weaponry.

"Any last-minute emergencies?" He frowned. Adelaide had been with him long enough to know he didn't stick around longer than necessary after a loss.

He needed to start preparing for their first regular-season game. A game that counted. But he recognized a certain stiffness in her shoulders, a tension that wouldn't come from a defeat on the field even though she hated losing, too. She'd mastered hiding her emotions better than he had.

"There is one thing." She wore an earbud in one ear, the black cord disappearing in her dark hair; she was probably listening for messages from the public relations coordinator already in the media room. "It will just take a moment."

Adelaide rarely requested his time, understanding her job and his needs so intuitively that she could prepare weeks of his work based on little more than his daily texts or CCing her on important emails. If she needed to speak with him privately—now—it had to be important.

"Sure." He waved her to walk alongside him. "What do you need?"

"Privately, please," she answered tightly, setting off alarms in his head.

Commandeering one of the smaller offices along the hallway, Dempsey flicked on a light in the barren, generic space. The facilities in the building were nothing like the team headquarters and training compound in Metairie, where the Reynauds had invested millions for a state-of-the-art home. They played here because it was downtown and easier for their fans. The tiny box where they stood now was a fraction the size of his regular work space.

"What is it?" He closed the door behind him, sealing them inside the glorified cubicle with a cheap metal desk, a corded phone from another decade and walls so thin he could hear the lockers slamming and guys shouting in the team room next door.

"Dempsey, I apologize for the timing on this, but I can't put it off any longer." She tugged the earbud free, as if she didn't want to hear whatever was going on at the other end of her connection. "I've tried to explain before that I couldn't be a part of this season but it's clear I'm not getting through to you."

He frowned. What the hell was she talking about? When had she asked for a break? If she wanted vacation time, all she had to do was put it on his calendar.

"You're going to do this now?" He prided himself on control on the field and off. But after today's loss, this topic was going to test his patience. "Text me the dates you want off, take as long as you need to recharge and we'll regroup later. You're invaluable to me. I need you at full speed. Take care of yourself, Adelaide."

He turned to leave, ready to get back to work and relieved to have that resolved. He had a press conference to attend.

She darted around him, blocking the door with her five-foot-four frame. "You aren't listening to me now. And you haven't been listening to me for months."

The team owned tackling dummies for practice that stood taller than Adelaide, but she didn't seem to notice that Dempsey was twice her size.

He sighed. "What did I not hear?"

"I want to start my own business."

"Yes. I remember that. We agreed you would draw up a business plan for me to review." He knew she wanted to start her own company. She'd mentioned it last winter. She'd said something about specializing in clothes and accessories for female fans. She hoped to grow it over time, eventually securing merchandising rights from the team with his support.

He worried about her losing the financial stability she'd fought so hard to attain and figured she would re-alize the folly of the venture after thinking it over. He thought he'd convinced her to reevaluate those plans when he'd persuaded her to return for the preseason. Besides, she excelled at helping him. She was an in-valuable member of the administrative staff he'd spent years building, so that when he finally had the right football personnel on the field, he could ride that tal-ent to a winning year.

That year had arrived.

"I've emailed my business plan to you multiple times." She folded her arms beneath her breasts, an unwelcome reminder that Adelaide was an attractive woman.

She was his friend. Friendships were rare, important. Sex was…sex. She was more than sex to him.

"Right." He swallowed hard and hauled his gaze up-ward to her hazel eyes. "I'll get right on reading that after the press conference."

"Liar," she retorted. "You're putting me off again. I can't force you to read it, any more than I can make you read the messages and emails from your former female companions."

She arched an eyebrow at him, her rigid spine still plastered to the door, blocking his exit. It had never pleased her that he'd asked her to handle things like that from his inbox. But he needed her help deflect-ing unhappy ex-girlfriends, preventing them from talk-ing to the press and diverting public attention from the team to his personal life. Adelaide was good at that. At so many things. His life frayed at the edges when she wasn't around.

Plus, he was devoting every second possible to the task of building a winning team to secure his place in the Reynaud family. It wasn't enough that he bore his father's last name. As an illegitimate son, he'd always needed to work twice as hard to prove himself.

And Adelaide's efforts supported that goal. He was good at football and finances. Adelaide excelled at everything else. He'd been friends with her since he'd chased off some bullies who'd cornered her in a neighborhood cemetery when she was in second grade and he was in third. She'd been so grateful she'd insinuated herself into his world, becoming his closest friend and a fierce little protector in her own right. Even after the time when Dempsey's rich, absentee father had shown up in his life to remove him from his hardscrabble life in the Eighth Ward—and his mother—for good. His mom had given him up for a price. Adelaide hadn't.

"Then, I'll resume management of the personal emails." He knew he needed to deal with Valentina Rushnaya, a particularly persistent model he'd dated briefly. The more famous a woman, apparently, the less she appreciated being shuffled aside for football.

"You will have no choice until you hire a new assistant," Adelaide replied. Then, perhaps realizing that she'd pushed him, she gave him a placating smile. "Thank you for understanding."

Hire a new assistant? What the hell? Was she grandstanding for something, like a raise? Or was she actually serious about launching her business right now at the start of the regular season?

"I don't understand," he corrected her, trying to talk

reason into her. "You need start-up cash for your new company. Even without reading your plan, I know you'll be depleting the savings you've worked so hard for on a very long shot at success. Everyone likes an underdog but, Addy, the risk is high. You have to know that."

"That's for me to decide." Fierceness threaded through her voice.

He strove to hang on to his patience. "Half of all small businesses fail, and the ones that don't require considerable investment. Work for one more year. You can suggest a raise that you feel is equitable and I'll approve it. You'll have a financial cushion to increase your odds of growing the company large enough to secure those merchandising rights."

And he would have more time to persuade her to give up the idea. Life was good for them now. Really good. She was an integral part of his success, freeing him up to do what he did best. Manage the team.

The voices and laughter in the hallway outside grew louder as members of the media moved from the locker-room interviews to the scheduled press conference. He needed to get going, to do everything possible to keep their future locked in.

"Damn it, I don't want a raise—"

"Then, you're not thinking like a business owner," he interrupted. Yes, he admired her independence. Her stubbornness, even. But he couldn't let her start a company that would fail.

Especially when she could do a whole hell of a lot of good for her current career and for his team. For him. He didn't have time to replace her. For that matter, as his longtime friend who probably understood him better than anyone, Adelaide Thibodeaux was too good at her job to be replaced.

He reached around her for the doorknob. She slid over to block him, which put her ass right over his hand. A curvy little butt in a tight pencil skirt. Her chest rose with a deep inhale, brushing her breasts against his chest.

He. Couldn't. Breathe.

Her eyes held his for a moment and he could have sworn he saw her pupils widen with awareness. He stepped back. Fast. She blinked and the look was gone from her gaze.

"I'm grateful that working with you gave me the time to think about what I want to do with my life. I got to travel all over and make important contacts that inspired my new business." She gestured with her hands, and he made himself focus on anything other than her face, her body, the memory of how she'd felt pressed up against him.

He watched her silver bracelet glinting in the fluorescent lights. It was an old spoon from a pawnshop that he'd reshaped as a piece of jewelry and given to her as a birthday present back when he couldn't afford anything else. Why the hell did she still wear that? He tried to hear her words over the thundering pulse in his ears.

"But, Dempsey, let's be honest here. I did not attend art school to be your assistant forever, and I've been doing this far too long to feel good about it as a 'fill-in job' anymore."

He didn't miss the reference. He'd convinced her to work with him in the first place by telling her the position would just be temporary until she decided what to do with her art degree. That was before she'd made herself indispensable. Before he'd started a season that could net a championship ring and cement his place in the family as more than the half brother.

He'd worked too hard to get here, to land this chance to prove himself under the harsh media spotlight to a league that would love nothing more than to see him fail. This was his moment, and he and Adelaide had a great partnership going, one he couldn't jeopardize with wayward impulses. Winning wasn't just about securing his spot as a Reynaud. It was about proving the worth of every kid living hand-to-mouth back in the Eighth Ward, the kids who didn't have mystery fathers riding in to save the day and pluck them out of a hellish nightmare. If Dempsey couldn't use football to make a difference, what the hell had he worked so hard for all these years?

"You can't leave now." He didn't have time to hash this out. And he would damn well have his way.

"I'm going after the press conference. I told you I would come back for the preseason, and now it's done." Frowning, she twisted the bracelet round and round on her wrist. "I shouldn't have returned this year at all, especially if this ends up causing hard feelings between us. But I can send your next assistant all my files."

How kind. He clamped his mouth shut against the scathing responses that simmered, close to boiling over. He deserved better from her and she knew it.

But if she was going to see him through the press conference, he still had forty minutes to change her mind. Forty minutes to figure out a way to force her hand. A way to make her stay by his side through the season.

All he needed was the right play call.

"In that case, I appreciate the heads-up," he said, planting his hands on her waist and shuffling her away from the door. "But I'd better get this press conference started now."

Her eyes widened as he touched her, but she stepped aside, hectic color rising in her cheeks even though they'd always been just friends. He'd protected that friendship because it was special. She was special. He'd never wanted to sacrifice that relationship to something as fickle as attraction even though there'd definitely been moments over the years when he'd been tempted. But logic and reason—and respect for Adelaide—had always won out in the past. Then again, he'd never touched her the way he had today, and it was messing with his head. Seeing that awareness on her face now, feeling the answering kick of it in his blood, made him wonder if—

"Of course we need to get to the conference." She grabbed her earpiece and shoved it into place as she bit her lip. "Let's go."

He held the door for her, watching as she hurried up the hallway ahead of him, the subtle sway of her hips making his hands itch for a better feel of her. No doubt about it, she was going to be angry with him. In time, she would see he had her best interests at heart.

But he had the perfect plan to keep her close, and the ideal venue—a captive audience full of media members—to execute it. As much as he regretted hurting a friend, he also knew she would understand at a gut level if she knew him half as well as he thought she did.

His game was on the line. And this was for the win.

That went better than expected.
Back pressed to the wall of the jam-packed media

room, Adelaide Thibodeaux congratulated herself on her talk with Dempsey, a man whose name rarely appeared in the papers without the word *formidable* in front of it. She'd made her point, finally expressing herself in a way that he understood. For weeks now, she'd been procrastinating about having the conversation, really debating her timing, since there never seemed to be a convenient moment to talk to her boss about anything that wasn't directly related to Hurricane football or Reynaud family business. But the situation was delicate. She couldn't afford to alienate him, since she'd need his help to secure merchandising rights as her company grew. And while she'd like to think they'd been friends too long for her to question his support…she did.

Somewhere along the line they'd lost that feeling they had back in junior high when they'd sit on a stoop and talk for hours. Now it was all business, all the time. That didn't seem to bother Dempsey, who lived and breathed work. But she needed more out of life—and her friends—than that. So now she was counting down the minutes of her last day on the job as his assistant. Maybe, somehow, they'd recover their friendship.

She hated to leave the team. She loved the sport and excelled at her job. In fact, she'd grown to enjoy football so much she couldn't wait to start her own high-end clothing company catering to female fans. The work married her love of art with her sports savvy, and the projected designs were so popular online she'd crowd funded her first official offering last week. She was ready for this next step.

And she was very ready for a clean break from Dempsey.

Her eyes went to him in the bright spotlight on the

dais where coaches and a few key players would take turns fielding questions. The sea of journalists hid behind cameras, voice recorders and lights, a wall of devices all currently aimed at Dempsey Reynaud, the hard-nosed coach and her onetime friend who'd unknowingly crushed most of her dreams for the past decade.

He was far too handsome, rich and powerful. Dempsey might not ever see himself as fully accepted into the family, but the rest of the world breathed his name with the same awe as they did the names of the other Reynaud brothers. All four of them had been college football stars, with the youngest two opting for NFL careers while the older two had stepped into front-office roles in addition to their work in the family's business empire. Each remained built like Pro Bowl players, however. Dempsey's broad shoulders tested the seams of his Hurricanes jersey, his strong biceps apparent as he leaned forward at the podium to provide his perspective on the game and give an injury report.

With his dark brown hair and eyes a bit more golden than brown, there was no mistaking Dempsey's relation to his half brothers. But the cleft in his chin and the square jaw were all his own, his features sharp, his mouth an unforgiving slash. He spoke faster, too, with his stronger Cajun accent.

Not that she'd spent an inordinate amount of time cataloging every last detail about the man she'd swooned over as a teen. There was a time she would have done backflips to make him notice her as more than just his scrawny, flat-chested pal. But the only time she'd succeeded? He'd ended up noticing her as a tool for increasing his business productivity. He had honestly once referred to her in those exact terms. He hadn't even noticed when she'd ceased being much of a friend to him—forgoing personal exchanges in favor of taking care of business.

That hurt even more than not being noticed as a woman.

"Adelaide?" The voice of the PR coordinator sounded in her earpiece, a woman who had quickly seen the benefits of a coach with a personal assistant, unlike some of the front-office personnel in other cities where she'd worked. "I'm receiving calls and messages for Dempsey from Valentina Rushnaya. She's threatened to give some unflattering interviews if she can't arrange for a private meeting with him."

Adelaide's skin chilled. Dempsey's latest supermodel. The woman had been rude to Adelaide, unwilling to accept that her affair with Dempsey was over despite the extravagant diamond bracelet he'd sent as a breakup gift. Occasionally, Adelaide felt bad for the women he dated. She understood how it hurt to be kept at a distance after experiencing what it felt like to be the center of his attention—if only briefly. But she had no such empathy for Valentina.

Stepping to the back of the room, Adelaide spoke softly into her microphone, momentarily tuning out of the press conference as Dempsey wound up his opening remarks.

"I talked to Dempsey about this and he's agreed to handle it." She didn't see any need to share her plans to vacate her position. "Anything she says would either be old news, or blatant lies."

"Should we schedule a meeting to come up with a response plan, just in case?" Carole pressed. The woman stood on the far end of the room, her arms crossed in her navy power suit that was her daily uniform, her blond bob as durable as any helmet in the league. "Dempsey's new charity has their first major fund-raiser slated for next week. I think he'll be disappointed if this woman succeeds in deflecting any attention from that."

Adelaide would be equally disappointed.

The Brighter NOLA foundation had been her idea as much as his, a youth violence prevention initiative where Dempsey could leverage his success and influence to help some of the more gang-ridden communities in New Orleans. Like where they'd grown up. Or, more accurately, where he'd lived briefly and where she'd been stuck after he got out.

She'd had her own run-ins with youth violence.

"I'll make sure that doesn't happen." She would honor those words, even if it meant communicating with Dempsey after she walked away from the Silver Dome today. "She signed a strict nondisclosure agreement before she started dating Dempsey, so going to the press will be a costly move for her."

Dempsey had communicated as much to Adelaide in a one-line email when she'd mentioned it to him two weeks ago. He'd typed, She has no legal recourse, and attached a copy of the confidentiality agreement the woman had signed as part of his megaromantic dating procedure. In Adelaide's softer-hearted moments, she recognized that the single life could be difficult for an extraordinarily wealthy and powerful man in the public eye. He had to be practical. Careful. But the nondisclosure agreement, complete with enforcement clause and confidentiality protection, seemed over-the-top.

Given the number of women who still lobbied to be in his life, however, it must not deter many.

"Valentina is wealthier than some of the ladies he's dated," Carole pointed out. "But I hope she's just stirring trouble with us and not—" She stopped speaking suddenly and leaned forward. "Wait. Did he just say he has a personal announcement? What is he doing?"

From across the room, Adelaide noticed all of the PR coordinator's focus was on the lectern where Dempsey was facing down the media.

The audience sat in stillness, making her wonder what she'd missed. In the hushed moment, Dempsey held the room captive as always, but more anticipation than usual pinged through the crowd. She could see it in their body language, as the journalists sat straighter in their seats, all dialed in to whatever it was the Hurricanes' head coach was about to say.

"I got engaged today." He announced it as matter-of-factly as if he'd just read the latest update on a linebacker's injury report.

Murmurs of surprise rippled through the crowd of sportswriters while Adelaide reeled with shock. Engaged?

The floor seemed to shift beneath her feet. She reached behind her, searching for something to steady herself. He'd never mentioned an engagement. Her chest hurt with the weight of how little he trusted her. How little he cared about their old friendship. How much this new betrayal hurt, not to even know the most basic detail of his personal life—

"To my personal assistant," he continued, his gaze landing on her. "Adelaide Thibodeaux."

Two

Adelaide reeled back on her high heels.

Dempsey had just publicly declared an engagement. To her.

The man who was so cautious about every aspect of his personal life. The man who trusted her never to betray him even though he'd betrayed her in a million little ways over the years. How could he?

In her ear, Adelaide heard Carole squeal a congratulations. A few other members of the press who knew her—women, mostly, who were still vastly outnumbered in the football community—turned around to acknowledge her. Or maybe just study her to see what renowned bachelor Dempsey Reynaud would find appealing in the very average and wholly unknown Adelaide Thibodeaux.

Of course, the answer was obvious. She had no appeal other than the fact that Dempsey didn't want her to leave the team. And he was a man who always got his way.

She'd naively thought she could just turn her back on her job as his assistant and start a company that would rely upon good relations with the Hurricanes and the league in general for securing merchandising rights down the road. Something she couldn't afford to jeopardize if she wanted her company to be a success.

If she stood up and challenged him, she'd lose team support instantly. She didn't dare contradict him. At least not publicly. And no question, Dempsey absolutely knew that, as well.

Realization settled in her gut as smoothly and firmly as a sideline pass falling into a wide receiver's hands. She'd been outflanked and outmaneuvered by the smartest play caller in the game.

Her brand-new fiancé.

She needed time to think and regroup before she faced him and blurted out something she would regret. Adelaide darted out of the press conference just as a reporter began quizzing Dempsey about the quarterback's thumb. She didn't know what else to do. She lacked Dempsey's gift for complicated machinations that ruined other peoples' lives in the blink of an eye. Storming off was the best she could come up with to relay her displeasure and give herself time to think.

She tore off her earpiece even though Carole currently informed her she needed to stick around the building for any follow-up interviews.

Like hell.

Adelaide picked up her pace, heels grinding out a frantic rhythm on the concrete floor as she burst through a metal door leading to the stairwell. She headed down a flight to the custodial level of the dome, taking the route where she was least likely to encounter media.

The sports journalists hadn't really known what to do with the story about the Hurricanes' coach getting married. Sure—they would recognize the news value. But in that he-man room full of sports experts, no one would quiz the tersest coach in the league about his love life. They would hand that off to the social pages.

Who, in turn, would eat it up. All four of the Reynaud brothers had been in *People* magazine's Sexiest Men Alive list for two years running. The national media would be covering Dempsey's engagement, too. While she ran away.

She stumbled as her heel broke on the bottom step because her shoes were meant for work, not sprints. Hobbled, she shoved through the door on the ground level just as her phone started vibrating in her bag. She ignored it, trying to think of the most discreet way to reach her car two floors up.

A car engine rumbled nearby. It was the growl of a big SUV—a familiar SUV that slowed as it neared her. Dempsey's Land Rover, although it had probably never been operated by the owner himself.

Evan, his driver, lowered the tinted passenger window. He could have passed for a gangster with his shaved head, heavily inked chest and arms and frightening number of face piercings; his appearance gave Evan an added advantage in his dual role serving as personal security for their boss.

"Miss Adelaide," he said, even though she'd told him a half dozen times it made her feel like a kindergarten teacher when he called her that. "Do you need a ride?"

"Thanks, Evan," she huffed, out of breath more from runaway emotions than the mad dash out of the dome. "My car is on the C level, if you don't mind bringing me up there."

Relief washed through her as she limped over to the side of the vehicle. Before she could get there, Evan jumped out the passenger side and jogged around to help her, all two hundred sixty-four pounds of him. Before he blew out a knee, he'd been a top prospect on the Hurricanes' player roster, one she knew by heart.

She'd worked so hard to impress Dempsey over the years, memorizing endless facts and organizing mountains of information to help him with his job.

Only to be rewarded like this—by having him ignore her notice of resignation, refuse to discuss her concerns and announce a fake engagement to the very industry whose respect her future work depended upon.

"No problem." Evan tugged open the door and gave her a hand up into the passenger area of the vehicle specially modified to be chauffeur driven, complete with privacy screen. "Happy to help."

She waited for his knowing grin, certain he'd been listening to the press conference in the garage, but his face gave nothing away, eyes hidden behind a pair of aviator shades.

"I appreciate it." She tried to smile even though her voice sounded shaky. "I parked on the west side today. Close to the elevators."

Ticket holders had cleared out after the game, leaving the lot mostly empty now, save for a few hardcore fans that stuck around for autographs. The press parking area was separate, three floors up.

"Got it." Evan shut the door with a nod and she settled into the perforated leather seats. The bespoke interior was detailed with mother-of-pearl and outfitted with multiple viewing screens that Dempsey used to watch everything from game film to feeds from foreign stock exchanges to keep up with the Reynauds' family shipping business in the global markets.

Sadly, she knew the stats of most of the ships, too.

Her phone continued to vibrate in her bag, a hum against her hip where her purse rested, a reminder that her life had just fallen apart. Squeezing her eyes shut, she felt the Land Rover glide into motion and wished she could seize the wheel and simply keep driving far, far away from here. As if there was anywhere out of reach of the Reynauds, she thought bitterly.

Out of habit, she touched her right hand to the bracelet on her left wrist to feel the smooth metal that Dempsey had heated and shaped into a special present for Adelaide's twelfth birthday. The jewelry was worth far more than any of the identical diamond parting gifts he'd doled out to lovers over the years. Maybe she'd been foolish to see so much meaning in those years they'd spent together when his life had gone on to change so radically. She'd always thought she would do anything for him.

But not at this price. Not when he stopped being her friend and started thinking he was the boss of every aspect of her life. He couldn't dictate her career moves.

Or her choice of fiancé, for crying out loud. The funny part was, there had been a time in her life when she would have traded anything to hear him announce their engagement. But she'd grown up since the days she'd harbored those schoolgirl hopes. Once his father's limo had arrived to take him out of her world and into the rarefied air of the Reynaud family compound in Metairie, things had never been quite the same between them. Sure, he'd checked up on her now and then when the family was in Louisiana and not one of their other homes around the globe. Yet he always seemed acutely aware of the expectations of his family, and they did not include hanging out with a girl from the old neighborhood. For that matter, Dempsey had put all his considerable drive into becoming a true family heir, increasing his workload at school and throughout college. Eventually, he'd dated women in his same social circles, and Adelaide had remained just a friend.

Peering out the dark tinted windows, she noticed that Evan had exited onto the wrong floor of the parking garage. She reached for the communications panel to buzz him even as the SUV slowed by the east side elevators a floor below where she needed to be.

"Evan?" she said aloud when he didn't answer right away. "Can you hear me?"

"Yes, Miss Adelaide?" His voice sounded different. Sheepish?

Maybe he knew he'd made a mistake.

"We're in the wrong spot—"

She stopped when the elevator doors opened. Dempsey strode out, a building security guard on either side of him.

"Sorry, ma'am. The boss called."

Of course Evan hadn't made a mistake. He'd come here to pick up the man who called all the shots. Or had he been sent downstairs earlier to retrieve her? Either way, she was screwed. Her escape plan was over before she'd even gotten it off the ground.

At almost the same time, the stairwell door opened

and a small throng of reporters raced out, camera lights spearing into the parking garage gloom as they shouted Dempsey's name and called out follow-up questions he must not have addressed in the televised press conference.

"Coach Reynaud, have you set a wedding date?"

"How do you think this will affect your team?"

"How long have you been dating your assistant?"

The last question came from a thin woman who reached him first, her voice recorder shoved toward his face. One of the security guards warded her off easily enough, opening the door of the Land Rover so Dempsey could step up into the vehicle.

"Does Valentina know?" the skinny reporter shouted, banging on the window of the SUV as Dempsey closed the door and locked it behind him.

Adelaide scooted to the far end of the seat as he lowered himself beside her, the soft leather cushion shifting beneath her as the vehicle started into motion again.

"Hello, Adelaide." He made the greeting sound like so much more than it was, his deep voice tripping along her senses the way it sometimes did when he used her whole name.

She hated that he could inspire those feelings even now. It was as if he'd sucked all the air out of the small space so she couldn't catch her breath. She watched in silence as he tugged off his team jersey, tossing the Hurricanes gear onto the opposite seat and leaving him clad in a simple black silk T-shirt with his black pants. He looked like a very hot hit man.

A hit man who'd targeted her business. Her future. All for his own selfish ends.

"Can you call Evan and remind him my car is on

the C level?" She glared at him, reminding herself with every breath not to get too emotional. Not to let all the anger fly, as much as she wanted to do just that.

She'd seen him in action for years, knew him well enough to understand that no one won battles with him by acting on feelings. Dempsey ran right over adversaries who couldn't negotiate with the benefit of cool reason.

"It might not be wise to drive when you're angry." He set aside his phone and stretched an arm along the back of the seat.

Almost touching her. Not quite.

Not the way he had back in that vacant office before the press conference when she'd inserted herself between him and the door. When she'd felt the warmth of his hand on her hip. Brushed up against him chest to chest in a moment that had almost caused cardiac arrest. She swallowed hard and refused to think about all that wayward attraction, which had always been one-sided.

"It might not be wise to kidnap the assistant you're dating either." She couldn't keep the bitterness out of her voice.

"We're not dating. We're engaged." He reached to tug a lock of her hair, as easily as if she still had pigtails. As if she would still follow him anywhere just because he said so. "I'll send someone back for your car later. It will be safer to stick together."

"Safer for who exactly?" She tried not to wrench away from him, would not let him see how much this cavalier treatment got under her skin. Even now, despite the anger inside, another heat simmered right along with it. "And who made you lord of what I can and can't do? Turn the damn car around."

Being trapped beside his powerful presence in the back of a private luxury vehicle only stirred to life those other potent feelings she'd tried so hard to stamp out long ago.

"I don't think either of us wants to create a firestorm around the team right now," he reminded her.

"Seriously? Which is why you chose to announce an engagement to the press when you knew I couldn't contradict you." She clenched her fingers tight and contained her temper as Evan drove the SUV out of the parking garage and into the early-evening traffic heading west, away from her home.

Toward the Reynauds' private compound in Metairie. She didn't need to ask where they were headed, any more than Evan needed to ask. The world simply moved according to Dempsey's wishes.

"I realize you think I did this just for me. For the team. But I did it for you, too." His golden-brown eyes remained on her even when the viewing screens built into the overhead console flipped to life with game updates from around the league.

Being the focus of his undivided attention had the power to rattle any woman.

"We've been friends for too long for you to trot out that kind of BS with me." She folded her arms tight across her chest, her body reacting all kinds of erratically around him today. "Can we at least be honest with each other?"

"I am being honest." He shifted in his seat, turning toward her. Moving closer. "Adelaide, I don't want to see you fail at anything. Ever. And I promise you, if you stick this out with me—just this one more season—I will ensure that your company gets off the ground with all the benefits of my connections."

It was a lot to promise her. Worth a heck of a lot more than those diamond bracelets he passed out like consolation prizes.

"I don't want a company that is a glorified Reynaud hand-off. I want the satisfaction of developing it myself." There had been a time when he would have understood that. "Don't you remember what it feels like to want to build something that is all your own? Without the benefit of—" she waved her arm to encompass his custom-detailed world in a vehicle that cost more than most people's homes "—all this?"

His phone rang before he could answer her. And worse?

He held up a hand to indicate that he needed to take it.

"Reynaud," he growled into the device.

Tuning him out, she fumed beside him. This was precisely why she needed to leave. She understood that he worked eighteen-hour days every day and that he took his business concerns as seriously as his team. But it had been too many years since he'd even pretended to make time for her or the friendship they'd once shared. He spoke to her as his assistant, not like the girl who had once been privy to all his secrets.

He had no idea about the strides she'd made in her business over the past few weeks—the way she'd pulled off funding for a short run of her first clothing item. He hadn't been there to applaud her unique efforts or otherwise acknowledge anything she did, and she was sick of it. Sick of his whole world that could never pause for one moment. Even for the conversation they'd been having.

By the time Dempsey disconnected his call, she could barely hold on to her temper.

Enough was enough.

Setting aside his phone after clearing up some problems in Singapore, where it was already Monday morning, Dempsey hoped the time-out from the confrontation with Adelaide had helped her to cool off and see his side. She sure had backed him into a corner by quitting out of the blue.

What else was he supposed to have done when she'd forced his hand like that? The engagement was simply a countermove.

"Adelaide," he began again, only to have her swing around in the seat to glower at him.

"How kind of you to remember we were in the middle of a conversation." Her clipped words suggested her temper wasn't anywhere close to cooling down. "Do you need a refresher on what we were discussing? One, our ridiculous engagement." She ticked off items on her fingers. "Two, your sneak attack of having Evan lying in wait for me in the garage so I couldn't make a clean break from the stadium today. Three, your inability to understand why I want to build my own company from the ground up, without the almighty Reynaud name behind me—"

"How can you, of all people, suggest I don't understand what it's like to want to develop your own company? To build your own team?" His voice hit a rough note even as his volume went softer. "You know why I went into coaching. Why it means everything to me to win a championship for this town."

He remembered shared rides home that weren't in the

back of a Land Rover. Shared rides in a cramped bus full of bigger, stronger kids who amped up their street cred by converting new gang members or beating the living crap out of nonconverts. Of course he knew. He was giving back with his foundation. Constructing a positive environment with the Hurricanes for a community that needed an identity. Creating a team to root for that wore football jerseys instead of gang colors.

Adelaide didn't answer, though. She stared at him with a stony expression. He didn't have a clue what she was thinking. When had he lost the ability to read her? His gaze dipped to her mouth, set in a stubborn line. He read that well enough. Although, after that brush up against her before the press conference, he suddenly found himself wondering what she'd taste like. He hadn't let himself think along those lines in years, always protecting their long-standing friendship. Something had gone haywire inside him after he'd touched her today. He couldn't write it off as passing awareness of her as a woman, the way he had a few times as a teen. This attraction had been fierce, making him question if he'd ever be able to see her as just a friend again. It rattled him. He'd grown to rely on her too much to have an affair go wrong.

And it would. Adelaide was not the kind of woman to have affairs, for one thing. For another? Dempsey only conducted relationships that came with an expiration date.

With an effort, he steered himself back to his point.

"I've got controlling shares in businesses around the globe," he reminded her as they got off I-10 and headed north toward Lake Pontchartrain. "But being CEO of this or vice president of that doesn't mean as much when it's handed to you. With coaching, it's different. I earned a spot in this league. I am putting my stamp on this team, and through it—this town. I'm creating that right now, with my own two hands."

He pulled his eyes away from her, needing a moment that wasn't filled with the distracting new view of her as more than just his friend. He did not want to think about Adelaide Thibodeaux's lips.

"You're right." She reached across the seat and touched his forearm. Squeezed lightly. "I'm upset about…a lot of things. But you deserve to be proud of your efforts with the team and with Brighter NOLA." Her hand fell away, briefly grazing his thigh.

Then she pulled back fast.

He wished he could will away his reaction just as quickly.

"I understand you're angry." Maybe that was the source of all this tension pinging back and forth. Passions were running high today between the team's loss, the start of the regular season and her trying to quit. "But let's hammer out a plan to get through it. You want to build your own business, fine. Just wait until after the season is over and I'll at least help you finance it. I can offer much better terms than the bank."

The moon hung low over the lake as the SUV wound around the side streets leading to the family's waterfront acreage. The lake was shallow here, requiring boat owners to install long docks to moor their watercraft. Dempsey couldn't recall the last time he'd taken a boat out, since all his time was devoted to football and business.

"That's very generous of you. But I can't stay a whole season." Briefly, she squeezed her temples between her thumb and forefingers. "I posted a design of my first shirt and won crowd funding for the production. I need to honor that commitment after my followers made it happen for me."

And he had missed that milestone, even if it was just enough capital for a small run of shirts and not the launch of an entire business. He admired that—how she'd started off things so conservatively that her potential buyers had bought the clothes before she'd even made them. She was smart. Savvy. All the more reason he needed her. He could help her with her business after she helped him solidify his.

"Congratulations, Addy. I didn't know about that. So give me four weeks." He did not want to compromise on this. But four weeks bought him more time to convince her to stay longer. To show her that she had a place with the team. "The deal still stands. I'll help you with the startup costs. You retain full control. But you will stay with me for another month to get the season underway."

"What about the engagement? What happens to that ridiculous fiction next month?"

"You can break it off for whatever reason you choose." He trusted her to be fair. He might not have been paying much attention to her for the past few years in his intense drive to lead his team, but he knew that much about her.

When the time came to "break up," she wouldn't drag him through a scandal the way Valentina had threatened. Especially since he and Adelaide would still be working together, because no way in hell was he losing her. Four weeks was a long time to win her over now that he understood how high the stakes were. A season like this might only come around once in a lifetime. If he didn't make the most of it and secure the championship now, he might never get another shot.

"And until then? What will your family think of this sudden news? Will you at least tell them the truth so we don't have to pretend around them?" She bit her lip as they drove through the gates leading to the Reynaud family acreage along the lake.

She'd never seemed at ease here, not from the first time she'd set foot on the property for his high school graduation party and spent most of the time searching for shells on the shore.

The SUV rolled past the mammoth old Greek Revival house where Dempsey had spent his teen years, now occupied by his older brother, Gervais. Henri and Jean-Pierre split an eleven-thousand-square-foot Italianate the family acquired when they'd bought out a former neighbor. Neither of them stayed with the family for long, since Henri and his wife had a house in the Garden District and Jean-Pierre spent the football season in New York with his team.

Dempsey's place was slightly smaller. He'd specially commissioned the design to repeat the Greek Revival style of the main house, with four white columns in the front, and a double gallery overlooking the lake in back.

Evan parked the vehicle in front, but Dempsey didn't open the door. "My family doesn't need to know the truth about our relationship." He reached for her hand to reassure her, guessing she would be bothered by the lie. "It will be simpler if we keep the details private."

Her hand closed around his for a moment, as though it was a reflex. As though they were still friends. But damned if he didn't feel that spark of awareness again.

Whatever had happened between them back at the stadium was not going away.

"Your family won't believe it." She shook her head. "We've kept things strictly platonic for too long to feel...*that* way."

She withdrew her hand from his. Either he was really losing his touch with women, or they'd both been feeling "that way" today. Was it the first time it had happened for her, or had she thought about him romantically in the past?

It bothered him how much he wanted to know.

"It's none of their business." He didn't care what anyone thought. His brothers were too caught up in their own lives to pay much attention to Dempsey outside of his work with the Hurricanes. He'd been the black-sheep brother ever since their father had shown up with him in tow as a scrawny thirteen-year-old. "The engagement is important, since Valentina threatened to cause trouble for the Brighter NOLA fund-raiser by going to the media with some story about my nondisclosure agreements. The announcement of my marriage to you trumps her ploy ten times over. No one will care about her story, let alone believe it."

"Ah. How convenient." Adelaide wrenched her purse onto her lap and started digging through it. Finding a tube of lip balm, she uncapped it, twisted the clear shiny wand upward and slicked it over her mouth until her lips glistened.

His own mouth watered. Then he recalled her words.

"It is useful." He watched her smooth her dark hair behind her ears, the primping a sure sign of nerves. "The engagement helps me to keep you close and prevents Valentina from sabotaging something you and I

worked hard to develop. That foundation is too important for her to derail our efforts."

"Well, I don't find it useful. Or convenient."
Adelaide's eyes flashed a brighter jade than normal,
her cheeks pink with a hint of temper. "I am not an ac-
tress. I can't make an engagement believable to your
family when they've hardly noticed me in all the time
we've known each other."

"We can address that."

"If you think I'm going to start tossing my hair—"
she exaggerated some kind of feminine hair fluffing
"—or slinking around your house in skintight gowns to
convince anyone that I'm the kind of female who could
capture your attention…"

"You think that's what I notice in a woman?" He
couldn't say if he felt more amused at her attempt to toss
her hair, or dismayed that she perceived him as shallow.

Her shrug spoke volumes.

"Your challenge could not be clearer if you'd thrown
a red flag on the field." Something stirred inside him—
something deeper than the earlier flashes of attraction.

A bone-deep need to prove her wrong. He was not a
shallow man. He'd simply dated women who could go
into a romantic relationship with eyes wide-open. He
refused to give any woman false expectations.

"I'm not challenging you." She bit her lip again, her
shiny gloss fading as her anxiety spiked. "Simply pointing out what has historically intrigued you about the fair
sex. I won't be the only one who finds our decision to
marry a total farce."

She reached for her door handle as if to end the conversation on that note.

He reached for her, bracketing her with his arms. Stopping her from exiting the vehicle.

"No one is going to doubt that you have my attention." The space around them seemed to shrink. He noticed she remained very, very still. "That much is going to be highly believable."

She swallowed hard.

"Do you believe me, Adelaide?" He wanted to hear her say it. Maybe because it had been a long time since someone had questioned his word. "Or shall I prove it?"

Her eyes searched his. Her lips parted. In disbelief? Or was she already thinking about the kiss that would put an end to all doubts?

"I believe you," she said softly, her lashes lowering as her gaze slid away from his.

He had no choice but to release her then, his argument won. He should be relieved, since he didn't want to give Adelaide false expectations of their relationship. But as they exited the SUV and headed into the house, he couldn't help a twinge of disappointment that she hadn't challenged him on that last point, too.

He'd been all too ready to prove that the attraction he felt for her was one hundred percent real.

Three

Everything about this day felt off-kilter to Adelaide as she followed Dempsey up the brick steps onto the sprawling veranda of his house. Fittingly, she limped up the steps in her broken heel, unable to find her footing around him.

He'd commissioned the home when he'd first taken the head-coaching job in New Orleans, though it hadn't been completed until last spring. As if the Reynaud family complex hadn't been impressive enough before, now Dempsey's stalwart white mansion echoed the strong columns of the main house where he'd grown up. His place, just under ten thousand square feet, was only slightly less intimidating than Gervais's historic residence on the hill that had been built in the same style two centuries prior. She could see the rooftop from here, although the live oaks gave the structures considerable privacy. It helped to have the billions from Reynaud Shipping at their disposal, though the generations-old wealth was one of many reasons Adelaide had always felt out of place here.

Today, she had even more reason to feel off her game. From the erratic pounding of her heart to the all-over tingle of awareness that lingered after their talk in the back of the Land Rover, she felt too dazed to don her usual armor of professionalism. What had he been thinking to focus that kind of sensual attention on her? She'd been so breathless when he'd bracketed her between those powerful arms, his chest just inches from her own, that she hadn't been able to think straight. Hadn't been able to question why they needed to enact this crazy charade for his family that had always intimidated her.

She slipped off her unevenly heeled shoes at the door and walked barefoot into his house. Once she shook off this fog of attraction, she would talk sense into Dempsey and leave. She'd wanted a clean break from him, and now he'd changed the playing field between them so radically she didn't know what to expect. Should she put her product launch on hold? Or should she keep fighting to end her commitment to the Hurricanes? She needed to sort through it all without the added confusion of this new sensual spark between them.

"You might remember from the blueprints that there's an extra bedroom upstairs and one downstairs." He led her through the wide foyer past a grand staircase. He used an app on his phone, she realized, to switch on lights and lower blinds as they moved through the space. "Both have en suite facilities. I can send Evan to your place to pick up some things for you when he retrieves your car."

They paused in an expansive kitchen at the back of the house, connecting to a dining area with floor-to-ceiling French doors that opened onto the yard overlooking the lake. There was another set of French doors in the family room, also accessing the back gallery and lawn. It was a perfect place for entertaining, although she would be surprised if Dempsey had hosted many people here. She certainly hadn't been invited to any private parties at his home even though she'd helped choose any number of fixtures and had spoken with his contractors more often than he had.

But in all fairness, Dempsey had always spent the majority of his time on the road or at the office. She doubted he'd spent many nights here himself.

"The house is beautiful," she said finally. "You must be pleased with how it turned out. I know I looked at the plans with you when you first approved the blueprints, but seeing the real thing… Wow."

She shook her head as she took in the ceiling medallions around matching chandeliers that were either imported antiques or had been designed by a master craftsman. The natural-stone fireplace in the kitchen gave that space warmth even when it wasn't lit, while another fireplace in the family room had a hand-carved fleur-de-lis motif that matched the ceiling medallions.

"Thank you. I haven't spent much time here, but I'm happy with it. Why don't I order some food and we can hash out a plan for the next few weeks while we eat?" He set his phone on the maple butcher-block top of the kitchen island, one of the elements of the house she'd helped choose, along with the appliances.

But when she'd been comparing kitchen options on her tablet, she'd simultaneously been investigating a wide receiver's shoulder injury and a competing team's new blitz packages. No wonder she'd all but forgotten the details until now.

"Anything is fine." She wasn't in the mood to eat, her body still humming with awareness and a sensual hunger of a more unsettling kind after those heated few moments earlier.

Even in this giant house, Dempsey's magnetic pull remained as potent as if they were separated by inches and not feet. When he walked toward her, her breath caught. Her heart skipped one beat. Then two. It had been one thing to ignore her reaction to him when he'd always treated her as a friend. But now that he'd opened that door to a different kind of relationship, teasing her with hints of the possible chemistry they might have together…her whole being seemed to spark and simmer with the possibilities. That kind of distraction would not make figuring out her professional life any easier.

First she needed to strategize a method for dealing with him and this fake engagement, then find a way out of the house as soon as possible. She couldn't survive spending twenty-four hours a day with him, especially when she wasn't sure if he genuinely felt some kind of attraction, too, or if he'd always known about the feelings she thought she'd kept well hidden. Would he be so cruel as to use that attraction now to his advantage?

"Gervais has a full-time chef at his place now that Erika is having twins." He gestured in the general direction of the house on the hill where his older brother had settled his soon-to-be wife, a beautiful foreign princess who would fit right into the Reynaud family. "It's easy to have something sent over."

"I'm too wound up to eat." She shrugged. "I would make some tea, though." She peered around the kitchen, not seeing a kettle or any other signs of basic staples.

"Tea." He typed in something on his phone and shook his head. "I'll ask for a few things." He set the device aside. "Evan will bring it over in half an hour or so. I'll show you the rooms so you can choose one. You'll be safer from the press here. You have to know that my family's security rivals that of Fort Knox."

The very last thing she wanted to do was choose a bedroom in Dempsey's house, especially when her pulse fluttered so erratically just to be near him. It didn't matter to her body that she was angry with him and his high-handed move. Some fundamental part of their relationship had shifted today; a barrier that she'd thought was firm had caved. She felt raw from having that defense ripped away.

He stalked through the family room into the western wing of the house and pushed open the door of an expansive bedroom with carpet and walls in blues and grays, a king-size modern bed with a pristine white duvet and a white love seat in front of yet another fireplace, this one with a gray granite surround.

The en suite bath on the far end of the room had a stone bathtub the size of a kiddie pool, spotlighted with an overhead pendant lamp on a dim setting. Gray cabinets and white marble were understated accents to the dominant tub.

"You didn't take this one for your room? I thought you had chosen that tub especially for you," she asked over his shoulder, realizing as she said it that she'd allowed herself to stand very close to him to better see the whole space. If she leaned forward just a little, she could rest her cheek against his back where broad shoulders tapered to a narrow waist.

It didn't help that she'd been thinking about him lounging in that huge custom tub, muscles glistening.

"The view is better from the suite upstairs." He turned to face her and it was all she could do not to scuttle backward. She did not need to have both Dempsey and a bed in her field of vision. "I'll show you the bedroom near mine."

"No. I mean—there's no need." She would sleep downstairs by herself if it meant they could end this tour faster. "I can sleep here tonight."

She wasn't committing to spending any more time than that in this house. One night was bad enough, but she had too much to work out with him to leave just yet.

"Are you sure you'll be all right alone down here?" He frowned. But then, he knew when they traveled she preferred a room close to his. Her house had been broken into as a teenager—after he'd moved away from her. And she felt jittery at night sometimes.

"I'm certain. Your family's security rivals Fort Knox. Remember?" She nodded, knowing she wouldn't sleep well under Dempsey's roof for entirely different reasons than that long-ago robbery where she'd hidden under her bed for half an hour after the thieves had left. "But you mentioned discussing a plan for the next few weeks?" She backed up a step now, out into the hallway away from the warmth of his broad shoulders. "I'll rest easier once we talk through this. Actually, if we can come up with a plan, I'll say good-night and leave you to watch your game film."

She knew his habits well. Understood how he spent most nights after a day on the field, watching the action on the big screen where he could replay mistakes over and over again, making notes for the next day's meetings so the team could begin implementing adjustments.

"Come upstairs first." He turned off the light and headed back toward the front of the house, where she remembered seeing the main staircase. "I want you to see my favorite part of this place."

Something in his voice—his eyes—made her curious. Maybe it was a hint of mischief, the same kind that had once led them into a haunted house, which turned out to be the coolest spot in their neighborhood after she got over being scared of the so-called voodoo curse on the place. Besides, she needed to see hints of her old friend—or even her boss—inside the very hot, very sexy male she kept seeing instead. So she focused on that "I dare you" light he'd had in his eyes as she padded up the dark mahogany stairs behind him, the two-story foyer a deep crimson all around them.

He'd come a long way from the apartment on St. Roch Avenue where he'd battled river rats as often as his mother's stream of live-in boyfriends, each one more of a substance abuser than the last. His mom had been a local beauty when she'd had an anonymous one-night stand with Dempsey's father after meeting at the restaurant where she'd waitressed. She hadn't read the papers enough to recognize Theo Reynaud, but when she'd seen him on television over a decade later, she'd remembered that one night and contacted him.

Adelaide hadn't been at all surprised when Dempsey's real father had shown up to claim him. She'd known as soon as she'd met Dempsey—way back when he'd saved her from a beat down in a cemetery where she'd gone to play—that he was destined for more than the Eighth Ward. In her fanciful moments, she'd imagined him as a prince and the pauper character like the fairy tale. He had the kind of noble spirit that his poor birth couldn't hide.

And even though she wanted to think she was destined for more than her tiny studio still a stone's throw from St. Roch Avenue, she was determined to make it happen because of her hard work and talents. Not because of all the wealth and might of Dempsey Reynaud.

"Through here." He waved her past the open door to another bedroom, the floor plan coming back to her now that she'd walked through the finished house. She recalled the two huge bedrooms upstairs and, down another hall, the in-law suite with a separate entrance accessible from outside above the three-car garage.

She didn't remember the den where he brought her now. But he didn't seem to be showing her the den so much as leading her through it to another doorway that opened onto the upstairs gallery. As he pushed open the door, moonlight spilled in, drawing her out onto the deep balcony with a woven mat on the painted wooden floor. A flame burst to life in the outdoor fireplace built into the exterior wall of the house, a feature he must have been controlling with the app on his phone. An outdoor couch and chairs surrounded the fireplace, but he led her past those to the railing, where he stopped. In front of them, Lake Pontchartrain shone like glass in the moonlight, a few trees swaying in a nighttime breeze making a soft swishing sound.

"I haven't spent much time here, but this is my favorite spot." He rested his phone and his elbows on the wooden railing, staring out over the water.

"If this was my house, I don't think I'd ever leave it."

There was so much to take in. Lights from Metairie and a few casino boats glittered at the water's edge. Long docks were visible like shadowy fingers reaching out into the lake, while the causeway spanned the water as far as she could see, disappearing to the north.

"I wish I had more free time to spend here, too." He turned to face her, his expression inscrutable in the moonlight. "But someone might as well make use of it. Move in for the next few weeks, Adelaide. Stay here."

Normally, Dempsey wouldn't have appreciated an interruption of a crucial conversation. But Evan's announcement of dinner had probably prevented another refusal from Adelaide, so he counted the disruption as a fortuitous break in the action.

Now they ate dinner in high-backed leather chairs in the den, watching highlights from around the league. They attempted to name the flavors in the naturalistic Nordic cuisine with ingredients specially flown in to appease Gervais's fiancée's pregnancy cravings. The white asparagus flavored with pine had been interesting, but Dempsey found himself reaching for the cayenne pepper to bring the flavor of Cajun country to the salmon. You could take the man out of the bayou, but apparently his palate stayed there. Dempsey's birth mother may have been hell on wheels, but before she'd spiraled downward from her addictions, she'd cooked like nobody's business.

"I can't believe you have Gervais's chef making meals like this for you." Adelaide took more asparagus, finding her appetite once she'd glimpsed the kind of food prepared by the culinary talent being underutilized by Gervais and his future wife. "That is another reason I could never live in this house. I'd weigh two tons if I could have dishes arrive at my doorstep with a phone call. What a far cry from takeout pizza."

"I think you're safe with asparagus." He'd always thought she'd eaten too little, even before he started training with athletes who calculated protein versus carb intake with scientific precision to maximize their workout goals.

His plan for dinner had been to keep things friendly. No more toying with the sexual tension in the air, in spite of how much that might tempt him. He needed Adelaide committed to his plan, not devising ways to escape him, so he would try to keep a lid on the attraction simmering between them.

For now.

If she moved into his house, he would spend more time here, too. He'd keep an eye on her over the next few weeks, solidify their friendship and learn to read her again. He'd taken her friendship for granted and he regretted that, but it wasn't too late to fix it. He'd find time to help her with her future business plans, all while convincing her to stick out the rest of the season.

"You don't understand." She pointed her fork at him. She'd put on one of his old Hurricanes T-shirts about six sizes too large for her, her dark hair twisted into a knot and held in place with a pencil she'd snagged off his desk. She still wore her black pencil skirt, but he could only see a thin strip of it beneath the shirt hem. "I peeked in the dessert containers while you were finding a shirt for me and I already gained twelve pounds just looking at the sweets. There is a crème brûlée in there that is…" She trailed off. "Indescribable."

"This you know just from looking?" He remembered how much she loved sweets. When they were growing up, he'd given her the annual candy bar he'd won each June for a year's worth of good grades. Now that he could have bought her her own Belgian chocolate house, though, he couldn't recall the last time he'd given her candy.

"I may have sampled some." She grinned unrepentantly. Then, as if she recalled whom she was talking to, her smile faded. "Dempsey, I can't stay here."

"Can't, or won't?"

"I've already told you that I don't want to pretend we are engaged in front of your family, and this puts me in close proximity to them every day," she reminded him. Then she pointed wordlessly to a screen showing a catch worthy of a highlight reel from one of the players they'd be facing in next Sunday's game. It was a play that he'd already heard about in the Hurricanes' locker room.

He admired how seamlessly Adelaide fit into his world. He'd had a tough time bridging the gap between life as a Reynaud and his underprivileged past, acting out as a teen and choosing to work his way up in the ranks as a coach rather than devote all his attention to the family business. But Adelaide never acted out.

Or at least, not until today.

"I saw that catch," he said, acknowledging her. "We'll definitely keep an eye on that receiver." Then, needing to focus on Adelaide, he shoved aside his empty plate. "But regarding staying in the house, you don't need to worry about my family. I will spend more time here, too, so I'll be the one to deal with any questions that come up."

"Can you afford to do that? I know you often sleep at the training facility."

The schedule during the season was insane. He was in meetings all day, every day. He talked to his defensive coordinator, his offensive coordinator, and addressed player concerns. And through it all, he watched film endlessly, studying other teams' plays and tailoring his game plan to best counter each week's opponent. Yet he couldn't regret that time, since it was finally going to pay off this year in the recognition he craved, not just for himself but for the people he'd brought up with him. People who had believed in him.

"You are important to me. I will make time."

He'd surprised her, he could tell. For the first time, he was seeing how much he'd let her down in recent years, focused solely on his own goals. His own friend was surprised to hear how valuable she was to him.

"That's kind of you, but I know you're busy." She frowned. "It's no trouble to simply enjoy the comfort of my own home."

He made an exaggerated effort to look around the room.

"Is this place lacking? Hell, Addy. Upgrade my sheets if they're not to your liking."

"I'm sure your sheets are fine." She set aside her plate and made a grab for her water, taking a long swallow.

He watched the narrow column of her throat and wondered how he'd ever look at her in a purely friendly way again. Just thinking about her under his sheets was enough to spike the temperature in the room. To distract himself from thoughts of her wrapped in Egyptian cotton, he stood, stalking around the table to sit on the otto-man right in front of her, turning his back on the game.

"But?" he prompted, an edge in his voice from the pent-up frustration of this day with her.

"But no matter how lovely your home is, I'd rather be close to my own things. I don't see the benefit of being here."

"The benefit is the complete privacy as well as safety, since the family compound is absolutely secure. No media gets through the front gate." He knew she valued privacy as much as he did. This angle would be more effective than telling her the truth—that he wanted her close at all times so that he would never miss an op-portunity to push his agenda over the next four weeks. "You know as well as I do that public interest in our en-gagement will be high, especially after how thoroughly the press covered my split with Valentina."

"So I hide out here because of a manipulative ex-lover?" Her expression went stony. "I have business to conduct."

"Use my office," he offered, hitting the button to mute the sound on the television. "The facilities are excellent."

She frowned. "I do not like being put in this posi-tion."

He hoped that meant she was done arguing. He couldn't remember ever arguing with Adelaide before today—or at least not since she'd worked for him. "I don't like you leaving, but I'm trying to find a work-able solution."

She opened her mouth to speak and then closed it again.

"What?" he prodded her, wanting to know what was going on in her head.

"I'm not looking forward to being in the public spotlight with you."

"You've been there a million times." He knew because he usually met her gaze a few times during his press conferences, her hazel eyes wordlessly communicating to him if he was staying on track or not.

"Not in a romantic way." She shook her head, a few tendrils of dark hair sliding loose from the haphazard knot she'd created. "We've got the Brighter NOLA fund-raiser coming up, and no matter what you say about how convincing I'll be as your fiancée, I definitely don't look the part."

"Because of all the hair tossing and slinky gowns." That comment of hers still burned. He didn't care for that view of himself. "I believe we've covered that. And if you're correct that I've become too predictable in my dating choices, I'm glad for the chance to shake up public perceptions."

"I didn't mean to suggest you only dated women for their looks." She bit her lip. "The sad truth of the matter is a far more practical concern. I have the wardrobe of an assistant. Not a fiancée."

He tried to hide his grin and failed. "So you're saying we actually need the slinky gowns to pull this off?"

"You don't have to look so damn smug about it," she fired back, making him realize how much he'd missed their friendship.

He held up both hands to show his surrender. "No smugness intended. But I sure don't have time to dress shop this week, Addy, what with our first opponent being the defending National Conference champions and all."

"Wiseass," she chided, shaking her head so that the pencil holding the knot in her hair slipped. She reached up to grab it as the dark mass fell around her shoulders.

He'd seen that move before in private moments with her. Never had it made his mouth water. Or kicked his lust into a full-throttle roar.

Some of what he was feeling must have shown on his face because the hint of a smile she'd been wearing suddenly fled. Pupils dilating, she stood up fast, letting go of her hair and setting aside the pencil.

"I'll figure something out." She stared down at him, her face bathed in the blue glow from the television playing silently in the background, her delicate curves visible through the thin fabric of his too-big T-shirt. "With the wardrobe and with my business. I'll use your office and stay here. It's just for four weeks anyway."

She'd just conceded to everything he'd been angling for, but the reminder of the four-week time limit on their arrangement sure stole any sense of victory he might have felt. Slowly, he got to his feet before she bolted.

"Thank you." He wanted to seal the deal with a hand-shake. A kiss. A night in his bed. But putting his hands on her now might shatter the tenuous agreement they'd come to in the past few hours.

She deserved so much better from him.

She nodded, the big T-shirt slipping off one shoulder to reveal her golden skin. "I'm going to let you watch your film now."

Edging back a step, she moved away from him, and it took all his willpower not to haul her back.

"For whatever it's worth—I'm proud to call you my

fiancée. To my family, the media. The whole damn world." He thought she deserved to know that much. Today had shown him that he'd taken her friendship for granted too often.

He hadn't paid attention to her—really paid attention—in far too long.

He paid attention now, though. Enough to see the mix of emotions he couldn't read cross her face in quick succession.

"Good night," she said softly, her cheeks pink with confusion.

Watching her retreat, Dempsey turned on the television even as he knew the game film wasn't going to come close to holding his attention the way Adelaide did.

Four

"Sweetheart, stop fidgeting," Adelaide's mother rebuked her, a mouthful of pins muffling the words.

"I'm just nervous." Adelaide stood on a worn vinyl hassock in the one-bedroom apartment on St. Roch Avenue where she'd grown up.

With less than an hour before her first official public appearance with Dempsey, she had realized the gown she'd chosen for the Brighter NOLA foundation fundraiser was too long despite her four-and-a-half-inch heels. She could have phoned the exclusive shop where Dempsey had given her carte blanche, but the price tag had nearly given her heart failure the first time around. She couldn't bring herself to request an emergency tailor visit simply because she'd forgotten her shoes the day she'd chosen the dress.

So instead, she brought the pink lace designer confection to her mother's apartment for a last-minute fix. And perhaps she also craved seeing her mom when she was incredibly nervous. She hadn't been home since her "engagement" had become front-page news in the New Orleans paper and she hated that she couldn't confide the truth to her mother. But she could at least soak up some of her mom's love while she got the hem adjusted—with Evan waiting for her out front in the Land Rover.

"Addy." Her mother straightened, tugging the pins out of her mouth and setting them in the upside-down top of the plastic candy dish on the coffee table. "You're engaged to one of the richest, most powerful men in the state. You could have a dozen seamstresses fixing this gorgeous dress instead of your half-blind mama. You know better than to trust a woman who needs bifocals to do this job."

Guilt pinched Adelaide more than her silver-and-pink stilettos.

"You're not half-blind," she argued, leaning down to kiss her mother's cheek and breathing in the scent of lemon verbena. "And you could sew stitches around anyone working on Magazine Street. But I'm sorry to foist off the job on you last minute. I just missed you and I didn't want a snippy tailor frowning at my choice of shoes or thinking how my breasts don't suit the elegant lines of the gown."

Her mother gave her a narrow look. Taller than Adelaide, her mother was a commanding woman who had worked hard to raise Adelaide after her father died in a boating accident when she was just a toddler. Della Thibodeaux had given Adelaide her backbone, but there were days when Addy wished she'd gotten more of that particular trait. Her creativity and her dreamy nature were qualities she'd inherited from her father, apparently. But it was her mother's unflinching work ethic that had helped Adelaide excel at being Dempsey's assistant.

"Bite your tongue," Della said. "How will you survive your future mother-in-law if you can't put an uppity dress-shop girl in her place?"

"I know. I'm being ridiculous." She blinked fast, trying to control her emotions. It had been a crazy week fulfilling her duties as Dempsey's assistant while maintaining her commitments to her new business. And now she had a role to play as his fiancée, all the while fighting off waves of nostalgia for what she'd felt for him in the past. "Living the Reynaud life with Dempsey has put my emotions on a roller-coaster ride. I'm not used to the way the Reynauds can just…order the world to their liking."

From personal chefs to chauffeurs, there was no service that wasn't available to Dempsey around the clock. And now to her, too. While she'd witnessed that degree of luxury from a business standpoint for years, she hadn't really appreciated the way there were no limits in his personal life. He'd offered to have designers send samples from Paris for tonight's gown, for crying out loud.

And the ring he'd ordered for her… She'd nearly fainted when she'd opened the package hand delivered by a courier who'd arrived at the house with a security escort earlier in the day. The massive yellow diamond surrounded by smaller white ones had literally taken her breath away.

Between the ring—temporarily stashed in her purse,

since it seemed over-the-top for her mother's house—and the dress, she'd started to understand how closely scrutinized she would be as Dempsey's fiancée. It increased the pressure for tonight tenfold.

"My sweet girl." Her mom spared a moment to put a hand to Adelaide's cheek. "If you *are* emotional, is there any chance you could be pregnant?"

"Mom!" Embarrassed, she fluffed the hem to see how the length was coming. "There is no chance of that."

Her mom studied her for an extra second before bending to her task again. Della took up the needle and continued to make long stitches to anchor the hemline.

"Well, you must admit the engagement came a bit out of the blue. People are bound to talk." Her mother straightened, still wearing purple scrubs from her shift at the hospital where she'd worked for as long as Adelaide could remember.

She hadn't thought about that. "Well, it's not true, and the world will know soon enough when I don't start showing. I just want tonight to go well." She kicked out the sagging hem of her gorgeous dress. "I feel as if I'm off to a bad start already since I lost time to do my makeup and my hair when I realized I had a wardrobe malfunction."

Her mother frowned. "Addy, you just got engaged. You should be glowing with joy, not running to your mother and fretting about your makeup. Are you going to tell me what's wrong?"

Closing her eyes, she realized her mistake in coming here. Her mother didn't suffer fools lightly. And Adelaide was taking the most foolish risk of her life to put herself in close proximity to Dempsey every day and night. What if her old crush on him returned?

Actually…what if it already had? Remembering the

way her thoughts short-circuited whenever they had spent time alone together this week, she had to wonder.

"You know I've always liked Dempsey," she began, unwilling to lie to her mother.

She could at least confide a little piece of her heart to the woman who knew her best.

"I would have to have been blind not to see the adoration in your face from the time you were a girl." Her mother went back to sewing, taking a seat on the chair next to the hassock. "Yes, honey. I recall you've always liked him."

"Well, his proposal caught me by surprise," she admitted, her gaze rising over the sofa and settling on the wooden shelves containing her mother's treasures—photos of Adelaide, mostly. "And I want to be sure—" she cleared her throat "—that he asked me to marry him for the right reasons. I don't want to just be convenient."

Her mother paused and then resumed her sewing. Adelaide waited for her mom's verdict, all the while focusing on a chipped pink teacup Adelaide had painted for her for Mother's Day in grade school.

"Damn straight you don't," her mother said finally. "That boy's whole life has been *convenient* ever since he was whisked out of town in a limo." She knotted the thread once. Twice. And snapped it off. "Maybe you should ruffle his feathers a little? Catch *him* by surprise."

"You think so?" Adelaide worried her lip, remembering she'd better start her makeup if she didn't want to be late.

Evan had made her promise she'd be finished in time to meet Dempsey outside the event promptly at 7:00 p.m. so they could walk in together. A shiver of nerves—and undeniable excitement—raced up her spine.

"Honey, I know so." Her mother held out a hand to help Adelaide down to the floor. "You've made yourself very available to that man—"

"He's my boss," she reminded her.

"Even so." She shook her finger in Adelaide's face. "He's not going to be the boss in the marriage, is he? No. Marriage should be a partnership. So don't let him think you're going to be the same woman as a bride that you are as his assistant."

Easy enough advice if her engagement were real. But for the next few weeks, she was still more an employee than a fiancée. Then again, he had looked at her with decided heat in his eyes ever since that accidental touch in the stadium last weekend. And truth be told, it stung that he thought he could boss her into an engagement when they were supposed to be friends.

"Maybe I will surprise him." She picked up her makeup and went to work on her eyes, hoping to look more like an exotic beauty and less like an efficient, capable assistant.

Mascara helped. Besides, she'd gone to art school. If she couldn't create a good smoky eye, she ought to turn in her degree.

"No maybe about it." Her mother went to work on Adelaide's hair, her fingers brushing through the long caramel-colored strands. "This dress is a good start." She winked at Adelaide's reflection in the hallway mirror. "You don't look like anyone's assistant tonight."

"How close are you?" Dempsey shifted the phone against his ear as his hired driver pulled up to the venue in Jackson Square.

He'd left the Land Rover and Evan with Adelaide

this week, trusting his regular driver to keep her safe. By safe, Dempsey had meant keeping reporters away. He'd never imagined his temporary fiancée would have a sudden desire to visit the old neighborhood.

A tic started behind his eye as he thought about her there without him. She'd moved to an apartment closer to the French Quarter after college, but her mom had never left the place on St. Roch. Even Dempsey's mother had found greener pastures nearer the lake.

But then, his mother had the financial cushion of whatever his father had paid her to keep clear of Dempsey.

"Two minutes, max," Evan assured him. "I'm right behind the building, just crawling with the traffic."

"I'll walk toward you." Dempsey exited the vehicle close to Muriel's, the historic restaurant chosen for the event. Then he sent the driver on his way.

He would have preferred to pick up Adelaide personally tonight, but practice had run long and the meetings afterward had been longer still. There was unrest among some of the younger guys on the offensive line, but Dempsey was leaving the peacekeeping to his brother Henri, their starting quarterback. Henri had mastered the art of letting things roll off him, which was key for a player who operated under a microscope every week.

But the same quality could tick off other guys in the locker room, the players who took every setback like a personal affront, the athletes who were competitive to the point of obsessive. The media loved to key in on crap like that.

And with the press hinting at marital trouble in Henri's private life, the team's front man wasn't exactly feeling friendly toward the local sports journalists.

Dempsey just hoped he would get through the fundraiser tonight. No matter what was going on in Henri's personal world, he trusted the guy to lead them to a win Sunday.

"I see you." Evan's voice in his ear brought him back to the present, where he damn well needed to stay. "I'm going to pull right up to the curb for the sake of Miss Adelaide's shoes."

Looking up the street, Dempsey spied the Land Rover headed his way. He pocketed the phone and moved toward the red carpet that had been laid on the sidewalk. Players were already arriving along with prominent local politicians, artists and philanthropists. A lone trumpeter in a white suit serenaded the guests on their way into the Jackson Square landmark venue.

A staffer from the Brighter NOLA foundation hurried toward Dempsey to pin a flower to his jacket and update him on the guest list so far. He thanked her and waved the woman off as the Land Rover arrived in front of the carpet.

He didn't care about protocol, so he didn't wait for Evan to open Adelaide's door. Dempsey tugged open the handle himself and extended a hand to…

Wow.

All thoughts of guests, players and philanthropy vanished at the sight of Adelaide. She wore a pink dress that might possibly be described as "lace," but it was a far cry from a granny's doily. Beaded and shimmering, the gown hugged her curves all over. It wasn't low cut. It was long-sleeved and it fell to her toes. Yet the lace effect made strategic portions of her honey-toned skin visible right through the rosy-toned mesh. Her thighs, for example. The indentations above her hips.

Intellectually, he'd always known she was an attractive woman. Of course he had. He wasn't blind. But maybe her workday wardrobe had helped minimize an appeal that damn near staggered him now. With an effort, he dragged his attention away from her body to meet her gaze.

Only to find a simmering heat there that matched his own.

This engagement charade of his was feeling far too real. And if he wasn't careful, he would end up following that heat where it led and hurting Adelaide in the process. That was the last thing he wanted.

The very last thing he could afford.

"You look beautiful." He tugged her closer, wrapping an arm around her waist to escort her inside.

She smelled fantastic. Like night-blooming roses. Her hair was gathered at the back of her head, some of it coiled and braided, with strands left loose to curl around her face. She wore her waist-length hair up most days, wound into a simple knot. The soft curls trailing to the middle of her back made him wonder when was the last time he'd seen her with her hair let down.

"Thank you." She kept a tight hold on a beaded pink purse, the engagement ring he'd produced for her glinting on her left hand. "And thank you for the ring," she added softly, for his ears only as they walked toward the entrance behind slow-moving attendees meeting and greeting one another. "I've never seen anything so gorgeous."

He'd ordered it immediately after announcing the engagement to ensure the custom design would be crafted in time for tonight's party. He hated that he'd had to have it shipped to her at the house instead of giving it to her in person, however.

Then again, with their roles feeling a little too real, it was probably for the best he hadn't personally slipped that big yellow diamond onto her finger.

"Adelaide!" someone on the street called out to her, and she halted. Turned.

A camera flash popped nearby as a woman snapped a photo of them.

"Are you aware that Valentina Rushnaya will be attending tonight's event?" the photographer shouted over the trumpet music and din of nearby conversation.

Dempsey tensed, ready to respond. Addy beat him to it.

"How kind of her to support a Brighter NOLA future." Adelaide smiled as she lifted a hand to his chest and tipped her head to his shoulder as if they were a couple in love.

Was she simply posing for another photo? Or showing off the ring?

He followed her lead, kissing the top of her head possessively before ushering her toward the door.

"Nicely done." He wished he could pull her into a dark corner and talk to her. Make sure she was solid going into this event if Valentina truly put in an appearance. But there was no time now as people were already headed their way. "Let's stick together for the first half hour."

"Of course." She smiled her public smile, already waving to one of their biggest donors. "But you're dancing with me tonight," she warned him. "It's the perk of being your fiancée."

Normally, Dempsey worked the floor of a fund-raiser

with precision, glad-handing the necessary parties and then leaving, never giving in to Adelaide's invitations to stay longer and have fun. But this was his foundation and he was here for the long haul.

"The perk is all mine." The words fell out of his mouth before they were surrounded by well-wishers, potential patrons and community bigwigs.

Dempsey noticed Adelaide went into work mode as quickly as he did, but his focus was nowhere near his usual level. Even as he made conversation, his thoughts went back to those moments on the red carpet with Adelaide. The way she'd looked when she stepped from the Land Rover and every soul in Jackson Square had let out a collective breath. The way she'd curled against him when that photographer wanted a picture, as though she'd been born to be in his arms.

The idea bothered him.

There was no doubt in his mind that Adelaide looked different tonight, from how she wore her hair to that dress of hers that was killing him. And as the night wore on, he couldn't take his eyes off her. He wondered who she was talking to and if they noticed that she looked like a walking fantasy. Part of him wanted confirmation that something about her had changed, but another part of him wanted to make sure every other man in the building wasn't looking at her, because he didn't want anyone else thinking about her thighs.

Maybe he really had been blind all those years they'd just been friends.

Two hours into the event, the night seemed to be running smoothly enough. Casino tables had opened around the rooms blocked off for the party. The red walls and decadent furnishings of Muriel's legendary

Séance Lounge made an appealing backdrop for black-jack as the crowd loosened up. The gaming was strictly to raise money for Brighter NOLA. It was so packed that guests stood out on the balconies in the heat, snapping photos of themselves with Jackson Square in the background. The dance floor was filled and the band—as always in this town—sounded fantastic.

He was about to seek out Adelaide when a feminine voice purred in his right ear.

"My lone wolf looks on edge tonight." The low tone and soft consonants of Valentina's Russian accent made him tense.

Turning, he avoided her attempt to kiss his cheek.

"If I'm on edge, it's only because you've taken up the valuable time of my staff with empty threats and games." He gave her a level look, noting that her barely there silver gown was completely over-the-top for a charity event that raised funds for underprivileged and at-risk youths.

"Your staff? Or your fiancée?" She tossed her head in a dismissive gesture meant to be insulting.

Dempsey had to smother a mirthless laugh because—damn it to hell—Adelaide had been correct about him dating theatrical women in slinky gowns. When had he become such a cliché?

"Both." He was grateful they stood in the shadows, since he didn't need photos of them together showing up in the paper. "And I trust the only reason you're here is to write a big, fat check to the foundation, since we specifically agreed to go our separate ways."

"Agreed? There was no agreement!" She pulled a glass of champagne off a passing waiter's tray and helped herself to a long sip. "You dictated every detail of our time together, and then disappeared before my bed even had time to cool down—"

"Ms. Rushnaya, how beautiful you look." Adelaide appeared at his side, slipping an arm through his. "I'm so sorry to interrupt, but, Dempsey, we did promise a quick word with the representative from *Town and Country* before they leave."

She nodded meaningfully toward the other side of the room.

"Of course." He had always counted on Addy for well-timed interruptions, and she delivered yet again. Still, he didn't like that she'd overheard the bit about running out of Valentina's bed. He didn't treat women that way. "Please excuse us."

"Yes, do take your turn with *Town and Country*." Valentina emptied her glass and set it on a nearby table, her movements unsteady. "I have my own press to speak with, Dempsey."

She turned on her heel to march away, right toward a woman who had a camera aimed at them. Again.

"Dempsey." Adelaide laid her hand on his cheek and turned his face toward her, commanding his attention before the camera flashed. "There isn't actually an interview," she confided. "I was just trying to give you some breathing room."

The look in her hazel eyes stole all his focus. Or maybe it was the gentle press of her breasts as she arched closer.

"Thank you." How many times had she served as a buffer for him with the media or with football insiders he didn't particularly like? She ran interference like a pro.

"Dance with me?" she asked, a hint of uncertainty in her gaze.

Had he put that vulnerability there? He hadn't spent much time with her this evening, handling the room with the same "divide and conquer" approach they'd used in the past at events he'd needed to attend. But tonight was different. Or at least, it should be. If he'd had Adelaide by his side earlier, Valentina might not have tried to ambush him in a dark corner.

"With pleasure." He lifted Adelaide's hand to his mouth and brushed a kiss along her knuckles. Her skin smelled like roses.

He'd done it to reassure her that he wanted to be with her. To thank her for sending Valentina on her way.

At least, the kiss started out with good intentions. But as the slow blues tune hit a long, sultry note, Dempsey couldn't seem to let her go. Adelaide was getting under his skin tonight, and it wasn't just that damnable dress. So he flipped her hand over and placed a kiss in her palm, where he felt her pulse flutter under his lips. Which made him think about all the other ways he could send her heart racing. All the pulse points he could cover with his mouth. In turn, his own heart slugged harder inside his chest.

Every damn thing got harder.

"My song will be over by the time we get out there," she whispered, though she didn't sound terribly disappointed.

Her pupils dilated so wide there was just a hint of color around the edges.

"It's less crowded right here." He wanted her to himself, he realized. Craved her, in fact. "Plenty of room to dance."

"Really?" She peered around them. "I guess it's the kind of thing an engaged couple would do."

"Exactly." He pulled her into his arms, fitting her curves against him, close enough to catch her scent, but not nearly as close as he'd like. "No sense letting anyone think Valentina caused any drama."

At the mention of the woman's name, Addy's gaze dropped. He cursed himself for being an idiot as he backed them closer to the open doors leading out to the balcony.

"Is that what this whole charade is about?" she asked when she looked up at him again. "Have I been promoted to your round-the-clock protection from the she-wolves of the world?"

She couldn't be jealous. Yet the thought nearly made him miss a step.

"No." He lowered his voice, knowing how the walls had ears at events like this. "You and I have a whole lot more at stake between us and I think you know it."

"If there's more at stake, you might want to up your game while we're in public, since newly engaged men don't tend to prowl the perimeters of parties alone." She practically vibrated in his arms as he drew her out onto the balcony and into the farthest deserted corner.

He couldn't remember the last time she'd spoken to him with so much fire in her eyes.

"You're jealous." He tested the idea by saying it out loud as he studied her in the moonlight. The song came to an end.

He didn't let go of her.

"And you're *mine* for four weeks, Dempsey Reynaud." She tipped her chin up at him. "I suggest you act like it if you want to pull off this ruse of your own making."

Heat rushed up his spine in a molten blast. The need to offer her what she'd asked for made him grip her tighter, pulling her hip to hip, chest to breasts.

And if that was a little too much PDA for a charity event, too damn bad. It wasn't anywhere near enough for what he wanted to do with her. She felt even better up close than he'd imagined, and his head had been full of inventive scenarios all week.

"Careful what you wish for, Addy," he warned her, grateful for the night shadows that kept them hidden.

He'd been a gentleman for her sake. At least now she would know exactly how much he was feeling like her fiancé. Her hips cradled the hard length he couldn't begin to hide.

And that was when things got crazy. Because instead of storming off like his affronted best friend, Adelaide gripped the lapels of his tuxedo and pressed a kiss to his lips.

Five

Adelaide saw stars.

Clutching Dempsey's jacket, she fulfilled a secret dream as her lips brushed along his. They stood under the night sky, his back shielding her from view. Behind her, the iron bars of the balcony pressed against her spine. In front of her, warm male muscle was equally unyielding but oh-so-enticing.

She'd seen a chance to surprise him—just as her mother had suggested—and she'd taken it. She knew better than to think this fake engagement was going anywhere. But she could use this time to indulge herself and her long-standing fantasies about Dempsey. Because in less than four weeks, things were going to change between them forever when she left her job with the Hurricanes.

Her senses reeling, she broke the kiss, needing to

put some distance between them. He didn't move far from her, though. It took another long moment before he released her.

"Let's go," he urged, threading his fingers through hers and claiming a hand.

Blinking through the fog of desire, Adelaide followed him, her steps smaller and quicker by necessity due to the fitted gown. Her lips tingled pleasantly, her nerve endings humming with awareness of the man beside her.

"Are you sure we should leave?" She glanced around the private rooms at the full dance floor, the crammed gaming tables, the busy bar stations. "As hosts of the event—"

"We've done our part," he assured her. "The event planner will take it from here. And I'm dying to get you alone."

To explore what she'd started? She hadn't missed the indication of attraction when she'd been pressed up against him. But she couldn't afford to trade her heart for a night in his bed, and she knew herself well enough to know that was a very real possibility. Her feelings for Dempsey had always been strong. Complicated. And this engagement wasn't exactly simplifying matters.

"I didn't mean to send mixed signals." She hated to have this conversation here, in a quiet corridor as they waited for an elevator. But it was too important to wait. "I got caught up in the moment—" She bit her lip to refrain from telling him about her mother's suggestion that she surprise him.

She'd taken the gamble, but she wasn't sure she was ready for the payout he had in mind.

"Will you promise me something?" His eyes searched

hers, as if he could see straight through to her heart. "Will you think about how rewarding it could be to get caught up in another moment? Not tonight, maybe. But we've got a lot of days to spend together and I think there's something worth exploring in that kiss."

Her heart did a little flip that made her feel woozy and breathless at the same time. She settled for a nod, unable to articulate an answer just now.

He pressed a button for the elevator and stepped into the cabin behind her when it arrived. His grandfather, family patriarch Leon Reynaud, stood against one wall inside the elevator. Adelaide didn't know him well, but he attended all of the Hurricanes home games and she'd seen him in the owner's suite on the fifty-yard line a few times.

He'd been a big man in another era, playing football and becoming a successful team owner of a Texas franchise until he'd sold it to be closer to his grandsons in Louisiana. But the years had bowed his back and he'd grown much thinner. Dempsey had told her once that Leon had never considered himself a good parent to his own sons and because of that, he tried harder to be a presence for his grandsons. Adelaide knew for a fact the older man held far more of Dempsey's respect than his philandering father, Theo.

"Hello, Mr. Reynaud," she greeted him while Dempsey clapped him on the shoulder.

"We're heading home, Grand-père. Do you need a ride?" Dempsey asked.

"No need. I want to try my hand at blackjack and see if the Reynaud luck holds." He gave Adelaide a rakish grin and straightened his already perfect tie. "My dear, did you know my own grandfather won his first boat in a game of cards? From there, he grew the Zephyr Shipping empire."

It was a much-loved bit of Reynaud lore.

"Adelaide probably knows the family history as well as I do." Dempsey met her gaze for a moment and she drank in the compliment.

He rarely handed out praise, especially publicly. The elevator bell chimed, and the door opened to the first floor. She stepped out into the crowd while Dempsey held the door for his grandfather.

"Adelaide, you say?" Leon frowned as he moved slowly toward the bar, his expression blank for a moment before his gray brows furrowed. "Be careful with the ladies, son. You wouldn't want your wife to find out."

"But, Grand-père—" Dempsey called after him as the older man disappeared into the crowd. Turning toward her, Dempsey pulled out his phone. "He's been getting more confused lately."

"Should we stay with him?" Adelaide hadn't heard about Leon having any moments of confusion, but then, Dempsey didn't share much about his family outside of business concerns.

Some of the magic of their kiss evaporated with the reminder of how removed she was from his private life. Even as his so-called fiancée.

"I'm texting Evan. He has a friend here tonight providing extra security. I'll have him keep an eye on Leon and make sure he gets home safely."

"One of your brothers might still be here." She peered back into the party. "I saw Henri with some of the other players—"

"It's handled." He tucked his phone in his pocket and pressed a hand to her lower back.

A perfunctory touch. A social nicety. She could feel that his attention had drifted from her. From them.

Ha. Who was she kidding? There was no *them*. Dempsey maneuvered her now the same way he orchestrated the rest of his world. He wasn't the kind of man to be carried away by a kiss, and right now he clearly had other things on his mind.

Forcing her thoughts from the chemistry that had simmered between them, Adelaide promised herself not to act on any more impulsive longings. She'd wanted to shake things up a bit between them and she had. But his silence on the ride home told her all she needed to know about the gamble she'd taken with the kiss.

It hadn't paid off.

From now on, she would take her cues from Dempsey. If he wanted their relationship to be focused on business, she only had three and a half more weeks to pretend that old crush of hers hadn't fired to life all over again.

The next day, she balanced two coffees in a tray and a box of pastries from Dempsey's favorite bakery as she strode through the training facility toward his office. She reminded herself she'd done the same thing for him plenty of other times in her years as his assistant. When they'd been in Atlanta together and Dempsey had still been an assistant coach, they'd shared a secret addiction to apple fritters and she'd grown skilled at sneaking them into the training complex so the health-minded nutritionists wouldn't discover them.

Now that they were back in New Orleans, Adelaide knew to pick up beignets on game days when they were downtown. But in Metairie, for an occasional treat, she bought raspberry scones. Technically, procuring pastries wasn't on her formal list of duties. And maybe it was her sweet tooth that had driven this one shared pleasure. But after last night's awkward end to the evening, she found herself wanting to put their relationship back on familiar ground.

It wasn't as if she was offended that her kiss hadn't made him realize he'd always loved her from afar or had some other fairy-tale outcome. But maybe she'd dreamed once or twice that such a thing could really happen if they ever kissed. That Dempsey would see her with new eyes and forget about the Valentinas of the world.

Right. He'd made it clear she would be welcome in his bed, but he hadn't seemed inclined to consider what that would mean for them—their friendship, their work together or even this farce of an engagement. How could she knowingly walk into an intimate relationship with him when she'd seen the devastation he left in his wake?

The sun hadn't even risen that morning when she'd awoken to an empty house, and she'd known that Dempsey had left for work. He'd been restless when they'd arrived home after the charity fund-raiser, excusing himself to call his brother Jean-Pierre in New York. She'd thought then that maybe he was more upset about his grandfather's mistake than he'd let on. Why else would he call Jean-Pierre when it would have been after midnight in Manhattan?

Unless he'd been fighting the riot of yearning that had plagued her.

She backed into the double doors leading to the front

offices and nearly ran into Pat Tyrell, the Hurricanes'
defensive coordinator.

"Well, good morning, Miss Adelaide." He tipped his
team hat to her since, even at seventy years old, the griz-
zled old coach was still a flirt. "Those wouldn't happen
to be illicit treats in that white pastry box of yours?"

The older man knew her well. He held the door open
for her.

"I figured I didn't have to hide them at this hour since
the trainers won't be in until at least nine o'clock." She
lifted the box toward him. "Want a raspberry scone?"

"You speak an old man's language." His black-and-
gold windbreaker crinkled as he reached into the box
to help himself. "Dempsey ought to be ready for breakfast soon. I came in this morning to find him running
up and down the bleachers like a kid in training camp."

Her mouth went dry as she envisioned Dempsey in
his workout routine. He was as fit as any of his players, even if she did manage to tempt him into an occasional scone.

"Maybe he's getting ready to run a few plays himself on Sunday." She sidestepped Pat to head into her
office. "He's always saying we need more discipline
on the field."

"Damn shame that boy didn't have a shot to play
in the NFL. When you get that kind of football mind
combined with talent, it's a beautiful thing to watch."
He raised his pastry in salute. "Thanks for the sweets,
Addy."

Settling into her small office next door to Dempsey's
massive suite, Adelaide set down the coffees and
dropped her purse on the floor beside the desk. She'd
only been joking about Dempsey getting ready to run

plays. Maybe because she wasn't a football player she hadn't given much thought to the fact that Dempsey's decorated college career as a tight end had never gone to the next level. He'd told her once that he'd chosen to coach because he could bring more to the game that way, and she believed him.

But she also knew from articles in the media that an injury in his youth had never mended properly and that another hit to his spine could paralyze him—something that his college coaches hadn't known about, but had been quickly discovered in a physical by the team that had drafted him. Dempsey had been on a plane back to Louisiana the next day and, Adelaide recalled, Leon Reynaud had threatened to sue the college where he'd played.

At the time, she'd been busy finishing up her fine arts degree and debating whether to apply to a master's program. She'd also been in recovery mode from her crush on Dempsey and had been trying to ignore the stories about him.

The knock on her office door startled her from her thoughts. Dempsey appeared in the doorway in cargo shorts and a black team polo shirt that fit him to perfection. His hair, still wet from the shower, was even darker than usual. He hadn't shaved either. The jaw that had been well groomed just twelve hours ago for the charity ball was already heavily shadowed.

"Morning." He strode past her desk to stand by the window overlooking the training field, where a few players were loosening up even though official warm-ups wouldn't start for another hour or more. "I didn't expect you today."

She'd worked overtime this week, as she did most

weeks. But he seemed to understand her desire to devote some hours to her own business because he'd told her last night that she should take the day off.

She watched him now, struck anew by his masculine appeal. After all the years she'd known him, she would have hoped to have been used to him. Some days, when they were embroiled in work, she managed to forget that he was an incredibly magnetic male. Other times, the raw virility of him made her a little light-headed, like now.

"You seemed so distracted last night, I wasn't even sure you would remember saying that." She handed him his coffee and joined him at the window. She tracked the movements of two new receivers racing each other down the field.

Every day she encountered virile, handsome men. Men that other women swooned over on game days. What was it about Dempsey alone that drew her eye?

"I meant it." He sipped his coffee and stared at her until her skin grew warm with awareness. "I'm worried about Leon."

That shifted her focus in a hurry. She couldn't remember the last time he'd shared a personal concern with her.

"He thought he was speaking to Theo last night when he told you to be careful your wife didn't find out about me." She knew that Theo Reynaud had a notorious reputation, dating back to his years as a college athlete and straight through his time as a pro.

His wife had left him shortly after Dempsey—the son of an extramarital affair—arrived in her household. She'd told Dempsey that he was her "last straw."

"Right." He shook his head. "We've known that he

has episodes of confusion, but he claimed he saw a doctor who diagnosed it as a thyroid problem. I looked it up, because I wasn't sure if we could believe him, but that is a possibility."

"So either he's not taking the right medicines for it—"

"Or he's been BSing us the whole time and he's never seen a doctor. He's as hardheaded as they come and he doesn't put much faith in the health-care system."

"He is always telling the trainers not to coddle the players." She'd heard him bark at the medical staff often enough, imparting a "tough it out" mentality.

"Exactly." Dempsey frowned. "I asked Jean-Pierre to try to spend some time down here this season so we can present a united front to get Leon evaluated and, if necessary, into more aggressive medical treatment."

Reaching toward her desk, she pulled the box of scones closer.

"Jean-Pierre will have to come home for Gervais's wedding." She'd tracked the wedding talk on social media as part of her duties managing Dempsey's profile pages online. With the Hurricanes' owner marrying a foreign princess, the topic had more traction than any other team news.

The fact that there'd been no official announcement only fueled the rumor mill until speculating on the whens and hows of the nuptials filled page after page of gossip blogs.

"That's still six weeks away." He relinquished his coffee to grab a couple of paper plates from her stash near the minifridge. "I think we need to act soon. I don't want something to happen to Leon because we're all too damn busy to pay attention to the warning signs.

We owe him better, even though he's not going to be happy about us strong-arming him."

"Will you invite your dad to be there?" She took a plate and a scone and passed him the box. "Or any of the rest of the family?"

Leon had another son who lived in Texas, and one out on the West Coast, and there were cousins as well, but the relationships had been strained for a long time.

"No. If Theo happens to be in town, fine." His jaw flexed at the mention of his father, a tic shared by all of Theo's sons. "But I'm not going to seek him out for a family event that will be stressful enough as it is." He set aside his breakfast.

Then slipped hers from her hands and set it on the desk.

"Is that a hint?" she asked, her gaze following the bit of raspberry heaven now out of reach. "Am I indulging my sweet tooth too often?"

"Of course not. I wanted to apologize for last night." He took her hand between his and gave her his undivided attention.

Making her whole body go on full alert.

"You don't owe me any apologies." She hadn't expected a discussion about what happened and, consequently, was completely unprepared.

"I do. I didn't pick you up last night to bring you to the event. I didn't deliver your engagement ring personally. And then the episode with my grandfather distracted me from one of the most shockingly provocative kisses of my life."

"Oh." Completely. Unprepared. "I—"

"Can I ask you a personal question?"

Her heart hammered so loudly in her ears she wasn't

entirely sure she'd hear it, but she nodded. The warmth of his palm on the back of her hand sent sparks of pleasure pinging around her insides.

"Have you thought about us that way before? Or is this a whole new experience, feeling all that chemistry?" His golden-brown gaze captured hers.

Her cheeks heated and she cursed the reaction bitterly even as she shrugged like an inarticulate teenager. But answering the question felt like a "damned if she did, damned if she didn't" proposition.

"Right." He let go of her hand. "Maybe I have no business asking you that. But I'll admit I'm having a tough time concentrating today. I came in early just to hit the gym and try to work off some steam because I damn well couldn't sleep."

That got her attention.

"Because of me?" Her voice sounded as though she'd been sucking down helium. She grabbed her coffee and took a healthy swig.

"Things got heated last night, wouldn't you agree?" His voice lowered. Deepened.

The words felt like a stroke along her skin, they were so damn seductive. But she needed to proceed with extreme caution. She'd heard Valentina's accusation the night before. Dempsey had left her bed before the sheets cooled, according to her.

"That's what happens when you play games and pretend things you don't feel." She kept her cool, needing to make herself heard before she did something foolish, like respond to all that simmering heat she felt when he touched her. "You can't tell where the game ends and reality begins."

For one heart-stopping moment, she imagined what

would happen if he kissed her this time. If he laid her on her desk and told her the games ended here and now. She could almost taste the moment, it felt so real.

"Why does it have to be a game?" He edged back from her, his gaze level. "We've always been good together. We respect each other. Why not enjoy the benefits of this attraction now that it's becoming a distraction?"

She could hear the influence of his Reynaud roots in his word choices. It took a superhuman effort not to roll her eyes.

"Maybe because I don't think of relationships in terms of benefits. We're talking about intimacy, not some contractual arrangement. And I definitely don't want to be pursued for the sake of a distraction."

"I wouldn't be so quick to write off the advantages." He took a step closer. Crowding her. "Perhaps we should make a list of all the ways you would directly benefit."

Her heart galloped. Her skin seemed to shrink, creating the sensation of being too tight to fit. She didn't think she'd make it through a discussion of the ways having Dempsey in her bed would reward her.

"Maybe some other time." She tossed her empty coffee cup in the trash and stood. "Now that I know you were serious about that day off, maybe I'll just head back to the house and do some work on my designs." She would preserve some dignity, damn it.

Although she did take the box of scones.

The light in his eyes told her that he was on to her. That he understood why she needed to beat a hasty retreat.

"Good. I'm coming home early tonight. I'll take you out for dinner."

Alone?

Her mouth went dry.

"Maybe," she hedged, backing toward the door. "I've got a meeting with a fabric company downtown later. But I'll text you afterward."

She didn't wait for his response as she walked out into the corridor. Her skin hummed with awareness from being around him and from the knowledge that he wanted her. Her kiss—practically a chaste brush of lips—had shifted the dynamic between them more than she'd imagined possible.

Dempsey wanted her.

And maybe, for now, that ought to be enough. She couldn't expect him to fall head over heels for her when he'd hardly seen her as a woman up until earlier in the week. Was she a fool to run away from the firestorm she'd created?

Part of her wanted to march back into her office and strip off all his clothes. Request that detailed list of relationship benefits after all.

Except, of course, she had little experience with men. And baiting a Reynaud was a dangerous business when she wasn't a man-eating Valentina type who could deal with the fallout. She was just Adelaide Thibodeaux and she had a feeling she might never recover from a night in Dempsey's bed. Knowing her overinflated sense of loyalty, she'd probably be lovesick for life, stuck in a job as his assistant in the hope he'd one day crook his finger in her direction so she could repeat the mind-blowing experience.

No, thank you.

Dempsey might have started this game on his terms, but she planned to finish it. On hers.

Six

Dempsey made no claim to being an intuitive man.

But even he could sense that he'd made some headway with Adelaide earlier in the day. Sure, he understood her reluctance to jeopardize their friendship. And he meant what he'd said about respecting her. Caring about her.

Yet the flame that burned between them now wouldn't go away just because they ignored it. She might not be ready to address it, but he sure as hell would. So now he found himself driving around downtown New Orleans in search of the fabric supplier she was using as a pretext for not meeting him for dinner.

He'd rearranged his day and moved his nonnegotiable meetings earlier in the afternoon. His practice had gone well. His game plan for Sunday was solid. Nothing was going to stand in the way of spending time with her tonight. He would make a case for exploring this attraction in a way he hadn't been prepared to do last night after that unsettling talk with Leon.

He needed to get to know her better—a damn sorry thing to admit when he ought to know her as well as anyone. But he'd been too caught up in his own career the past few years to pay attention to Addy. If he wanted to persuade her to let her guard down and give him a chance, he needed to understand what made her happy. What pleased her.

Spotting the storefront of the warehouse, Dempsey steered his BMW sedan into a spot on the street. Evan had driven Adelaide to this location, so Dempsey had it on good authority she was still inside.

The least he could do was show an interest in the business she wanted to start. He'd looked over her business plan briefly before driving out here and he'd been both impressed and worried. Her goals were sound, but fulfilling them would mean a lot of hands-on involvement to get it up and running. Maybe if he discussed the clothing company with her in detail, he'd see a way for her to hand off some of the less important tasks. There had to be a way to free her up enough to keep working with him.

He needed Adelaide.

In the ten steps it took to hit the front door he was already sweating, the heat still wet as a dishcloth even though it was six o'clock. The man seated at the desk out front pointed Dempsey in the right direction, and he went into the warehouse to look for Adelaide.

He found her in front of a display of laces, draping an intricate gray pattern over her calf as if to see what the material looked like up against bare skin. Making him wonder what kinds of garments she had in mind for her next design project.

A vision of her high, full breasts covered in nothing but lace and his hands blasted to the forefront of his brain, making him hotter than the late-afternoon sun had. She wore different clothes from the ones she'd had on at the training facility, trading dark pants and a Hurricanes T-shirt for the yellow-and-blue floral sundress she now wore. Wide-set straps and a square neckline framed her feminine curves. Her hair was rolled into some kind of updo that exposed her neck and made him want to lick it. So much for keeping his thoughts friendly.

"Dempsey?" She straightened, a smile lighting up her face for a moment before a wary look chased after it. "What a surprise to see you here." She gestured to the soaring shelves of fabric samples on miniature hangers, sorted by color and material. "Are you here to redesign the Hurricanes jerseys?"

He scanned a section of striped and polka-dotted cotton.

"I think the guys will stick with what we have." He peered around the warehouse to gauge their level of privacy. He'd seen one other shopper on his way in, but other than that, the space appeared empty. "I'm here for you."

The lace dropped from her fingers. "Is there a problem with our opening day? I checked my phone—"

He caught her hand before she could dig in her purse for the device.

"No problems. Things are running just as they should for the regular-season opener."

He couldn't even touch her anymore without images

of that tentative kiss of hers heating him from the inside out. He didn't know how he'd found the willpower to let her retreat to her own room last night when the need for a better taste of her rode his back like a tackle he couldn't break.

"Then, what did you need?" She slid her hand away from his, making him wonder what she felt when they touched.

"What do I need? To see you." He huffed out a breath and braced an elbow on one of the nearby shelves. "I came here to insist on that dinner I offered since it seemed as though you're being elusive today, and it's bugging me that I don't know why."

She busied herself with returning the lace to its small hanger and finding the proper place to reshelve it. When she didn't respond, he continued, "But now that I'm here, it occurs to me that the bigger reason I needed to see you is that I can't seem to think about anything else."

He watched as her busy movements slowed. Stopped. Color washed her cheeks, confirming his suspicion that she suffered from the same madness as he did. And yes, it gave him tremendous amounts of male satisfaction to think he wasn't the only one feeling it.

She clutched a handful of indigo-colored silk and squeezed.

"You made it clear that I've become a *distraction*," she reminded him, a hint of bitterness creeping into the words.

"Is that why you're avoiding me? Because I didn't make a more romantic gesture?" His hands were on her before he'd thought through the wisdom of touching her again.

Spinning her away from the fabric display, he turned her to face him, his palms settling into the indent of her waist. Hidden from view, he wrestled with the urge to feel more of her, to mold her to him and put an end to the damnable simmering distraction.

If she'd been anyone else, the next move would have already been made. But this was Addy.

"No. Thinking about romance will not help get us through the next few weeks," she told him evenly. "I'm not one of your girlfriends with a legal agreement you can keep renegotiating, okay? You laid out the terms when you put me on the spot with this engagement. I'm not sure why you think you can keep rewriting those terms to give you more *benefits*."

The bitterness in her voice had vanished. Taking its place was a trace of hurt.

An emotional one-two punch that he'd never intended.

His hands tightened on her waist. His throat dried up.

"You're right." Closing his eyes, he dragged in a deep breath and only succeeded in inhaling a hint of night-blooming roses. "I haven't thought about how this is affecting you. That day you told me you were quitting, I was completely focused on making sure that didn't happen. I came up with the only short-term solution I could."

Dempsey became aware of the sound of a woman's high heels clicking on the concrete floor behind him. She was heading their way.

"Ms. Thibodeaux, do you have any questions—" A tall blonde woman in a dark suit rounded the corner and came into view. "Oh. Hello there." She blushed at the sight of them together, making Dempsey realize how close he'd gotten to Adelaide during this discussion.

How much closer he still wanted to be.

"I put the last sample back," Adelaide told her, edging around Dempsey and straightening. "I'll give you a call once I have a better idea of what I might need."

The woman was already backing away. "Of course! No problem. And congratulations on your engagement."

As soon as the sales clerk disappeared from view, Adelaide swung around to face him.

"So now that you've acknowledged this engagement was a mistake, are you ready to call it off and maybe life can go back to normal?" Her hazel eyes seemed greener in this light. Or maybe it was the combination of anger and challenge firing through them.

"Not until I have a better short-term solution." He understood they needed to have this discussion since this attraction was proving far too distracting at a time when he needed absolute focus. "But you can help me brainstorm alternatives. Over dinner."

Two hours later, Adelaide sat cross-legged on a wooden Adirondack chair behind Dempsey's house overlooking Lake Pontchartrain. A blaze burned in the round fire pit in front of them as they finished a meal of Cajun specialties obtained by Evan from a local restaurant. Adelaide hadn't wanted to risk a public outing, unwilling to smile and lie politely about her engagement to Dempsey when the man was hell-bent on taking their relationship into intimate terrain.

And that's a problem...why? some snide voice in her head kept asking.

Sure, she wanted him. Desperately. But since a corner of her heart had always belonged to him, she feared this new development could have devastating consequences when the time came to return to their regular lives. And the time would come. She'd witnessed Dempsey's parting gifts to his exes enough times to know that relationships came with an expiration date for him. Still, she simmered with thwarted desire. While she finished her meal, she tormented herself with fantasies about touching him. Agreeing to his offer of sensual benefits. Bringing this heat to the boiling point. Even now she wanted to cross over to his chair and take a seat on his lap just to see what would happen.

From her vantage point, his thighs appeared plenty strong enough to bear her weight. Those workouts of his seemed to keep him in optimal shape.

Was she really ready for him to relegate her to friendship for life when she had this opportunity of living with him for the next few weeks? When he'd admitted he couldn't stop thinking about her? She'd nearly melted in her shoes when he'd confessed it at the fabric warehouse.

"Remember when you stole a crawfish for me and I was too afraid to eat it?" she asked, deliberately putting off the more serious conversation he'd promised over dinner.

She wasn't ready to help him brainstorm solutions to their dilemma. And right now she wanted a happy memory to remind her why she put up with him and all that driven, relentless ambition, which kept him from getting too close to anyone. She blamed that and his need to prove himself to his family for his unwillingness to take a risk with the relationship.

Although maybe she just needed to tell herself that to

protect her heart from the more obvious explanation—
that he saw any attraction as a fleeting response doomed
not to last.

"I didn't steal it." He sounded as incensed about it
now as he'd been when he was twelve years old. "If a
crawfish happened to walk over to me, it was exercis-
ing its free will."

Laughing, she set aside the jambalaya that had made
her think of that day. They'd walked to a nearby crawfish festival. When one of the restaurants selling food
at the event refilled its tank of crawfish, a few escap-
ees had headed toward Dempsey and Adelaide, who'd
been drooling over the food from a spot on the pavement nearby.

"I don't know what made you think I would eat a
raw mudbug." She shivered. "Sometimes I still can't
believe I eat them when they're cooked."

"A hungry kid doesn't turn his nose up at much,"
he observed. "And I figured it was only polite to offer
them to you before I helped myself."

Adelaide had never gone hungry the way Dempsey
sometimes had. His mother could be kind when she
was drug-free, but even then the woman had never had
any extra money thanks to her habit. When she'd been
using more, she'd even forgotten about Dempsey for
days on end.

"You were very good to me." When Adelaide looked
back on those days, she could almost forget about how
much he'd shut her out of his personal life since then.

He stared into the flames dancing in the fire pit.

"I still try to be good to you, Addy."

She bit back the sharp retort that came to mind, pur-
posely focusing on the friendship they used to have so

as not to bad-mouth the turn things had taken over the past five years.

"I take it you don't agree?" he asked.

"We've had a strict work-only relationship for years." She traced patterns in the condensation on her iced tea glass. "You convinced me to take this job that furthered your career while delaying mine. You've ignored our friendship for years at a time, going so far as referring to me as a 'tool for greater productivity.'" She wanted to stop there. But now that the brakes were off, she found it difficult to put them back on. "Or maybe you think it's *kind* of you to toy with the chemistry between us, pretending to feel the same heat that I do and using it to your own ends to convince me to stay?"

She knew she'd admitted too much, but sitting in the dark under the bayou stars seemed to coax the truth from her. Besides, if she didn't put herself on the line with him now when he'd admitted to being "distracted" by her, she might never have another chance to find out where all that simmering attraction could lead.

"Damn, Addy." He whistled low and sat up straighter in his chair, his elbows on his knees. Firelight cast stark shadows on his face. "You must think I'm some kind of arrogant, selfish ass. Do you really think that's how I perceive things? That I created a position for you just to benefit me?"

"You're putting words in my mouth."

"Nothing you didn't imply." He rose to his feet, his agitation apparent as he paced a circle around his vacated chair. "And I can assure you that you were not the most obvious choice to work with me in this capacity. There aren't many assistant coaches who bring an administrative aide with them when they take a new job, but I did it just the same because you needed a job at the time. And I'm the only coach in the league with a female personal assistant, so I'm breaking all kinds of ground there."

"You can't honestly suggest that you created the job for me to further my career. I wanted to be an artist."

"Yes. An artist. And your work led you to a studio in an even worse part of town than where we grew up. A place I warned you not to take. I offered to rent another space for you. But then—"

"The break-in." She didn't want to think about that night when gang members, high on heaven knew what, had broken into the studio and threatened her.

They'd destroyed her paintings when they'd realized there was nothing of value in the place to steal. Then they'd casually discussed the merits of physically assaulting her before one of them got a text that they needed to be elsewhere. The three of them had disappeared into the night while she'd remained paralyzed with fear long afterward.

"Those bastards threatened you. And I suggested every plan under the sun to help you, Addy, but you were too stubborn and proud to let me do anything."

Crickets chirped in the silence that followed. A log shifted in the fire pit, sending sparks flying.

"You wanted to build me a studio in the country." She recalled a fax from an architect with the plans for such a building, including a state-of-the-art security system. "How on earth could I have ever repaid you for such a thing? I was barely out of college."

"Like I said. Too stubborn." He spread his hands wide. "I was just a few years out of college myself and I was dealing with a lot of family expectations. The studio would have been easy for me to give you and I was happy to do it, but you wouldn't hear of it."

"I'd never take something for nothing. And don't you blame me for that, because you wouldn't either if our positions were reversed." Maybe she hadn't let herself remember that time in detail because it had taken a long time to recover from the emotional trauma of that night.

Seeing her canvases hacked to bits had been different than having her computer stolen or her phone smashed. Her art was an extension of her, a place where she poured her heart.

"So I gave you a job. That, you would accept."

"And now, years after the fact, I'm still supposed to kiss your feet for the opportunity?" She shot out of her chair, a restless energy taking hold as she closed the distance between them.

"Absolutely not."

His quick agreement didn't come close to satisfying her.

"I worked hard in an industry I knew nothing about," she pressed. "I left my home and everything I knew to go to Atlanta with you." Her first task had been finding housing for them.

Relocating to a new city had been so simple with Dempsey's seemingly limitless resources and connections.

Unlike starting over in New Orleans, which had seemed impossible after her sense of safety had been shredded and her body of work reduced to scraps.

"Yes. And you proved yourself invaluable almost right away. My work was easier with your help. You never needed direction and understood me even on days

I was so terse and exhausted I could only snap out a few words of instructions for you."

"I had a long history of interpreting you." A wry grin tugged at her lips, but she wasn't going to let nostalgia cloud her vision of him. Of them.

"But we'd scarcely seen each other for a decade." He reached toward her, as if to stroke her cheek, but he must have thought better of it when his hand fell to his side. "I was surprised how well we got back into sync."

"You might be more surprised to know how much more in sync we could be." The words leaped from her mouth.

One moment they were in her head. The next they were in the air, with no way to recapture them.

She saw the instant that full understanding hit him. The instant he heard the proposition underlying those words. His gaze shifted to her mouth, the heat in his eyes like a laser in its intensity.

"Of course it would *not* surprise me. That's exactly what I've been trying to tell you." He focused all his attention on her. "You've occupied every second of my thoughts today. You've got me so damn distracted, I can hardly think about football."

Still he didn't move toward her. Didn't give in to the current that leaped back and forth between them. Her cells practically strained toward the sound of his voice.

"Then, maybe you ought to call off this engagement charade before you tank a season that means everything to you." She wouldn't make the first move again. Being impulsive with him the night before had only complicated things between them.

"I don't think so." He reached behind her and tugged a pin from the knot at the back of her head. Then, sifting through the half-fallen mass, he found two more and pulled them free.

Her hair tumbled to her bare shoulders and covered her arms. She shivered despite the warmth of the night, awareness flooding through her like high tide.

"Why not?" Her voice rasped low from the effort of not stepping closer. She wanted him to touch her the way he had the night before. Craved the feel of his body against hers.

"Because I have a better solution for all this distraction you're causing." He combed his fingers through the ends of her hair, smoothing it along her back.

Sensation shimmered over her skin, nerve endings dancing to life. Desire pooled in her belly as her gaze roamed over his powerful arms and shoulders, the solid wall of his chest that would be warm to her touch.

"A way to stop all this distraction?" She needed to know what he was thinking before her thoughts smoldered away in the blaze erupting between them.

"I'm beginning to think that's a lost cause after last night." His hands moved to her hips as he stepped into her space, crowding her in the most delicious possible way. "That dress you wore last night flipped some kind of switch in my head and I can't stop thinking about this spot." He palmed the front of her thigh. "Right here."

Her breath caught on a hard gasp. Pleasure spiked. Her breasts beaded under the bodice of her dress.

"Do you remember where I mean?" His eyes were dark and lit by firelight, reflecting the bright orange flames beside them. He traced a pattern on the front of her leg, fingering gently. "There was a sheer place in the lace. Here."

He increased the pressure of his touch and she

couldn't swallow a strangled sound in the back of her throat. He hadn't even kissed her yet and she was utterly mesmerized.

"I remember." Her words were a breathless whisper as she steadied herself against his shoulders, anchoring her quivering body with his strength.

"If I'm a bad friend to you, Addy, you only have that dress to blame." He shifted his hold on her to align their hips, allowing her to feel how much he wanted her. "But I damn well can't resist any longer."

Seven

Dempsey's control had snapped the second she'd suggested they could be even more in sync. He'd been hanging on by a thread before that moment, willing himself not to think about the tender brush of her lips on his the night before. Not to think about that damn siren's dress she'd worn or the way she'd melted in his arms.

So by the time she'd made that one coy, flirtatious taunt, his restraint had simply incinerated.

From that moment on, he'd been plagued with sweaty visions of them moving together in perfect sensual accord. Now that he had his hands on her, molding her sweet, curvy body to his, he didn't have a prayer of putting a lid back on this combustible attraction.

He kissed her. Hard. With deliberate purpose. Need. Seeking entrance, he explored every nuance of her mouth, claiming it with a hunger and thoroughness he couldn't hold back. The way she opened for him, swayed into him, encouraged him all the more.

Unleashed, his emotions fired through the kiss until he all but devoured her. She clutched his shoulders, her nails biting ever so slightly into his skin through his shirt. He wished he could torch their clothes so he could feel the sting of that touch without barrier.

He bent to nuzzle her neck, tasting the skin all along her throat and under her ear until he found the source of her fragrance. The scent of roses made him throb with teeth-jarring need. He nipped and licked his way down her collarbone along the strap of her dress and peeled the fabric free. He had to feel more of her.

But right before he helped himself to one of her breasts, he remembered they were still outdoors. And even though it was nighttime, the fire might make them visible to one of the houses dotting the lake if someone was so inclined to spy. The porches of plenty of coastal homes were furnished with telescopes.

"I want to take you inside." He nudged the strap of her dress back up her shoulder, his hand unsteady and his breath uneven. The ache from wanting her still heated his veins.

"I want to take you anywhere I can have you." She loosened her hold on him as she edged back a step. "So that's definitely fine with me."

Her words fanned the flames hotter inside him. Aching to have her, he swept her up in his arms and charged over the lawn toward the house.

"Your room is closer." He said it to himself as much as her, directing his steps toward the downstairs bedroom. "But the condoms are all upstairs." He changed direction, cursing himself for the mansion's extravagant square footage when it delayed having Adelaide.

She nipped at his neck while he covered the distance, those delectable breasts of hers pressed tight to his chest as she clutched him. She made a luscious armful, her thighs draped over one arm while her hip grazed the erection that had hounded him the better part of the day.

"I can't wait to feel you without the barrier of clothes," she murmured against his ear, her breath puffing a silken caress along his skin.

"That's good." He ground the words out between clenched teeth as he finally reached the door to his suite. "Because I don't think we're going to leave this room until the game on Sunday."

He needed to wear himself out with her. To excise this hunger spilling over into every aspect of his life until all he could think about was Adelaide.

Setting her on her feet, he backed her into the nearest wall, yearning to feel more of her. Light spilled into the room from low-wattage sconces on either side of the bed that came on automatically at sunset. He toed the door shut behind them and took another valuable second to flip the lock into place. Then all of his focus returned to Adelaide.

Immersing his hands in all that long, caramel-colored hair of hers, he shifted the length of it over one shoulder in a silky veil. His body pinned hers in place, hips sinking into hers where they fit best.

He was dying to have her. It was as if he'd been holding back for years instead of days, and maybe subconsciously he had been. That friendship wall could be a strong one. Mistresses were plentiful. Friends, true friends, were few. But the time for restraint was long gone as he tugged the straps of her thin sundress down and exposed a pretty turquoise-colored bra that wouldn't be nearly as enticing as what was underneath. Applying his hands to the hooks, he swept that aside, too, so he could get his mouth around the tight buds of dark pink nipples he'd felt right through her clothes.

Her back arched to give him better access, her body straining toward his while he laved and licked at one and then the other. She made soft sexy sounds that told him how much she liked what he was doing, and her hands worked the buttons on his shirt until she was touching bare skin. He hauled the shirt off his shoulders and let it slide to the floor, his eyes never leaving her. With her dress tugged down and all that goddess hair draped over her shoulders, she made one hell of a vision.

Lifting her against him, he slid a hand up her skirt to wrap her leg around his waist. Positioned that way, the vulnerable, hot core of her came up against his rock-hard erection. She shuddered against him, a subtle vibration he felt right there, a sensation so damn good he cupped her hips and moved her against him again and again. A sensual ride he wanted to give her for real.

"That feels…" Her words broke on a small cry of pleasure as she braced herself on his shoulders.

"Tell me." He wanted to know everything she liked. Exactly how she liked it.

While he'd always striven to pleasure the women in his bed, this was different. He needed this night to be perfect because this was Adelaide and *she* was different. So much more important to him.

And he wasn't ready to think about what that meant or all the ways that was going to complicate things for them.

"It feels so good." Her eyes flipped open long enough

for him to see the haze of desire there, her gaze unfocused. "I'm so close. Already."

Knowing that only cranked him higher. He kept up the friction beginning to torment him and fastened his lips back on one breast. He drew on it. Hard. Then, finding the edge of her panties with one hand, he slid beneath the satin to stroke the drenched feminine folds. Once. Twice.

She came apart with a high cry she muffled against his shoulder. The force of it, combined with the way she went boneless in his arms, made him sway back on his feet a little.

Damn. He used that moment to watch her, to soak up the vision she made with her cheeks suffused with color and her chest heaving with all that sensation.

Giving her a moment—giving himself one, too—he tried to catch his breath before he carried her over to the bed and deposited her there. His own release was close and he hadn't even taken off his pants. Leaving her just long enough to retrieve a box of condoms from the bathroom cabinet, he dropped it on the nightstand.

Then he went to work on his belt while he watched her slide off her heels. He dropped his pants while she wriggled out of her dress. He was left wearing only his boxers at the same time she wore nothing but turquoise-colored satin panties.

"I'll show you mine if you show me yours," she dared him, hooking a finger in the lace waistband about as substantial as a shoelace.

He slid off the boxers.

"I'm going to see yours, all right," he warned her, edging a knee onto the bed and stretching out over her. "Up close and personal."

She let go of the panties, her hand moving to his chest as he shifted closer.

"Oh?" Her breathless question told him exactly how much she liked that idea. "Well, I'm going to revisit on you all the same pleasure that you give me." She arched an eyebrow at the sensual promise.

Laying a hand on her hip, he slipped the satin down her thighs and off.

"Not a chance. This isn't like a favor where you can keep an accounting. In this bed, I get to give and give and give all that I want." He stroked the soft curls just above her sex, sliding touches lower and lower while she drew in a breath between her teeth.

"Dempsey." She arched her hips toward him, a silent plea.

One he was powerless to resist.

Parting her thighs, he made room for himself there. She watched him with wide eyes, biting the soft fullness of her lower lip while he found a condom and opened the packet. She stole it away from him, rolling it into place herself and positioning him where she wanted.

Where they both wanted.

When he entered her, she tightened her grip on him. Her arms wrapped around his shoulders. Legs tightened around his waist. And her inner muscles squeezed him with sensual pulls that had him gritting his teeth against the sweetly erotic feel of one hundred percent Adelaide.

For a long moment, he held himself still, breathing in the scent of her hair and giving her time to adjust to him. When he thought he could move again without unmanning himself, he levered up on his arms and began a slow, steady rhythm. Addy held herself still for a moment, and then, as if she'd just been waiting for the right time to join him, she swiveled her hips in a way that rocked him.

Heat blazed up his spine as she undulated beneath him, meeting his thrusts and making him see stars. She locked her ankles behind him, her heat, her softness and her scent surrounding him. He wanted to draw this out, to make the pleasure go on and on, to explore every facet of what she liked. But not this time. Not now when just being inside her was enough to send him hurtling over the edge.

Next time, he'd find some self-control. Some way to make the pleasure last. Right now the need to come inside her was the most primal urge he'd ever felt. He closed his eyes, cued in on her breathing and synced his movements, causing her to gasp and arch. He moved faster, needing to focus solely on her. On pleasuring her.

He wouldn't let himself go until then.

She called his name with a hoarse cry as her whole body went taut. Her release pulsated through her and freed his. He kissed her to silence, the shout poised in his throat as wave after wave of pleasure pounded through him. The moment went on and on until they were both spent and lying side by side, their breathing erratic and heartbeats pounding crazy rhythms. He knew because one of his hands rested on her throat, where he could feel her pulse hammer.

She must know, too, because her hand lay on his chest, where his heart thrummed so hard it felt as though it wanted out.

Long minutes passed before their skin began to cool and Dempsey thought he could move again. He drew her into his arms and stroked her hair, smoothing tangles and skimming it to one side of her beautiful body.

"I'm speechless," she murmured, her breath a soft huff on his chest.

"We could make talking optional for the next few hours," he suggested, already wanting her again.

She peered up at him through long lashes. "Save all our energy for the important things?"

"Exactly." He cupped her cheek and tilted her face to kiss her. "You can practically read my mind anyhow. You can probably guess what I'd like to do next."

She sidled closer, her hips stirring him to life with a speed he hadn't experienced since his teens.

"I have an excellent idea. But I stopped being your dutiful assistant when you gave me the day off. So I won't be fulfilling your every need tonight." She ran a lazy hand up his biceps and onto his chest. Then trailed her nails lightly down the center of his sternum.

"No?" His voice rasped on a dry note.

"I might give a few orders of my own," she teased.

"Is that what I do? Order you around?" He found a ticklish spot on her side and made her laugh.

"Definitely." She gripped his wrists and pinned them to the bed. Climbing on top of him, she let all that glorious hair fall around him. "Now it's my turn."

Adelaide couldn't resist teasing him. She stared down into Dempsey's impossibly handsome face and wondered how long he would let her play this game.

Judging from the impressive erection resting on his abs, he was liking it well enough so far.

"I can't imagine what you'd ask me to do when I've already put so much thought into pleasing you, Ms. Thibodeaux." His dark eyes wandered over her in the most flattering way.

"I already like your deferential tone." She kissed his cheek and brushed her breasts against it. "Why don't you tell me about this effort you say you've put into pleasing me? I'd love to hear all about that."

Kissing her way down his chest, she paused now and again to look up at him. Make sure he was still watching. Still liking what she was doing. Because honestly, she had little enough experience with men, and none with a man like Dempsey. She could only trust her instincts to guide her and have fun with him in this rare moment to play and tease.

And enjoy his sinfully delicious body.

"I've taken all my cues from you tonight," he informed her, his muscles flexing under her as she slid down him to kiss his abs.

"How do you mean?" She peered up to find him shoving a pillow under his head.

Making himself comfortable? Or getting ready to watch the show? Nerves danced along her skin, mingling with anticipation. When he put his hands behind his head, it was a devastating look for a man with his build, emphasizing the way his upper body tapered to narrow hips.

"You get a sexy look in your eyes when you're thinking wicked thoughts, Addy. I know that's when to make my move."

"A sexy look?" She stroked a light touch up the hard length of him.

He hissed a breath between his teeth. "Definitely." He shifted under her, his whole body tensing.

She climbed back up him to whisper in his ear, "I've never done this before. Feel free to offer instruction." She paused to kiss his lips and wander her way down

his body again, taking his incoherent groan as a good
sign that he was on board with her plan.

She listened to every intake of his breath, repeating
the things he liked best. When she traced the indents
between his abs with her tongue, he almost came off
the bed.

That was when she experimented with how she
touched him, discovering it was easy to know what he
liked. Tasting him received wholehearted approval. In
fact, the more of him that she took into her mouth, the
more encouraging his reaction.

"Addy." His tone warned her more than his words.
And he would have hauled her up to kiss him if she
hadn't paused to remind him who was in charge.

"Let go," she commanded, meeting his gaze one last
time before she returned to the kisses he liked so well.

When his release came, she savored it, loving that
rare moment of seeing him lose control. Of knowing
she'd given him that pleasure.

But when the hot pulses halted and a final groan
ripped from his throat, Dempsey reached for her and
dragged her back up his body. His golden-brown gaze
seared her. As if he'd taken her game as a personal
challenge, he settled between her thighs and kissed her.

The sharp jolt of sensual pleasure was like an electric
shock, rippling through every part of her. He dipped one
shoulder beneath her thigh and then the other, finding
just the right angle to slowly drive her to the edge of
madness. Each stroke of his tongue sent quivery ribbons
of pleasure to her belly. Fingers twisting in the sheets,
she held on as he nipped and licked, making her fly
apart in hard spasms that went on and on.

She wanted to say something about that, the intensity of the orgasm unlike anything she'd ever felt. But the hungry look still lurked in his eyes as he stretched out over her, kissing her mouth while he found another condom and seated himself deep inside her.

Any words she'd been about to speak dried up in her throat. All she could do was hold on and trust him to take care of her body, which was in the grip of a hunger that seemed bigger than both of them. Tucking her cheek against his chest, she closed her eyes and got lost in the feel of him inside her.

Dempsey. Reynaud.

She felt as if all her life had led to this moment. This joining. This wild heat that shook her to her core. And when at last he found his release, taking her with him yet again, Adelaide kissed him hard in a tangle of tongues and pleasure.

Afterward, she could barely move, but she didn't need to. Every part of her felt sated. Happy. And—at least in the physical sense—well loved. She knew they'd taken an irreparable step away from friendship toward something potentially more dangerous. But with the heavy feeling in her limbs and Dempsey's naked body wrapped around hers, she refused to have any regrets tonight. They would come, she guessed, as sure as the sunrise.

For now, however, she was going to squeeze every moment of pleasure she could out of this fake engagement and their time together. There was always a chance Dempsey could learn to care about her as more than a friend before their four weeks were up.

If sex was a way to make that happen, she would just have to sacrifice her body for the greater good.

And if her gamble didn't pay off? Adelaide would

have some incredible memories to keep her warm at night. She told herself it was a good plan. The only plan she had. But a little voice in her head kept reminding her that Dempsey didn't have affairs without an expiration date. How many times had Adelaide shipped off one of those extravagant tennis bracelets to a former lover?

She ought to know better than anyone. The only reason Dempsey had initiated this unwise relationship was because she was quitting soon. Yet knowing how their affair would end before it happened wasn't going to make it any easier when Dempsey walked away.

Eight

When Dempsey's alarm chimed before dawn, he slammed the off button and hoped it hadn't woken Adelaide. They hadn't slept much with the fever for each other burning in their blood. He didn't want to wear her out, but the last time they'd been together had been her idea after they'd headed into the kitchen to refuel after midnight. She'd made crepes from scratch and they'd been amazing. Including the part when she'd taunted him to find the hint of raspberry sauce she'd dabbed on her bare skin while he wasn't looking.

That game had ended deliciously, but it had required a shower, where he'd gotten to wash her long hair himself. He'd wanted her then, too, when he'd carried her damp, freshly washed body back to his bed. But he hadn't wanted to exhaust her.

Studying her face in the shadows cast from the

bathroom light—they'd fallen asleep without shutting it off—Dempsey wondered what it would be like to work side by side now that they'd shared this incredible night. He'd never touched a woman he did business with. It was a rule he'd kept all through the years as he'd learned about the Reynauds' shipping empire from his grandfather, unwilling to have anyone draw a comparison between Dempsey's personal ethics and his parents.

"I can hear you thinking," Adelaide whispered, her eyes still closed.

"Maybe I'm thinking about how good you taste." He stroked her hair, still damp in places from their late-night shower. In other spots, strands had turned kinky, a phenomenon he remembered from when they were kids and she'd let it run wild.

He kissed her bare shoulder, breathing in the scent of roses that lingered even now that it mixed with his soap.

"My female intuition suggests there's more going on in your brain than that." She captured his hand where he touched her and threaded her fingers between his. "Do you really need to go to work already?"

"No. But I received a text last night from Evan that one of the players I cut in training camp—Marcus Wheelan—was picked up by the cops for getting into a fight in a local bar. I need to talk to him. See if I can get through to him before he heads down a path that he can't recover from." Dempsey had been saved from choosing that kind of life by a fluke of birth, a lucky chance. But if Theo Reynaud hadn't shown up to pluck Dempsey out of his old life, what were the chances that it would be Dempsey who spent the occasional Friday night in jail?

Or worse.

"Won't that attract the kind of publicity you don't want around the team?" Adelaide shifted, turning to meet his gaze.

"I'll get a lawyer to look at the bail situation and pull Marcus out of there so I can speak to him privately." Dempsey wasn't clear on the charges yet, but hoped they were no more serious than disorderly conduct or resisting arrest—the kinds of things police leveled at drunken, noisy athletes.

But according to Evan, who kept in touch with a lot of the players who'd been invited to training camp, Marcus had been out with a rough group. He'd taken it hard when he hadn't made the Hurricanes' regular-season roster after getting cut by a West Coast team last spring.

"That's good of you." She feathered a light touch along his cheek, her expression troubled. "I hope he listens."

"Me, too." He kissed her forehead and waged an inner battle not to slide his hands beneath the sheets and lose himself in her one more time. "And I hope you can get some more sleep."

She ignored his efforts at restraint, sidling over to him and slipping a slender thigh between his.

"I'll sleep better knowing you left the house happy." Her whispered words were like a drug, finding their way into his bloodstream and sending a fresh wave of heat through him.

"I could get used to this in a hurry." He gripped her hips and molded her curves to his, her breasts flattening against his chest.

He needed to be inside her, exploring her heat and hearing her soft moans in his ear. He'd never felt this way about a woman before, when every time with her made him want her even more. Again and again. He'd barely be able to walk by tomorrow at this rate.

But he didn't even care.

She pressed kisses along his shoulder and skimmed a hand down his chest. Lower.

"Good. Because I want you thinking about me at work today. And I want you to rush home early because you need to be with me all over again."

They both knew that was exactly what would happen, too. Already he couldn't imagine spending hours away from her. For a moment, he felt a pang of conscience that he was allowing this kind of relationship to grow unchecked, the kind where they could lose themselves in each other completely. He wondered how he would handle it once that heat finally burned itself out, but far more important, he should be thinking about Adelaide.

What would it do to her?

Not ready to consider that right now when they were only just beginning to discover all the ways they could drive one another to new heights of pleasure, Dempsey shut down his thoughts. He let the magic of Adelaide's touch carry him into a sensual world that was all their own.

Afterward, Adelaide walked along the lakeshore at sunrise as Dempsey showered and prepared to drive into the training facility. The grounds all around the Reynaud homes were breathtaking, the landscaping exotic and a little wild. She'd never gardened much herself, but she knew well how fast things grew in this kind of weather, and that it would take a whole fleet of full-time gardeners to meticulously maintain all of the dense plantings around the low-rock retaining walls and fountains, or the vines crawling up some of the outbuildings.

And, to her way of thinking, the rich greenery and abundance of flowers looked more natural than precisely trimmed boxwoods or well-spaced English gardens. Turning her attention back to her path along the lake, she spied a feminine figure walking toward her.

Princess Erika Mitras was engaged to Dempsey's older brother, Gervais, and she'd recently moved into his home near Dempsey's place. Adelaide had met her a few weeks ago when she'd first arrived and been thoroughly dazzled. Refined, royal and incredibly lovely, Erika was the kind of woman who would always draw stares, but there was much more to her than that. She'd served in her country's military, defying her parents' wishes to fulfill a call to civic duty.

Smiling, the princess navigated the walking path in glittery gold sandals and a gauzy white sundress. Her cool Nordic looks and platinum blond hair were shielded by a wide-brimmed hat.

"Good morning," Adelaide greeted her. "Did you happen to see the sunrise?"

Even now, the sky streaked with bright pink light.

"I was awake and waiting for it." She covered a yawn. "It is the curse of pregnancy that I can only sleep when I do not want to."

Adelaide turned to walk in the same direction as the other woman. In the distance, she saw a shirtless Gervais running toward them.

"Well, you look fantastic for someone who didn't sleep well."

"Maybe it is the pregnancy glow," Erika said wryly.

"Or else just plain happiness. I cannot believe how lucky I am to have Gervais in my life. I told him how beignets settle my stomach in the morning, and now he has fresh, warm beignets for me every day."

"How thoughtful. And romantic." Adelaide wondered if Dempsey would do things like that for the mother of his child one day. She paused to pick up a piece of driftwood with an interesting shape, thinking she might find a spot for it in one of the gardens.

"True. Although that is why I have taken to walking in the mornings. I will need the exercise to bear the many, many pounds I plan to gain over the next months."

Adelaide laughed. "You must have so many plans to make to prepare for your baby."

"Babies, actually. Did you not hear that I am having twins?" Erika rested a hand on Adelaide's forearm, a friendly touch that made her realize how few close female friends she had in her life.

Of course, she'd been living and breathing work and football these past four years.

"Oh, Erika." Adelaide's chest ached with a longing for the kind of happiness this woman had found. "How incredible. Congratulations." She hugged her gently. "Please, please let me know if there's anything I can do to help."

"Gervais already treats me as though I am carrying the weight of the world on my shoulders." Her good humor was contagious. "I have to tell him I am a healthy, strong woman. I do not need to put my feet up every moment of the day." She leaned close to lower her voice. "I am telling him that an active sex life will lead to happier babies."

"Well, it must have worked." She pointed to where Gervais had paused to do a cycle of push-ups along the path. "He looks as if he's in training for a marathon."

"As I said, I am a lucky woman." Erika winked and shared her plans for decorating a nursery as they walked.

Adelaide listened attentively, all the while wondering what it would be like to be expecting a first child. She had never stopped to think much about babies, since she had never come close to finding a lasting love relationship and, of course, that needed to happen first.

But all the talk of babies and parenting tugged at her heart. She couldn't help but wonder what would happen if she were to become pregnant. Would Dempsey be excited? More likely he would not be pleased. He'd made it clear their relationship would have boundaries. For years, they had just been friends. Then, she'd been his assistant.

Now she was his lover.

After that? She feared she would be very much alone.

When Dempsey left the house that morning, he spotted Adelaide down by lake, walking with Gervais's future wife. For all that Adelaide had resisted getting close with his family, she looked comfortable enough, pausing in her walk to give the other woman a hug.

The sight did something peculiar to his insides. She was so naturally warmhearted and caring. Of course she would befriend the pregnant foreign princess who must be struggling to adjust to life in New Orleans as she prepared to be a mother.

Dempsey crossed the driveway to reach the detached garage when he caught sight of a familiar figure jogging toward him, his only neighbor right now while Henri spent the season in the Garden District house with his wife.

"Gervais." Dempsey lifted a hand in greeting.

The eldest Reynaud brother, like Dempsey, had walked away from football after college because of injuries. He still ran every day, though, and Dempsey had caught sight of him in the players' gym after-hours some nights, working out to the point of exhaustion. Dempsey had never fully understood his brother's demons, since Gervais had always been the heir to a billion-dollar corporation and he'd been born with the innate business sense to run it well. But then, Gervais had always been the most coolly controlled one of them.

"Congratulations on your engagement." Sweating and shirtless, he slowed his pace to run in place. "Sorry I haven't been by to welcome Adelaide to the family. It's been a busy week in the front office while we prepare for the regular season to start."

"I wouldn't have chosen the week of our home opener for the engagement announcement if it hadn't been necessary." If Addy hadn't decided to quit on him, that is. Although it was tough to regret her decision now, knowing it had led to the most incredible night of his life.

Gervais raised a brow. "Necessary? As in, I won't be the only one trying to navigate the challenges of fatherhood next spring?"

"No." Dempsey hit the remote to raise the door to the farthest right bay in the garage. "You're on your own with that—double dose. Adelaide and I got engaged for different reasons, but the timing was unavoidable."

"Spoken like the romantic soul you've always been," Gervais said drily, clapping him on the shoulder. "But at least Adelaide understands you well. You two want to come up to the house for dinner tonight? Erika is used to having her sisters around. I know she would be glad to get to know her future sister-in-law."

"I'll check with Adelaide, but given how they seem to be enjoying their conversation on the beach now, I think that'll be a good plan." Surprised at the invitation— they'd never extended such invites to one another as bachelors—Dempsey wondered for a split second how family dynamics would change with women around. But then, that wasn't really a concern for now, since Adelaide wouldn't be under his roof for long. He would return to his usual role as the Reynaud black sheep then.

"Good. We can sneak away to watch some game film after dessert." Gervais started jogging again, backward. "You can let me in on the highlights of Sunday's game plan."

"Of course." So it would be a working dinner. Still, he appreciated the offer. "I'll text you once I speak to Adelaide."

Since the four Reynaud brothers had gone off to college, they hadn't spent much time together outside of family gatherings that their grandfather insisted on. Even now, Leon was the most likely to bring them together. Dempsey hated to think that their grandfather's decline in health would be the next thing to put Gervais, Dempsey, Henri and Jean-Pierre in the same room together.

Maybe tonight would be a step toward having a stronger relationship with Gervais—they had a working partnership to protect in the Hurricanes if nothing else. The only drawback would be that Dempsey would have to share Adelaide for a few hours, and with their time together limited, he didn't like the idea of giving up any of it.

They'd been together intimately for less than twenty-four hours and already Adelaide had gotten under his skin deeper than any other woman he'd ever known.

"I love your earrings." Erika lifted a hand toward Adelaide's ear as they sat outside by the pool behind Gervais's breathtaking home that evening. "May I?"

They were sipping virgin margaritas under a pergola heavy with bright pink bougainvillea. Adelaide had mixed feelings about the evening, since getting closer to Dempsey's family would only make their breakup more difficult when it happened. But visiting with Gervais's fiancée this morning and this evening had been surprisingly fun. There was nothing pretentious about this Vikingesque princess who, apparently, was one of five daughters in a family of deposed royalty from a tiny kingdom near Norway.

Their casual outdoor dinner had made Adelaide all the more committed to building a business and a life for herself outside the male-dominated world of football. She craved more girl time.

"Of course." She scooted closer on the massive side-by-side lounger they shared, since Erika had wanted to put her feet up and insisted Adelaide should, too. "These are a sample from an accessory collection I hope to design for female sports fans."

"Sports fans?" Erika frowned, a pout that didn't come close to diminishing her stunning good looks. "They do not look like sports paraphernalia."

Close up, Adelaide marveled at the other woman's skin tone. But then, maybe living so far north the sun couldn't wreak the same kind of havoc. She'd rather take the freckles, she decided, than live for months in the cold.

"That's because they are intended to offset other team-oriented clothes. Most women don't want to dress in head-to-toe gear like a player. So I have some pieces that are very focused on team logos, and some accessories that pick up the colors or motifs in a more subtle way so that fans can be coordinated without being cartoonish."

"So when I buy Henri's jersey to wear—just to tease Gervais, of course—" she gave Adelaide a conspiratorial grin as she released the jewelry "—I can wear gorgeous black-and-gold earrings with it."

"Exactly." Sipping her icy-cold cocktail that made good use of fresh oranges and limes, Adelaide winked at her new friend. "And how can your future husband argue when the jersey has the Reynaud name on it?"

"There is a bit of competition among them. Have you noticed this?"

Adelaide nearly choked on her drink after the unexpected laugh. "I've noticed. You'd be surprised to know it was even worse when they were teenagers."

"Tell me." Erika peered over her shoulder where the brothers had sat a few minutes before. "It is safe. They are watching their games on television."

"When I first met Dempsey's brothers, I was thirteen." It was a year after he'd been living with the Reynauds and she'd been so excited that he'd invited her to his fourteenth birthday party. The day had been a disaster for many reasons, mostly because she'd realized that her friend had become someone else since leaving

St. Roch Avenue. "And they knew I was Dempsey's friend, so they decided to vie for my attention."

"Because when you have a sibling, you enjoy irritating them. Trust me, I understand that part a little too well."

As an only child, Adelaide hadn't. She wished she'd understood because she'd handled the attention all wrong.

"One of them decided they should have a race to see who was fastest. On that particular day, fastest was synonymous with best."

"I would bet Gervais won because he was eldest." Erika sipped her drink, adjusting her blue-and-white sundress around her legs as she shifted to her side.

"Well, he would have, except Dempsey tripped him." She'd been so disappointed he'd cheated that she'd failed to see the significance of him needing to win for her. At least, that was what she'd decided it meant later.

"Of course he did. You were *his* friend." She stirred the ice in her glass with the red straw and waved over a maid who had emerged from the house to pick up the dishes from their dessert. "May we have some waters?" she asked the server, passing off her glass. "And the men are in Gervais's study. I believe he keeps brandy in there, but will you see if they need anything?"

The woman nodded before disappearing into the house.

"I didn't really understand how competitive they were at the time. I just thought it meant Dempsey had turned into a bully and I spent the party being kind to Gervais."

Erika laughed. "So he won after all." Her blue eyes sparkled. "What a clever clan we are marrying into,

Adelaide." She reached to squeeze her hand. "I'm so glad I will have a new sister here."

Adelaide swallowed, her throat and eyes suddenly burning. Tricking nice people did not sit well with her. She blinked fast.

"I've never had a sister." She cleared her throat, grateful for the maid's return so she could accept a fresh glass of sparkling water with lime. "Let's not be competitive, though," she added.

"Deal." Erika clinked her water glass with Adelaide's. "Now, will you order me some of your earrings? And whatever else I need to be a stylish sports fan?"

"Of course." Flattered, Adelaide wondered if she would still want the items once her engagement was broken. "Thank you."

"But I'll need some things in blue and white, too, in addition to the Hurricanes gear."

"Blue and white?" Puzzled, she turned to see Gervais and Dempsey headed down the steps from an outdoor deck on an upper story.

"Some days I'll have to root for Jean-Pierre's team, of course. He *is* family." She pantomimed zipping her lips and throwing away the key.

The princess was a firecracker in couture clothes. It made Adelaide happy for Gervais, who seemed as if he could use more fun in his life. But as they said their good-nights and walked back across the landscaped properties separating their homes, she couldn't help a hollow feeling in her chest.

"Thank you for spending time with my family." Dempsey slid an arm around her waist as they passed a line of Italian cypress trees and rounded a courtyard with a fountain at the center.

"You don't have to thank me. I had fun." She held her hand out as they neared the fountain so she could feel a hint of the cool spray drifting on the breeze.

"Did you?" He halted their steps on the gray cobblestones and tipped her chin up. "You look troubled."

She took comfort in his concern. "Erika was so kind to me. It feels wrong to deceive them about us." She searched his expression for clues to what he was thinking.

"An unfortunate necessity," he admitted, his handsome face revealing nothing while his hands smoothed down her back in a reassuring rub. "What do you think of Erika?"

"I like her. She's witty and sharp. I think she will liven up Gervais's world, and I bet she'll be a fabulous mother."

"That's good. He deserves to be happy." Palming the small of her back, he turned her toward his house again.

"Why? What do *you* think of her?" She knew Dempsey well enough to understand when he wasn't saying everything on his mind.

"I didn't get to speak with her one-on-one the way you did, but I trust your judgment. I researched her when Gervais announced the engagement, and her family—for all that she's royalty—has come close to bankruptcy in the past. So I wondered—"

"That's a horrible thought." Defensiveness surged at the insult to their lovely hostess. "And incredibly cynical."

"My grandfather taught us to be wary of fortune hunters from an early age." He kept to the cobblestone path until they reached his driveway. "Said he worked too hard building the company to have it torn apart by that kind of infighting."

"So is it safe to assume your brothers and grand-father are all reviewing my financial information this week?" She didn't like the idea of being held up to scrutiny for a fake engagement. She quickened her step as they neared the front door. "Because if a foreign princess rouses suspicion of gold digging, I can only imagine what the Reynauds think of a struggling artist from your old neighborhood."

"No one questions our relationship when we've been friends for more than half my lifetime." He circled around so he could hold the door open for her. "Every single member of my family knows you're important to me."

Some of the frustration eased out of her at the reassurance. She was important to him. But would she remain that way once she was no longer his fiancée?

A ball of panic bounced through her at the thought, but now they were inside and Dempsey's golden-brown eyes were already alight with desire as he stared down at her in the foyer.

"All through dinner, I was thinking about the moment when that door would close behind us." He crossed the polished Italian marble floor to eliminate the distance between them. "You know what else I was thinking about?"

"No." Her heartbeat did a crazy dance, and she was all too willing to let go of her doubts and worries about the future. This time with Dempsey was precious. A chance she'd been awaiting for half a lifetime.

Oh, what this man could do to her. With his hands. His sinful lips. The powerful thrust of his hips. He was better than any fantasy she'd dreamed up in the days when she'd had a crush on him.

"I was obsessed with this." Reaching behind her, he hooked a finger in the loop of the tie for her dress's halter top. "Do you have any idea how provocative it is to wear an outfit that allows a man to get you naked with a single tug on a lace?"

Her skin tightened like shrink-wrap.

"I hadn't known." Her neck tingled where his knuckles grazed it. "But now that I do, I will put the knowledge to work the next time I want you thinking about me."

Keeping his finger threaded through the loop, he didn't pull it free, but simply palmed her bare back and drew her closer.

"I'm thinking about you lately, no matter what you're wearing." He breathed the words in the hollow under her ear, right before he kissed her and then licked a trail across her most vulnerable places as he headed lower toward her shoulder.

The rasp of his jaw was a gentle abrasion on her skin, a sexy contrast to the wet heat of his lips and his tongue. She liked knowing that she was on his mind as much as he lingered in hers. Against all reason, she wanted to stay there.

"Are we alone in the house?" she asked, an idea coming to mind to help her stay in Dempsey's thoughts.

With only three more weeks of working as his assistant remaining, she wanted to fill his home with memories of her. Of them.

"Absolutely." He lifted his head from his task, eyes flaming with heat. "Why? Afraid of being an exhibitionist?" He tugged on the tie to the halter top of her dress.

"I'd prefer tonight to be for your eyes only," she admitted, clutching the dress to her breasts before it could fall. "And actually, the reason I wore this dress was just in case dinner by the pool turned into a pool party."

She let go of the fabric, and it fell away. She wore a simple strapless red bikini beneath.

If Dempsey was disappointed she wasn't naked under her clothes, he sure didn't show it. In fact, he stared at her body in a way that felt deliciously flattering.

"Damn." He whistled softly as he slid a finger beneath the tie in the center of the bandeau top. "You mean I could have been watching you cavort around the pool in this?"

"It's not too late for a swim." She backed up a step and then another. "We could head outside—" she clutched the knot between her breasts and tugged it "—and skinny-dip."

Dempsey made a strangled sound as he came after her. She pivoted on her toes and raced through the kitchen and toward the back door with the hottest man she'd ever met on her heels.

Sprinting through the rear of the house, she found one of the French doors leading out to the pool. Only the underwater light illuminated the surface, although the grounds were decorated with low-wattage bulbs around the trees and bushes. The pool was well hidden from any prying eyes on the other side of the lake, the landscaping planted to provide natural privacy.

Adelaide slipped off her shoes and jumped in wearing only her bikini bottoms. Dempsey surprised her by diving in a moment after her wearing...nothing.

Her breath caught as the low lights reflected off his impressive frame. Strong thighs. Powerful shoulders. A butt that had no business being so appealing. And then a splash engulfed her and she had no more time to admire the man swimming across the pool toward her.

She made a halfhearted effort to get away because, of course, she couldn't wait to be captured.

When she felt a hand wrap around her ankle and drag her back through the water she welcomed the heat of his touch.

"That's not skinny-dipping," he accused, seizing her hips and dragging her bikini bottoms off before she could protest.

He flung them onto the deck with a wet splash, then backed her against a wall in the shallow end. Despite the slight chill of the water, his body was like an inferno against hers. He wrapped her in his arms, warming her, his erection trapped against her belly as he kissed her deeply. Thoroughly.

She got so lost in him she didn't know how long they stayed there, hands gliding over slick skin, tongues tangling as they moved together. She watched, fascinated with the way their bodies looked beside one another, his muscles so impressive in the moonlight.

"I want you inside me." She shifted her hips to stroke him with one hand as she circled his waist with her leg. "Please."

"I don't have any protection out here," he said in her ear, nibbling her earlobe and driving her mad with need.

She bit her lip against the hunger, already so close to release. She could just let go and enjoy the sensations he could pull from her so easily with his talented hands. But she wanted to hold out for having him deep inside her.

"Let's go in," she pleaded, the hollow ache almost painful.

Dempsey lifted her into his arms and climbed the built-in stairs while water sluiced off them. He must look like Poseidon, rising from the depths, but she was too busy kissing him to see for herself. He paused near a deck box and withdrew two prewarmed towels, laying both of them on her as he carried her against his chest.

"I can walk." She pulled back as he edged sideways through the open French door. "You can let me down."

"And risk having you run?" He nipped her ear. "I already caught my prize. I'm not letting go now."

He bypassed the main staircase for the narrow steps up from a butler's kitchen, probably because the thick rubber treads provided traction when they were still dripping wet.

"You're crazy if you think I'd run now." She delved her fingers into his wet hair and brought his lips to hers. "I keep thinking that I must have been dreaming last night and that sex couldn't have been as incredible as I remember. I want to see for myself. Again."

"I like a challenge." He angled into his bedroom and fell onto the bed with her, taking her weight on him as they rolled. Together. "Why don't you keep track of how many times I make you scream my name tonight?"

She might have laughed or teased him about that, but his hand was already between her legs, the heel of his palm pressing where she needed him most.

Desire shot through her like a Roman candle, a bright burst that fired again and again. She clung to him, calling out his name just as he'd promised she would. It was only the beginning, she knew. She hadn't imagined how thoroughly Dempsey would dominate her world, her thoughts, her nights.

She had gladly given him her body. But as tender feelings crowded her chest for this man, Adelaide feared she was giving him much, much more.

Nine

Dempsey awoke to the scent of coffee just how he liked it, thick and strong. Still half-asleep, he reached for Adelaide, only to find her side of the bed cold.

Coming more awake, he realized she must be responsible for making the coffee. He would have to tell her that he would far rather wake up to her in his arms, but he did appreciate the gesture on a game day. It was still dark out, but he needed to get to the stadium for their home opener—a banner moment in a career-making season. He could feel it in his bones.

And damn, but he would have liked to share that good feeling with Adelaide.

Shoving out of bed, he shrugged on a clean T-shirt and boxers, thinking he could coax her back upstairs. Then again, the kitchen table would do just fine. Last night had been so wild. So unexpected. He picked up his pace to find her.

When he reached the kitchen, he found her making breakfast in his shirt, her legs bare and her hair restrained in a messy braid that rested on her shoulder. But as he got closer, he could tell something was off by the way she moved. She fried eggs at the stove, her movements jerky and fast.

"Everything okay?" he asked as he passed the walk-in pantry. He might have lost his ability to read her more subtle emotions, but he'd have to be blind not to correctly interpret anger.

"No." She pulled down two plates from a cupboard and slid the eggs onto them. "I got up early because of a notification on my phone. I keep alerts on various buzzwords in the media as they pertain to you and the team." She pointed toward the kitchen table. "Have a seat and check out the morning paper."

Worry stabbed him hard in the gut as he headed toward the table.

"Is Marcus back in trouble?" He'd sprung the kid from jail on good faith, offering him a job helping Evan with some work for the Brighter NOLA foundation. Dempsey needed extra hands for a renovation project on a building that would house a local recreation center for the kids.

"No. Not this week anyway." Her clipped response gave nothing away as she retrieved silverware and linen napkins from a sideboard near the breakfast bar.

"Hurricanes Coach Muzzles Stormy Girlfriends." He read the headline aloud from the social section's front page. "Old news, right? Did she offer anything different than the rumors that have been around for years—that I rely on confidentiality agreements for some of my personal relationships?"

Was this what had Adelaide so riled? They'd seen worse and weathered it in the past.

"No." She put his eggs down on the table and tugged out a chair to sit across from him. "But nice timing on a game day, isn't it?"

"Whoa." He reached for her, bracketing her shoulders with his hands. "What am I missing? Why is this so upsetting?"

"Why?" Adelaide's eyes widened. "Because for all she knows we really *are* getting married. And what kind of evil witch does that to someone who is newly engaged?"

She blinked fast, emotions swirling through her eyes quicker than he could register them.

"Someone selfish." He shrugged, still not sure he saw what the big deal was, although he knew better than to say as much. "Someone who doesn't give any thought to who she hurts to get her own way. I'll bet you any money she wants to tout a new contract or sponsor or has some kind of promotional angle—"

He let go of her to turn the paper toward him so he could read the story.

"She has a part in a new action-adventure film," Addy admitted. "She mentions it toward the end."

"You see? Self-centered and trying to scam off the Hurricanes' publicity when a lot of people are paying attention to the team." He kissed Adelaide's cheek and pulled her to him again, holding her close, savoring the feel of her wearing precious little under that T-shirt. "C'mon. Let's have this breakfast you made. It smells fantastic."

"It's just eggs," she grumbled. Then her lips curled upward a bit. "Although I did make use of the cayenne pepper, which is why you like the scent, you crazy Cajun."

She hadn't called him that in a long time. Memories of their past—her friendship and unswerving loyalty—stirred along with it. Reminding him he didn't want to hurt her. She'd made him breakfast long ago when there'd been no food at his place. Eggs were a cheap meal, and even though he had access to the most exotic foods in the world, there was nothing he'd rather share with her right now than the eggs she'd cooked for him herself.

Taking care of him.

"Some spice in life is a good thing." He tugged her back and kissed her harder, more comfortable thinking about the chemistry they shared than that other, deeper connection. "And speaking of which, last night was incredible."

"I had fun, too." She shot him a flirtatious look as she took her seat at the table. "I'm glad you're not upset about the article in the paper—even if I'm still steaming a little."

He flipped it over and shoved it away.

"Not at all." He tucked her chair in and then sat beside her. "Valentina is annoying but predictable. I'm only upset for you."

He took a few bites before he noticed Addy had gone quiet. Glancing up, he noticed her studying him.

"Is that a plus when you're dating?" she asked, carefully cutting a piece of her egg and sliding it onto her toast. "Predictability trumps selfish and annoying?"

And just like that, he stood alone in a minefield with no foreseeable path out.

"You must know that I've deliberately simplified my

personal life these past few years in order to focus on my career." He set down his fork, realizing he should have paid more attention to the nuances of this conversation.

It wasn't about the article in the paper. Or about a potential distraction for him on his season opener.

Adelaide was more than a *little* angry about Valentina.

"You want simple *and* predictable." She tapped the heavy band of her engagement ring on the table. "It's strange that you opted to stage a relationship with me right now since it's both complicated and unexpected."

Didn't she understand that she was nothing like other women he'd been with? He wouldn't trade this time with her for anything.

"But you're not like other women, Addy. I trust you not to turn our private affairs into a three-ring circus for your own ends." He wanted to salvage a good day. He wanted to get back to where they were yesterday, when they'd had dinner with family and then driven each other wild all night long.

"You trust me to keep this simple and be predictable, too." She shook her head, a smile that was the opposite of happy twisting her lips. She shot out of her chair. "Unbelievable how the Reynaud arrogance has no bounds."

"Wait a minute." He stood as well, scrambling to follow her, to understand how he'd hurt her when that was the last thing he'd intended.

"No." The word was sharp. A short warning that her emotions were seething close to the surface.

He could see it in her face. In her eyes.

"Addy, please. Let me explain."

"No." She shook her head, her braid unraveling as she moved, since she hadn't bothered to wrap a tie around the end. "I'm going to drive separately to the stadium. And when I get there, I will be an excellent assistant, as I've always been. I'll even keep the ring on my finger. But don't ask me to pretend with you, Dempsey. Not today."

For a moment, he felt stunned, as if she'd kicked him in the solar plexus.

"What do you mean? You can't end our agreement—"

"Please." She held a hand up to stop that line of discussion. "I'm not ending anything except this conversation. But I'm asking you—don't put me on the spot today, okay? I might not be as predictable as you'd like to think."

Members of the media rushed onto the field after the Hurricanes won 21–17 in their home opener against the defending Super Bowl champs. Adelaide watched from the sidelines, a rare spot for her, since her duties were more behind-the-scenes. But after her exchange with Dempsey over breakfast that morning, she had been reminded that in three more weeks, she would no longer have a role on the team. She might never have the chance to witness a game from this vantage point again.

Rap music blared from the speakers in the stands, adding to the celebratory mood. Fans whooped it up with one another. While some headed out to the parking lots to party or drive home, many hardcore followers remained in the stands, getting as close to the field as ushers would allow.

A photographer with a camera and a big plastic sound shield shuffled past her, his lens trained on Dempsey where he shook hands with the opposing team's coach. A coach who did not look happy. The guy's face was still red after a screaming match with a ref about a pass-interference call that had not happened.

But the Hurricanes' game one was in the books. Dempsey and his team were off to the start he'd wanted for this season, the start that meant so much to him. Logically, she understood why. He'd always felt like an outsider in the Reynaud family, working relentlessly to prove he belonged, that his father had not made a mistake in plucking him out of that crappy apartment down the street from hers.

Yet, she couldn't help but think that if St. Roch Avenue wasn't good enough for him, then she wasn't good enough for him either. He'd dated one beautiful woman after another for years, never looking at Adelaide twice until she tried to quit. Hearing his easy defense of Valentina this morning had brought that hurt to the surface. When Adelaide's time with Dempsey was through, he'd go right back to women who were simple, predictable and from a much different world than hers.

She had no illusions about his ability to move on. She'd seen him do that plenty of times. But she seriously doubted hers.

Heading for the door that led into the medical staff's offices and bypassed the locker-room area, Adelaide picked up her pace when she saw a female reporter charging toward her, a cameraman in tow. Seriously?

The press on the field were normally big-time sports reporters, not from the social pages.

"Adelaide!" the woman called. "Excuse—"

Arriving at the door, Adelaide hauled it open and

risked a glance back to see what had happened to her follower.

Henri Reynaud, the Hurricanes' quarterback and Dempsey's younger brother, had planted himself between Adelaide and the woman. Addy's heart fluttered a bit. Not that she thought Henri was Mr. Dreamy the way the rest of the female fans did. But because Dempsey's brothers had made her feel as though she mattered this week. Gervais by inviting her to dinner. Henri by running interference.

Seeing how she might have been accepted into their world made her chest ache for the things she wasn't going to have with Dempsey. She would be walking away from so much more than a job in three weeks. So why was she spending this window of time second-guessing herself—and Dempsey—every time she turned around? Why couldn't she just enjoy the moment?

Maybe she needed to stop worrying about the future. Starting tonight, she wasn't going to look beyond three weeks from now.

She would save up her memories of being the woman who got to be on his arm and in his bed. The memories of being part of a family. They wouldn't be enough, but if they were all she would ever have of him, she would make each moment count.

Dempsey drove the fastest street-legal BMW produced to date, but it didn't get him out of downtown any quicker after the game.

Had he ever felt so uneasy after a win?

He switched lanes to pass a slow-moving car, his G-Power M5 Beemer more than ready to launch into overdrive at the earliest opportunity. Too bad the ribbon of brake lights ahead meant he only succeeded in hurtling headlong from one stop-and-go lane to the next.

He'd asked the public relations coordinator if she'd seen Adelaide, but Carole didn't know where his fiancée had gone after the game. Now he gave in and phoned Evan. Hitting the speed-dial icon on the dashboard, he listened to Evan's line ring via Bluetooth.

"Hey, Coach. What's up?" Evan had lost his roster spot due to injury, but unlike most guys who'd been in the league for any length of time, he hadn't been in a hurry to rehab and look for a new team in the spring. He understood well the hazards of being a player and had been content to simply stick around the team.

Dempsey had asked him about returning to school for sports medicine and coming aboard as a trainer, but Evan called himself a "simple guy with simple needs," insisting he liked driving the Land Rover.

"Just checking to see if you're taking good care of my future wife." The comment didn't roll off his tongue the way he thought it would.

His wife.

The idea made his chest go tight and he wasn't quite sure why.

"She's teaching me about the garment business at the moment. Just a sec." Clearly holding his hand over the phone, Evan spoke to someone else—Adelaide, presumably. But a man's voice came through in the background, too. Then Evan came back on the line. "We're just finishing up a tour of a manufacturing facility. She's hoping that with some customization it might work out for producing her apparel line."

Her apparel line. Dempsey ground his teeth together, biting back a retort.

Apparently he hadn't made any headway yet convincing her to stay with the Hurricanes—with him—for the rest of the season. But then, he'd spent all his time romancing her after being surprised by an attraction he hadn't accounted for.

He needed to get their relationship back on track.

"I'd like to surprise her with dinner," he improvised, although maybe that wasn't a bad idea. "Are you bringing her home soon?"

Dinner aside, he just wanted to know when he would see Adelaide. She hadn't picked up her phone or answered his text after the game.

But then, she obviously took her start-up business more seriously than him.

"Definitely," Evan returned. "I think she's finishing up her meeting with the Realtor now. We're about half an hour away."

"Good deal. Thanks." Disconnecting the call, Dempsey pulled into the driveway of his house.

The outdoor lights were on, along with a few indoor ones. He had everything on timers, and he'd increased the periods when the grounds were lit, wanting to make the place as hospitable as he could for Adelaide.

Had her decision to tour a manufacturing facility been made this morning, spurred by her frustration regarding Valentina? Or had Addy been quietly taking care of her own business concerns all week, in spite of their agreement that she'd devote her time to the Hurricanes?

To him. This upset him far more than it should have.

His phone rang after he'd parked the BMW and headed into the house. Juggling his keys in one hand, he didn't check the caller ID before he thumbed the answer switch.

"Reynaud." He didn't need team problems. He had enough personal ones, since Addy was giving him the runaround.

"Hey, bro." The voice of his youngest brother came through the airwaves. "Congrats on the win."

"You, too, Jean-Pierre. I saw you put up some hellacious stats today." Dempsey hadn't been able to watch any film highlights on the way home, since he'd had to drive himself, but he'd checked for updates on the other one o'clock games before he left the stadium.

"Perfect football weather in New York. The ball sailed right where I wanted it to all day." The youngest Reynaud was the starting quarterback for the New York Gladiators and currently the only member of the family who wasn't a part of the Hurricanes organization. "Tomorrow's practice is light. I could head down there afterward if you think we need a powwow about Gramps."

"That'd be good. I think it's going to take all four of us to figure out how to approach him." Dempsey stepped inside the house, which was too quiet without Adelaide there.

Already, all his best memories in this place were with her.

Undressing her in the foyer. Chasing her out to the pool. Carrying her up to his bed.

"He's getting worse?" Jean-Pierre asked, pulling Dempsey's thoughts away from Addy.

"He thought I was Dad at a fund-raiser event the other night. Implied I needed to be careful my wife didn't find out about the woman on my arm."

On the other end, Jean-Pierre let loose a string of soft curses.

"That sucks," he finally said, summing it up well. "I'll be off the practice field by noon. I can probably be at the house by four." A perk of being in New York was that private planes were plentiful. Jean-Pierre didn't come home often, but he could make the trip in a hurry when he needed to.

"Sounds good. We practice at noon, but I'll make sure we finish up in time. See you then." Disconnecting the call, he knew he'd have to go in early to meet with his assistant coaches and watch game film.

Hell, he'd be watching game film tonight, too. But first, he would order dinner for him and Adelaide. Do something nice for her to make up for all the things he'd said wrong over breakfast. Maybe then he would be able to confront her about that trip to see a potential manufacturing facility. The capital investment for a start-up business would compromise her operating costs. She had to know that.

Her role with the Hurricanes aside, it was too soon for her business to launch in that kind of direction. Small growth was wiser. Subcontracting the manufacturing would give her more cushion for expenditures. As much as he understood she didn't want him interfering with this company she wanted to build, he simply couldn't let her fail.

Ah, hell, who was he kidding? He might be a selfish bastard, but he couldn't ignore the truth.

He didn't want her to leave.

Ten

"No one could hold a grudge after that dinner." Adelaide swirled a strawberry through a warm chocolate sauce served in a melting pot over an open flame. "I might have to pick fights with you more often if this is the aftermath."

Dempsey had ordered an exquisite meal to be catered for them, and considering it must have been on short notice, the food was outrageously delicious. Her scallops had been prepared in a kind of sauce that took them from good to transcendent. The grilled vegetables were hot and tender, perfectly seasoned. But the dessert of exotic fondues was inspired.

She couldn't get enough of the chocolate sauce with a hint of raspberry liqueur.

"Are you sure?" Dempsey asked her, reaching under the mammoth dining room table to skim a touch along her knee. "I know you were upset this morning."

They were seated diagonally from one another—he was at the head of the table and she was to his right. The table was a chunky dark wood handcrafted in Mexico, the coarse finish making the piece all the more masculine and right for the house. Adelaide liked all the decor even if—in her fanciful imaginings—she pictured what she would do if she lived here. She'd put a vase of birds of paradise on the table, for one thing. Bright splashes of color to warm up this cool, controlled world.

"I was upset," she admitted. "But as I stood on the sidelines today, it occurred to me that I don't want to spoil this time with you. Working for you has been an incredible opportunity and I will miss it... I have to confess I will miss working with you, as well. Seeing you."

"Tell me what else you'll miss." He pulled her bare foot into his lap and massaged the arch.

"That feels amazing." She settled deeper into the red leather cushion on her high-backed wooden chair. Popping a raspberry into her mouth, she told herself she could have one more chocolate treat if she ate two plain berries.

Those were actually delicious as well, the juicy fruit almost tart after the sweetness of the chocolate.

"Turn your chair and I can do both feet." He nodded toward the side that needed shifting. And sure enough, pivoting toward him made it more comfortable to give him her other foot, too.

His thumbs stroked up the centers, over and over.

"What else will I miss?" She repeated the question to remind herself what he'd asked her before she slipped into a foot-massage-induced trance. "Always having a seat for the big games. The scent of barbecue in the

parking lot from the tailgaters before home games. Seeing the young players at training camp and watching
them horseplay because they're overgrown kids."

He was quiet for so long she wondered what he was
thinking.

But hadn't she promised herself to simply enjoy this
time with him? To make the most of every day of these
next few weeks?

"I'll bet chocolate sauce would taste good on you,"
she observed lightly, dragging the warm pot closer.

That captured Dempsey's attention completely. He
slowed the foot massage.

"The catering staff is still here," he reminded her,
peering over his shoulder toward the kitchen.

They hadn't seen anyone since dessert was brought
out, but two servers waited behind the scenes to clear
their dishes and put away the leftovers.

"I'll bet they won't mind billing you for a fondue pot
if I bring it upstairs with me."

Releasing her feet, he pushed back from the table in
a hurry. He took the sauce from her, securing it under
one arm, and then pulled out her chair to give her more
room to stand.

A gentleman.

"No." He put a hand on her back and guided her
away from the staircase. "Your room this time. You've
got that big tub for afterward, and I think we're going
to need it."

A thrill shot through her. Something about this new
pact she'd made with herself—to live in the moment and
store up these memories—made her bolder. More willing to take chances with him and see what happened.

He was already prepared to walk away from their

engagement in three more weeks, so why not at least ask for the things she wanted in a way she never had before? Chocolate sauce all over Dempsey... It was the stuff of fantasies.

Except once they closed the door to her bedroom, he set her decadent treat on the glass top of a double dresser, and then spun her in his arms. A whirlwind of raw masculinity, he hauled her up in his arms and carried her toward the large bathroom, his eyes blazing with undeniable heat.

"Dessert?" she asked, walking her fingers up his chest, her breathing unsteady at the feel of his arms around her.

"It's going to have to wait," he growled. "If you wanted slow and sweet, you shouldn't have looked at me like that over the dinner table."

A laugh burst free, but it turned into a moan as he settled her on the vanity countertop and stepped between her legs.

"I have no idea what you're talking about," she teased, her mouth going dry as he bunched up the fabric of her skirt and snapped the band on her panties with a quick tug.

Fire roared over her skin.

"The look you gave me?" He passed her a condom a second before he dropped his pants. "It said you wanted me right here." He slid a finger inside her.

The condom fell from her fingers. She wound her arms around his neck, needing more of him. All of him. Her heartbeat pounded so fiercely she felt light-headed. She pressed her breasts to his chest, doing her best to shrug out of the bodice. He must have retrieved the condom because she could feel the graze of his knuckles against her while he rolled it into place.

And then he was deep inside her.

His thrusts were hard, fast, and she loved every second of being with him. She held on tight, meeting his movements with her own as she caught glimpses of them moving together reflected in the mirrors all around. His powerful shoulders all but hid her from view from the back. But from the side, she saw her head thrown back, her spine arched to lift her breasts high. He ravished them thoroughly, one hand palming the back of her scalp while the other guided her hip to his.

Again and again.

"Let me watch you, Addy," he whispered in her ear, his breath harsh. "Come for me."

And she did.

Pleasure burst through her with fiery sparks, one after the other. He followed her, muscles flexing everywhere as he joined her in that hurtle over the edge.

His hand swept over her back, holding her close, his forehead falling against hers. She clutched at the fabric of his shirt, amazed that he was still half-dressed.

When she caught her breath, she pulled back, looking up at him. She wasn't sure what she expected—a smile, perhaps, for the crazy bathroom sink encounter. But she hadn't expected the seriousness in his eyes. Or the tenderness.

There was a connection there. A moment of recognition that sex hadn't been just about fun and pleasure. Something bigger was happening. She felt it, as much as she didn't want to. Did he?

Maybe he did. Because just then he blinked. But the

moment had passed. The look had vanished. His expression was now carefully shuttered.

She knew it would be wisest, safest, to pretend that moment had never happened. To keep things light and happy and work on stockpiling those memories before she left to start over—a new career, a new life.

But it took every ounce of willpower she possessed to simply call up a smile.

"Where did that come from?" She walked her hands down the front of his chest, admiring his strength.

His beautiful body.

"I missed you today," he said simply. "It didn't feel right, starting our day off arguing." He shifted positions and helped her down from the counter.

They cleaned up and she followed him into the bedroom. She sprawled on the California king–size mattress beside him, pulling pins out of her hair and setting them on the carved wood nightstand.

"Well, I sure don't feel like arguing after that amazing meal and the…rest." She laid her head on his chest and listened to his heartbeat.

In some ways, she would miss these moments even more than the torrid, tear-your-clothes-off encounters. A swell of emotions filled her, and she couldn't resist kissing the hard, muscular plane.

This, right now, was her best memory so far. Being cradled in his arms and breathing in the pine scent of his soap.

"All day it was on my mind, how much I wanted to get home and fix things with you." He stroked fingers through her hair.

That moment of connection in the bathroom? Could he feel it even now?

But she knew him well. Knew that he'd pushed away his other lovers once they started to get too close. Expect more from him. As his friend, she wouldn't follow that same path. There had to be some way to salvage at least their friendship when this was all over.

"I have the perfect stress reliever that will make you feel better about your day." She sat up on the bed, letting her hair fall over her shoulder now that she'd taken it all down.

Light spilled in from the bathroom, casting them in shadows. They'd eaten dinner late after the game and she knew he'd have to watch his game film soon.

"My stress faded as soon as I got you alone." His wicked grin made her heart do somersaults.

"Take off your shirt and turn over," she commanded, already plunging her fingers under the hem of his T-shirt.

"Yes, ma'am," he drawled, his eyes lighting with warmth again as he dragged the cotton up and over his head.

"You know how they say chocolate is good for the soul?" She retrieved the dessert sauce and dipped a finger in the warm liquid.

"I think it's books that are good for the soul." He propped his head on a pillow, his elbows out.

"Well, chocolate is good for mine." She traced the center of his spine with her finger, painting a line of deliciousness and then following it with her tongue. "But I think you're going to like this, too."

An hour later, she'd proved chocolate was good for everyone. Dempsey had bathed her afterward, whispering sweet words in her ear while he washed her hair.

She felt sated and boneless by the time he slipped

from her bed to put in the necessary hours at his job. She hated that he couldn't sleep with her all night, but in some ways, she wondered if it was for the best. She could tell herself that he had to work to do, and maybe that would make the hole he'd left in her heart a little more bearable.

Dempsey was still thinking about Adelaide the next day when he arrived at Gervais's house to meet with his brothers. Physically, he stood outside the downstairs media room and made himself a drink at the small liquor cabinet in the den. But mentally, his brain still played over and over the events of the night before.

Mostly, he thought back to that electric shock he'd felt when he'd looked into her eyes and the earth shifted. He couldn't write off that moment when he'd never experienced if before with any other woman. He had feelings for Adelaide. And that was going to complicate things in more ways than he could imagine.

"Dude." Jean-Pierre strode into the den behind him. "You're getting old when that passes for a drink. I come to town once in a blue moon. You can do better than—" he held up the bottle to read it "—coconut water? You'd better turn in your man card."

"I get the last laugh when I live longer." Dempsey set down his drink to give his brother a light punch in the stomach, a favored family greeting that their grandfather had started when they were kids.

Jean-Pierre returned with a one-two combination that—while still mostly for show—made Dempsey grateful he maintained a rigorous ab workout. Of all his brothers, he was closest to Jean-Pierre, making him the only one in the family he still punched.

"You'll be a hundred and five and wishing you'd had more fun in your life," Jean-Pierre joked, going straight for the scotch decanted into cut crystal. "I've got transportation home tonight, so I don't mind if I crack open the stash Gervais likes to hide at the back of the cabinet."

"You have no idea where I hide my real stash." Gervais stalked out of the media room, where game film seemed to run on a continuous loop during the regular season. "I leave the swill out when I know the hard drinkers are coming."

Gervais hugged their brother.

"Did someone say swill?" Henri ambled out of the media room, where he must have been already watching film with Gervais. "Sounds like my kind of night—as long as I don't have to drink with any holier-than-thou New York players."

Even as he said it, he one-arm hugged Jean-Pierre. The two of them were more competitive with the rest of the world than each other. It had always made Dempsey a little sick inside to see them go up against one another on the field, since he genuinely wanted both of them to win. They were incredibly gifted athletes who, in a league full of gifted athletes, walked on a whole different plane.

"Sit," Gervais ordered them. "You are busy and it's rare we're all together. I'd like to deal with the issue at hand first so we can relax over dinner."

"Relax?" Jean-Pierre lounged sideways in one of the big leather club chairs arranged around the fireplace in the den. "Who can relax while Gramps is struggling to remember his own grandsons?"

The mood shifted as they each gravitated toward the

spots they'd always taken in the room from the time they were kids and Theo would call them in for talks. Or, more often, when they had run of the house because their father was on an extended "business trip" that was code for a vacation with his latest woman.

When the house had still belonged to Theo and Alessandra, most of the rooms had been fussy and full of interior-decorator additions—elaborate crystal light fixtures that hung so low the brothers broke something every time they threw a ball in the house. Or three-dimensional wall art that spanned whole walls and would scrape the skin off an arm if they tackled and pushed each other into it.

The den had always been male terrain.

Now Dempsey got them up to speed on his exchange with Leon at the Brighter NOLA fund-raiser.

Silence followed, each one of them ruminating on the possibility that Leon was in the early stages of dementia.

"You do take after Dad the most," Henri offered from his seat behind the desk, Italian leather shoes planted on the old blotter. He lifted a finger from his glass to point at Dempsey.

His shoulders tensed. Every muscle group in his arms and back contracted.

"Henri," Gervais warned.

"Seriously, he looks more like Dad. He has his walk, too. Grand-père might have been—"

"I am nothing like our father." He had to loosen his hold on the cut-crystal glass before he shattered it.

He'd done everything to distance himself from Theo from the moment he'd arrived in this house as a teen. He could count the number of drinks he took in a year

on one hand. As for women? He'd had contractual ar-
rangements with every single one but Adelaide, and the
time frames had never overlapped. There would never
be a surprise child of his who would be raised alone.
Separated from family.

"I know, man. But you've got the whole drama with
the model going on the same week you get engaged.
Maybe Leon just got a little muddled and—"

Dempsey was across the floor and knocking Henri's
feet off the desk before the sentence was done.

"Not. The. Same." Fury heated the words.

"Seriously?" Henri put his drink down. "Are we
going there? Because I'm not getting bounced off the
team for some bullshit argument in the den, but if I have
to pound you, I will."

Dempsey had more to say to that, since any pounding that needed doing would be meted out by him. But
Gervais clapped him on the shoulder.

"Henri just doesn't want to face the fact that Leon
isn't indestructible. Maybe give him a pass today." Gervais spoke calmly. Rationally.

And, probably, correctly.

No one wanted to think about their grandfather going
downhill. They all loved the old man.

"I would never cut you for an argument in the den."
Dempsey extended the olive branch. "But just so we're
clear, I could still kick your ass."

"Not responding." Henri returned his feet to the desk.
"So no one else thinks it could have been a momentary
lapse for Leon? One mistake and he's an Alzheimer's
patient?"

"It's not just one. There were signs this summer, too,"
Gervais reminded them. "He was going to see his doctor

about it and he said it was a thyroid condition. If that's the case, he needs to get his meds checked. But at this point, we might need to consider the idea that he's not really taking care of himself."

Dempsey drained his water, trying to focus on the conversation and let go of the dig about his overlapping affairs. Not that Henri had worded it that way, but damn. He'd worked so hard to distance himself from his father's philandering ways. Did his brothers still see him as some kind of playboy type?

Clearly they had no idea how far gone he was over Adelaide. He couldn't even imagine letting her go at the end of their engagement. By now he wasn't even as concerned about replacing her as his assistant.

He couldn't replace her in his bed. Or if he was honest with himself, his heart. She made him laugh. She understood his lifestyle and the huge demands of his job. She even made it easier for him to be around his family. That dinner with Gervais and Erika had been one of the most stress-free times he'd ever had with one of his brothers as an adult, perhaps because he wasn't reading slights into the conversation the way he did today with Henri.

"Dempsey?" Jean-Pierre's voice knifed through his thoughts. "What do you think we should do?"

"Spend as much time with him as we can." It was all he knew how to do with people who weren't staying in his life forever. He knew it was a crap plan even as he proposed it, but he hadn't figured out anything better for keeping Addy around either.

Throughout the meal he shared with his brothers, he kept coming back to that point. He had no plan for convincing Adelaide to stay. He respected her for wanting to build her own business and he couldn't in good conscience prevent it from happening for his own self-ish ends. He had to find a way to help her that would be an offer she couldn't refuse. A way to help her that wouldn't make her feel as if he was taking the power out of her hands.

He understood that much about her.

But their time shared as a newly engaged couple had shown him how good they could be together, and he refused to walk away from that without giving the re-lationship more time. Every day he couldn't wait to be with her. Even sitting around with his brothers in a rare meal where they were all in the same place, Dempsey was still picturing that moment when he would head home and see Addy.

She made sense in his life and she always had.

He would make a case for extending their engage-ment. No, damn it. He would propose to her for real. They had been friends. They'd worked together. He counted on her.

Now? Their chemistry was off the charts and they brought each other a level of fulfillment that he'd never experienced before. Adelaide was a smart woman. She would understand why they worked together.

She had to.

Eleven

"I think it's a great space, Adelaide." Her mother walked through the riverside manufacturing facility that Adelaide could use for mass-producing knitwear. Della's purple flip-flops slapped along the concrete floor.

"The square footage for offices is nice, too." She headed toward the back of the building to show her mother. Her Realtor had opened the door for them as long as Adelaide would lock up behind them.

She was already subcontracting out a short run of shirts after her success with crowd funding, but the time had come to think bigger. And this space would be ideal, already containing a few machines she would refit for the kind of textile production she needed. She'd been approved for a small-business loan that would cover the cost of the building and her biggest start-up expenses, but it was still a big step and she wanted her mother's opinion.

Lately, it felt as though her life was on fast-forward, and while it was exciting to have so many new options open to her, a part of her wished she could just stop for a minute and be sure she was making the best decisions. Dempsey jumbled all her thoughts lately, the passion they shared so much different from her old crush. She wasn't sure if she trusted herself to move forward in any direction.

"What does Dempsey think about it?" Della asked, examining the floor-to-ceiling windows overlooking the Mississippi in the largest of the offices.

"He hasn't seen it yet." She hated to admit as much, but he'd been so dismissive of her dreams before, so ready to leap in and save her from her own mistakes, that she wasn't ready to share this with him.

Then again, maybe moving ahead with her business simply signaled an end to her time as Dempsey's fiancée and she wasn't sure if she was ready for it to be over.

Della's brows arched. "Too busy to make time for my girl's work?"

"No. Nothing like that." She closed her eyes, hating the lies. And would it really matter if she told her mother the truth? Della Thibodeaux didn't exactly have a history of running to the press with gossip. "He didn't want me to tell anyone, but the engagement is just for show. I did it to help him."

Or because he'd put her in a ridiculously awkward position, take your pick.

But she couldn't regret it after how close they'd grown. The only problem was, now that she'd seen how amazing it was to be with him—even better than she'd ever imagined—she had no idea how she'd ever go back to their old friendship.

"Just for show?" Della folded her arms, leaning into the window frame as she studied her daughter, deep concern in her eyes.

Sunlight spilled in all around her, catching the grays in her dark hair. Her mother was a beautiful woman and so wise, too. Addy couldn't deny being curious to hear her mother's opinion on the fake engagement. Would she tell Adelaide she was the most foolish woman ever?

"He announced it in public and made it difficult for me to argue it without humiliating him."

"Of course you didn't argue, because you've always wanted to make him happy." She strode closer and put her hands on Adelaide's shoulders, her heavy silver bracelets settling against Adelaide's collarbone. "And is it still for show now, after you've been living with him for almost two weeks?"

Her cheeks heated, which was silly because she was a grown-up and could live with whomever she wanted.

"I think I'm in love with him," she admitted, the words torn from her heart, since she knew that level of emotion was not reciprocated.

"Oh, sweetheart." Her mother opened her arms, gathered her close and squeezed tight. "Of course you do. At least one of you has admitted it."

Adelaide's eyes burned. Tears fell as she rested her head on her mother's shoulder. She didn't want her mother's pity for loving a man who didn't—

Wait. She stopped crying, her mother's words sinking in.

"What did you say?" Her thoughts caught up with her ears and she pulled back to look into her mom's hazel eyes, which were lighter than Adelaide's.

"You heard me." Della kissed her cheek and stepped

back. "You two were meant to be. You just needed the right time to come along. Why do you think he's thirty-one years old and dating fluff-headed women with more boobs than brains?"

Adelaide choked on a much-needed laugh. "Mom. That's not fair."

Even if, in her meaner moments, Adelaide might have been equally unkind in her thoughts. Mostly about Valentina.

"All I mean, daughter dear, is that he has never dated a woman seriously. I think it's because he's been waiting for the right woman. He's been waiting for you, my girl." She looped her arm around Adelaide's waist as they headed for the exit and shut off the lights.

Adelaide's yellow-diamond engagement ring caught the sun's rays, sending sparkles in every direction.

"That's such a mom thing to say." Still, it warmed her heart even if she knew Dempsey far better than her mother. "Does parenting come with a handbook of mom sayings to cheer up dejected daughters?"

She wanted to trust in her mother's words but she was scared to believe that Dempsey could care about her like that.

"Mothers know." She tipped her temple to Addy's, the scent of lemon verbena drifting up from her hair.

"Well, I'm not sure about the engagement or where that's going, but I'll tell him about this manufacturing space tonight. The Hurricanes play in Atlanta tomorrow and I'm going with him. After the game, we'll have some time together to talk and I'll see what he thinks." Or she hoped they would have time together.

Last Sunday, after their home opener, they'd had a nice dinner. But Dempsey had seemed distracted this week, ever since his dinner with his brothers. She knew he was worried about his grandfather, but it seemed as if he'd been busy every night since, only falling into bed with her at midnight and sleeping for a few hours.

He also made hot, toe-curling love to her until she couldn't see straight. She couldn't complain about that part. But she did wish she had more time with him, since it felt as though the clock was ticking down on their arrangement.

And no matter what her mother said to cheer her, Adelaide had seen no sign from Dempsey that he'd fallen in love.

"I'm dying to know where you're taking me." Adelaide glanced over at Dempsey sitting beside her in the limo he'd booked after the game. "I've never known you to be so mysterious."

When she'd checked into the hotel where the team was staying the night before, the concierge had given her a card from Dempsey, who had on-site duties at the Atlanta stadium when they'd landed. The card had invited her on a date to an undisclosed location after Sunday's one-o'clock game against Atlanta. A jaw-dropping Versace gown awaited her in their suite, burgundy lace with a plunging neckline that kept everything covered but—wow. The Louboutin sky-high heels that accompanied it were the most exotic footwear she'd ever slid on, the signature red sole dazzling her almost as much as the satin toes with hand-crafted embellishments.

If she looked down her crossed legs now, she could see the pretty toes peeping out from the handkerchief hem of the tulle skirting.

He folded her hand in his, the crisp white collar of his

shirt emphasizing his deep tan gained from spending every day on the practice field. "I owed you a date night. You were kind enough to be my date for the Brighter NOLA ball, so it seemed like you ought to have a night that was just for you."

His Tom Ford tuxedo was obviously custom tailored, since off-the-rack sizes never fit an athlete's body, and the black fabric skimmed his physique perfectly. The black silk-peaked lapels made her itch to run her hand up and down the material.

Later.

For now she just wanted to know where they were headed. She'd never seen Dempsey race out of a stadium so early. She hadn't even attended the game, taking her time to dress in the hotel, then taking the limo to the VIP pickup outside the stadium. Traffic had been slow at first, but it wasn't even six o'clock yet. Almost two hours before sunset.

"I'd be surprised if there are many restaurants out this way," she observed, peering out the windows as they drove toward Stone Mountain, winding through quieter roads.

It was early yet, but her invitation had mentioned a special "sunset dinner."

A mysterious smile played around his mouth. A mouth that had brought her such pleasure.

"There's a surprise first. I hope you're not too hungry."

"I think I'm too excited to be hungry." She felt the first flutter of nerves, because Dempsey looked so serious for a date night.

She wanted to ask him about that. About his grandfather's health. Maybe that was what had been bothering him all week. But just then, the limo came to a clearing in the trees and a flash of rainbow-colored silk fluttered through the sky.

"How beautiful!" She clutched his arm, pointing to a hot-air balloon being inflated on a nearby field.

At the same moment, the limo slowed and turned into the field, heading right toward the balloon.

She stilled.

"Don't tell me…" She turned toward him, and saw the first hint of a smile on his face. "Is this the surprise?"

"Only if you'd like it to be." He squeezed her hand.

She squealed, scarcely able to take her eyes off the huge balloon that looked as if it would burst into flames any moment from the blazing blasts that shot into the bottom, filling it with air. Or helium. Or whatever did that magic trick that made it go from half on the ground to a big ball in the sky.

"Yes!" She risked her lipstick by kissing him through a shocked laugh. "It's amazing! I've never seen anything like it."

"Here." He produced a satin drawstring bag as the car rolled to a stop and their driver came around to open the door. "Better wear these for now and save your pretty shoes for later."

Opening the sack, she pulled out a pair of silver ballet slippers. Just her size.

"You thought of everything." She had to have him help her because she fumbled the shoes twice, distracted by the sight of yellow, blue, red and orange silk rising higher just outside the car.

"I would have tried to get us here earlier if I'd known you wanted to see this part." His warm hands tugged her shoes into place before he helped her out of the car. He reached back in the limo and withdrew a length of fuzzy mohair and cashmere that at first she thought was a blanket, but he unfurled it and laid it around her shoulders. A burgundy-colored pashmina fell around her. "The pilot said it will be cooler once we're up there."

A red carpet lined her path from the car door to the balloon basket. While the limo driver exchanged words with the crew that operated the balloon, Adelaide had a moment to catch her breath and take in the full extent of her surprise. Blasts of heat passed her shoulders in rhythmic waves each time the pilot pulled the cord to unleash flames into the air that kept the balloon filled.

"I just can't believe how huge it is up close." She'd seen hot-air balloons in the sky before and admired their beauty, but she'd never dreamed of riding in one. "And I can't imagine what made you think to do this tonight, but I'm so excited I feel…breathless."

He tucked her close to his side as they walked the carpeted path together. "The best part hasn't started. I hear it's incredible to go up in one of these things."

"You've never done this either?" That made it feel all the more special, that she could share a first with him. She felt like a medieval princess, traipsing through the countryside in her designer gown, the layers of handkerchief hem blowing gently against her calves as they walked.

"No. This is just for you, Adelaide." He stopped as they reached the balloon basket, his eyes serious. Intense.

"Any special occasion?" Curious, she wasn't sure why he'd put so much effort into a special night for them now.

As much as she wanted to believe that he'd planned a fairy-tale date just to romance her, a cynical part of her couldn't help but wonder why.

"I'm sorry I put you on the spot when I announced our engagement. Consider this my apology, since that's not how I should have treated a friend." He lifted her hand to his lips and kissed the back of it.

Her heart melted. Just turned to gooey mush. She would have swooned into his arms if the pilot hadn't turned to them right then and introduced himself.

While the pilot—Jim—went over a few safety precautions and briefly outlined the plan for their hour-long flight, Adelaide stared at Dempsey and felt herself falling faster. She'd tried to keep herself so safe with him, from him. But her mother was right, and this man had always had a piece of her heart. How on earth could she maintain her defenses around a man who bought her a Versace gown to take her on a hot-air balloon ride?

She hadn't heard any of Jim's speech by the time Dempsey lifted Adelaide in his arms and set her on her feet inside the basket. He vaulted in behind her, their portion of the basket separated from Jim's by a waist-high wall. Moments later, the ground crew let go of their tethers and the balloon lifted them into the air so smoothly and silently it felt like magic.

Her heart soared along with the rest of her.

Impulsively, she slid her arms around Dempsey's waist and tucked her head against his shoulder. He'd said he wanted to apologize for not being a better friend. Could that mean he wanted to be…more?

"Do you like it?" His hand gripped her shoulder through the pashmina, a warm weight connecting them.

They stared out their side of the basket while Jim

took care of maneuvering the balloon from his own side. It felt private enough, especially with all the open air around them.

"I love it." She peered up at him as the world fell away beneath them. "I've never had anyone do something so special for me."

"Good." He kissed her temple while the limo below them became a toy-size plaything. "Because the past two weeks have been something special for me. I wanted you to know that, even if this engagement got off to an awkward beginning, it's been…eye-opening."

She reached for the edge of the basket and gripped it, feeling as though she needed an anchor in a world suddenly off-kilter. What was he saying? Had her mother guessed correctly that Dempsey cared more than she'd realized?

"How so?" Her voice was a thin crack of sound in the cool air, and she tugged the pashmina closer around her. The landscape spread out below them like a patchwork quilt of green squares dotted with gray rocky patches and splashes of blue.

"We make a great team, for one thing." He turned her toward him, his hands on her shoulders. "You have to know that. And you've spent years helping me to be more successful, always giving me far more help than what I could ever pay you for. I want you to know that teamwork goes both ways, and I can help you, too."

He withdrew a piece of paper from the breast pocket of his tuxedo. It fluttered a little in the breeze as the temperature cooled.

"What is it?" She didn't take it, afraid it would blow away.

"The deed to the manufacturing facility you looked

at with Evan last week." He tucked the paper into her beaded satin purse that sat on the floor of the balloon basket and straightened.

"You bought it?" She wasn't sure what to say, since she'd told him she didn't want this to be a Reynaud enterprise. "You haven't even seen it. I was going to ask you what you thought when we got back home—"

"I toured it Thursday before practice. It's a good investment."

The balloon dipped, jarring her, but no more than his words.

He'd toured it and bought it without speaking to her. She didn't want to ruin their balloon ride by complaining about what he'd obviously meant as a generous gesture. But she couldn't help the frustration bubbling up that he hadn't at least spoken to her about it.

"I hadn't even run the numbers on the operating costs yet." She didn't want to feel tears burning the backs of her eyes. She understood him well enough to know his heart was in the right place. But how could he be friends with her for so long and not understand how important it was for her to make her own decisions regarding her business? "I hadn't decided for sure yet—"

"You showed me the business plan, remember? I ran the numbers. You can afford the expenses easily now."

Except she needed to make those decisions, not him. Didn't he have any faith in her business judgment?

"Perhaps." She watched an eagle soaring nearby, the sight so incredible, but more difficult to enjoy when her world felt as if it was fracturing. "But I can't accept a gift—"

"I know you don't want anything handed to you, Addy, but this is no more of a gift than all the ways you've anticipated my every need for years. How many times have you worked more than forty hours in a week without compensation?"

"I'm a salaried employee," she reminded him, still feeling off balance.

"In a job that you took to help me. Don't try to make the deed mean more than it does, Adelaide. You've worked hard for me and I'm finally in a position to achieve everything I've always wanted with the Hurricanes this year. Let me be a small part of your dream, too."

Some of her defensiveness eased. She had to admit, it was a thoughtful gesture. A generous one, too, even if a bit high-handed. And the way he'd worded it made her feel a teeny bit more entitled to the gift, even though it far surpassed the monetary value of what she'd done for him. Still, the gift left her feeling a little hollow inside when she'd just convinced herself that he'd taken her on a balloon ride because he'd realized some deeper affection for her.

"Can I think about it before I accept it?" She cleared her throat, trying not to reveal the letdown she felt. The wind whipped a piece of her hair free from her updo, the long strand twining around her neck.

"No. You can sell it if you don't want to use the facility. But it's yours, Addy. That's done." He reached to sweep aside the hair and tucked it into one of the tiny rhinestone butterflies that held spare strands. "I have one other gift for you, and I want you to really consider it."

That seriousness in his eyes again. The look that had made her nervous all week. What on earth was on the man's mind?

When he reached into his breast pocket again, her heart about stopped. He pulled out a ring box.

Her heartbeat stuttered. Her gaze flew back to his.

"Adelaide, these two weeks have shown me how perfect we are together." He opened the box to reveal a stunningly rare blue garnet set in…of all things…a tiny spoon ring design that replicated the spoon bracelet he'd given her all those years ago when he'd had to forge a gift for her with his own hands.

"Dempsey?" Her fingers trembled as she reached to touch it, hardly daring to believe what she was seeing. What she was hearing.

"It's not meant to replace your engagement ring. But I wanted to give you something special."

"I don't understand." She shook her head, overwhelmed by the generosity of the gift.

"We're best friends. We're even better lovers. And we're stronger together." He tugged the ring from the velvet backing for her and slid the box into his pocket. "This ring is my way of asking you to make our engagement a real one. Will you marry me?"

Her emotions tumbled over each other: hope, joy, love and— Wait. Had he even mentioned that part? Of course he must have. She just hadn't heard it in the same way she'd missed the pilot's preliftoff speech because she'd been marveling at how perfect a date this was. She hadn't been paying attention.

Her hands hovered beside the ring.

"Did you…?" She felt embarrassed. Flustered. She should leap into his arms and say yes. Any other woman would. But Adelaide had waited most of her life to hear those words and she didn't want to miss any of it. "I'm sorry. I was so mesmerized by the ring and the setting and—" She gestured to the balloon above them and the scenery below. "It's all so overwhelming. But are you saying you want to get married? For real?" Happy tears pooled in her eyes already. "I love you so much."

And then she did fling herself into his arms, tears spilling onto the beautiful silk collar of his tuxedo. But she was just so happy.

Only…he still hadn't said he loved her. Her declaration of love hung suspended like a balloon between them. In fact, Dempsey patted her back awkwardly now, as if that was his reply.

She hadn't missed the words in his proposal, she realized with a heart sinking like lead. He simply hadn't said them. She knew, even before she edged back and saw the expression on his face. Not bewildered, exactly. More…unsure.

It wasn't an expression she'd seen on his face in many years. Her Reynaud fiancé was used to getting what he wanted, and while he might want Adelaide for a bride, it wasn't for the same reason that she would have liked to be his wife.

"Adelaide. Think about the future we can have together. All the things we can achieve." He must have seen her expression shifting from joy to whatever it was she was feeling now.

Deflation.

"Marriage isn't about being a team or working well together." She wrapped a hand around one of the ropes tying the basket to the balloon, needing something to steady her without the solid strength of Dempsey Reynaud beside her.

"There are far more reasons than that."

"There's only one reason that I would marry. Just one." She stared out at the world coming closer to them now. Dempsey must have signaled Jim to take them back down.

Their date was over.

"The ring is one of a kind, Adelaide. Like you." His words reminded her of all she was giving up. All she would be turning her back on if she refused him now.

But she'd waited too long for love to accept half measures now. She owed herself better.

"We both deserve to be loved," she told him softly, not able to meet his gaze and feel the raw connection that was still mostly one-sided. "You're my friend, Dempsey. And I want that for you as much as I want it for me."

When the balloon touched down, it jarred her. Sent her tumbling into his arms before the basket righted itself.

She didn't linger there, though.

Her fairy tale had come to an end.

Twelve

Three days later, back home at the Hurricanes' training facility, Dempsey envied the guys on the practice field. After the knife in the gut that had been Adelaide's rejection, he would trade his job for the chance to pull on shoulder pads and hit the living hell out of a practice dummy. Or to pound out the frustration through his feet with wind sprints—one set after another.

Instead, he roamed the steaming-hot practice field and nitpicked performances while sweat beaded on his forehead. He blew his whistle a lot and made everyone else work their asses off. Fair or not, teams were built through sweat, and he'd played on enough teams himself to know you balanced the good times—the wins—with the challenges. And if the challenges didn't come on the field on Sunday, a good coach handed them up in practice.

"Again!" he barked at the receivers running long patterns in the heat. Normally, Dempsey focused on the full team as they practiced plays. But today he had taken over the receiver coach's job.

In a minute, he'd move on to the running backs, since he'd already been through all the defensive positions.

Adelaide had not publicly broken their engagement yet, but she had moved out of his house. Which shouldn't have surprised him after the epic fail of his proposal. He'd planned for the moment all week. Spent every spare second that he wasn't with his team figuring out how to make the night special. Yet it had fallen short of the mark for her.

Of course, they hadn't gotten to half of it. He'd ordered an outdoor dinner set up in the mountains with a perfect view of the sunset. He'd had a classical guitarist in place, for crying out loud, so they could dance under the stars.

And she hadn't even taken her ring.

Of all the things that had gone wrong that night, that bothered him the most, given how much thought he'd put into the design. Sure, he was to blame for not understanding that he could have scrapped the balloon, the limo and the guitarist to simply say, "I love you." Except, in all his planning, that had never occurred to him. He'd known what he felt for Addy was big. But was it love? He'd shut down that emotional part of himself long ago, probably on one of the nights his mother had locked him out of the house, claiming some irrational fault on his part, but mostly because she was high.

Love wasn't part of his vernacular.

That had worked out fine for him in the Reynaud house full of men. Caring was demonstrated through externals. A one-two punch for a greeting like what he and Jean-Pierre still exchanged. Covering up for Henri when his younger brother had broken a priceless antique. His first well-executed corporate raid had won the admiration of Gervais and Leon alike.

Dempsey understood that world. It was his world, and he'd handed it to Adelaide on a silver platter, but it hadn't been enough.

And now he'd lost her in every way possible. As his friend. His lover. His future wife.

Stalking away from the receivers, he was about to put the running backs to work when his brother Henri jogged over to match his steps.

"Got a second, Coach?" Henri used the deferential speech of a player, a sign of respect Dempsey had never had to ask for, but which had always been freely given even though Henri thought nothing of busting his chops off the field.

"I probably have one." He kept walking.

Henri kept pace.

"Privately?" he urged in a tone that bordered on less deferential. "Practice was supposed to end an hour ago."

Surprised, Dempsey checked his watch.

"Shit. Fine." He blew his whistle loud enough for the whole field to hear. "Thanks for the hard work today. Same time tomorrow."

A chorus of relieved groans echoed across the field. Dempsey changed course toward the offices. Henri still kept pace.

"You're killing the guys," Henri observed, his helmet tucked under one arm, his practice jersey drenched with sweat. "Any particular reason?"

They were back to being brothers now that practice was done and no one would overhear.

"We have a tough game on Sunday and our first two wins have not been as decisive as I would have liked." He halted his steps and folded his arms, waiting for Henri to spit out whatever was on his mind. "You have a problem with that?"

"I'm all about team building." Henri planted a cleat on the first row of bleachers. "But you've run them long every day this week. Morale is low. The guys are confused in the locker room. I know that's not what you're going for."

"Since when do you snitch on locker-room talk about me?" Dempsey shooed away one of the field personnel who came by to pick up a water cooler. He didn't need an audience for this talk.

"Only since you started acting like a coach with a chip on his shoulder instead of the supremely capable leader you've been the whole rest of my tenure with this team."

The rare compliment surprised him. The complaint really didn't. There was a chance Henri was correct.

"I'll take that under advisement." He accepted the input with a nod and tucked his clipboard under one arm to head inside.

"So where's Adelaide?" Henri asked, stopping Dempsey in his tracks.

"Running her own business. Having a life outside the Hurricanes." Without him.

The knowledge still gutted him.

"Since I'm on a real roll with advice today, can I offer a second piece?" Henri brushed some dirt off his helmet.

"Definitely not." Pivoting away from his brother, he noticed some of his players were lying on the field.

Were they that tired? Had he run them that hard?

The idea bothered him. A lot.

"Dude, I'm not claiming to be an expert on women." Henri hovered at his shoulder, carrying the water cooler inside. "Far from it with the way my marriage is going these days."

The dark tone in Henri's voice revealed a truth the guy had probably tried hard to keep quiet.

"Sorry to hear it." Because even though Dempsey was waist high in self-pity right now, he felt bad for his brother.

"My point is, I know enough about women to know you're going about it all wrong."

"Tell me something I don't know."

Henri laughed, a loud, abrupt cackle. "How much time do you have, old man?" Then, tossing his helmet and the water cooler on the ground, he pantomimed a quick right hook to Dempsey's gut. "Seriously. Don't let Adelaide go."

And then he was gone, scooping up the helmet and shouldering the cooler to go hassle the slackers left on the field. No doubt reinstalling the team morale that Dempsey had single-handedly shredded.

He wasn't sure what had shocked him more. He'd never been particularly close with Henri, sensing that the guy had resented Dempsey more than the others as kids because Henri had been close with their mother. The mother who'd left as soon as Dempsey had set foot in the Reynaud house. But that was a long time ago, and maybe he needed to shake off the idea that he was a black sheep brother. Figure out how to be a better brother.

How to show he cared about people beyond stilted words about being good teammates.

Henri was right. It was time for Dempsey to stop expecting Adelaide to read between the lines with him. Just because she understood him better than anyone didn't excuse him from spelling out his feelings for her. She deserved that and much, much more.

So damn much more.

But he was going to lay it on the line for her again, without any distractions or big gestures. And hope like hell he got it right this time. Because the truth of the matter was he couldn't live without her. His championship season didn't mean anything if he couldn't share it with her.

The woman he loved.

Adelaide dug to the bottom of her pint of strawberry gelato while seated on her kitchen counter in the middle of the afternoon, wishing strawberry tasted half as good as chocolate ice cream.

Except everything chocolate reminded her of Dempsey after their chocolate-sauce encounter, and if she thought about Dempsey, she would cry. And after three days back home alone in her crappy apartment, she did not feel like crying anymore.

Okay, she did a little. Especially if she thought about how much effort he'd put into romancing her on Sunday after the game. How many other women would trade anything to be treated the way Dempsey treated her? Yet she'd discounted all his efforts in the hope of hearing he loved her.

Dumb. Dumb. Dumb.

Except that she'd do it all over again because she was

one of those romantic girls who believed the right guy would hand her his whole heart forever and ever. She didn't think she could go through life if that turned out to be a myth. Then again, she wasn't sure she could go another day without Dempsey.

But she could probably go through a few more single-serving-size gelatos. She'd bought every flavor that didn't contain chocolate, determined to find some new taste to love.

Her doorbell rang as she was on her way back to the freezer.

No doubt her mother on a mission of mercy to lift her spirits. Little did Della know that Adelaide was only going to stuff her with gelato to avoid hearing any kind platitudes about waiting for the right one to come along.

She yanked open the door, only to have the safety chain catch, and remembered too late she was supposed to look through the peephole. She didn't live in Dempsey's ultrasafe mansion anymore.

He stood on her welcome mat.

The man who hadn't left her thoughts in days wore black running shorts and a black-and-gold Hurricanes sideline T-shirt like the ones the players wore. He must have come straight from practice, because he made a point not to wander around town in team gear that made him all the more recognizable. He looked good enough to eat, reminding her why all the gelato in the world was not going to satisfy her craving.

"May I come in?" he asked, making her realize she'd stood there gawking without saying anything.

"Of course. Just a sec." She closed the door partway to remove the chain, then opened it again, more than a little wary.

She told herself it was just as well he'd stopped by, since she had wanted to give him that damn deed back to the manufacturing facility. Except he looked as tired as she felt, the circles under his eyes even darker than the ones she knew were on her face. The rest of him looked as good as ever, however, his thighs so deliciously delineated as he walked that she thought about all the times she'd seen them naked. Against her own.

"How'd practice go?" Her voice was dry and she cleared it. She'd continued to work for the team from home, not wanting to leave him in the lurch.

He hadn't said anything about her absence at the training facility, acknowledging her work-related emails with curt "thanks" that had been typical of him long before now.

"Poorly. I haven't been myself this week and I've been pushing the guys too hard. Henri called me on it today. I'm going to do better." He wandered around her living room, touching her things, looking at her paintings over the ancient nonfunctional fireplace.

She was surprised that he'd admitted to screwing up. No, that wasn't true. She was more surprised that he'd screwed up in the first place. He normally put so much effort into thinking how to best coach a team, he didn't make the type of mistakes he had described.

"I'm glad. That you're going to be better with the team, that is." Nervous, she wandered over to the refrigerator that was so old that modern retro styles copied the design. "Would you like a gelato?"

She pulled out a coconut-lime flavor and cracked open the top.

"No, thank you." He set down a statue of a cat that she used to display Mardi Gras beads. "I came here to bring you this. You left it behind when you moved out your things."

He set a familiar ring box on the breakfast bar dividing the living area from the kitchen. Her on one side. Him on the other. A ring in between.

As if her heart wasn't battered enough already.

"That stone is worth a fortune." She hadn't taken the yellow diamond either, of course. That one, she'd left on his bathroom vanity.

"And you're worth everything to me, so you can see you are well suited." He opened the box and took out the ring. "It's not an engagement ring. I'd already given you one of those. Adelaide, this one is the grown-up version of that bracelet I made you. Something you've worn every day of your life since I gave it to you."

"Friendship is forever," she reminded him, something he'd told her the day he gave it to her.

He came into the kitchen and eased her grip on the coconut-lime gelato, then set it on the linoleum countertop.

"I'm glad you remember that." He held the ring close to her bracelet. "Look and see how the patterns match."

"I see." She blinked hard, not sure what he was getting at. But she couldn't wear that beautiful ring on her finger every day without her heart breaking more.

"The spoon part is supposed to remind you that you're still my best friend. Forever." He slipped his hand around hers. "The rare blue garnet is there to tell you how rare it is to find love and friendship in the same place. And how beautiful it is when it happens."

Her gaze flipped up to his as she tried to gauge his expression. To gauge his heart.

"That's not what you said when you gave it to me."

She shook her head. "It's not fair to say things you don't mean—"

"I do, Adelaide." He took both her hands in his. Squeezed. "Please let me try to explain. I got it all wrong before, I know. But it was not for lack of effort."

"It was a beautiful date," she acknowledged, knowing she'd never recover from loving him. There would never be a man in her life like this one.

And it broke her heart into tiny pieces if he thought he could win her back by trotting out the right phrases.

"I spent so much time thinking about how to make the proposal perfect—how to make you stay—I never gave any thought to what *you* might want. What was important to *you*." He shook his head. "It's like spending all my time shoring up the defense and ignoring the fact that I had no offense."

She tried not to mind the sports metaphor. And, heaven help her, she did understand exactly what he meant.

"So I was just caught off guard at how much I missed the mark that day. It must tell you something that a mention of love threw me so far off my game I didn't even know what to say in return."

"You would know what to say if you felt it, too." She stepped back, needing to protect herself from the hurt this conversation was inevitably going to bring.

"No. Just the opposite. I didn't understand what I felt because I don't say those words, Addy." He looked at her as if he was perfectly serious.

And beneath the trappings of the wealthy, powerful man who was the CEO of international companies and would one day coach a team to the Super Bowl, Adelaide saw the wounded gaze of her old friend. The boy who hadn't been given enough love as a child yet still found enough kindness in his heart to rescue a little girl from a trouncing because he was an innately fair and honorable person.

He blinked and the look vanished as though it had never been, but she was left with an understanding that should have been there all along. She, who thought she knew him so well, hadn't seen the most obvious answer.

Dempsey Reynaud had never been in love. Had probably never spoken the words in his life to anyone. There was certainly never a mention of love in those notes she'd written to accompany the parting gifts to his old girlfriends.

"I understand." She nodded, the full weight of his explanation settling on her, yet still not quelling her concerns about the future, the ache of her heart. "But you can see why I'd want to feel loved and to hear that I'm loved if I was going to be your wife?"

She edged closer to him again, understanding now that she didn't need to worry about protecting her heart. If anything, she ought to think about his.

"I understand now. But it took three days of hell—not sleeping, not eating, missing you every second and damn near killing every guy on a fifty-three-man roster—to get it through my head." He swallowed hard. Tipped his forehead to hers. "So please, Adelaide, let me slide this ring on your right hand. And I want you to wear it forever because our friendship is even more beautiful now than when I gave you that bracelet so long ago."

She took a moment to think, to look in his eyes and see the truth. That they were bound together through years of love and friendship, tied together in a way that was strong. Lasting.

"Yes." She nodded. Kissed his rough cheek and liked it so much she kissed the other one, too. "But it's going to be hard being just friends after—"

He produced the second ring.

She made an unintelligible sound that might have been a cry of relief, hope or pure joy. She wasn't sure. She could feel her legs going unsteady beneath her, though.

"I brought this back with me, too." He held it between them, their foreheads still tipped together.

"It hurt leaving it behind." A few of her tears splashed down on it.

"It tore my heart from my chest to find it." He leaned back to kiss her forehead. Her temples. "But since I didn't get to personally put it on your finger the first time, I'm looking at this as my chance to do something right."

He got down on one knee in her tiny, ancient kitchen, his handsome face so intent on her that her heart did backflips.

"Adelaide Thibodeaux," he continued. "You are my heart and I am not whole without you. I love you more than anything. Will you do me the honor of being my wife?"

Speechless because her heart was in her throat, she nodded. But as the beautiful yellow diamond slid into place on her left hand, Adelaide recovered enough to fling her arms around him.

"I love you more than anything, too. And that was my favorite proposal yet." Her voice was all wobbly, along with the rest of her.

Her big, strong future husband lifted her off her feet and pressed his lips to hers, his arms banded around her waist. He took his time with the kiss, making up for the days and nights they'd missed each other. Heat tingled over her skin, awakening every part of her. She was breathless and a little light-headed by the time he broke contact.

"I meant it as a compliment that I wanted you to be on my team." He smiled up at her and she laughed.

"I am complimented." Her heart swelled with love for him. She bracketed his face in her hands while he carried her into her bedroom. "But thank you for letting me be more than that."

"I'm going to be the best husband you can imagine," he promised, his golden-brown eyes dazzling her more than either of the rings on her fingers.

"I'm going to remind you every day that I love you," she promised him in return, her body sinking into the bed as Dempsey laid her down.

He stretched out next to her, his muscular frame filling her small bed so that he crowded her in the most delicious ways.

"I'd like to start now, by adoring every inch of you." His words were warm on her neck as he kissed that vulnerable spot.

"That's perfect, because every inch of me has missed you." She trailed a hand through his dark hair, knowing she was the luckiest woman on earth.

Her fairy tale hadn't ended. The best part was just beginning.

* * * * *

MILLS & BOON®

PASSIONATE AND DRAMATIC LOVE STORIES

A sneak peek at next month's titles...

In stores from 10th March 2016:

- **Take Me, Cowboy** – Maisey Yates *and*
  His Baby Agenda – Katherine Garbera

- **A Surprise for the Sheikh** – Sarah M. Anderson *and*
  Reunited with the Rebel Billionaire – Catherine Mann

- **A Bargain with the Boss** – Barbara Dunlop *and*
  Secret Child, Royal Scandal – Cat Schield

Available at WHSmith, Tesco, Asda, Eason, Amazon and Apple

Just can't wait?
Buy our books online a month before they hit the shops!
visit www.millsandboon.co.uk

These books are also available in eBook format!

MILLS & BOON®

Helen Bianchin v Regency Collection!

MILLS & BOON®

Let us take you back in time with our Medieval Brides...

The Novice Bride – Carol Townend

The Dumont Bride – Terri Brisbin

The Lord's Forced Bride – Anne Herries

The Warrior's Princess Bride – Meriel Fuller

The Overlord's Bride – Margaret Moore

Templar Knight, Forbidden Bride – Lynna Banning

Order yours at
www.millsandboon.co.uk/medievalbrides

MILLS & BOON®

Why shop at millsandboon.co.uk?

Each year, thousands of romance readers find their perfect read at millsandboon.co.uk. That's because we're passionate about bringing you the very best romantic fiction. Here are some of the advantages of shopping at www.millsandboon.co.uk:

* **Get new books first**—you'll be able to buy your favourite books one month before they hit the shops

* **Get exclusive discounts**—you'll also be able to buy our specially created monthly collections, with up to 50% off the RRP

* **Find your favourite authors**—latest news, interviews and new releases for all your favourite authors and series on our website, plus ideas for what to try next

* **Join in**—once you've bought your favourite books, don't forget to register with us to rate, review and join in the discussions

Visit **www.millsandboon.co.uk**
for all this and more today!

MILLS_WEB